SLAUGHTER HOUSE PRAYER

JOHN KING is the author of eight previous novels: *The Football Factory*, *Headhunters*, *England Away*, *Human Punk*, *White Trash*, *The Prison House*, *Skinheads* and *The Liberal Politics Of Adolf Hitler*. *The Football Factory* was turned into a film and his books have been widely translated abroad. He has written short stories and articles for a number of publications, and edits the fiction fanzine *Verbal*. He lives in London.

JOHN KING

SLAUGHTERHOUSE PRAYER

LONDON BOOKS BRITISH FICTION

LONDON BOOKS
39 Lavender Gardens
London SW11 1DJ
www.london-books.co.uk

A catalogue record for this book
is available from the British Library

ISBN 978-0-9957217-2-2

Printed and bound in Great Britain by
CPI Group (UK) Ltd, Croydon, CR0 4YY

Typeset by Octavo Smith Publishing Services
www.octavosmith.com

THIS NOVEL IS DEDICATED TO

MARTIN KNIGHT, PETE MASON and PAUL WILLETTS

For their support, encouragement and friendship
during some difficult years

Wonderful World

THE MAN MOVED along the ridge, his eyes focused on the way forward, heart tapping out a marching beat, and when the path narrowed and the slope to his right steepened, threatening to kill him if he lost his nerve and tumbled, he didn't slow down but instead walked faster – in control of his life for the first time in much too long. And once the fall was behind him he kept up this quicker pace, knowing the harder he pushed his body the stronger his mind would become. He was little Michael Tanner, a boy full of dreaming; Mickey Moo, a youth doing his best to fight his anger and believe in the power of words; plain old Tanner, a disillusioned, middle-aged adult who saw this long-distance walk as some sort of rebirth. He liked the idea of being born a second, third, maybe even a fourth time.

It was still early in the day, not yet ten o'clock, but he was already soaked in sweat. The sun was scorching the land, salt forming fractals on a tattered Subhumans T-shirt, the Munch-like skull cracked and gasping. He imagined the heat falling in pancake layers, its pulse linking to his heartbeat, and as he did this he willed more blood into his brain, doing his best to drown the last dregs of depression. Too much thinking had definitely damaged his health.

It was a week since the sunshine had broken into his flat and reminded him that he was one of the lucky ones. His body and soul were his own, not controlled or denied by businessmen, politicians, priests. He had to be strong and stand tall. It was Sunday morning and he ignored the temptation to roll over and savour this surge of positive energy, instead hurrying out of bed and opening windows and filling the bath and scrubbing his skin and shaving his face and cleaning a sink's worth of dishes with a lemon-scented liquid. Seven days later and here he was on a cross-country journey, revelling in the incredible space, silence and peace.

The land began to rise and he firmed his boots inside steps cut out across the centuries, straining muscles as he followed the hunters and gatherers and shepherds and soldiers and pilgrims and all the other creatures who had created this path. His heart thumped faster and he was out of breath when he reached the top of the slope. Stopping, he leaned forward, resting his hands on his knees. Bile churned and he thought he was going to puke up the breakfast he'd eaten two hours earlier.

Baked beans on toast – cooked on a portable stove outside his tent – was meant to balance the drink he'd had in a village pub the night before. The Stag did a nice pint of cider, and he'd tried the perry as well, welcomed by locals who made sure they told him about the spirits haunting the ridge. He listened to their stories and played along. It had taken a while to find his tent at closing time, but he was relaxed and unafraid, felt a flush of happiness now as he remembered the pub, which only lasted a moment.

He was suddenly light-headed and dizzy and seemed to be swaying, his mind numb so he hardly knew where he was or what he was doing. For a split second he thought he was falling, that he hadn't made it across that narrow stretch of path, but then his life flashed back up from the fields below in a rush of euphoria that raced into his feet and legs and filled his torso and finally his head. The nausea was gone and his mind was clear. He felt fantastic.

Stretching his spine and rolling a tight neck, he continued walking, and it wasn't long before his rhythm returned, and this was so smooth and natural he felt as if his feet were barely touching the ground. When a breeze brushed his face he was tempted to lift his legs up and let the current carry him into the sky where he would fly with the birds, an albatross of a man, cumbersome in comparison yet strangely graceful, dipping down as he traded an ocean for grass. He was sailing through space, a weightless adventurer circling his own blue-marble planet, a purist feeding on the cleanest air, captain of his very own spaceship. Coming to a wider plateau he slowed down as he passed through thousands of dandelions and daisies, their yellow-and-white heads the stars from last night.

He had positioned his tent near a copse that shielded it from other walkers but gave him a view over the surrounding country-side. Back from the pub, he had sat in front of it eating cereal from a plastic mug, the clouds clearing so the sky was clear, the moon nearly full. Amazed by the number of stars that were visible, he had picked out the brightest one and stared at it for ages, then searched for meteors burning up as they entered the earth's atmosphere. When he was a boy he had done the same thing, and not so far from here. It made sense that the ancients looked to the heavens for their gods.

The drinkers in the village swore there was a beast on the ridge, as well as the ghost of a traveller and the spirit of a horse. It would be dangerous to fall asleep. But he had always wanted to believe in fairy tales and knew some of the area's history. Pagans had built stone circles and buried their dead in barrows, Christians follow-ing with churches and graveyards. Their sacrifices crossed over. He had listened for the roar of the beast, the call of a man, the clatter of hooves. He imagined families searching for their loved ones, unaware that they too were dead. Small creatures watched from the darkness. A single human would be a problem, but he'd love to see a ghost. He couldn't let his mind wander. Not last night and not today. He continued walking. It was forty-five minutes before he stopped.

At a high point on the track he decided he'd earned a rest and the chance to properly appreciate the scenery. His rucksack puffed up dust when he dropped it to the ground, his shirt separating from his skin so he felt the coldness of the sweat. He wiped his face with a hanky and squeezed out the water, watched brown earth turn black. Moving away from the path he sat on a ledge padded with soft grass, legs dangling over the side of the hill. The slope was gentler than elsewhere, but if he went over he would die. He was perched on the side of an older world. A man on the edge.

Shading his eyes with his right hand he scanned the fields, found green patches sectioned by bulging hedges and open ditches and strips of piled stone, a range of shades and colours and textures sewn together in uneven blocks, and these fields ran into clumps of oak heavy with leaves, smaller trees he couldn't identify on a hill three or more miles away. There were meadows and hollows and tangled brambles that had never been cut, mustard shining bright yellow, two brown oblongs of freshly dug soil on either side, black triangles hopping as birds searched for seed. A crooked path led to a crooked barn, a box he hoped had been used for hay. Chalk pressed through banks near the horizon, as if a giant had worn out the elbows of his jacket. There were no houses and no people. It was the perfect picture. A brilliant painting.

He squinted and made out fifty or so white dots, guessed they were lambs and ewes, quickly shifted his eyes towards the long grass at the foot of the hill, a home for rabbits and mice and badgers and the deer that maybe came across from the woods late in the day.

There was a fairy mound behind him and he eased back, sunk his head into a ready-made pillow. His body relaxed, but the scenery was fixed in his head, and he thought about Paul Nash and his brother John, who had recorded the First World War and painted English fields when it was over. The mechanised killing had affected Paul so badly he'd suffered from depression for the rest of his life. The younger war artists tended to show the slaughter of men through the ruined land over which they had fought, and despite the horror their work was inspiring. Nash was a romantic. A modernist.

He felt the grass pushing against his hands, a miniature jungle where insect armies patrolled in silence, unseen by spotter planes and bombers, and he wondered what tipped certain people over the side into depression while others thrived. He covered his eyes with a forearm as beetles roamed, dragonflies circled, butterflies flapped, ladybirds balanced on green blades. Last night's cider had been cold and refreshing and he could have done with a pint now. Drink lifted him up, but there were negatives. One pint too many could shorten his temper. He was fine talking about meat and dairy, explaining his veganism, listening to other views, but there had been a couple of times last year when he'd lost control. Every meat eater's excuse was predictable. The jokes were unoriginal and had turned from pathetic to insulting. A lack of respect was enough.

He remembered his punches connecting and heard the breaking of glass as a grasshopper snapped a twig, another insect soldier left to rot on the streets of a grateful nation.

This ridge ran through land he had spent time in as a boy and a youth, and he thought of that chunk of life since his early twenties – a blur of work, love, marriage, divorce, sickness, death. It was five years since he'd seen his ex-wife and two since he'd been made redundant. He had made mistakes, but seeing the two people he loved most suffer and eventually die had hit him hard. There had been no escape, nothing he could do to save his parents' lives. This just made all the unnecessary cruelty in the world seem much worse. The daily routine of work and then caring for them had blocked out the horror he'd tried to confront when he was younger, and this returned with a vengeance once he was alone and unemployed. For a while he'd wished he could just go to sleep and never wake up.

He jolted as a stun-gun flashed, the electric shock opening his eyes. A knife shone. He sat up and saw a silver cross floating across the sky. He waved, stood up and tried again, using both arms, moving them side to side above his head, but couldn't see if the glider pilot responded. He was always amazed by the miracle of flight, didn't need to know what was inside the person's head. There was no more room for arguments.

When he got home he was going to live a different sort of life. He would tune into his radio and TV and lose himself in their wisdom, embrace the biggest of the group-minds, surf the internet and agree with thousands of new friends, accept the baby-talk of his leaders. He was going to laugh at all those unfunny comedians who had traded general humour for specific targets, treat news as twenty-four-hour entertainment, revel in his decency as he agreed with the dominant view and nodded his head. There were special offers and bonus points to save, trivia and the intricacies of endless upgrades to master, and he would exercise and become healthy and ask no more questions. Feeling angry had done him no good. He didn't want to be sad.

Heaving his rucksack onto his back, he adjusted the straps until it was comfortable. A column of light appeared, as if Turner had added a stroke of white paint to the scene, drawing his eyes back to the sky. It was a single small cloud responsible. The mothers of Nash and Turner had both died in asylums and he wondered what this meant. He felt as powerless as they would have done, and for the first time in his life it was a comfort. He was a small man who could change nothing, so why bother trying? Everything happened for a reason. That's what he had heard.

The man known as Tanner started to walk, picking up speed and loving the thump in his chest and the rhythm in his wrists and the heat of the sun on his head and arms, and it wasn't long before his mind was clearing and his spirit soared. He was a tiny speck on a huge canvas. A boy and a youth and a man – marching together if not in time. Water filled his eyes. He wasn't sure if it was sweat or tears, but he did know that he was happy. Nothing could hurt him. It was a wonderful world.

Hunters cornered the youth on a quiet country lane and kicked the fuck out of him. Two terrier-men with pickaxe handles stood in front, a shotgun-carrying farmer behind, thick hawthorn hedges and nettle-filled ditches boxing the lad in as they stepped forward to deliver a lesson that would never be forgotten. The silly bugger had become separated from his friends and it was their lucky day. It was their right to manage the land as they saw fit, and hunting was an important part of this, as well as a basic freedom. They really did hate these hunt saboteurs.

For some reason the youth kept grinning, but they'd soon wipe the smile off his face. He mooed like a cow. Maybe he was a bit slow in the head. Mickey treated them to the chorus of 'Sabotage The Hunt' by The Business. Or was he taking the piss? Now he was barking. It didn't matter. There was nowhere to run. No escape. Christmas had come early.

Their own faces were flushed red, skin raw and laced with tiny veins, eyes bright with the joys of the bloodsport brigade. Townies had no respect for the countryside. These sabs were anarchist scum who wanted to destroy traditions that had existed for hundreds of years, a bunch of layabouts with nothing better to do with their lives than worry about animals. When the youth started to oink they hesitated, felt uneasy suddenly, but knew that this was a golden opportunity.

Mickey was nineteen and no weakling, but the men closing in on him were older and used to violence. He punched the first one in the mouth and knocked him backwards, which seemed to outrage his friend, who probably expected him to cower like one of the foxes they spent their spare time terrorising. Or at least keep to the non-violence code of the ALF. But Mickey was different. He was no pacifist. Neither was he going to give his attackers the satisfaction of trying to get away. The odds only made him more determined to stand and fight. He was big, strong and angry.

He whacked the second terrier-man on the nose, heard a crack and saw blood. This pleased him. He did a donkey impression. These men killed rabbits as well as foxes, chased down hares and all sorts, probably worked with the badger baiters and blinded babies with acid. He hit the first one again, nearly putting him down, preferred a physical fight to insults and mental violence. He had been trying to turn the other cheek, listening to the more experienced hunt saboteurs and animal-rights activists, but this was self-defence. He'd forgotten the farmer, though, who was cunning and patient and moving in from behind. The shotgun's butt connected with the back of his head.

Human beings could justify anything. They gave speeches and delivered sermons, debated and decided, wrote billions of words down on paper and into computers, produced reports and books, passed complex laws only a well-paid elite was meant to understand, boasted about clarity, invented rules of engagement and humane slaughter, consulted friends and enemies, shook hands and slapped backs and swore eternal loyalty, lectured the masses on civilised behaviour and the rights of the individual, the limitations placed on interrogation and torture, the conditions of confinement, the double-speak of rape, castration, murder. Mickey knew it was bollocks.

People loved an easy target. The more defenceless their victim, the greater the violence. Humans rarely fought fair. Too many of them were bullies dealing in physical, verbal and mental abuse. They preyed on the young and they preyed on the old, closed in fast when they saw their chance.

Mickey was on his knees, dazed and unable to dodge the first kick that crashed into his face. He moved his hands up to protect his eyes, a second blow connecting, his jaw taking the full force. The third kick came from the opposite direction, a heavy boot to the back of his head. He felt stones on the side of his face as he fell forward, scared as he imagined the shell protecting his brain cracking, a coconut split by a hammer. He tried to curl into a ball and cradle his skull, widening his palms and stretching his fingers, but the next kick was to his balls, the pain filling his mouth with vomit. He pulled his legs up tight and tucked his head in the best he could.

The terrier-men kept going, kicking him up and down his body, taking their time as they picked weak spots. This was a methodical attack and they taunted him as they worked, told him about the fox cubs they killed and how they ripped the hearts out of the mothers for trophies, that badgers made a racket and thrashed about when their eyes were burnt out, the money they made on dog fights, the rabbits they caught, the way they treated the hounds and the fact the courts would release a hunt supporter who committed GBH but give a non-violent saboteur five years for denting a car. He was a fucking idiot to think he could ever change anything.

This was the countryside and they could do what they wanted, and they kept hurting him for these same reasons – because they could and because they wanted to – at least until they became tired, huffing and puffing and pausing. Mickey was semi-conscious. He hoped they were done.

They started using their pickaxe handles next. Heavy wood battered his flesh. They said it was like tenderising meat and laughed. The sound of the blows was hollow and repetitive. They grunted and groaned, the punches he'd landed driving them on. But the animal impressions had spooked them, if only for a few seconds. There was something not quite right about this one. They didn't want him getting back up.

When they paused again, Mickey peered through his fingers and found the farmer staring at him, the shotgun resting on his hip. Their eyes connected and the man raised the barrels so they were pointing at Mickey's head. For a moment he thought he was going to die and was scared, and later he would decide that without the law to protect him he would have done, but the farmer was never going to risk a murder charge and prison. Instead he lifted the shotgun so it was leaning against his right shoulder, as if he was a sentry on guard duty, told the terrier-men to stop now, they didn't want to kill the lad. That was enough. A warning to all those other interfering cunts.

The terrier-men dragged Mickey to the side of the lane, stones cutting his hands and neck, releasing him at the top of a ditch and pushing with their boots so he rolled into it, over and over like he used to do in the park when he was a child, told he was going to be sick if he wasn't careful, that he would end up with a headache that would last for hours. He didn't feel the stinging nettles and thorns as he rolled, and at the bottom he rocked side to side, riding a seesaw, landing on his back.

A voice was telling him to fuck off and never come back. The words echoed and died. Footsteps crunched. The sound faded. He was alone.

The water in the bottom of the ditch was thick with decaying plants, a sugary sweetness softening the rancid smell, and being down here meant his kicking was over. The solution was clammy against his skin, a mass of rotting leaves and bark, a soapy compost heap. The slime was warm and he had that feeling of climbing into bed cold and exhausted and knowing he could sleep late in the morning. He rested for a minute, didn't want to hang around, tried to move but couldn't. His body was stiff. Maybe he had been paralysed. It was hard to think straight.

The water was soaking through his clothes and running into his ears, wrapping itself around him as he closed his eyes. There was a ringing in his head that became a shrill whistle before returning as a steady throb. His body was starting to ache. The reality of what had just happened sent a delayed shock through his system. He had been fighting for survival on the lane, hadn't expected more than a few punches and kicks, realised he could have died up there, and that he might be seriously injured. Again, he tried to move. Again, he couldn't.

His chest heaved and he was starting to panic, knew he had to calm himself down, move to a better place. The water on his face came from a sprinkler in a huge glasshouse, a gentle mist that floated in the air, settling on the leaves of palm trees and banana plants. He was inside the protective walls of his favourite botanical gardens and safe from predators. True, this ditch was home to spaceship pods and time-travelling seeds, long genetic threads that slipped out from under his fingernails and merged with the spawn of reptiles, but he had read a lot of science fiction as a child and didn't need to worry. He heard a frog croak and realised he was in a prehistoric pool, muddy and clueless, branded pond life, fins wedged into amputated arm sockets, legs tapering into a rudder. His attempt to escape had failed. He was a subspecies non-human beaten to a pulp. His brain was bleeding.

Perhaps he had been sedated and taken by ambulance to a hospital where the nurses were coaxing him through the initial trauma, doing their best to bring him back to some form of life. There were dedicated doctors from every part of the world keen to help. He had wet the bed and was ashamed, didn't want to wear the nappy the nurses brought, and he realised that the chemicals they were injecting weren't going to make him better, could only ease his pain.

He opened his eyes. Skeletons linked arms high above his head, bones turning to branches and creating a canopy, a natural dome that held in the moisture. Millions of brilliant green leaves slow-danced on brown limbs, balancing billions of teardrops. He didn't want to die in a ditch. It would be like drowning in a puddle. He could see beads running along the surface of the leaves, shaking loose and falling into his face. His ears were thick with glue. He was stuck. It took huge shots of willpower to climb out of the gutter, a superhuman determination to stand tall and plan ahead.

When he finally managed to sit up he tried to shake the goo from his hands, but it was sticky, elastic and congealing, and he stopped. Moving to the side of the ditch he cried out. Leaning against a log he held his fingers up and found them webbed with mucus. His ears were mushy and he tilted his head left and right so the water could run out, pulling himself straight, groaning as he did so. Looking across to the other bank he saw a path of crushed nettles where he'd rolled down the slope. His stings and cuts were starting to hurt, and when he put a hand to his face and wiped at the green gunk it was laced with red.

It was the sheer unfairness of life that forced him to his feet and sent him scrambling up the bank and out of the ditch and into the lane where he stumbled and fell. It took him a while to recover, but he was upright and swaying and finally steady. He was bleeding more heavily now, the blood in his eyes and covering his clothes and hands. Mickey was worried, but still noticed how the attack had left little impression on the land. Out of sight and out of mind. This was why the hunters and butchers could keep on killing.

He looked both ways and it really was as if nothing had happened. The nettles would recover and anyway, who could guess what that flattened path in the ditch meant? His beating only existed in his injuries and the memories of those involved.

He was dizzy, the pain sharper, and when he put a hand on his chest he recoiled, sure he had broken some ribs. His head would need stitching. Yet he had been lucky. His attackers had held back. They would have killed him if he was a fox or a rabbit. Mickey Moo gritted his teeth and hobbled down the lane, wincing as he went, and once he was mended he swore he was going to find those three men and get even, and the knowledge that he would keep his promise drove him on.

It was the boy's grandfather who told him about the animals – the *non-human* animals. Michael was nine years old, wide-eyed and open-mouthed, following the flow of the old man's words, the gruff but musical sounds that chopped into each other and created films in his head, and while he took in the meaning he couldn't stop staring at the creases on that leathery face opposite. He remembered dead leaves raked and stacked in his local park, brittle skeletons inside green wax crumbling to brown, black and yellow. He bounced back to the fossils he'd seen at the seaside the summer before. Broken rocks held the bones of small fish and birds. A pixie danced, squashed in slate. He wasn't sure if this last fossil was real or not, asked the man behind the counter. Did he *want* it to be? Michael nodded. The shopkeeper said in that case it *is*. And cheap at the price.

Grandad Pop eased forward in his chair, creases catching the glow coming off the bulb above his head. Michael knew about the canals on Mars from his comics and the light turned to liquid silver, and each time Pop moved it swished along the grooves and ran into ditches that linked to the main channels. The last natives survived here, sheltering from week-long electrical storms, only coming to the surface when they were over. Martians loved to visit the craters where their ancestors had lived, wishing themselves across the sand and rock, and when they were travelling at the right speed these half-spirits were invisible to the mechanical insects patrolling the planet. Hiding in the darker valleys were chainmail frogs and dogs with human heads, paper-clawed birds and purple mouse girls, all of them hunted by steel-head controllers and their bronze spider regiments. Robot assassins hid in the tiny holes that dotted the deserts. He followed the canals back to his grandfather's mouth.

Pop was explaining how the smallest souls could find their way into a building – sliding down chimneys, climbing through letter-boxes, swimming along pipes. Just because he couldn't see them it didn't mean they weren't there. It was the same as electricity. They couldn't see it, could they, but electricity existed. Spirits lived in the wires that helped them see at night. There was probably a pixie sitting inside that bulb on the ceiling right now. Michael raised his eyes and felt a thrill run through his body. The kettle whistled and Pop winked and ruffled his hair, stood up and left the room, taking his bottle of beer with him to the kitchen.

There was a clank as crumpets were placed on a tray, the scratch of a match as the grill was lit. Staring into the fireplace, Michael watched coal, wood and paper burn, most of the smoke leaving through the chimney, but it hadn't been cleaned for a long time and the smell hung in the air. This was his second night at Elm Cottage, and it had felt strange being so far from his parents at first, but he was glad he'd come to stay. Pop's brother had died and he was clearing his belongings out of the family home. There was some of their parents' stuff here as well. Pop wanted to get it done and return to London as soon as he could.

Elm Cottage was three miles from its nearest neighbour, next to a country lane that nobody seemed to use. Michael had never known anywhere so quiet. Dad said Pop had always found it a sad and lonely place, leaving when he joined the army and settling in London when he was demobbed. The silence made him think too much. And there was something on Michael's mind as well, lingering from last night when they were sitting at the kitchen table eating the pie Pop had made.

Michael liked pies. The pastry was the best bit, along with the gravy inside, and while he never thought too much about the filling he had noticed the difference in this one and mentioned the mushrooms. Pop asked what sort of pies he normally ate. Michael had to think – meat, chicken, steak and kidney. He cut two chips in half, lined them up on his fork, dipped this in ketchup and put it in his mouth. Pop said he didn't eat animals. Didn't eat meat. There was a pause. He mentioned someone called Harry King, his voice trailing off.

A short silence followed, broken when Pop had thought about the beer loosening his tongue and tried to change the subject, asking Michael about his train journey again – they had already talked about this on the way back from the station – if he'd been worried travelling on his own without Mum or Dad. It was a long trip. Michael was chewing so he didn't reply, knew not to speak with food in his mouth, but he was remembering how the houses thinned out and that he'd seen a canal with locks and then woods and hills in the distance, sheep and cows in fields and these huge pigs in a dusty area with huts to live in and bales of straw to eat, and as he thought about this he kept wondering what Pop had meant, because he didn't eat animals either.

A day had passed and his grandfather was coming back into the living room, placing a tray on the table in front of the couch, crumpets piled up next to a jar of jam and a pot of tea. He poured as Michael helped himself, the boy adding strawberry jelly before sitting back and raising his knees to form a platform for his plate. They watched the fire as they ate and every so often Michael glanced at his grandfather, studying the way the light moved across his face, and then looking up at the lightbulb. A pixie was waiting for them to go to bed so he could leave his glass ball and sit on the couch and watch the fire die down. Michael asked Pop what would happen to the planet if all the people moved to Mars. The old man made a show of considering the question.

Well, the meek were supposed to inherit the earth, so they would take over and do a better job of running the place. Yes, it would be great if everyone left for Mars, or somewhere further away, just kept on going, went and lived in a different universe they couldn't come back from to ruin things again. Michael didn't know who the meek were and Pop tried to explain. They were the humble souls. Quiet and shy. Didn't want any bother. Human and non-human animals. Michael laughed. Humans weren't animals. Pop frowned. Yes, they were. And because the meek were gentle they were easily bullied. Michael was confused. Didn't meek mean weak? Scared? A coward? Pop shook his head.

Everyone was scared. Deep down inside. A brave man was one who faced up to his fear. He had seen pacifists serving as medics in wartime, and while some called them cowards they were as brave as anyone. Braver maybe. They saved lives. Saw the same terrible things as those who fought. Everyone suffered. Civilians. Animals. Pop's voice had dropped. He was mumbling and his leathery face buckled, the creases tightening, and for a moment it seemed as if the ditches were overflowing and water was running into his eyes, but he raised a hand and wiped the light away.

Thinking about it, Pop admitted that he had probably never seen a truly meek person, but he was certain they existed. If humans moved to Mars it wouldn't take long for nature to reclaim the earth, to break down everything that mankind had invented and built. It was like this house. The wind and rain would destroy it over the coming years, once they were back in London and it was empty. Good riddance as well. Water would get into cracks in the bricks and slate and make them bigger. Seeds would arrive in the wind or be dropped by birds, land in the holes and grow, their roots spreading and causing more cracks. Nobody would ever know Elm Cottage had existed. The rabbits in the field behind might even move into the garden.

Rabbits were meek. Deer and mice as well. Pop wasn't sure if he could call farm animals such as chickens, sheep, pigs, cows, donkeys, horses and goats meek exactly, but they *were* innocents, more like mild maybe. Most of them were still children when they died. Lambs were meek. Mary meek, Mary mild... Piglets, calves, foals, kids. There were other innocents. Exotic creatures. Zebras, gazelles, giraffes, elephants. He'd always liked monkeys and had stroked one at a fair when he was a boy, but they could have a fight, though it depended on the species. Elephants weren't so mild he supposed, but they were magnificent. And vegetarian. In the vegan sense of the word.

Pop had always wondered why people were so attracted to lions and tigers, and why every nature programme had to show them killing the more peaceful animals. Carnivores ate herbivores. Maybe that would change when the rockets left for Mars. Cameras followed crocodiles and sharks, yet the rivers and oceans were full of passive fish, huge shoals of tiny lives burning in a kaleidoscope of colours and shapes, tuned into each other's thinking in a way humans could never match.

Michael liked it when Grandad talked this way. He had always told him bedtime stories, making up adventures in which Michael was the hero, insisting it was fine to believe in fairy tales when you were old as well as when you were young. He never mentioned the war, even though he had fought in one, and Dad had told Michael that it was best not to ask him about his time as a soldier.

One day Michael was going to sail to the middle of the ocean, wear a scuba suit and go down to the bottom and discover galleons loaded with gold and silver. He would swim with the dolphins as well, and when he was a man he was going to get a good job and earn lots of money and take Pop on a plane to the other side of the world and they would go on safari and find the wild animals in Africa. Pop thought about this and asked if they could go to Australia afterwards to see the kangaroos. He had forgotten about the kangaroos and wallabies. He might not be around then, so Michael had to make sure he went on his own or with his wife, as Pop would be with him in spirit, even if he was invisible. Yes, Michael was going to be busy. He had a good soul and would turn into a fine man.

Pop sighed. Life passed so fast. When he was a boy he had watched the rabbits in the field behind the house, and all these years later there were still burrows there. He was sure they were full of the same families, which could have lived in them for hundreds of years. In the springtime tiny heads would poke out of the holes and babies would sniff the air and after a while become more daring, move into the warm and hop around and start getting into mischief. Rabbits used to raid his dad's vegetable patch and Pop had built a scarecrow to keep them out, as he didn't want anything bad to happen.

When it was bedtime Michael washed his face and scrubbed his teeth and was soon tucked up with Pop turning off the light and going back downstairs. The door was left open a crack and light from the landing formed patterns that played across the walls, small souls chasing each other and jumping and doing somersaults, and he watched them play for a while before lying flat so he stared at the ceiling where clouds moved like water and plaster canals hid Martians.

It started to rain, the wind rattling the glass in a rotting window-frame, and he saw a big bad wolf huffing and puffing and trying to blow the house down. He was a piglet who had come in from the sties outside, and he wondered what real pigs thought when there was a storm, if they liked the thunder and lightning.

Maybe they were taken into the barn, but he doubted it, and Pop had told him to keep out as it was dangerous – a bad place. Real pigs wouldn't have been allowed into the house as they would make a mess, but in a story anything was possible.

Michael heard claws scratching at the window. Paws tapped on the walls and sent rabbit code into the bricks. He liked animals. *Non-human* animals. The sense of dread building up inside him came from something else, and he dropped out of bed and went over to look into the night, the land black but the sky full of stars. It was a magical sight.

Tomorrow morning he would ask Grandad Pop what he had meant about not eating animals, and before he fell asleep he put his hands together and said his prayers, making sure that he included the meek and the mild and all the innocents.

Run Rabbit Run

MIKE TANNER RAISED a glass in a private toast, his attention moving from the storyteller holding court at the bar to the buses stacked up at the junction outside, their heavy-duty engines sending tremors skimming across the pub window, some serious sub-bass scuffing the names of brewers and distillers, two rows of letters carved in flamboyant shows of family pride. The four- and five-storey buildings towering above the crossroads had changed little over the last century, and while the passing transport may have switched from horse-drawn carriages to trams to open-topped and open-backed and closed-in buses he didn't believe the people riding these clever inventions had altered much either. Every generation needed the same essentials – food, water, shelter, warmth. They craved acceptance. It was important to fit in. Nobody wanted to travel through life alone.

It was three months since his cross-country walk and things were going well. He had returned to London feeling physically and mentally strong, a string of painting and gardening jobs keeping him busy and stopping his mind from wandering. He'd had a couple of wobbles, that was true, but nothing major. Lapses of concentration. He pressed the rim of the beer glass against his lower lip. He was in a reflective mood.

Dipping into the nearest bus he saw damp brown and blonde and black and white hair cut short and hanging long, skulls blushing red and orange, every purple-lipped person present sweating in the sauna conditions. The bottom deck was packed tight, hips brushing and shoulders rubbing, ribs tinkling as people breathed in time, riding a common rhythm, the machine easing them along. Some of these good citizens dozed. Others held up newspapers and screens and studied the important issues of the day. Many followed uplifting melodies on their phones, thin plastic cords running into plugs that fitted inside ears and delivered messages of love, hope and freedom. Humans were creative and brilliant. Technology was the new magic.

He pulled back and scanned the outside of the bus. A superman fired shells into a dark valley, flares illuminating horned heads on semi-human bodies. The hero's features were highlighted so he could be more easily identified by his fans. The monsters snarled. Fangs and claws dripped blood. The scene was promoting *Part 4* of the *Destroy All Evil* franchise, a line of subtext announcing that *Part 5* was in pre-production. The war on terror continued. It might never end.

Above this movie advert, human faces lined the windows of the top deck, and he returned to the inside of the bus, to a small army of peace lovers exhausted by their hard day's work. This was a wholesome tiredness and he knew how they felt. The system was fair and rewarded loyalty. Each individual was free to push a button and pause their ride, at liberty to dismount and stroll through safe city streets, greeting neighbours and commenting on colourful flowerbeds outside flats and houses, rows of neatly clipped hedges and freshly painted railings, and when they entered their homes they would slip into the arms of those who had promised to love them forever. Refrigerators were opened and bottles of lager and cartons of fruit juice and cans of pop removed. Glasses were three-quarters filled. Small plastic trays left freezers and heart-shaped ice cubes were dropped into these drinks one after the other – plonk, plonk, plonk.

He focused on a slender character in his late-fifties. The head was tanned and firmly held, the expression proud yet humble. A white shirt was fixed by a brown tie. Tanner identified a great mathematician, a boy genius who had dedicated his gift to the collective good but preferred to remain unknown, content that he was helping others. It wouldn't be long before he too could relax, removing shoes and socks and settling into his favourite armchair, a luxury model with a lever that allowed him to raise his feet into the air. The wine he had been looking forward to would be tipped inside a crystal glass, the mathematician concentrating on the process, rinsing the grape around his mouth before letting it slide down a parched throat. Reaching for the remote control he would turn on his TV and surf a hundred-plus channels of cutting-edge culture, a magnificent merging of entertainment and education that was vital to the health of the nation. Choosing a documentary about London during the last war, he might find the narrator questioning stories he had heard from his own grandparents, tales of courage and self-sacrifice dismissed for a more progressive interpretation of history, yet he would not mind in the slightest. He trusted the producers.

The woman sitting behind him seemed less confident. She was younger and her skin was very pale, the clothes she wore shapeless, a sleepy head nodding as she fought to stay awake. Her work was less glamorous, involved the hoovering of offices and the mopping of corridors, the emptying of bins and the scrubbing of toilets, yet society valued her as highly as it did the mathematician. Once safely indoors she would lift various letters from the floor and feel the weight of the paper, study her name and address and note the efficiency of the postal system, opening these small wonders with a special knife, thrilled by messages from friends and family, gentle reminders of unpaid bills, an invitation to borrow from a well-known and well-meaning bank. She would remove half her clothes and put on a dressing-gown, sit comfortably with a nice cup of tea and a small plate of biscuits, turn on the radio and immerse herself in the flexing of intellects, a relaxing clash of positions, each speaker acknowledging the other's viewpoint as they dismissed those who could never be allowed to join the debate. She was looking forward to this time alone, willing the bus to continue on its way.

Tanner looked at the traffic lights. People filled the crossing, avoiding each other as they respected personal space, the black-and-white stripes of the zebra pattern long gone, even if he saw it for a second or two, his memory playing tricks. He remembered zebras in the zoo when he visited as a boy, cousins to the horses who used to pass through this junction, but nobody tried to ride a zebra or make it pull a carriage. In his school geography lessons Africa meant zebras and giraffes, elephants and monkeys, rhinos and hippos. It was lush jungles and lunar deserts, mountain gorillas and migrating flocks of birds. Pink flamingos standing on a single leg and gazelles bouncing in long grass, the midwifery of the elephants and their secret graveyards. Lions were symbols of pride and strength. They were the kings. There were no big-game hunters and no dictators.

A middle-aged white woman struggled with her provisions, a yellow cauliflower wobbling on the edge of a plastic bag, ready to fall to the ground. An older brown man moved around her, deep in thought, oblivious to the vegetable, a betting slip hanging from his back pocket, and when it slipped and floated in the air it was spotted by a young black man who reached out and caught it and said a few words and saved the gambler his winnings. Two teenage girls paraded skinny legs and peeling faces, a laughing youth bumping the tallest of the two and slipping an arm around her waist. Tanner stayed on the bright side. Love, marriage, children. They would all live happily ever after.

The traffic lights changed colour and the crowd stopped moving, backing up on itself, people leaving the road and mounting the pavement. Some of them jostled each other, nervous of the buses which roared and pumped black fumes into the air, the pub window shaking as one, two, three double deckers rolled forward. A car followed the last bus through the junction, speakers blaring, lyrics sparse. Tanner thought about the slow changes, the move from horsepower to diesel. There was a photograph at the back of the pub – blown up big and framed and screwed to the wall – that showed the junction a century before, and when he was a boy he'd have assumed that each horse in the picture was rewarded for its labour when it reached retirement age, taken into the countryside to live out the rest of its life in a lush green field.

A voice tugged him back inside The White Hart. Back into the moment.

The storyteller hadn't noticed Tanner's lack of attention until now, as he was busy building a plot, the sort of man who had spells when he had to keep talking or his brain would fill with words and explode. Tanner understood his nature, found it easy to sympathise, tuning back into Big Tony and the tale of a fifty-pound ring, two bright-red bows and a good-looking lady known as Punk Rock Penny. Tanner picked up the thread, tried to imagine her face, using the name according to the custom. He breathed deep on the pungent air filling the bar, the sweet smells of beer and spirits, perfume and aftershave, the savoury fragrances of salted peanuts and salt-and-vinegar crisps.

He heard how Tony had been put in his place after he tried to con Penny on the price of the ring, how she had left him standing with his trousers around his ankles, and there was a proper punch-line as well, but of course it was all made up. Penny didn't exist and Tony was a much better man than he made out. He could be noisy, but really he was shy and eager to please. Tony stood back and caught Tanner's eye, still a little wary following their row last year. Even so, they liked each other and had quickly made up. Tanner guessed that deep down Tony knew the truth. He had been testing Tanner on his vegan argument, but had gone too far. The drink had played a part. It was something that shouldn't have happened, but it was the storyteller's fault. He had deserved the black eye.

Leaving his glass on the bar, Tanner passed through the drinkers filling the front of the pub. He was polite as he headed towards the Gents, tapping shoulders and saying excuse me, seeing as good manners cost nothing. He slipped through a snug left over from the pub's heyday, cut-glass sitting inside varnished wood panels, walls dotted with racehorse drawings – thoroughbreds stretched out of shape, coats lacquered and manes tight-knotted – and he had pointed these out to Tony, directing him to the space between their hind legs. He had talked about the use of language. What it meant to be a gelding. The reality of castration. The motivations of those responsible. Tony hadn't laughed. Plenty did. But he couldn't start thinking about these things again.

The temperature dropped when he entered the back bar. There were no windows here, but a glass dome dominated the ceiling, a low-watt glow behind the patterned design. During the day the room was brighter as light filtered through from the street, but whatever the hour this was where the purists gathered. Cool in summer and warm in winter, it was removed from the year-long rattle of the junction. This was the place to brood. Loners did their heavy thinking in the semi-gloom, for the most part a different breed to those who congregated in the front of the pub. They needed company, conversation and sunlight. Tanner could see the appeal of both these bars.

He reached the door in the far wall and walked down a short hall lined with fading faces, photos put up by a former landlord, and these people would have been regulars who had died or moved away, others disabled by age, stuck indoors and unable to go outside. Pictures kept their memories alive for a while, but they were nameless now, and without a name did they really exist? He went into the Gents and stood in front of the urinal, closing his eyes as the pressure eased and water bounced off the porcelain, drawn back to the racehorses, wondering why zebras had ended up with stripes, the reason for their camouflage. He thought of the horses that had passed through the junction, the harnesses and heavy loads, the strain on their hearts and minds.

He had to love The White Hart regulars and the travellers on those big red buses, had to love how they dodged the hardest questions, preferring humour and rumour and a moan and a gossip. He had no choice but to love and understand his fellow human beings. That was the path to happiness. He was part of the whole, replaying Tony's story in his head. Penny'd had him running around on her behalf – *running around like a headless chicken* – that's what the storyteller had said, pleased to show himself up, to be seen as clueless if it would get a laugh, and she had treated him badly – *the dirty cow* – taken the ring and left him sweating – cock out, jaw bruised. Except it was a shaggy-dog tale. Just a joke. A clever use of words. Men and women. Us and Them. The peck-peck-pecking order of those headless chickens. The moo-moo-mooing of mankind's moaning herd. *Headless chicken... dirty cow... smelly pig...*

He finished and buttoned up and went to the sink, washed his hands in cold water, adding liquid from the dispenser and frothing it up, smoothing the potion into his palms and rubbing hard, rinsing the suds off and drying his skin on thick paper towels. He looked towards the sound of hot air blowing on the fists of a short-haired youth, leather boots layered in dust, a grafter fresh from work, looking forward to a session. Tanner wanted to talk to him about the skin he wore on his feet, the brutal nature of the animal's death, but instead he left the Gents, catching the door as it flapped, a drunk brushing past, oblivious to the contact, and Tanner took no notice, was back in the passage and passing the faces on the wall.

The door at the end of the corridor opened and he glanced at the approaching figure, a faint memory turning to recognition. He wasn't sure if he should feel pleased or not, realised that he could keep going and not be seen, instead stopped and blocked the way, felt as if his head had expanded and he was rubbing his scalp on the ceiling, the other man's expression changing from surprise to worry to relief to joy. Ronnie held his hands in the air as if he was being robbed. Two brains clicked as they tried to remember how things had been left. There was a pause and then they moved aside so the young builder leaving the Gents could pass, his skull pushed into a mobile phone. Ronnie reached out and shook Tanner's hand, moving his head left and right. He was still full of energy, jerking his shoulders, eyes burning, with a grip that was solid like the stubborn streak he hid behind a cheerful manner. Tanner had always admired his inner strength.

Ronnie said he was desperate for a wee, that he would be back in a minute and not to go away, and he hurried into the Gents. Tanner returned to the back bar and waited near the door, next to a fruit machine where two hard men were busy feeding in change, and he watched the oranges and lemons spinning, thinking of Ronnie as they urged strawberries to deliver a jackpot, and he was picturing his local fruit-and-veg market now, its colour and characters, the tiny Rasta cafe with its Ital menu, a place for rotis and doubles, reggae music and the words of Benjamin Zephaniah.

One of the hard men noticed him staring, shifted his position and glared over, eyeballing Tanner who returned the compliment.

The man was a chancer, a small-time bully who couldn't follow things through, saw something in Tanner's eyes, moved foot-to-foot pretending he'd meant nothing by it, face flushed as he returned to the machine. Tanner shrugged and greeted Ronnie, who was pushing through the door. They moved to a quiet corner by the entrance to the front bar.

Ronnie talked fast, features jumping under a block of black hair specked with grey, genuinely pleased to see his old friend, shaking his hand a second time to emphasise the point. He was explaining how he was married with two children, a boy and a girl, and that they were great kids, the best in the world. They meant everything to him. He was working for the council, looking after his family like a good parent should, living four or five miles away from The White Hart, a short bus ride, had just popped in to use the toilet. He shook his head at some of the things they'd got up to, like that raid on the vivisection lab when they'd worn plastic masks. Did he remember that? His words trailed off. Ronnie was suddenly serious.

He'd had some bad times, done five years in prison for saving nine dogs from a torture chamber. Rapists got less than that. Beasts and nonces... He did the full term as well, had gone a bit mental when he was inside. Too much time to read and think... Tanner knew how it worked. If a society was judged on how it treated its weakest members... Ronnie talked about the new terror laws and how they were being misused. You couldn't win. But life had been sweet these last ten or so years. He still had his beliefs, but apart from talking to people and trying to turn them vegan, and some handing out of leaflets, he kept his head down. What else could he do? What could any of them do? He bit his lip and Tanner nodded. They were older and wiser. Following similar paths. He wondered why he had thought to ignore Ronnie, but pushed the thought away, listened to him talk excitedly about his wife and children and a job in a housing department.

When Tanner's turn came he skimmed the surface, said he'd had his ups and downs as well, but was doing fine, keeping his news short and positive. Ronnie dipped a hand inside his jacket and waved his arms about as if he was making a presentation, pressed a card into Tanner's palm. There was a phone number and email address below his name. It came with the job. He was sorry he couldn't stop and have a drink, but he was in a hurry, needed to collect the kids from their gran, asked Tanner to call him so they could meet up and have a proper chat. And then he was gone. Off to catch a bus.

Slipping the card in his pocket, Tanner returned to the front bar. His head was spinning. He picked up his glass. Tony was telling another story and the traffic lights had turned red again, another crowd of people crossing the road. Tanner studied the nearest bus. Its exhaust was hanging low, fumes drifting towards the pavement, forming a mist that cut through the years and pushed at the pub windows, chemicals seeping under the door, terrifying a youth gassed in the trenches of a dirty war, the smell of manure mixing with diesel and the high-tech singe of smart weapons, the cloud heavy with the faces of press-ganged horses.

He moved from the killing of the past to a reinvention of the present, settling on the driver of the bus, a bright face he identified as a Rwandan refugee. A scarred head bent forward, bobbing gently, appreciating this fresh start in a peaceful part of the world. Tanner didn't want to imagine the tribal genocides, the mass rapes and mutilations. New waves of people were fleeing new wars and new massacres. Yet none of it was *new*. The killing was relentless. Wildlife programmes kept showing lions ripping at gazelles, never seemed to tire of the slaughter. He preferred *Meerkat Manor*.

He looked to the passengers on the bottom deck of the next bus. Men, women, boys, girls were happy, sad and content. They smiled, sulked, floated. He tried to guess their thoughts, the degrees of self-obsession, levels of empathy. The crowded nature of the city suited him and it suited Ronnie. He could lose himself in London, remain anonymous, understood why his grandfather had found the countryside depressing. Lonely people did not want to live in lonely places.

The buses crept forward and he searched for his friend, but couldn't see him. These great machines moved away, and he knew that everything good about mankind could be found in London. The streets were heaving with expression. Invention filled the air. If he couldn't be happy here he had no chance. People left him alone. Nobody was interested. The drinkers in this pub took him at face value, didn't know or care too much about his past or what he planned for the future. He had his opinions, liked a pint, a chat and a laugh. Nothing else mattered.

He compared Tony and Ronnie. On the surface they were different, and yet he saw similarities. Tony was big physically, a ginger-haired chap who was a show-off in his manner and generous when he was at the bar, the sort who knew his football and enjoyed a bet. His philosophy was simple. He looked after his own. Family came first, next were his friends, then his country. Ronnie was shorter, a wiry character who also liked to talk and was quick-witted, but his subject matter was political. He was an anarchist and didn't believe in nations. Despite Tony's front, Tanner guessed he was the more frightened of the two, putting on masks to hide his fear. Ronnie had left himself wide open and paid the price. Tony played it safe. Even so, Tanner saw a desire to hear another point of view, even if his defences meant it had to be rubbished.

Laughter rumbled around the storyteller. Tony's face was purple and he seemed to be having trouble breathing, his wide chest heaving at his own humour. Tanner had missed the punchline, but the mood was infectious and he lifted his glass in another toast, this time to the brotherhood of the hop, the ability to live in the moment for a while and only see the good things in life. He was a lucky man. Maybe the world wasn't as picture-perfect as he had thought when he was on that long-distance walk, marvelling at the landscape and thinking of Turner's skies and the fields of Nash, but it wasn't far off. He loved the changing scene outside on the junction, the way the buildings were being chopped up by the twilight, redesigned in cubist patterns, and beyond this were the steel girders of the railway bridge, the long rows of housing, the stacked hutches and pens of the city.

The pub window was vibrating again. A bus stopped and the ripples widened, but he was the only one hearing the whispers. The transporter was busy but not packed, and he recognised familiar faces that were also unique. But he didn't linger on personalities this time, drawn instead to the vibrancy of the clothes being worn, impressed by the brightness of the various shirts, blouses, jackets. He couldn't help admiring the fine lines – the crisp stitching of a dedicated seamstress, the fine scissor strokes of a master tailor. He imagined these clothes hanging in a wardrobe. Scented with lavender. Lovingly ironed. Men and women suspended from the same hangers. Everything was in its right place. There were no loose threads. No fading dye, torn fabric, flapping skin. No smashed ribs, hacked limbs, broken hearts.

He lowered his eyes and washed this thinking away with a mouthful of beer. Self-discipline was another necessity. Without it the average person became confused and strayed, ended up lost and scared. The old questions followed – why was he alive; what was the point of living; why was life so unfair? He repeated the answers he had invented, raised his head and returned to the bus, pleased to see that every single face was beaming in the best cartoon style.

The daylight was starting to fade and there were fewer people on the pavements. Electricity clicked on and the first bulbs set off a chain reaction, showers of colour forming fireballs that roared along the bricks and into the lamp posts. The junction was burning with positive energy, transformed into a fairground that offered entertainment and comradeship. Fresh waves of people would soon arrive, adding new layers to the spectacle. Tanner emptied his glass and turned towards the bar, nodded at the storyteller and asked him what he wanted to drink.

Standing at the traffic lights, Mike Tanner heard a siren and looked up the slope running away to his right, saw a flashing light coming his way. He reached for the nearby railings and placed both hands on the frame, conscious that he was adding his fingerprints to the collection. The ground was thick with DNA, flakes of skin and strands of hair stamped into the concrete. CCTV recorded the scene. The police car grew in size as it accelerated downhill, over-taking a bus and slowing at the junction, veering left towards the railway bridge and the high-rise estate beyond. He remembered the food waiting for him at home and was hungry, the thought of it making him move.

He crossed the road and headed up the hill to his left, pausing to admire the brightly lit display in a department-store window. Three mannequins were having fun on a tropical island. The two females wore bikinis and sarongs, had garlands around their necks and drinks in their hands, the cocktail glasses topped with slices of plastic pineapple. The male was decked out in a Hawaiian shirt and knee-length shorts. He wore designer sandals while the ladies balanced on heels. Their skin was smooth and they looked confident, with their wry smiles and blank eyes. A range of clothing was positioned around them, the focus of an exciting summer collection. The mannequins seemed very tall, the same height as the imitation palm tree, and Tanner wished he could join them in Bali, Barbados or Honolulu – he didn't mind where.

Getting home would have to do him for tonight, and he continued past the shop selling carpet off-cuts, the art supplier with the neat shelves and fussy owner, the messy charity shop fighting heart disease. Drunks came from the opposite direction, some walking in silence and others shouting. One man was singing a Kaiser Chiefs song and wanted a riot. A couple kissed on a bench. He saw a middle-aged woman hurrying with her head down, staring at the ground, hoping that this would make her invisible. By her manner and dress, he decided she was sober and returning from work. He tried to guess her occupation, but his imagination failed.

Another siren sounded and he wondered if it was the same police car, or an ambulance or fire engine… a doctor carrying an organ for transplant. He thanked the police for their protection; the ambulance crews for racing to help the sick; the fire-fighters for risking death to save lives. Nurses, doctors and soldiers were more real-life heroes, servants of a state in which he believed. These people were actually doing things that mattered. They were examples to the rest of the population, could only make him stronger as he pushed his legs and fought the tiredness left by the alcohol.

Reaching the top of the hill he picked up speed on the level surface, traffic cones diverting him so that he found himself in the road passing piles of paving stones, part of the council's plan to help wheelchair users and the elderly. A kerb could be an obstacle and a danger, and lowering them to improve mobility was a simple enough solution, but it needed awareness and a willingness to act.

The post office on the other side of the road was plain and functional in its appearance, but even in these digital days it was busy from the moment it opened to the second it closed. The staff dealt out stamps, weighed parcels, managed forms, changed currencies and linked the world. This was another of society's wonders. And next to him now that he was back on the pavement was the local library, a grand building offering books, internet access and rooms in which to meet. It had been offering knowledge across the generations and gave him access to the finest minds on the planet.

He left the main road for a long side-street, the two-storey houses compact and well kept, their boundaries marked by clipped hedges and low walls topped with railings. The front gardens slowed him down again as he admired a mass of hebes, blooming roses, ferns mixed in with rotting tree stumps, a mature wisteria covering a wall. The lamplights could only show shades and outlines, but he knew this street well and was familiar with the gardens. Further along was a house with cacti on every single windowsill, another one with a palm that had huge machete-like leaves, and finally a collection of packed alpine troughs at the top end. He noticed a face at a window and realised he had stopped walking. Tanner hurried on.

Black bin-bags were stacked in small heaps, ready for their morning collection. There were orange versions as well, ecologically aware citizens recycling paper, cardboard, bottles and cans. There were so many great systems in operation that it was easy to take them for granted. Waste disposal was essential. Dustmen did a lot more for society than estate agents. Diseases had been fought and defeated. Workers supplied clean water, gas and electricity. Society was alive with good intentions. He had heard a piano being played on this same street, the window open and the curly haired young man responsible so absorbed in the music that Tanner had decided to buy something similar, a hospice charity selling him albums by Chopin, Schumann, Shostakovich and Rachmaninov.

A fox came out of a garden a few doors up, looked at him and trotted off in the opposite direction, glancing back several times to make sure there was enough space between them. Tanner had seen plenty of foxes locally, as they lived on the common and in some of the overgrown gardens of the more run-down houses, and were confident enough to roam the streets after dark. They did no harm that he knew of and lived longer in the city than in the country. There was more food available for a start. And no hunts. The fox stepped behind a van and when Tanner reached the spot it was gone.

He reached the common and followed the path that kept him near the road and its lights. The outline of a playground was just visible, and during the day it was always busy with children, but dark and empty it looked eerie. There was a path running through the middle of the common, but he wouldn't want to cross it now. He had been fine camping on his own in the countryside, but it was different in a city. He thought of that classical pianist again, the albums he had bought and how he hadn't played them for at least a year, and there were others he should listen to, but the likes of Knock Off and the East End Badoes weren't going to keep him calm, never mind Conflict and the Subhumans. Shostakovich wasn't easy listening either. Back when they were married, Kate used to tell him that he was angry because of the music he listened to and the books he read. He agreed. It was easier to watch TV.

Turning away from the common, he reached a small parade of shops. There was a late-night takeaway here and the smell of spices made his mouth water, but it was dedicated to meat and chicken and had nothing to offer. Anyway, he was nearly home, reached his street of once-noble houses long ago broken up into flats, recessions changing the nature of the area, boom-and-bust economics shaping the city. The houses were shabbier here and he was taking his keys out of his pocket and opening the front door, pushing a light on and hauling himself up the stairs, hands on rickety banisters, the dark varnish lightened by a century of returning tenants. He trod the same steps as pre-war servant girls and depression-era spivs and post-war tarts, navvies, drinkers, smokers, grafters. He reached the top landing and inserted a second key, jiggled it in the lock and went inside his flat.

It was hot and stuffy, so he opened the kitchen window, took a bottle of lager from the fridge and opened it, had a refreshing swig and placed it on the tray he had prepared earlier. He often made himself something to eat before he went out drinking, as the nearest takeaways had little to offer a vegan. A stack of hummus sandwiches, a bowl of olives and a packet of crisps were ready and waiting, and he carried his food into the living room, put the tray on the table while he turned on a couple of lamps and let more fresh air in, sat in his armchair with the football highlights on TV. The sourdough and hummus went down a treat, likewise the chilli-soaked olives and his favourite crisps, and he dipped in and out of the beautiful game, the commentary barely registering as he followed the ball and savoured his food but couldn't help thinking about Ronnie.

It was Ronnie who'd taken him on his first raid and out to sabotage the hunt, introduced him to a lot of dedicated people, and like most of those in animal-rights groups he was committed to non-violence. They had argued about that a few times, and maybe it was why he'd hesitated in the pub, or it could have been a feeling of guilt for backing away from the movement. It was a long time ago and his memory was hazy, but their lives had moved on. You couldn't beat the system. It worked for a reason. And while Tanner was pleased to see Ronnie doing so well, bumping into him like that wasn't what he needed right now. Instinctively, he would have known this in the pub.

He thought about that time when he was in his late teens and early twenties, the music that matched what they believed, or more likely helped shape their activism, all those records and lyrics he had put in a box. He could feel the old arguments stirring, reached in his pocket and took out the card Ronnie had handed him, tore it into tiny pieces and piled them up at the side of his tray. He would not see him again.

There was no real breeze and the air was still close, and when he finished eating he put his tray on the table and turned off the television, went over to the window and stuck his head out, breathing deeply as he peered into the empty street below. He heard a helicopter in the distance, looked across the rooftops and saw a band of clouds lit up by the moon, shortly after a searchlight appearing. He couldn't see the chopper, but he followed the beam as it moved forward, stopped and started, changed its angle, the noise of the engine and blades growing louder. Someone was running for their life, innocent or guilty they were making a dash for freedom, tracked by airborne Old Bill and their heat-sensitive technology, AirCav chopper coppers chasing spirits.

He thought of other machines, of the lorries moving under cover of darkness, out beyond the lights of the city, the stop-start drone of buses and helicopters replaced by the smooth hum of the lorries transporting lambs to their slaughter. Pigs, chickens, steers, donkeys… He pictured Upton Sinclair's boxcars in the great stockyards of his steak-eating democracy, the death-camp trains of the fascists and communists, the slave ships of the sugar kings. The horror continued in the right here and right now, but the masses drank and ate and went to work and didn't want to know. That searchlight should have been on the lorries. People needed to confront the reality.

The helicopter started to move away from Tanner, but then it stopped and hovered. The police must have cornered the person they were chasing. Maybe an arrest was being made. The chopper didn't leave the scene, stayed there for a good ten minutes, and he wondered about the inventor, the team responsible for the first models, was sure they loved birds and insects, dreamed of hovering like a bumble bee over a lavender flower. He wasn't working in the morning and could handle a hangover, but had things to do and should really go to bed. His head ached and his thoughts were straying. He'd had enough. Even so, he kept watching the search-light until it finally snapped off.

Tanner had first come to the Bell Street allotments a week or so after Ella's stroke. He got stuck into the weeding and did the watering while she was in hospital worrying, then when she was back at home but too frail to go outside he had built cane pyramids and put her beans in, since her recovery continuing to help out. She was the brains, he was her muscle – that's what he said. Sowing seeds and seeing them sprout from soil he had prepared was one of life's many miracles. He loved double-digging, turning and break-ing up the earth, adding loam, working until he was worn out, finally drinking tea with Ella and talking into the twilight.

The allotments had been her favourite place since she was a girl, back when her father had the plot. It kept her going after her hus-band Ted died, his ashes scattered under the vine her dad had planted more than six decades earlier. She was here most spring and summer days, less so during the autumn and rarely in winter. That was the season to stay warm and make plans, and by February she couldn't wait to get going again. The allotments were beautiful when the snow settled, an oil painting of frozen flower-heads and fuzzy old sheds, but she couldn't come on her own, scared she would slip on the ice and end up back in hospital.

Ella had only started to mend properly on the day Tanner took some groceries round and decided that he had to act. She'd been stuck indoors for a month after two weeks on the ward, and her world was shrinking fast. He felt her fear, the claustrophobia of the flat, recognised the haunted look in her eyes. She had deteriorated in the two days since he'd last seen her and was starting to give up, but he couldn't accept death, and like Dylan Thomas raged against the dying of the light.

He persuaded Ella to trust him, picked her up like the doll she was turning into and carried her down the stairs, eased her into his car and drove straight to Bell Street. Gripping his left arm as they walked through the gates, she moved in closer as they started up the slope, relying on his strength the same as his mum and dad had done towards the end of their lives. Trusting and childlike. Grateful for any sort of kindness. Ella didn't notice the tears filling his eyes, was just relieved when she reached the white metal table by her brown wooden shed and was able to sit down. Out of breath and exhausted, she knew she had achieved something important. It was a cloudy day, but within minutes Ella was glowing, and when the sun broke through she seemed to straighten and revive in a matter of seconds.

Four years on and here he was earthing up potatoes while she stood nattering with Sid from the next allotment, having swapped a bag of runner beans and rhubarb for two of his marrows wrapped in newspaper. Ella Brown – seventy-two years old, full of energy and speaking fast, her right hand squeezing Sid's left wrist, retired but with every minute a busy one, repeating daily that she didn't know how she'd ever had time to go to work. It was almost impossible to remember her as that frail lady knocked sideways by a stroke.

Sid was slower in his delivery, tilting his body forward when he listened to someone speak, and at first Tanner had thought he was hard of hearing before realising it was a sign of pure concentration. The man was genuinely interested. But when Sid was trading veg he changed, stood straight and became cautious, glancing left and right, checking over each shoulder as if he was selling guns or drugs. This impressed Tanner. He knew little about Sid's life away from the allotments, other than that he did shift work and would come straight to his plot during the summer, some days arriving as early as five or six in the morning.

Sid was a squash fanatic. He was king of the courgettes and marrows, a lover of pumpkins with a longing for flamboyance. He was a connoisseur of shape, colour and texture. Turbans and gourds – he had exotic tastes. Atlantic Giant met Jack Be Little. He was a butternut nut, a Turk's cap craver, revelled in the sheer style of the goldarc, pattypan, sweet dumpling. On occasion, he described himself as a cultivator, and emphasised the term, breaking it into four sections, and when he was going into detail about his squash he seemed to grow in height.

On his third visit to Bell Street, Tanner had paused to admire the mystical kingdom next to Ella's more functional plot. A jungle of green foliage glistened after an early water, while the orange bodies below looked as if they were ready to explode. The patch was boxed in by corrugated-iron walls, ridged and rusting panels laced together by white rope turned to grey. He replayed films set in the American Deep South. Hot and humid locations – Mississippi, Louisiana, Tennessee. Huge hillbillies in dungarees grew enormous pumpkins. Sun and water worked their magic, the walls raising the temperature. Sid had appeared carrying a coiled hose, introduced himself, his handshake as firm as any Tanner had felt. He was shocked when he heard about Ella's stroke. That evening he went to visit her in hospital.

Later, when they knew each other better, Tanner had told Sid how his allotment reminded him of *Invasion Of The Body Snatchers*, a Seventies film starring Donald Sutherland. He explained how spores landed from space and grew into pods, which produced lookalike humans as aliens replaced individuals and started taking over the planet. Sid didn't know the movie and seemed concerned. A week later he came over and said he had watched the film and thought it was very good. Brilliant, in fact. If there *was* going to be an attack from outer space then the invaders were bound to infiltrate the human population via the plant world. It made perfect sense, even if the film mirrored some old Cold War tensions.

Sid leaned in very close. He had seen the original. In his opinion it was far better than the Sutherland version of 1978, which he had also watched. Made in 1956, it starred Kevin McCarthy and Dana Wynter, and was directed by Don Siegel, who had worked with the brilliant Clint Eastwood on a number of occasions. Siegel was the director behind *Dirty Harry* – Sid's all-time best film. Interestingly, the Sutherland remake was directed by Philip Kaufman, who Clint had fired from *The Outlaw Josey Wales,* going on to direct Sid's third-favourite movie himself. That was another gem. Yes, the body-snatcher takeover was logical, if a little ridiculous. He would watch the Siegel masterpiece again and had ordered the Jack Finney novel on which it was based. He liked the idea of pod people being born in his pumpkin patch. It was just a shame they weren't more friendly.

Last month Tanner had been invited to sit on Sid's bench. A mug of strong black coffee was served and five photo albums produced, each one filled with pictures showing a year's worth of squash. Sid explained how he would never enter a competition. He was not competitive. Never had been. It would change the way he looked at things, shift his attention from the process to the prize. Really, it would ruin everything. He tried to enjoy each day in its own right. When Tanner had been through the books and finally stood to leave, Sid handed him a twenty-page pamphlet. He had written the recipes inside himself and had it professionally printed – the inner pages were recycled off-white 100gsm, the cover a thicker orange card. This featured a drawing of a pumpkin. *Squash* was numbered. Tanner's copy had been marked '148'. The author had not added his name.

Ella was whispering in Sid's ear as he leaned as far forward as he could without falling over. His head was turned on its side so Tanner could see his eyes scrunch as he strained to make sense of what he was hearing. He snapped back to his normal height. They both roared, Ella doubling up and bending into the space he had left empty, while Sid's eyes were now closed. Ella put a hand to her mouth. They kept on laughing, their faces turning bright red, and as the sound died down their shoulders shook. When they were finally calm, Ella patted Sid's arm as he turned to leave, and he raised a hand in the air as he went.

Tanner returned to his work and Ella disappeared inside her shed. He dug methodically, each movement exaggerated, occasionally breaking his rhythm to pick up a worm and put it in with the spinach, so it was hidden from the birds. Almost done, he paused to stretch his back and look across the waves of vegetation rolling down the slope, a green sea dotted with splashes of red and white, the wooden structures built for climbers reminding him of masts. A scarecrow stood to his left, over near the fence.

He spotted Bunny outside the gates, closing the boot of his battered Mondeo, lifting two bin bags off the ground and heading towards the entrance. Tanner hadn't seen him since before Christmas and would go and say hello once he'd finished earthing up this last row. The man was a reformed crook from a family of villains and could still get his hands on anything from a vintage Cadillac to an unused firearm, but more importantly had promised Ella some of the fertiliser he brewed, which would be perfect for the spuds. Tanner worked fast and was soon driving his spade into the ground and admiring a job well done. He went over to the shed to look for Ella, but she'd wandered off. He rubbed his hands on a rag and left.

It could take ages to get anywhere on a day like today. The weather was perfect – hot and still – and the regulars were out in force. These people were largely retired, self-employed, unemployed or worked unusual hours, and normally he would stop and chat, happy to go with the flow, as this was part of what made the place so special, but he wanted to catch Bunny before he left again, so hoped those nearest the path would be too busy to notice him passing by.

To his right, Pat was examining a tomato plant, reaching into his pocket and taking out a knife and ball of cord, measuring it as far as one of the taller canes he'd pushed into the ground, doubling the length, stopping and thinking and adding extra for the loop he started to tie. Like most people here, he grew a range of vegetables, but his tomatoes stood out. Tanner felt hungry remembering the last lot, eaten like an apricot or sliced thick on olive bread. Cooking and even grilling Pat's tomatoes was a waste. Looking to his left, he saw the Guptas crouching as they tended their aubergines. They had been together for over sixty years, and while they produced a huge amount of fruit and veg Tanner always married them to the ginger and garlic Mrs Gupta grew. She had shared some of her tricks, telling him about their properties and how they could be best used when he was cooking. The aubergines were pretty special as well.

Pat and the Guptas didn't see him, but Maggie did, waving as he approached, a hammer in one hand and a jar of nails sitting on the shed roof she was repairing. Propped at the top of a ladder, she stood back to catch his attention, the angle and sunlight turning her into the star of a Fifties propaganda poster. Bold and brash, the photographer shot from the ground up to emphasise the heroism of a single representative of a unified people. Everyone was pulling in the same direction as they built the perfect society. The red-and-white scarf covering Maggie's blonde hair added to the effect. The nobility of labour was magnified. The workers were winning. East or West, communist of capitalist, the dream was Utopian. Maggie's pose may have struck Tanner, but not as strongly as the smell of her latest crop.

Maggie didn't bother with the basics such as potatoes and leeks, nor the more exotic pumpkins and tomatoes, instead concentrating on lavender. The flowers gave her oils that could be extracted and used for aromatherapy and massage. Tied inside material, cuttings were sold for scent and cures. Her land was neat and regimented, different species blocked together. He knew the blue flowers of Hidcote and the white of Arctic Snow, recognised the French lavender Maggie used for potpourri. The scent of her lavender garden really was incredible. Bees buzzed as they hovered around the flowers, butterflies lazily flapping their wings and searching for a breeze.

There was a section where Maggie had planted bamboo and exotic grasses, the canes forming a semi-circular wall to the side of her shed. Two heavy chairs sat in the space, facing the sun, her pond to the left with its ring of rocks and reeds, clumps of blue grass to the right. He had sat with her there last summer, drinking cider and hearing something about her life. This was unusual, as the people here tended to exist in a single dimension, much as they did in the pub, taking each other at face value, living freely in the moment. Deeper friendships did develop, but the wide range of backgrounds and ages meant they didn't always have so much in common in the outside world.

He was a different person to different people, their impression of him based on a small number of interactions, or a single location. How could anyone know what he thought unless he told them? It would be easy to vanish, to create different identities.

Maggie was much more than a lavender grower, had been a policewoman and then a detective, the horrors of the job leading to her resignation from the force. Her belief in human beings had been shattered by what she had seen them do to each other. He was surprised by her openness, put it down to the cider, but later he started to wonder if she sensed that he felt the same way about things. She had moved on. Maybe she was encouraging him to do the same.

He thought of the great grasslands of the USA and USSR, the conflicting philosophies and similar faces on the posters, and he thought about the essential oils that came from lavender plants, and how Maggie made part of her living from her plot. She may have gone green, but was organised and efficient, knew how lavender grew and what it carried inside it, and Tanner always wondered who worked these things out in the first place. Where did the knowledge come from? He assumed trial and error, experiment after experiment, and that involved a certain sort of mind, an incredible determination, but there had to be a spark that started a person thinking that way. There were lucky discoveries, but how many? Someone had to see into the future and imagine fire and electricity. Surely?

When it came to computers and digital technology, that really did seem like more magic, and so he understood the mobile-phone addiction, the new obsessions and reliance on social media, but knew it was a corporate scam as well. Had the web changed the world for the better? Could it? How did people first think to draw and paint, create cameras and shoot movies? Where did the ideas of the greatest artists come from, and especially those who had moved beyond reproduction? He again thought of the Nash brothers and Turner, added Van Gogh, who lived the extremes, saw the nature of human beings and went insane.

That knowledge had to be inside a person already, in the subconscious and unconscious, learned or part of a greater awareness that went beyond the individual, and if that was the case then surely it had to link into non-human animals as well, maybe even non-animal life. He had heard it said that trees screamed when they were cut down. The same happened with root vegetables. There were fruitarians who would never eat a potato or a carrot, and he wondered if he was a coward not doing the same. But part of him already felt like a coward, hiding in the everyday and not fighting for the animals. Right now, though, he was elated, his mind full of the shapes, colours and smells of his surroundings, and he left Maggie to line up another tack, trailed by the scent of her lavender and the noise of her hammer connecting.

Wendell saw him and called out, Tanner stopping and waiting for the older man to hobble over. He had something cupped in his palms and nodded downwards when he was close, slowly lifted his upper hand. Sitting in the thick brown ridges was a tiny green frog. It didn't hop forward or try to escape, just stayed perfectly still as it stared ahead. The eyes and feet were oversized, and Wendell squinted as he talked about the suckers, the beating of the creature's tiny heart, while his own breath croaked inside his smoker's lungs.

He had found the frog on the path. Nearly trod on it. It just sat there not moving, waiting to be squashed. He had caught it with a plastic bowl over the top and a thin sheet of wood underneath, turned it over and removed the board, put the bowl in the shade while he decided what to do. He was thinking now that it must have come from Maggie's pond. That was only two plots away, even if it seemed like a long distance for such a small creature. It could have got lost, but why sit out in the open? Was it on a suicide mission? It looked happy enough. Maybe frogs liked to roam, didn't always want to stay in one place. Was it a boy or a girl? Perhaps it was lonely and looking for a Mr or Mrs Frog? Well, he should maybe take it over to Maggie. Tanner reckoned that was a good idea. Wendell nodded, mentioned how he had come to the allotments at Christmas and seen the surface of the pond frozen over. It was important to break the ice. Did he know that birds died of thirst when the water froze? It might be the same for frogs. He would mention it to Maggie.

Wendell loved the allotments in winter, and his Brussels sprouts were as special then as Sid's summertime squash and Pat's tomatoes. As a Jamaican boy new to England, seeing snow for the first time had left an impression, the thrill somehow linking to parsnips and sprouts connected to the stem. His uncle was a grocer catering for the older Londoners and newly arrived West Indians, and so he had seen these sprouts and other root vegetables along with more familiar provisions.

His sprouts couldn't be frozen or overcooked. He wanted them fresh and firm, and had started adding chestnuts, a combination to which Tanner had been converted. Wendell grew lots of broccoli and kale, but for Tanner the callaloo was his tastiest crop. There was a system of nets that kept the birds off, and around October the Bell Street scarecrow came over and stood guard thanks to Wendell's sister Mary, who had told Tanner she'd given up on finding a decent man and decided to build her own.

Worried the frog would dry out or die of shock, Wendell started up towards Maggie's allotment, and with no more than a couple of waves and hellos Tanner was soon approaching Bunny's plot, his friend standing with his back to him, arms stretched out as he struggled to empty the last leaves from one of the bags he'd been carrying. Bunny's leaf-mould cage was easily the biggest here, with chicken wire nailed to six stakes, and Tanner had been out collecting leaves with him in the past, a surreal couple of hours in a wood that he wasn't in a hurry to repeat. Bunny shook the black plastic harder, stopped and reached inside to pull out the last handfuls.

If Ella, Sid and Maggie preferred the summer – like most people – and Wendell looked forward to his winter brassicas, then Bunny had a craving for the autumn. Plants started to die back, meaning there was more raw material for his compost. Leaves were kept separate in the cage as they broke down more slowly and had fewer nutrients, the end result used for potting and as a mulch. It was the process that appealed to Bunny, the philosophy involved. He used less than half his land, and in truth enjoyed having a quiet shed to come to when the weather was nice. In that sense he was with the other summer-lovers, at peace with the world as he sat in his deckchair enjoying his daydreams.

Beyond Bunny and his leaves were two compost heaps. Sturdy and made from wood, he had told Tanner to think of them as huge hotels, but ones in which the residents worked as well as lived. They weren't in the league of Trump Tower, say, or the skyscrapers in Docklands, had nothing in common with a Gherkin or a Shard. There was no gold-plated lift zipping The Donald up and down as he fired off angry tweets. No, this was more Margate than New York or London. Your everyday Blackpool B&B extended – slowly – layer on layer, floor by floor. These hotels doubled as factories, home to worker ants and worms, great armies of insects and slugs, billions and billions of microbes. He talked about the importance of a good nitrogen–carbon balance. Manure and grass raised the temperature and speeded up the conversion process. Bunny rubbed his hands together and pulled a satisfied face.

As well as the towers, nine strategically placed hobbit houses provided accommodation that was less industrial and more inti-mate. A builder by trade these days, Bunny had taken some Victorian ridge tiles from a skip at a grand old villa he'd been working on, sticking them in the boot of his car and bringing them straight to his shed. They were perfect for the wildlife shelters. Three bricks formed a solid foundation, with blocks of wood on the longer sides acting as walls, the interior stuffed with sticks, twigs, moss and leaves, one of the big V-shaped tiles creating a natural roof. Warm and dry, they were soon full of insects. They looked good as well, like something off a Monopoly board. There was an ornate chimney, but he had left this empty.

Bunny did dabble in roots – potatoes, parsnips, turnips – but it was the making of humus that mattered. He saw the creation of fresh earth from rotting vegetation as a sort of alchemy. Or an act of reincarnation. He was bringing the dead back to life. At times he had to control himself, when he spotted a wilting plant and wanted to cut it down and feed his ever-hungry heaps, but knew he had to wait, didn't want to end up like Burke and Hare. His comfrey grew back fast every time he cut it, which fed his interest in liquid fertiliser. Twenty pink plastic buckets stood in a long line, their contents slowly fermenting.

Tanner coughed and Bunny turned his head, the remains of the bin bag left for later. The kettle had already boiled and they were soon sitting down and drinking tea, munching biscuits as they filled in the time since they'd last seen each other. Tanner talked about his trip to the country without mentioning how he'd been in the months before, while Bunny had been away as well, working for a friend in Taunton, attending a Sixties weekender in nearby Minehead. That sounded good to Tanner, and he waited to hear about it, but more important to Bunny was the seaweed he had collected from a beach further down the coast in Cornwall.

He had filled eight reinforced bags with the stuff. The seaweed came in thick rubbery bands that were so full of iodine he reckoned he could taste it in the air. Bursting with nutrients, it would crank up production back in London. Two days later, when he opened his boot outside the allotments, he found that it had rotted into a congealed ball, like something out of *Alien,* but worse. The stench almost made him puke. It was disgusting. He pointed to a raised mound, which looked as if it held a couple of bodies.

Tanner wanted to hear about the weekender, but Bunny hadn't finished talking seaweed. A lesson had been learnt. He now knew that this sea vegetable had to be moved quickly, and he mused on what it would have added to his compost if it hadn't solidified, how his soil would have reacted if he'd been able to cut it into small pieces and space them out evenly, part of a double-digging extravaganza. He ran through a number of crops he could grow, but probably never would. Tanner was a strong man who could help with the soil if he wanted. His visitor didn't mind, but wanted to move the conversation on.

At the allotments, Bunny was one more scruffy gardener. When he was at work or lazing in front of the TV, he was just another everyday herbert. If he went to the pub he would put on a clean Ben Sherman and a Harrington, but even then it was hard to imagine the transformation that took place when he went out properly. Nobody was going to guess that his wardrobe included seven five-hundred-pounds-plus, made-to-measure suits. When he was in the mood he didn't so much scrub up as polish himself until he shone. Bunny turned into Mark Simpson, and while the same character was driving them both, Mark The Mod had another set of rules.

Tanner guided Bunny back to the weekender, heard about the chalet he'd shared with his new friends from Somerset. They drank too much, listened to the bands and DJs, tried to chat up a few women. Bunny had even bumped into an old girlfriend and they'd had a couple of dances. But he'd been disappointed, wished there were more stalls, Q&As with the musicians. Tanner nodded. Stories kept the world turning. Experiences were passed on. People elaborated, exaggerated, invented, lied. Oral traditions morphed into literature, poetry, lyrics. Drink stimulated thought. Never mind, Bunny knew there were plenty of good times to come, and they talked about music as they often did, and it would have been easy to sit here for the rest of the day but Tanner had a cargo to deliver, stayed for another half-hour before forcing himself back to work.

With a bucket of liquid comfrey in each hand he headed up the slope, doing his best not to spill the contents. He could hear the solution slopping around, and when the sound became louder he slowed down, really didn't want to splash it on his clothes. He concentrated on his aching arms, drove the pain away, straightening his back when he was tempted to slouch, stretching muscles and imagining them taut under his skin. He could make himself strong if he wanted. The slope was a positive. It gave Ella a view over the allotments.

Watching his step on an uneven section of the path, where a leaking tap had eaten into the soil and exposed the stones below, when he raised his head he saw Maggie up ahead, a pint glass in each of her raised hands. He was happy to stop now he'd seen Bunny, and especially glad it was Maggie waiting. She called for him to hurry up, before the ice melted, but she wasn't impressed by the smell of the rotting comfrey when he reached her, Tanner imagining the clash of liquid fertiliser and lavender scent, an invisible fizz followed by a silent explosion.

He put the buckets down on her land, didn't want anyone falling over them on the path, and as he did so the pain in his arms seared for a second and was gone. He looked at the marks the handles had left on his palms, followed Maggie to the chairs next to the pond where he hoped Wendell's frog was swimming, or had at least settled in and was watching from the rocks. Maggie handed him his drink and they clinked glasses, the cider sending his good mood into orbit.

The weather forecasters had predicted the hottest day of the year and they had been proved right. The city rose and fell in hazy waves as the sun burned its streets and rooftops, radio DJs selecting some classic Beach Boys and Motown as a soundtrack. London had been created by craftsmen, its bricks and mortar fitted together by jigsaw masters, the arches and tunnels shaped by sculptors, and Tanner was grateful. He moved slowly, a heavy canvas bag wedged over his right shoulder, the heat coming out of the pavement filtering through his shoes and into his socks and feet. If he paused his soles were going to melt and fix him to the concrete, and then the sun would turn him to bones.

At the next corner he stopped in the shade of a billboard. He put his bag on the floor and crouched to tie a lace that had come undone. Standing and looking up, he saw a huge cow smiling down at him. She was trying to sell him butter. He was immediately angry, turned away from the advert and the dairy industry, made himself admire the surrounding buildings again, noticed several stained-glass windows that had been added to a newish house opposite, told himself a story, staying in the shade until he had cooled down.

Tanner considered a short cut, seeing as it would save him ten minutes on his journey back to the flat. The path might be a bit overgrown, but he would be off the main road and there would be some shelter from the sun. He made a decision and crossed the road, headed down a narrow drive running between the backs of two rows of houses, their gardens and rear windows protected by planks and ivy and the barking of a dog. He heard radio voices, the muffled conversation of neighbours over a fence. The drive led to some garages, and he been told about the short cut by a mechanic who operated out of a lock-up and had fixed his broken-down car.

The rain had started as soon as Tanner arrived, and after explaining the problem and the man agreeing to come and have a look at it the next day, they sat inside the open door of the lock-up drinking coffee and watching puddles form in the potholes outside, waiting for the downpour to stop. Thunder boomed as they talked for a good half-hour, the mechanic having finished for the day, and oddly having no wheels of his own there apart from the two attached to a pushbike.

Reaching the end of the drive, Tanner saw that the lock-up was closed. An Astra and a Škoda were parked outside, the first of these with its front lights smashed in and the bumper hanging off. He went to the end of the garages and into the alley he had been shown, moving the bag into his arms so he was cradling his supplies – big packets of rice and pasta, tins of beans and chickpeas, bottles of sauce and cans of beer. Most of his vegetables came from the allotment, topped up by fruit from a nearby grocer.

There was a brick wall to his left, the breeze-blocks of the garages to his right. The passage was dark and musty and smelled of piss, and he was pleased to come out at the other end and turn along what would once have been a lane but had been closed in by buildings and forgotten. This sliver of land was bordered by some seriously big houses and a mesh fence covered in ivy, part of a jungle at the edge of a park. The surface of the lane was cracked and overgrown, grass and flowers colonising the gaps.

He had only been this way once before, in the rain and under heavy clouds, and it was very different on a sunny day. Trees bent over the garden walls of the houses, branches swaying in a breeze that was too high for him to feel, leaves breaking up the light and creating watery patterns on the ground. He half-expected a fish to swim past. He noticed acorns on the floor, looked into the trees and found hundreds more in their shells, heard birds singing, which was odd because he hadn't noticed them before, but maybe they had been watching and were passing on warnings now that his head was raised in their direction.

The gardens became longer as he continued, and the brick walls gave way to lower fences so he could see inside. He couldn't help looking, as while he didn't have a garden of his own he wished he did, liked watching Monty Don on his television, seeing what the possibilities were, how it all worked. There were a handful of greenhouses, lots of smaller trees he couldn't name, beds filled with delphiniums and hollyhocks, a row of giant sunflowers. He saw an elderly couple sitting at a table eating, turned his face away as he didn't want to intrude.

He imagined having a house one day, a garden to design and look after, a lawn to mow and keep free of weeds, earth to dig and fork. The people on the allotments had taught him a lot, and he had his plans in his head. There would have to be a vegetable plot as well. Bunny would improve his soil, Maggie supplying lavender to attract bees and showing him how to make his own pond, and Ella would help in the summer and Wendell in the winter. Mr and Mrs Gupta could advise on his ginger, garlic and spices generally, fine-tuning the operation. Sid would run the pumpkin patch. He was going to get himself a couple of rescue dogs. When the leaves fell from his trees he would split them between mulch and hedgehog piles. He wondered if it would ever happen. Probably not, but he could dream.

He saw a man up ahead, at the bottom of his garden, in a small space separated from the lawn by a wall of latticework. There was a shed and what looked like a big metal drum, something to catch rainwater in for recycling and watering in summer. Tanner identified a hidden corner where a person could escape the stresses and do what they wanted, a private allotment a short walk from their back door. He couldn't see any vegetables, but maybe they were lower down, hidden by the fence. The man was washing his hands in the drum, or it seemed that way at first, but as he got nearer he realised he was cleaning some sort of material, a bundle of rags by the look of it, pulling them from the drum and shaking them dry.

He dropped the rags to the ground, which was silly, as they would pick up more dirt. But he must have a bucket there. It flashed into Tanner's mind that he might be a mechanic like the one who worked from his garage, though this bloke could be more interested in motorbikes – a stripped-down engine sitting in the nearby shed, a hobby rather than a living.

The figure turned and a lean face formed. Tanner smiled, but the response was cold. Almost angry. He felt guilty, as if he was spying, wouldn't like it himself, raising his head like that and finding a stranger staring. It was important to see the other person's point of view. Essential. Do unto others as you would have them do unto you – that was the law. Nothing but logical. Despite his own irritation, Tanner looked away and focused on the path. It was hardly ever used so he was bound to seem suspicious. People identified a prowler, burglar, rapist. What did he expect? Yet there was something wrong about that face. He couldn't accept the expression. It was too much. More than even an insult. He stopped and walked back towards the man, who had dismissed the passer-by and returned to his work.

Bending down, he disappeared from view, and when he stood up again he was holding more rags, and these were dry and bulkier. Jumble-sale fabrics, secondhand textiles... Tanner heard him mutter as he sorted them out, purring like one of those motorbikes he loved to tinker with in his private corner, this place where he was king. The man was massaging the material, head shaking as he pushed the bundle down into the rainwater. Two legs kicked and then they were under the surface.

Tanner dropped his bag and hurried to the fence, reached over the top of the gate and slid the bolt back, pushed to go inside. It wouldn't open as there was another lock below the latch, one that needed a key. He stepped back and kicked at the wood, using his heel, which caused the man at the drum to turn. The gate still wouldn't budge so Tanner used his shoulder and this time it smashed open, the ragman removing his hands from the water and dropping a rabbit to the ground before storming towards the intruder. He took ten or so steps and hesitated.

Tanner hit him in the face. Punched at the side of the head as he stumbled. Grabbed the shoulders and turned the body around. Pushed it up against the drum. Pressed his weight into the back and forced the head into the water. When the man tried to rock himself out he rammed a knee into his thigh, forced him further into the drum so only a stump of neck showed. Bubbles burst on the surface and Tanner watched the water roll away, mesmerised by the choppy little waves and the leaves, spores and bark they carried. Water splashed over the sides of the drum, the rest swilling back. Something inside his head had clicked and he felt like he had never felt before. He had lost control, but at the same time he was totally focused.

The bubbles were fading, resistance weakening, the killer panicking as he struggled to stay alive. Tanner could hear the steel drum vibrating, but this was no tropical island get-together. He was a mannequin with a banging pulse in his arms, the thump of the man's heartbeat inside him. The ripples were thinning out and the bubbles had stopped. He came out of his trance, didn't want anyone to die, wished everyone could live in peace and live forever. Pulling the body back he eased it to the ground, propped the man against the drum, heard him coughing and spitting.

Tanner went over to the rabbit. Its fur was stuck to its body and it was trying to stand, but kept falling down. He was wary of picking it up right away. Rabbits were timid and had frail hearts, easily killed by shock. There were two more nearby, both of them dead, their eyes half-open and glazed. He saw two plastic cages. There was another rabbit inside the nearest one, bigger than the others, but maybe that was because it wasn't wet. It sat back from the door and avoided his gaze. He checked the rest of his surroundings, noticed an empty hutch with an open door, decided he had to get out of here, picked up the injured rabbit as gently as he could, placing it inside the cage with its remaining friend. The rabbit lay on its side. Perhaps it was too late.

The man responsible was on his knees. Hatred thinned the face out further. He sneered when Tanner squatted and asked if he was some sort of pervert. Why was he hurting something so defenceless?

The man spluttered, literally shaking with rage. It was a fucking rabbit. A rodent. Tanner grabbed his throat and pushed the head back against the drum. A friend had bought a pet rabbit for his children and it had turned out to be pregnant. The babies had grown and so he'd said he would take care of them as he had the space, would find them new homes. They were vermin. They breed fast. Fuck like rabbits. He sniggered. Who cares? Really, who fucking cares?

Given the chance Tanner reckoned this wanker would happily drown him, smash a brick over his head and cut his throat. There were people who bought small animals so they could practise their sadism at home. Mice, hamsters, rabbits. Tinpot dictators. Horrible cunts. This was how a lot of serial killers started off. Why didn't he just let them go? The man shrugged. It was more fun this way. Tanner punched the rabbit killer again and left him half-conscious and silent.

Picking up the cage with the rabbits inside, Tanner took it out to the lane and placed it next to his bag. They had their backs towards him, the dry one acting as a shield. He was about to lift his bag back into position, wondering how he was going to manage, when a rock flew past his head. The man was back on his feet, swaying as he shouted that he was going to call the police, that those animals belonged to him. Tanner went back over and he cowered by the broken gate. Begged not to be hit again.

If he told the police, then Tanner swore he would return and kill him. He knew where he lived. Peace returned to the lane. He picked up his bag and wedged it over his shoulder, lifted the cage with his free hand and headed for home.

Safe in his flat, sitting in the sun, barefoot and wearing shorts and a polo shirt, Mike Tanner was pleased he had saved the rabbits but angry at himself for losing control. He was genuinely shocked by the level of violence he'd used. He had gone too far. Much too far... It was three days after the incident and he hadn't been outside since. If he'd been reported to the police, they would surely have picked him up on CCTV by now, come knocking on his door. Smashed it down more like. Maybe it took time to track him across their cameras, and they would have other cases stacked up. Police numbers had been cut. He wasn't in the clear yet, but felt confident.

The rabbits were next to him on the couch. Their closed eyelids flickered as they shared a dream, and he saw them frolicking in a meadow, the grass flush with bright greens and blues, red flowers thick with prehistoric petals, a version of paradise where they lived with an extended family in a luxury burrow. There were no predators. It was a cinematic feast, a 3D fantasy, some quality escapism for the masses. He reached out and lowered his left hand, rested it on the back of the rabbit he had saved from drowning. It didn't flinch.

Boys or girls, they needed names – Brer Rabbit was obvious, but there were two of them and he decided to honour a friend and call the other one Bunny. Without a name you didn't exist. Maybe they were brothers. That made sense. The mother on the butter advert was Daisy – Daisy Moo Cow. Another favourite straight from a children's book. Then there was Porky Pig, and his sons would have biblical references and keep the alliteration going with Peter and Paul. These animals represented the innocence of childhood and bedtime stories that led to the sweetest of dreams.

The meadow faded. A mannequin stood by a metal drum. Blank eyes and a plastic face. The smile was thin and spiteful. There was no way Tanner could have kept going and done nothing. He was in the right, saw himself as a human being forcing a dummy's head underwater, the mechanical heart inches from his own. It was hard to admit, but maybe they weren't so different, both members of a species that specialised in violence. If he had kept going their heartbeats might even have merged in a single rhythm, and yet the more he thought about it, the more he remembered how focused and calm he had been. The rabbit killer was panicking – *scared as a rabbit*...

That sneering, cunning, dismissive language... loaded expressions... sly, snide, sneaky sounds... sleazy sentences, sentiments, slogans... they echoed across the years... decades... centuries...

– Smelly pigs… dirty cow…

He had put the rabbits by his living-room window when he got them home, so that the sun was shining on their cage. He filled a bowl with water and sliced up some carrots and broke an iceberg lettuce apart, put this on a plate and placed it in front of the door, which he opened. He was hoping the food would draw them out, that the heat would encourage them to stay while the sun dried the wet one out. He had left them alone, gone to lie down on his bed. He was shaking with anger, fear, excitement – he wasn't sure which. He put the World Service on and found it surprisingly easy to stay with the BBC journalists reporting from Brazil, Zaire, India and Finland.

Two hours later and most of the food had been eaten and the rabbits were sunbathing. They turned towards him when he entered, twitched and looked as if they were about to move, so he went back into the kitchen and made himself a mug of black coffee.

He had a pile of CDs by the side of his bed, turned the radio off and chose Tricky's *Maxinquaye*. The recording crackled, as it was meant to do, a desert-island castaway on vinyl, and he noted the mix of vocals and their delivery, as he always did. Tricky was a genius. No doubt about it. He wished he had a similar skill, but the way he saw things he had little to offer. He was secure enough, owned the flat and had half of his redundancy money in the bank, but was alone and powerless, a proper Mr Anonymous. Tricky had lost his mother when he was young in tragic circumstances, but had fought back and created music that captured the sadness of life but was at the same time inspiring. Despite the adrenaline and caffeine in his system, Tanner was soothed by the album.

Three days later and Bunny – the rabbit who had nearly drowned – had made himself at home. He was assuming they were boys… Tanner could feel the faint tapping of his heart through warm fur, tracing the outline of a delicate spine. Moving his hand along the bone he draped it loosely around Bunny's neck. He could kill him whenever he wanted, skin and gut the corpse, stick chopped-up body parts in his freezer. Nobody was going to complain because nobody would know. He could do what he liked. The idea made him feel sick.

Bunny's fur was soft like a toy – a cuddly rabbit, grinning pig, fluffy lamb, cheeky monkey, floppy bear… Really, Bunny and Brer Rabbit should be running from him, looking for a place to hide, but despite what had happened they trusted him. He should have felt good about this, but he didn't. It was terrible – *run rabbit, run rabbit…*

The rabbit killer did as he pleased. He was a small-time sadist, a gnome at the bottom of the garden, the sort of person Tanner had been trying to pretend did not exist. He was right and the bully was wrong, but the law saw things differently.

– *Run run run…*

He looked at the blank screen of his TV set, knew he could press a button and choose a news channel and see how the goodies were killing the baddies and the baddies were killing the goodies and while there were goodies and baddies and baddies and goodies and sometimes the goodies were really baddies and the baddies were really goodies and all these goodies and baddies thought they were winning and losing, in truth there were no winners and no losers. Civilisations were being built, destroyed and rebuilt. Foreign wars. Domestic dramas. Leaders worked hard and played hard. The goodies and baddies had similar tastes. The two sides killed each other and celebrated by butchering the same animals. Straight lines were bent. Each to their own. Humans marched on two legs and held their heads in the air. Animals slouched on four with their noses in the gutter.

The temperature was rising, the sun high in the sky, and he went into the kitchen and took a pint of cold water from the fridge, drank it in one go, continued to his bedroom for some shade. He hadn't slept well the night before. He spread out and stared at the ceiling, wondering how Bunny remembered things. Scientists made grand statements, but most of them were mechanics, focusing on the machine instead of searching for the driver. Religious dogma still played a part, helped shape political opposition to genuine animal welfare, but money was the real drive, science responding to the demands of business.

As far as Tanner was concerned, dismissing everything a non-human animal did as instinct was as lazy as it was loaded. He understood instinct as part of a great unconscious, or a species memory that saw birds and fish migrate enormous distances, moving in huge, coordinated formations. The survival instinct was something human and non-human animals shared, yet Bunny and Brer Rabbit didn't hide from him as they had been domesticated. Broken… He closed his eyes. Maybe those species that were hunted, defined as prey, had short memories in order to cope with the constant terror.

Memory loss was a defence mechanism. He had seen it with the elderly. There had to be a part of the brain that filtered the past, and sometimes he wished it would not just ease his own sadness but end it completely. He placed a finger on his wrist and felt the beat of his life. There were times not so long ago, when he was trying to shut out the horror, that he would take a thick book and place it on his lap and drum. He found a rhythm and repeated it, beating faster and harder until the sound filled his head, fingers stinging and hands aching so badly the pain was all he could think about, only stopping when cramp locked his wrists. It was similar to roaming the streets of a city, walking on ridges, punishing his muscles, keeping on until his mind was as stiff as his body. But without his memories he wouldn't exist, end up a man without a name or a story. The lessons he had learned would be lost. His past had made his present and would shape his future.

He felt Pop squeeze his hand, reminding him of times he would never want to lose, and while he had often stayed with his grandad in London, that one visit to the country stood out. He saw himself as a boy traipsing along narrow lanes, crossing fields and climbing a hill, nervous at the edge of a wood and not daring to go inside. He wondered what had happened to the cottage, if it had fallen down yet. Pop died when he was fifteen. He had loved him as much as he had his mother and father.

Pop was a dreamer, saw things differently, but feared no one, spoke his mind. There was a farmer who had taken the boy back to Elm Cottage in his Land Rover, and Pop was rude to the man, the only occasion when Michael was embarrassed by his grandfather. Norris was his name. Pop had called him Farmer Giles. Tanner struggled to recall the Christian name. Frank... Frank Norris. No, Pop didn't like him at all, and he sang 'Old McDonald Had A Farm' later than evening, raising a beer bottle in the air, Michael joining in when it came to the animal voices.

Farmer Norris had seen Michael on the lane that passed his house on several occasions. Once, he stopped him for a chat, handed the boy a bar of chocolate from his jacket pocket – something to eat when he went on his way. The farmer was interested to hear about London, what it was like living in a city. Later, when Michael got caught in the rain, he had sheltered under an oak tree across from the farmhouse. Frank saw the lad and called him indoors. Mrs Norris dried his hair with a towel and heated up some soup, served it with thick slices of bread and butter, which Michael was encouraged to dunk in the bowl. It was so good he could still taste it a week later.

Tanner could remember holding a rabbit on his lap. Before or after he'd had the soup, he wasn't sure. He was sitting at the kitchen table and the farmer told him to grasp it firmly by the fur at the back of its neck, which he did, and the rabbit had allowed him to stroke it with his free hand. He wondered what he had thought at the time, a boy with no knowledge of the world, and it must have made an impression on him for the scene to return so clearly. There were hutches outside and he guessed the rabbits were kept for eating, but he only thought of that now. But the rabbit was a hare. It came back to him in a flash of memory.

The farmer had pointed to the back legs and explained how they were longer and more powerful than those of a rabbit. The hare was a magical creature. One of their children had found him collapsed on the ground and hardly moving, bleeding and dehydrated. He'd hurt one of those long legs and Mrs Norris was nursing him back to health. When he was ready they would set him free. Return him to the wild. Hares brought good luck. More even than a rabbit's foot. Once he was released the hare would run as fast as he could, keep going until he reached the safety of the nearest trees, and he wouldn't slow down or stop to look back, just keep on running.

Farmer Giles was a good man who loved the countryside in which he lived. His role was that of a guardian. A salt-of-the-earth, proud son of the shires of England and Great Britain, he was a relation of the pioneers who had travelled into the North American wilderness and Australian outback, a friend to the rural folk of Europe and beyond. He had raised animals his entire adult life, learning the necessary skills from his father, who had been taught by his father before him.

Farming was a family tradition that spanned the generations, and at his peak he had owned a herd of cattle, rising before the sun and working into the darkness. Spring, summer, autumn, winter – there was always something that needed to be done. He looked forward to the days when he went to market to sell his livestock. These trips rewarded his hard labour, and he would suck on a roll-up and fill his lungs with smoke as deals were struck, hands shaken and money exchanged. When the business was complete, he headed to one of the nine pubs on the main street to drink the night away with straight-talking, like-minded men.

It was a tough living, but an honest one, and while it could be lonely at times it had provided him with a deep sense of belonging. He was rooted to the land and changed with the seasons. There was a harsh, unspoken romance to his life. Nature was cruel and he could not afford to make mistakes or show any sort of weakness. Every person and every animal had to earn their corn.

Farmer Giles was not sentimental. He dealt in reality. His bulls were magnificent creatures, strong and full of youth, but they lacked intelligence. He wasn't a religious man, but did know that animals had been put on earth by God to feed Man. It was the duty of humans to exploit this bounty. They did not experience emotions in the same way. It was true that the females became upset when their young were taken from them, mourned for days afterwards, and every species hated the lorries that came to take them to slaughter – that was natural enough – but they were simple creatures and didn't have real memories. They were childlike, less than human, and while he had always been fascinated by their behaviour, enjoyed being around them during the day, they only existed to provide food.

When he grew older and his strength started to fade, Farmer Giles gave up his herd. And then his sheep and pigs. He had always kept chickens and rabbits, and for a while he raised more of these smaller animals as they were easier to control. They were cheap to feed and easily killed at home. His bulls had symbolised his success as a younger man. His family ate beef that he had raised, but now he bought it from a shop. Meat production was increasingly in the hands of large-scale, intensive operations. It was terrible to see animals being raised in factory conditions, unfair on the small farmers who couldn't compete.

He had never thought to produce vegetables for sale, but always grew enough for the needs of his family. When his income dropped, he had earned money putting up fences and clearing ditches, but it was exhausting work for someone of his age, and when he injured his back he relied on sickness payments for nearly a year. He had kept the farm going, but missed those busier days. Working stopped a man from thinking, and by now his children had grown up and left home, moving first to the nearest town and then further away to the cities. They had come back for visits at first, but these became less regular until he was lucky to see his son and daughter once a year.

He was left alone with his wife, a strong woman who had stood with him over the decades, working as hard if not harder, up even before he was in the morning to boil the kettle and make him a pot of tea and a filling breakfast. She was the one who lifted his spirits in the worst times, urging him to stay positive. They had taken on the world together. Their life had been hard, but it had also been worthwhile, and he missed her terribly now that she was buried in the churchyard with her family. He tried not to think of her too much as it only made him sad, but it was difficult. She had always been the brave one.

Farmer Giles had aged quickly after her death and never known such loneliness, his main focus looking after his chickens and rabbits. When it was their time he carried them to his shed and shut the door, did what needed to be done. There was no escape, and yet he had to smile at the way they flapped and hopped and tried to get away. They didn't understand what was happening, but there were odd moments when he did wonder. He worked fast, reassuring them that everything was going to be all right. God loved them, and he whispered as he would to a child who didn't know what was best for it, and he was still a proud man who made sure they didn't suffer.

His animals were lucky, would never know the worry a husband and father faced as he tried to feed his family and keep a roof over their heads. He had struggled through so many long winters, those heartless months when the wind screamed and cold air filled his chest and the trees were skeletons warning him of his future. He had buried his mother and father and younger brother before he was thirty, and eventually it was the turn of his wife, and soon he would go the same way.

The croaking of birds in a nearby copse was a death rattle he had heard his entire life and it still filled him with dread. When he was a boy he had been terrified of the crows and ravens living in the trees, his father giving him a clip round the ear and telling him not to be so bloody daft, but later his old man had thought again and gone off with his shotgun, Frank hearing shots and seeing three dead birds brought back and nailed to a shed. He had cried at the sight of them and his father had laughed and told him they were only animals and nothing to be scared of, and looking back he knew that it was an important lesson, one of many his father had passed on. He had been trying to make a man of his son, toughening him up, which was only right.

Frank had been taught to work fast when it came to killing. His father reached for a chicken, avoided the flapping wings and snapped its neck. It was easy. Job done, he moved on. There was no time to waste, no lingering over the past in those days. There were bodies to be plucked, skinned, gutted, butchered. From his early teens he had killed thousands of times. It was a mechanical process that fed him and his family. He saw wings flash, legs kick and eyes blaze, but experienced no strong feelings.

His animals were lucky that he was their owner. He was a decent man, but there were some who enjoyed the killing, made their beasts suffer, and he had heard a couple of stories involving sexual acts, which he did not believe, unable to imagine humans reduced to the level of an animal.

Now in his eighties, the farmer's hands were arthritic and he had become clumsy. He preferred killing in small batches, as he could freeze the meat and save work later on, but he only had a few chickens and rabbits left. He didn't care about freshness at his age. He had started using a knife, but made mistakes, one rabbit breaking free and hiding in his shed, slowly bleeding to death. It served the little bugger right for trying to escape, that's what he told himself, but he was upset by what had happened, which was ridiculous. He thought of the bones outside and imagined his own skeleton nailed to a tree, stripped by ravens and crows. He didn't want to die.

Alone at night he would sit in his kitchen with a bit of chicken or rabbit next to his potatoes and veg and remember his heyday, back when he had bulls in the field and vegetables in the soil and a loyal wife by his side. The earth where he used to have his veg was overgrown now, covered in weeds and grass, and he relied on packets bought from a shop and kept in his freezer. He had become weak and nature was taking advantage.

He had argued with his daughter the last time she came to see him, and later he thought about his animals and recalled their smells and habits, knew in his heart that they had been happy to serve his family. They really had been amazing creatures, never failing to surprise him with their odd little ways, and he could see them running to greet him when he came home, like his children used to do, before they grew up and went away and became selfish. Animals knew their place.

What the town and city people didn't understand was that farming was the foundation of country life. If men didn't dominate nature they would be overrun and destroyed. A firm hand was needed to keep order, but he was no longer strong, and his children had abandoned a family heritage that would soon be lost. He wished he was young again, running the farm properly, surrounded by life. Tears filled his eyes. Farmer Giles missed his wife and he missed his animals.

THE TERROR
FANTASTIC

IT TOOK TANNER a good minute to realise that The Terror Squad was pounding on his door. The bangs were urgent and loud. Sitting up in bed, he sent the commander a message urging him to go and find some real terrorists. His identity was fluid and he didn't exist in the traditional sense, and so the authorities would never find the evidence needed to convict him of crimes he hadn't committed. There were no electronic trails. No calls, texts, emails. He was only here in spirit. Satellites were unable to track his movements. Police helicopters stayed on the ground. He was operating outside of their corrupt legal system.

The police were individuals and would rather be hunting rapists, paedophiles and the perverts who mutilated the genitals of little girls. The commander passed his message on and the men at his door lowered their heads in shame, knowing that this raid was a political decision that came from the very top. They were only following orders, but decided to make a stand, had been reading a lot of PETA and Animal Aid literature in their spare time, said goodbye and sorry for bothering you, sir, jumped in their unmarked vans and went for a vegan fry-up. The banging continued.

Tanner rubbed his eyes and made sure he was really awake this time, realised that the sound was coming from under his bed. Hanging over the side, he found Bunny thumping the carpet with a leg while Brer watched. The rabbits had decided to sleep there at night, following him into the bedroom when he turned the lights off. It was incredible something so small could make such a racket. Seeing the man's upside-down face ended the thumping. It was early, just after six, but these two rose with the sun and didn't care that it was a Sunday.

He went into the kitchen, cut vegetables and put them on two plates, placed these on the floor. He changed their water and the cat litter he'd bought, which they had been using. A routine had already been set. The rabbits came in for their breakfast while he went off and had a bath and dressed and, once he was ready and had seen them settled by the living-room window, he left the flat. He moved his legs and swung his arms, breathed deep on the fresh morning air, as apart from a visit to the supermarket he had been cooped up inside for nearly a week. That was long enough. Bullies like the rabbit killer were generally cowards, and he was confident his threat had worked.

Tanner had thought about the incident every day since it happened, and now he was more surprised than shocked by what he'd done. He had no sympathy for the man on the receiving end. That hadn't changed. And he had to admit he'd enjoyed the punches – they were small explosions of bottled-up anger – but holding the head underwater was different. More worrying. Yet interesting. It had been a cold, efficient, automatic act. As if a button had been pressed. Another part of him had taken over. That must be how a professional soldier operated. They had to remain unemotional and decisive, resist the fury of a battle, avoid the chaos. He had felt strong. Powerful. Couldn't pretend he hadn't.

He wanted to believe he had been driven by more than just his anger and a desire to punish the killer. It had been a lesson. A deterrent. That man now knew what it felt like to be terrorised. True, Tanner had done unto others... Righteous eye-for-an-eye justice. He knew people's daydreams as he'd had plenty himself, especially at night when he was trying to get to sleep, half-dozing semi-dreams that he controlled, revenge scenarios where the bad people of the work paid for their sins. These were the foundations of some of the world's biggest religions. The roots of human culture.

A recent documentary on the ivory trade had seen a TV camera crew following African wildlife rangers as they tried to stop poachers shooting elephants for their tusks. Pictures of mutilated elephants were followed by images of their orphaned young. The poachers were known to remove the tusks while a wounded elephant was still alive. He wondered how many viewers were pleased when a poacher was shot and killed. He had been, but would have felt terrible if he'd kept going and the rabbit killer had drowned. It was a one-off, a loss of control.

Tanner focused on familiar streets, walking by shops that were locked and shuttered and full of treats. The launderette and bakery were noisy and fragrant when open, but closed no more than silent shells. He passed offices dealing in insurance, accommodation, healthcare and legal advice. More shops followed, and he was drawn to the one where he liked to browse, the interior rammed with everything from tiny trinkets to big panes of stained glass. He peered inside, his eyes adjusting to the darkness, scanning the nearest shelves with their piles of brushes, bottle openers, shot glasses, seaside spoons, coins, thimbles, beermats and postcards. Coloured pencils filled a cluster of mugs. Corgi and Dinky cars were parked in a crooked row. Plates, saucers and bowls stood in towers. Further into the shop were records by crooners and cowboys, vinyl that skipped from 33⅓ to 78rpm, Frank Sinatra meeting up with Jim Reeves. Heaps of CDs and cassettes teetered. There were metal and wooden boxes, toy soldiers and tanks, radios and puppets and lots of cameras.

His favourite display was the glass case packed with plastic animals. These were split into two groups. Lions, tigers and crocodiles had been mixed in with giraffes, zebras, elephants, hippos and monkeys – exotic wildlife for children who wanted to be zookeepers or go on safari. Next to these were the farmyard funnies, a motley crew of mainly sheep, pigs, cows, horses and chickens – for those who preferred to run a farm. The bodies were chipped and scuffed, paint flaking as if they had been loved half to death. There were show-offs – a green donkey and a big orange duck.

Tanner had never been a collector, but he did like this shop. Maybe he needed a hobby. There were plenty of men who bought stamps and coins from around the world, filled their time searching for rarities. When he was young, boys had built RAF fighters from kits and launched suicide attacks on Luftwaffe squadrons. Men glued bombers for long-distance raids on dams and factories. Romantics of all ages were still running railway networks, and it didn't matter if they were dedicated to steam or diesel as the real fun was in the laying of the lines, the fitting together of tracks and the building of stations. Snobs took the piss out of trainspotters, but he doubted many of them jumped in front of an engine. They seemed content with their sandwiches and flasks of tea, loitering at the end of station platforms, appreciating every individual train when so many took them for granted. Tanner wondered if he should buy himself a farmyard army, give his pacifist troops a fresh coat of paint.

He started walking again, navigating his way through the concrete blocks of an estate, the smaller ones balanced on legs like beach huts. He knew the dead ends and openings, and it was cool in the shade, the air sheltered and smelling of apple blossom. Early on a Sunday morning it held none of the threat it was known for locally. A boy had been murdered here earlier in the year, stabbed to death for no known reason. Drugs were dealt and people robbed, so the police carried out dawn raids, targeted suspects while they were asleep, breaking into their dreams. He didn't know if the killers had been caught.

Coming back out into the sunshine, he was soon nearing a retail park, passing through the entrance and crossing a flatland of parking bays, trolley shelters, domes that recycled paper and glass, a metal box for secondhand clothes that would raise money for the homeless. A billboard showed a supermodel posing in red leather heels and a leopard-skin bikini. He supposed it was better than the butter advert, but there were two types of skin in her outfit, whether real or imitation. Blonde and buxom, the model bit the lower lip of a pouting mouth that promised a happy ending for any young stud willing to buy the car she was selling. The bodywork was sleek and sturdy, blending top-end design with raw power. The woman was cat-like, red claws extended, a castrator of weaklings, all those failures who couldn't afford her favourite automobile.

He reached a dual carriageway lined with railings, followed the pavement that ran parallel, went down the ramp leading into a subway, the smell of kebab vomit speeding him up. The tunnel cut under the main road, its walls covered in graffiti, cartoon figures that mimicked American originals, oversized guns and trainers standing out. A pitbull snarled. On the other side of the carriageway, more early risers appeared, the buildings ahead tall and narrow, the bricks sandblasted, each dot of colour seeming as if it had been digitally applied. Controllers lived here, the sort of people who ran IT companies, the banks, local politics, the arts. Most of the curtains were still closed.

He was soon out on a common and slowing down, his legs heavy, and he looked around for a place where he could rest. There was a run-down bandstand, which hadn't been used for years, though there was a plan for it to be restored. Sitting on a nearby bench, he rubbed gravel around under his feet and listened to the crunch, noticed a line of seagulls perched on a fence watching him and suddenly felt very alone. He stayed for five minutes, couldn't settle, stood up and carried on walking, pleased to spot an elderly couple by the side of a big pond. He walked towards them and found another bench. They were busy throwing bread to a collection of excited ducks, pigeons and seagulls, two swans sailing in from the other bank. He watched the birds eat their way through the contents of a large bag. This went on for another ten minutes before the couple left.

He started to drift, heard a church bell ring. An hour had passed in a second. He got to his feet. Cars circled the common, two minibuses full of footballers stopping at a red light. Soon they would be running around on one of the pitches and more people would come to spread out on the grass and enjoy the good weather. Leaving the common behind he walked through a mixture of houses and flats, men and women passing him to buy newspapers and milk. He heard more bells, crossed over when he saw a congregation milling around in a graveyard. He was moving slowly, but had a destination.

The Bricklayer's Arms was open when he arrived. He ordered from the barman and chose a paper from the pile at the end of the counter, drank his first pint standing up and loved every drop, ordered a second and a packet of peanuts. Breakfast was served. He scanned the pub, saw that he was one of nine men already set up. Each of them was alone with a pint and a newspaper, except for the two pensioners at the other end of the bar who were talking in hushed tones.

He found a seat and started working his way into the broadsheet he had chosen. The news and current-affairs coverage was good, but the features were only going to appeal to the rich end of society. The football coverage was decent, the arts section elitist, the travel predictable. There was a superior air to much of the journalism, which was irritating, and when he flicked through a special supplement he came across a feature on organic farming, the musings of a celebrity who had moved into the countryside and was *farming* animals – mainly goats and llamas – and making yet more money from his hobby.

The man was part of an elite that presented itself as open-minded and liberal, but was in reality narrow-minded and bullying. 'Sustainable' and 'ethical' were used several times in the article, along with that old favourite 'humane slaughter'. He had noticed this high-end fashion for animal exploitation over the last few years, the broadsheets wrapping killing up in ethical and green rhetoric. The poison had to come out somewhere, and animals were the easiest target.

He bought himself another drink, returned the broadsheet and took a tabloid, went back to his seat. There was an early kick-off at St James' Park. Newcastle were at home to Manchester United. The game had been rearranged and there were the usual complaints about the timing, but it suited the lunchtime drinkers in The Bricklayer's. The landlord had muted the analysis in the build-up, put on some decent music that included The Jam and The Stone Roses.

Tanner sipped his pint as he read a spread about an MP with a taste for Polish rent boys and cocaine, a single-page article on a man who had fallen from a ninth-floor hotel balcony in Portugal and somehow survived, the shopping spree of a woman who had won more than a million pounds on the lottery. He flicked the pages, ignoring every celebrity and gossip column, came to an article about two men convicted of cruelty on a chicken farm. The headline read *Headless Chicken Derby* and they had been fined for cutting the heads off a couple of birds and racing their still-moving bodies. One had a previous conviction for torturing a dog. The tone of the piece was one of disgust, but there were several attempts at humour, a couple of puns and a dismissive final line.

Around a billion chickens were being killed each year in the UK. That wasn't counting the egg industry and the unwanted male chicks crushed and gassed in huge numbers. The figures were hard to grasp and not mentioned in the article. Chicken flesh was ridiculously cheap. Eight legs under cellophane, four frozen breasts... However, the article did reference a report on the radio the previous month where a journalist had visited a chicken farm and been inside a shed housing over forty thousand birds. They never went outside but were lucky, as they weren't confined to cages. It was the same in this case.

Tanner's thoughts raced. Only a handful of people were reacting to what they saw on the TV, read in the newspapers, heard on the radio. The evidence was out there on the internet, easily accessed, but where was the mass reaction to the mass slaughter of animals? He couldn't believe that the majority just did not care.

He looked around the pub again, tried to spot the men who would be drinking faster with their dinnertimes approaching, and when they got home and sat down to their traditional Sunday roasts the last thing they would do would be to connect the beef on their plates to the mechanics of the meat industry. The drinkers in this pub were big babies, overgrown kids, and he pictured them at takeaway counters ordering fish, burgers, chicken, kebabs. They needed to see what he saw – suffocating fish, shackled steers bleeding out, decapitated roosters, screaming lambs. He wanted to punch someone, but knew it would achieve nothing. He had to love his own species. If he hated humans he would hate himself.

The door opened and Bunny strolled in, ordered for them both and was soon sitting next to his friend. Tanner's mind cleared. It was an almost physical experience as his anger was washed away in a rush of friendship. His mood changed so easily – the rabbit killer swinging the pendulum to one extreme, the infectious excitement of

Bunny to the other. He had a kitbag open and was removing 45s, bought that morning from an original mod in a private sale. He had gone to the bloke's house at 9am as requested, enjoyed several cups of tea and slices of toast. The man concerned wanted a good home for the singles, to sell them to someone who loved the music as much as he did. He was converting to digital. It was a shame in one way, but great for Bunny.

The old mod had been there at the start, told more than an hour's worth of stories – a real treat it was – and Bunny was going to go for a pint with him in a couple of weeks. He'd talked about the clubs in Soho, the shops and cafes, Eel Pie Island, the time The Who played at Burton's in Uxbridge. He'd seen The Rolling Stones at a sports club in Richmond before anyone knew about them, and he had lots to say about the bank-holiday runs, special nights at the 100 Club. The man was still dapper, his cotton shirt neatly ironed, a treasure chest of information and experience. Bunny couldn't stop talking, repeating the stories which were as much about the flavour as any plot, and he was thinking he should record them maybe, just make sure they were never lost. The mod's wife was really nice as well, good looking and smartly turned out. Neither of them had let themselves go.

Tanner relaxed as Bunny ran through the singles, most of them in excellent condition, and he was in there with the trainspotters and amateur signalmen, although he wouldn't appreciate the comparison given his interest in fashion. Tanner had enough records, but he'd never been an obsessive, wasn't bothered about labels and rarity, although he did appreciate an independent such as Mortarhate, which had something extra about it with the animal-liberation focus. It was all part of the same culture he guessed, a wider unconscious.

The football had started, but the landlord kept the volume low, which was a plus, meant they could talk, taking turns to go to the bar as the time passed and the drink flowed, and they discussed the merits of renationalising the railways, the sad death of Bob Crow, the shortage of housing, space travel and new frontiers, Tanner's childhood interest in science fiction, an uncle of Bunny's who swore he had been abducted by aliens, crop circles and the Ridgeway, natural cures, Maggie at the allotments, the fact Bunny had first met the mod with the records at church.

Tanner had never taken Bunny for the religious sort, but it turned out he was a practising Catholic. They discussed heaven and hell as they drank, the nature of an afterlife, the desire for retribution on earth and the need for forgiveness, a natural justice that was beyond the power of human beings. Tanner wanted to compare Christian sects, discuss faith and free will, go into Eastern ideas and reincarnation, but sensed Bunny was fixed in his beliefs and becoming uncomfortable. He could be wrong, but didn't want any trouble. No arguments. He didn't want to upset his friend, instead asked about the seaweed situation. Bunny's eyes lit up.

Everyone needed friends and nobody was perfect. Tanner was fitting in and avoiding controversy, wondered if he could stop and see Ella later, but he'd had a drink and would go another day. He glanced at the newspaper on the table and saw the faces of the chicken killers Ricky Spears and Bob Cummings staring back, the photo taken outside a pub in a provincial town, the two men sneering at the camera, arrogant and untouchable. He pushed them to the back of his mind. Bunny was planning another seaside raid and needed his help.

It was nice enough having the rabbits in the flat, but Tanner didn't want to keep them cooped-up for too long, and maybe he'd become over-confident, because if he was arrested the police would probably give them back to the man he'd attacked. In a perfect world he could have released them on a common or in a field in the countryside, but he doubted they'd be able to fend for themselves. He knew of a sanctuary that had taken liberated animals in the past, so checked it was still going, found a phone number and talked to a cheerful lady called Sandy who said to bring them along whenever he wanted. He asked how about tomorrow and it was arranged.

He made sure the basket he bought for the trip was secure in the passenger seat of his car, fixed the belt so it was firm, set off on slow-motion roads, careful at the speed bumps, and when he checked on Bunny and Brer Rabbit through gaps in the wicker they seemed fine. He spent thirty minutes stopping and starting before getting stuck in a jam for another ten, right behind a refrigerated lorry. A huge, cartoon pig filled the back doors. He was promoting *Funhouse Foods... Quality Pork, Beef, Lamb... Happy Means Healthy.*

The pig was beaming, standing on two legs, a trotter raised in the air, its body a brilliant pink. The smile was carefree and a little cheeky, and Tanner felt his skull tighten. It was another insult. An obscenity. *Babe* had been remixed with *The Texas Chainsaw Massacre*. The container was moving bodies – hacked, drained, decapitated corpses. He wanted to get out and talk to the driver, ask him if he would have driven the train to Auschwitz as well, but it would be pointless, another flash of anger, this time recorded on the one-way system's CCTV. He had the rabbits to think about. A job that needed doing.

He placed his left hand on top of the basket, felt noses sniffing his fingers, a pair of innocents oblivious to the contents of the Funhouse lorry. He was relieved when the traffic started to move again and he could leave it behind, and reaching the flyover he felt as if the rabbits were already safe. Glass towers were being erected on either side of the elevated road, thousands of panels reflecting cranes, two huge screens advertising computers and mobile phones, an electronic board ticking out prices and temperatures and interest rates, and then this high-tech strip was gone as the flyover dipped back down to earth and he was flanked by scrap-metal yards and storage depots and miles of suburban houses.

When he joined the motorway he put his foot down, stucco and pebbledash thinning into trading estates and parcels of undeveloped land, fields boxed in by single-storey factories, small service roads in between. The houses returned. Millions of bricks followed the flow of the river, which they hid from his view. The smell of pine trees filled the car as plantations appeared on both sides of the road, and he hoped the rabbits noticed. The trees became thicker, a fast-growing forest planted by well-meaning souls doing their best to replace woodland destroyed in the past.

He thought about the ebb and flow of families over the centuries, from tribal invasions and feudal villages into the industrial, space and digital ages. He knew little of his own history and wondered if the rabbits remembered their ancestors in a way humans could not. Cynics insisted the rest of the animal kingdom was essentially stupid, that intelligence could only be judged according to human strengths, but he had never accepted this idea.

Birds followed migration routes across the planet, using the sort of inbuilt radar that companies spent millions of pounds trying to mimic. The fact that any creature could fly was a miracle in itself, but humans still clipped their wings and caged them and plucked out their feathers and removed their heads – chopped them off for fun. The oceans held enormous, tightly packed shoals of fish that moved in perfect time, as one huge telepathic being, while smaller groups travelled great distances to feed and breed. Incredible documentaries had been made about those who could travel in the air and under the sea and live the dreams of aviators and mariners, while the herds and prides and flocks and mobs who lived on land possessed survival and psychic talents way beyond a man or woman. Conservationists had gone to the poles and into deserts and across grasslands and through jungles to record the planet's wonders and to persuade the rest of humanity that these creatures and their habitats should be protected, and yet the killing and destruction continued.

Every species had its special talents, but Tanner was thinking of the locals now, the pigs and sheep and cattle who just wanted to be left alone. They had family bonds and emotions, yet these were denied. To say these creatures had no feelings and didn't suffer pain or long to be released from their prisons was perverted. He rolled these thoughts around as he drove.

Leaving the motorway, he took one of the old roads, moving at a reasonable speed until he changed to lanes that narrowed and became the width of a single car. He had his directions written down, but had to check where he was, stopped by an opening in a hedge and turned off the engine. He opened a window and let the smells and sounds of the countryside flood in, saw the basket lid move as the rabbits pushed against the lid. They were going to love living out here, he was sure of that.

He studied his map and followed more lanes, came to a landscape that rolled up and down and reminded him of the area he'd stayed in with Pop as a boy. Really, Elm Cottage wasn't that far away, under an hour maybe, but he didn't dwell on this, needed to find the animal sanctuary. At a tiny crossroads, where two vehicles would have struggled to edge past each other, he saw the sign for The Meadows he'd been told to look out for, there on the track that would take him to the house. He followed this for half a mile and came out of the overhanging trees into a lawned area where he was able to park in front of a large stone building.

Turning the engine off, Tanner got out and straightened up, went around to the other side of the car and removed the basket, placing it on the roof. Nobody seemed to be about. He didn't know what he had expected, but definitely something busier and not so remote. It was very quiet. He was tired after driving, but found the silence unnerving. The air was incredibly still. The house was well hidden, and if Sandy hadn't told him where to look for the sign he would have driven right past. She had said to be careful of the dogs when he arrived. They wouldn't bite, but could get over-excited. He couldn't see or hear any people or dogs.

The door of the house opened and an elderly man in a Hawkwind T-shirt came out, raising a hand to touch the top of the frame before introducing himself. Jeff invited Tanner to join him in the back garden for a cup of tea. Tanner collected the rabbits and followed, sat at a table in the shade of an arbour covered in clematis while Jeff said hello to Bunny and Brer through the wicker. He thought it best if they got used to the smell of their new home before they were released. Some people found the silence daunting when they hadn't been here before, so it was probably the same for a rabbit, and especially ones who had lived their lives in a city hutch. He went inside to make the tea.

Tanner was in a neat, formal garden, which included some deep flowerbeds and tall ornamental trees, the only disorder a pumpkin plant running across a trimmed lawn. Beyond this was rougher pasture where sheep and a couple of donkeys were working on the grass. To the right was a fence, and he could see a shelter and goats and bales of hay. He was surprised by the garden, which was precise in its lines. He heard pigs to his right, but couldn't see them through the bushes. There was a vegetable garden near the fence, which seemed to be doing well. He wondered what Ella would make of this place, the likes of Wendell and Maggie, and how would Sid feel seeing that rampaging pumpkin? He eased back in his seat and started to relax.

Five minutes later Jeff placed a tray on the table and sat down. He had a carton of soya milk for the tea and scones he'd baked himself. There was blackberry jam, which his wife Sandy had picked and made. She'd had to go and see her sister, who'd come down with flu, taking the dogs with her for a ride. She sent her love.

Tanner asked about the sanctuary and heard how Jeff and Sandy had bought the house more than forty years ago. It was falling apart and they'd done it up, and had been looking after animals ever since. That had been their dream. Volunteers came for a few hours or a day. Some stayed for a week or two. Youngsters mainly. They had three children who had grown up here, and they helped when they could. He earned a living designing websites, had always been good with technology. Sandy dealt with the day-to-day running of the place. The public was generous with donations.

He was a lucky man, woke up in the morning feeling as if he was doing something worthwhile with his life, and how many people could say that? There were challenges. Terrible stories of cruelty. They saw the results of beatings and torture first hand. A lot of their animals were badly traumatised when they first arrived, but usually recovered over time. Some had gone insane. It was heart-breaking to see.

His face fell, so Tanner remarked on his Hawkwind shirt, mentioned an album he had, and Jeff cheered up. He loved the blues, especially Sonny Boy Williamson and Leadbelly, liked British folk from the Sixties and heavy rock from the likes of Cream and Humble Pie. More than anything he was a Hawkwind fan. He'd been to the free festivals at Windsor Great Park, the Isle Of Wight, Stonehenge, the first ones outside Glastonbury. He'd lived in Warminster for a number of years, talked about the UFOs that had been seen in the area when he was young, the more recent crop circles that had appeared in Wiltshire.

They drank three cups of tea and ate all the scones. Jeff was kind and generous, but no fool. Tanner saw a free-thinker in the English rebel tradition, and animal rights had been part of a fight for justice that went back across the centuries. Jeff jumped up, said they really should get the rabbits out of the basket, introduce them to their new friends. He led the way to another field. There was a big shed in the corner, a section of fenced-in land. This was where the rabbits lived and Tanner counted twenty-three. He handed the basket to Jeff, who placed it on the ground and lifted the lid, took Bunny and Brer out and placed them on the grass. They sniffed and looked around, saw straw and carrots, the other rabbits, sniffed the air. Tanner felt sad leaving them, but happy knowing they were with their own kind and would be safe and well looked after.

Jeff showed Tanner around the sanctuary. There were sixty-one acres now, and every time they passed through a hedge or a line of trees more animals appeared. The Meadows looked after the sheep, goats, donkeys and rabbits he had already seen, and the dogs who were out with Sandy, plus there were several horses, the pigs he'd heard earlier, chickens and ducks, a cow and her daughter, a baby deer whose mother had been shot. Most stayed their entire lives, others were moved to better homes. Years ago there'd even been a monkey here for a while. Tanner thought back. So this was where Ronnie had taken Billy... He didn't say anything to Jeff, knew enough to avoid awkward questions, but he had always wondered where Billy ended up. He could still be alive. He liked to think that he was, and so he did.

Eventually they came to the meadows. Jeff explained how they had walked around the land that came with the house when they were thinking of buying it, arrived here and any doubts they had about the state of the property vanished. It was the only name for their sanctuary. They really were proper meadows as well, full of wildflowers and insects, lush and alive, almost a vision of a lost world, a pre-industrial England. Jeff wondered if he knew the work of Samuel Palmer, which he did, and they both agreed on the comparison.

Returning to the house, Tanner wanted to see how the rabbits were getting on before he left, found them sitting next to each other in a line with several others, munching away. He shook hands with Jeff and after giving him a hundred-pound donation was on his way, doing his best to retrace his route, looking at the land and trying to remember the name of the Palmer painting he really liked, imagining the hills and fields here under a full moon. He stopped concentrating, his mind drifting as he entered lanes from a David Hockney recording, cameras on wheels, crossing the seasons and continents, adding Polaroid collages of desert roads. He was driving through a distorted but more logical world, moving from Pearblossom Highway to Gallowby Hill.

Coming to a familiar crossroads, where The Meadows sign marked a track, he realised he'd gone in a circle. He continued, found space to stop, pulled over and turned off the engine. Opening his map right out, he recognised the name of a town, saw the railway running through it, searched and found the nearest village to Elm Cottage. He made a decision, an hour later noticing how the trees were bunching up, mounds rising on either side of him, and the sight or maybe the feel of the place triggered a series of memories. He saw himself walking this way when he was a boy, could picture his grandfather more clearly than he had for years. He wasn't far away now, the next lane the narrowest yet, barely used, and when he came around the tight little corner there was the house – smaller than he remembered. Run down and abandoned.

He parked where the lane widened, stayed in his car for a while, overcome with emotion. It felt as if Pop was right here with him, Mum and Dad as well, and he fought to compose himself. He hadn't planned this when he set off for The Meadows, but there again, maybe the subconscious part of him had. When he was ready he got out and stood staring at Elm Cottage. Stepping forward, he found that the gate was jammed, one end wedged into the wooden post, and while he could have knocked it through easily enough he walked along the wall and used the small footpath that ran down the side of the garden, overgrown with ivy but still there in the groove of the earth.

He automatically went around to the back, the front door never used when he had stayed or when Pop had lived here as a boy, and it was easy enough to push inside. He stood in the kitchen. It was bare and smelled of damp, the floor scattered with leaves that had blown in through a broken window. He went into the living room, remembered the fireplace he had sat in front of with Pop. The pattern on the peeling wallpaper had faded, and patches were warped by mould. He looked up the stairs, tested the first couple with a foot and found they were rotting. It was a long time since anyone had been inside the house. Pop was probably the last person, a week or two after his grandson had returned to London. He shivered, told himself it was because he was cold in the shade.

He went outside and walked away from the cottage, looked up at the roof and saw holes where the slates had caved in, a section of the wall facing him crumbling. The garden was overgrown but had a rugged beauty. Buttercups filled the field beyond the fence. He stared at these for a while, before turning towards the pigsty he had played in as a boy, leaning on the wall and inspecting the house and yard. Beyond the sty, over towards the woods, there was a small barn, and he struggled to remember this for some reason, stamped his way through blackberry bushes to reach it, and these were heavy with fruit and he thought about Sandy's jam, wondered if he should pick some and take them home.

With a bit of effort he was able to slide the bolt back and go inside the barn, the air musty but dry, with a rich woody smell that he liked. It was deeper than it seemed from the outside, streaks of sunlight sliding through gaps in the planked walls, slicing across the haze, illuminating millions of tiny dust particles, changing them into stars. Despite the cracks, the barn seemed secure, though it could do with some fresh air, which he added by pushing the door wide open. He thought again and pulled it shut, decided he shouldn't be changing the atmosphere.

There was a rusty machine that would probably have cut hay sometime in the past. He reached down and pulled at a sack which fell apart and revealed an axe, three knives and several other odd-looking tools. He lifted the chopper up and jumped at the sight of a skull, the axe falling from his hand. He recovered and moved closer, saw that the head wasn't human. It had horns and he guessed it had belonged to a ram. He was relieved, reached down and picked it up off the table it sat on, cradled the shell in his hands and stared into the empty eye sockets. He was wrong to feel relieved, as the ram would have been scared of dying too.

There was a noise above his head, which echoed briefly, his eyes darting up, and when the sound repeated itself he realised a bird was walking on the roof. A crow or raven maybe. Something big. He heard wings flap and realised he was still holding the skull, put it back on the table, those starry sunbeams moving faster as the barn creaked. A farmer could have killed animals in here, but the positioning of the skull seemed too posed, and the barn didn't feel heavy or sad. He imagined small faces watching him from the shadows, though, as he had done on his cross-country walk. He could shout and scream in this place and never be heard.

Back outside, he made sure the bolt was in place, and while it was still early, the hill to his right was blocking out the sinking sun. He felt a surge of fear and decided he wouldn't want to be out here in the dark, but he had time, took another path towards the house, past a rotting trunk that was feeding thousands of ants. A branch snapped and he turned to look into the trees, but could see nothing. Moving faster he heard something crack under his feet, bent down and picked up a bone. There were others in the dirt. A chicken maybe? What did he expect? It was an old farm, for fuck's sake. It was no good romanticising things. There would have been a time when animals were killed here, yet he had never thought of Elm Cottage in this way.

He went back inside the house, stood in the living room again. It was colder than before and felt different to earlier, as if Pop's time here meant little, earlier occupants reclaiming the premises. He liked the barn better. It was a shelter, a mini-sanctuary, but he guessed The Meadows had felt the same when Jeff and Sandy first bought it, and they had fixed it up and filled it with their spirit, turning it into something new.

Having done his best to secure the back door he hurried to his car and locked the doors as soon as he was inside, but instead of driving straight off made himself look at the house again. The holes in the roof would get bigger as more water worked its way inside, sinking into the wood and bricks until Elm Cottage collapsed. He was surprised it hadn't already happened. It must have been built well. But he wouldn't want to sleep in there. No chance. He would prefer the pigsty. If the weather was good he'd only need a sleeping bag and pillow. With a gas cooker he could make himself a hot meal. Baked-bean masala. Warm the beans, add spice, stir well. He could sleep in the empty trough if it was hot, but he thought of the pigs who had lived there and what would have happened to them, knew he would be mad to spend a night out here. The light was weakening and he checked his map, would continue along the lane rather than return the same way. It looked like a shorter route back to the road he wanted.

Five minutes later he was passing a farmhouse, slowed down by the gate, sure it was the one he had been inside as a boy, when he was caught in a storm. A light was shining in a downstairs window, so someone was still living there, and then he was past the entrance and it was gone. He looked at his dashboard. It was twenty past nine. He had been at Elm Cottage longer than he'd thought. He was in a valley, which meant an early twilight and he turned his lights on. It would be a nightmare trying to find his way out of here if he got lost, but he was okay, before long travelling on the road he'd wanted, reaching and joining the motorway, hitting seventy and cruising in the outside lane, pleased that he had found the rabbits a good home and dipped into his past.

Tanner reached over and turned the radio on, skipped the latest news, found a station dedicated to easy listening, lasted halfway through a corny ballad and thought fuck this... His day wasn't over yet. Opening the glove compartment, he pulled out some CDs and put them on the passenger seat, chose a compilation that included Conflict's 'Slaughter Of Innocence' and 'Meat Means Murder', the spoken-word delivery of the latter turning angry and frantic, focusing his feelings and putting him in the right frame of mind.

The two men were drinking heavily and their mood had darkened. It was Wednesday night and they were out of work, had no jobs to go to in the morning. They had been in the pub every day since their convictions, complaining about their treatment. When an elderly regular asked them if they were proud knocking those birds about, he was lucky to escape a beating. Fucking nerve of the cunt. Fucking cheek. Standing there all puffed up like a rooster that needed his throat slashed and head chopped clean off. Brain-dead old geezer running in circles kicking skinny legs and flapping saggy arms. Half-dead cunt telling them they should be ashamed of themselves.

The pensioner's mates were sitting at a nearby table, clucking like hens following the cock about, a fancy boy who strutted but didn't know he was about to be put in his place. Miserable fuckers, tutting their tongues, and the bigger of the two men told them it was only their age that was saving their lives. Horrible chickens they were, covered in lumps and bleeding sores, missing half their feathers. More than their age, it was the law that protected these old cunts from a dose of what they had given those birds.

Ricky Spears hadn't known how to respond to the remark, quietly moved behind Bob Cummings, knew there was no way his friend was going stand for that sort of talk. He was right as well. Bob finished the last of his lager and cradled the empty glass in the palm of his hand as if he was about to shove it in the old man's face, instead leaning forward and leering, telling him that he bet he liked his chicken like everyone else – tender breast, crispy legs, barbecued wings. He didn't ask too many questions when he was in the shop searching the freezers for a bargain, did he? Didn't turn his nose up when his dinner was ready. No, mate, you can piss off. It's got nothing to do with you. Nothing. I hope you choke on a bone. Get cancer and die. You and your wife. The man spluttered and went red in the face, finished his drink and left the pub, taking his friends with him. Good riddance.

Ricky felt great, but wished Bob had glassed the pensioner, or at least given him a slap, broken a brittle bone or two. He saw himself following the mouthy fucker home and stabbing him as he reached his front door. Ricky imagined the pain he could inflict if he had the courage, or if the law allowed him, if he lived in the sort of society where an obedient man was encouraged to hurt his enemies. He should break into the smelly old cunt's house and tie him to a chair, burn that crinkly face with a cigarette, get some acid and burn his nose off, really make him beg for mercy and scream until he shat himself. Fucking wanker embarrassing them like that in public.

It was bad enough standing up in court and being written about in the local paper, and then some of the big boys had picked up on the story and plastered their names all over the nationals. They'd been approached by a reporter from London in this pub, accepted the drinks he'd bought them, fifty pounds each to pose for photographs like a couple of idiots. That had been a mistake. The article hadn't been sympathetic, not like the journalist was in person. Ricky wasn't strong like Bob, but he did have brains, and this made him worry.

More than anything else, Ricky was angry about losing his job. It had been an easy number. There was plenty of work and as long as he did it ahead of time he could more or less choose his hours. What was the world coming to when men like him and Bob were fined and sacked for hurting a few birds who were going to die soon anyway? The world had gone mad. Those chickens were rotting inside and out, their skin rancid, bodies full of disease. They were well and truly fucked. Ugly, ugly cunts. So stupid they kept running when you cut their heads off. It had cracked him up seeing them racing like that. Only lasted a few seconds, but funny as fuck it was.

Their solicitor told them not to worry, they'd had a result, the old duffers presiding letting them off lightly. Truth was, they liked their chicken as much as the pensioner in the pub. As the chief magistrate had admitted, food production could be a dirty business, but people needed to eat, and their job had to be done by someone. The accused fulfilled a function, kept the system working, and while they were of low intelligence and not the sort of men he would want to associate with personally, they had found their place in life.

Ricky had felt insulted by these last comments, and thinking about them now he decided it was a cheek and wondered if they could seek compensation, but there again, the courts had to go through the motions. They didn't give a fuck about those chickens either, yet had to be seen to be applying the law in front of the single reporter who had turned up. That cunt needed sorting out as well. Writing her story for the local rag, stirring things up. Wankers, the lot of them.

The company wasn't bothered about the chickens. Treated them like shit. It was all about profit margins. They were saying all the right words just like the police and the courts. No, their real mistake was letting Terry Williams film them on his mobile, and he was the one who had stitched them up, putting it on the internet like that, but he had said sorry, only done it for a laugh. Stupid fucker went and put the name of the company on there as well, and their faces couldn't be missed.

Ricky had a mouthful of lager and leaned against the bar. Give it three months and he wouldn't be surprised if the firm took them back on, once the fuss had died down. A lot of people couldn't do that sort of work, but he didn't mind it at all. Those birds were fucked. He was doing them a favour. Half of them had probably gone mad. There was shit and piss everywhere, but they were too stupid to break out and make a run for it. It was like the Jews in the war. How many of them fought back? How could you respect anyone who wouldn't fight to survive? At least the Jews had learned their lesson and turned up the pressure when they got the upper hand in Israel. Look at what they were doing to the Arabs.

Kicking fuck out of the ragheads after stealing their land. Good luck to them. They did the old kosher job as well. Cut their animals' throats and bled their chickens to death without bothering to stun them first. No electrified water for those cunts. Same as the Muslims and their halal meat.

Bob was his best pal of the last two years. They'd met at work and had a laugh, bossing the birds about, taking the piss. Bob was slower than Ricky, took time to catch up with his ideas, but he was handy with his fists, short-tempered and easily led. Ricky liked this – he was the general and Bob was his squaddie. They made a good team. It was like having his own protection squad. Nobody pushed him about when Bob was there.

He had been surprised at Bob's anger after the magistrate fined them, hadn't expected him to take it to heart, going on and on about the chickens not being alive like a human and how they didn't feel any pain. It had started to get on his nerves after a while, but he kept his mouth shut. He was scared of what Bob might do in a rage, but knew how to bring him around. Bob was gullible and wrong about those chickens not feeling pain, but he kept the information to himself. Fucking hell, if they were just objects who felt nothing where would the fun be in hurting them? There was no point in it if they weren't scared.

Bob was trying to chat up the barmaid now, but he was slurring his words and Ricky reckoned she was disgusted with them as well. The slag needed a good seeing to, and he imagined his friend taking her out round the back of the pub and fucking her nice and hard. That would sort her out. They fucking loved it these local slags. Ricky liked this image, watched his idiot mate spluttering into his drink, but the pub was emptying out and he was tired. The barmaid went off to collect empties and he suggested they leave. Bob shrugged. He'd had enough. They headed home, ambling along, taking the path next to the recreation ground. It was still warm out, a nice evening.

There was a crunch of gravel. Ricky and Bob only saw their attacker as an outline, remembered none of his details when they were interviewed by the police. The man came out of the shadows, a baseball bat connecting with Bob's head. He dropped to his knees. Drunk and semi-conscious, he was unable to get back up. Ricky saw this and turned to run, panicked and stumbled, felt a blow to his back, fell to the ground, had time to look up and see a man standing above him, leg pulling back like he was going to take a penalty kick, the foot zooming in, growing and thumping into his face, sending him flying. He rolled over, raised his hands to his face and started whimpering, propped himself on an elbow, tried to get to his feet, but he was weak and shaking, watched as the figure walked back over to Bob and kicked him in the face, sent his protector back down to the floor. The bat was raised and brought down twice.

Ricky started to cry. The pain was unbearable. He was sure his nose was broken. He wished he could jump up and run away, but he could hardly move. The figure turned and walked towards him and Ricky begged to be left alone, reached in his jacket and offered his wallet, the keys to his flat, his attacker could have anything he wanted. Ricky had done nothing wrong. He didn't deserve this. The man kicked the wallet out of his hand. This was all wrong. Ricky tried to scream, but the sound was odd, more of squeak, reminded him of the hamster he'd had as a child, the noise it made when he crushed it in his fists. He'd had a lot of fun with that hamster.

His right knee exploded as the baseball bat struck. He began to lose consciousness, but a blow to his left leg brought him back. He waited for the bat to descend again, closed his eyes, wanted it to crack his head open and send him to sleep so the agony would end, but it didn't. He heard feet on gravel, and for some reason imagined the cluck of a chicken, and as the footsteps faded into the distance he was sure he was being tricked, that the man was still there, waiting to end his life, and so he stayed still, hands firm around his head, crying softly, but after a while he wasn't so sure and peeked out and realised that apart from Bob knocked out like a useless fucking lump he was alone.

Ricky's knees were burning. He started to scream, and this time he didn't think about his hamster, didn't care when he puked up the lager he'd drunk and the cheeseburger he'd eaten earlier. Pushing himself into a sitting position, he stopped screaming and started to cry again, softy at first, and then he was sobbing, his chest heaving, and finally he was begging for someone to come and help, to take him to hospital, but nobody heard and so nobody came.

The core of Tanner's meal was Mrs Gupta's ginger and garlic, chopped and mashed up with sliced green chillis. He was making himself chickpea masala. Tangy dhal on the side. She had given him a spice container which was the same as the one she used, a thank you for the digging he'd done for her and Mr Gupta. He loved his metal treasure chest, which was round with a glass lid, the six pots inside arranged in a circle, with a seventh in the middle. They held cumin seeds, turmeric, ground coriander, cloves, cinnamon bark, masala powder and poppy seeds. There were seven tiny spoons to go with them. When the bark ran out, he had refilled the pot with cardamom seeds.

One day he was going to pack a bag and go off and see the world, and India would be his first stop. It had to be the best place on the planet for a vegan, which was handy, as he loved his curries, but the attraction was as much to do with the thinking behind the food. He had read about Benares, wanted to visit the city and head further up the Ganges into the mountains, stay in Rishikesh, having heard about it in a documentary on The Beatles. He planned to travel in the Punjab and Gujarat, represented in his mind by the Golden Temple in Amritsar and the Jain religion.

South India was the home of the thali and the dosa, and he would maybe start there or in Sri Lanka. They didn't have the same Muslim influences as the north, and so the food was lighter and more vegan. He respected The Beatles for their interest in Eastern ideas, and Paul McCartney had stood firm on animal rights across the decades. He liked the way they had brought India into their music with the great Ravi Shankar. As Tanner cooked his dinner Talvin Singh played. Cornershop were up next. Until he left to see the world he would eat its food, listen to its music, watch its films.

Tasting the masala, Tanner decided it was ready. He cut one of Pat's tomatoes into four pieces and dropped these in, stirred and left them for a minute, squeezed in the juice from half a lemon, adding fresh coriander as he turned off the heat. Draining the basmati rice, he put this on a plate and added the contents of the pan. He owned a chapatti dish, but had been too lazy to make any and regretted it now. At least he had the dhal. Putting his meal at the place he'd set at the table, he took a bottle of lager from the fridge and sat down. He spooned on mango chutney and lime pickle and got stuck in. Yes, he'd done well. It tasted great.

As he ate, he pictured Jeff and Sandy doing the same in their garden, surrounded by dogs and all the other animals they had given a home. They'd dedicated their lives to a cause, started early as well, hadn't drifted as he had done, making endless compromises. They had grown up in the Sixties and were rooted in the counterculture of the time, believed in the inherent decency of every human being. He knew the theory, but could the sort of people who casually drowned rabbits and cut the heads off live chickens for fun really change? He hoped so.

Mike Tanner cooked for himself. Sat at his table eating alone. He insisted he didn't mind. It was how he had ended up. Down to his character. He'd had some good years with Kate, remembered their last holiday together, saw them on the beach linking Holkham and Wells, part of a North Norfolk coastline that ran from Hunstanton to Cromer. They were sitting on top of a dune looking out across the sand, which was as smooth and soft as any he'd ever seen. It was a long, wide beach, and near enough deserted. Most people stayed nearer the car parks, and it was a cold day, which made them less willing to explore. Blurred figures walked next to the sea, off in the distance where washed-up shells and stones formed a thin black line. A breeze blew and the grass next to Kate rustled. There was a pine wood behind the dunes, a second line of defence against the flooding the flat landscape couldn't stop. When the clouds moved and uncovered the sun, the sand turned to gold. It was a beautiful part of the world.

He had felt so good that day when they'd set off for Norfolk, leaving early on a Sunday morning, crossing a still-dreaming city, the streets more or less empty except for some late-night dancers and first-light cleaners. He had gone along Millbank. It was a direct route and meant they could see Parliament and Westminster Abbey up close. These buildings were always impressive, but more so when it felt like they were the only people in the world. The pressure eased right off. He guessed that solitude was what Jeff and Sandy had wanted.

He replayed their journey, slowing at Downing Street and the Cenotaph, turning right at Trafalgar Square and heading down the Strand to Aldwych, past the Law Courts and into Fleet Street. At the end he turned right to avoid Smithfield Market, took a left at The Blackfriar pub and crawled along, wary of the speed cameras. Dwarfed by the stone blocks of the City, they entered White-chapel, where he'd expected traffic heading for Petticoat Lane, but they were early enough to sail through. Commercial Road was slow, but he picked up speed when they turned off and passed the Olympic Park on the right, reaching the M11 and doing seventy, only feeling like they were really on their way when they had crossed the M25. They played CDs, but he couldn't remember which ones, even though the trip and holiday were fixed in his mind.

Kate had booked a cottage ten minutes inland from Brancaster, and most days they would drive up and stop along the coast. She always did them a picnic before they set off, loved the making of it as much as the eating. They had walked for miles, or if it was warm and sunny they'd settle down on the sand, reading and dozing. She ate the same food and put on a spread, stocking up before they left London, made all sorts of sandwiches and rolls – plain and flavoured hummus, Nutolene, mushroom and vegetable pâtés, peanut butter, vegan cheeses, avocado, a range of flavoured soya slices. And then there were the extras, and not just crisps and nuts, but vine leaves, sun-dried tomatoes, gherkins, olives, wax peppers, dried apricots, the works. There were cold salads – red rice, maca-roni, couscous, potato.

They had seen seals basking on the banks of an inlet, sat on the other side of the water and watched them for a good hour until they stirred and heaved themselves into the sea. They'd visited a grand house with brilliant formal gardens, played croquet on a specially prepared lawn. In the evenings they would sit in the garden of the cottage if it was warm, or drive into Hunstanton where there was a funfair on the seafront by a caravan park, which meant shops, stalls, music, the bustle of families. If it was raining they watched a film. They had driven over to Cromer one day, found a couple of good secondhand bookshops, one with a shelf of African fiction by authors he had never heard of before. They went to the lifeboat station and he looked out for Steve Ignorant, who he'd heard was living in Cromer and part of its RNLI crew.

That day they'd first seen the migrating geese was one of the best of his life. They liked to walk inland from the cottage as well, following easy paths through the fields, and late one afternoon they heard honking, turned towards a nearby wood and waited as the sound grew louder. A V-shaped formation appeared, at least a hundred birds arriving in a wave that filled the sky. As it passed over them they could see the necks of the geese stretched out, wings battering the air, urging each other on. Slowly, the noise became quieter and the birds smaller, and finally they vanished into a huge grey heaven. It was a magical sight, raw and real and majestic, and probably the peak of their relationship. They had both seen it as special, on a deeper level recognising what it represented.

Another, smaller wave had followed a few minutes later, and they stopped again to watch it pass, stayed where they were after it had faded away, and within minutes there was more honking. This third group was as big as the first, moving fast, flying lower so they could see the colour of their beaks. Kate pointed to a bird that was trying to catch up. It was flapping faster and even harder than the main group and calling out, its voice isolated, scared and frantic. The V was too fast and it was left behind, wheeled away and flew low across a stubbly field, seemed lost and doomed, and their hearts sank as it turned in a wide circle, closer to the ground, heading towards the trees, and then it began to rise up as another wave appeared and it pushed itself as it tried to link up with this new flock.

Kate held his hand as they willed the bird on, and then it was at one tip of the V, and maybe it was caught in the slipstream, but whatever happened it became part of the whole and was moving much more easily. They watched the geese soar into the sky and turn to the right before swooping around and heading left, and they became smaller and the line fainter, finally fading along with the light. Mike and Kate Tanner had been elated.

It was another day when they came across the pig farm, approaching it by chance, from the rear, on a path running next to another wood. They could hear the poor creatures inside the sheds, smell the waste they were forced to live in. It was a dirty farm, stunk of piss and shit, and he imagined a few rotting bodies as well. He was angry and upset, Kate urging him not to think about it, they would go back the way they'd come. There was nothing they could do. He walked in silence, unable to think of anything else for the rest of the day.

It was a year later that Kate decided she'd had enough. He couldn't relax, had become moody and increasingly on edge, his head full of conflicting thoughts and worries. Kate had been right to walk away. He must have driven her mad. She was a nicer person and better off without him. He hoped she was happy, hadn't had any contact with her since she remarried. It had been for the best. He had to believe it had been for the best.

When he had finished eating he left his plates and went into the living room, turned on the TV, skipped channels and settled on the news. A young woman had detonated a bomb outside a mosque in the Middle East, killing herself and as many as fifty others. Early reports said she was eighteen years old and had left a recording that detailed the reasons for her attack. She would be seen as a martyr and rewarded in the afterlife. The report was accompanied by rough footage of the bomb's aftermath. This had been recorded on a mobile phone. There were glimpses of people running, mangled cars and scorched stone. The dead had been edited out.

The next story was that of a soldier who had shot and killed an injured enemy fighter. He was going on trial, the evidence against him more grainy images and a distorted soundtrack. The dead man had been badly injured and was dying, but the soldier had pumped bullets into the body. It was being described as a breakdown in discipline. The reporter said that the accused had recently lost three of his friends to a road-side bomb. Revenge was mentioned. Tanner had met former soldiers over the years and took them at face value, had no idea what they'd done in uniform. Truly fighting for a cause had to involve channelling your anger and focusing on the end result. Again, he wondered if it was possible. He didn't know the answer, but was interested in the question.

Turning the sound down, he watched important politicians speak words he couldn't hear. The faces changed, fragmented, re-formed in mass-produced, Andy Warhol prints. For his part, he wanted to know how anyone could claim to be a socialist and eat meat. What sort of liberal let piglets die because they enjoyed the taste of their bodies? Why would a conservative condone the cutting of a child's throat? Where was the outrage of the religious leaders? All of these people peddled morality, promoted their self-images, but refused to challenge the meat and dairy industries. He hated their dishonesty.

He spread out on the couch and dozed, a half-sleep where the faces of these politicians, soldiers and suicide girls were cut up and glued back together. Adjusting his position he opened his eyes and saw adverts playing. A famous face filled the screen, advertising a range of pork sausages. There were lots of these characters about, each of them with their own selling point, a quirk to be marketed. They bounced around, full of energy and positivity. Cleanliness was a meat-industry obsession, the front for a dirty business. The broadsheet articles were repeated on television.

He turned up the volume. A celebrity chef had travelled to a remote spot where he was left alone with the elements and a production crew. A pig needed to die on a rustic homestead. The sun beat down on the chef, who was challenging his own reluctance to kill. He shot the creature in the head and felt good. This was real life. A freezing wind blew across the rocks of a bleak but beautiful island. The chef accompanied tough locals as they captured a wild goat. It was taken into a barn and the doors partially closed. Knives were shown. Cleavers displayed. There were kicking legs, a blood-filled bucket, a wry smile. This was serious programme-making. Nobody was forced to watch. The pig and goat were delicious. Sustainable. Organic.

Tanner felt he was a decent enough cook, but not exactly celebrity-chef material. He liked to use ingredients from the allotments where possible, adding flamboyant touches that made every dish unique. He was no good with formal recipes, preferred to improvise, and he had no interest in the sort of fame that would see his face splashed across the pages of a supplement or tabloid. He could sit and watch rubbish on TV, but didn't want to see his ugly mug filling its screen. His was the cleanest food going and it didn't need any of their fancy packaging.

There was a television series where a pair of critics travelled the world and ate the sort of food those at home would never touch. The camera recorded rats being caught on the edge of a paddy field by a local, taken from a drain and their front teeth pulled out with pliers. They were killed and roasted, offered to the two presenters who pulled funny faces and refused to touch the meat. Even they had standards. They would not eat rodents who swam in shit. They visited a snake farm. A cobra was taken from a cage and cut open with a knife, its heart removed while it was still alive and served to the stars. This was seen as a delicacy. Lips were licked and eyelids fluttered. Jokes were made. The heart was eaten and enjoyed.

Tanner kept an eye on the screen, flicking channels, but there was nothing about the men he had read about in the paper, no mention of Ricky and Bob here or on the internet. It was a shame, but showed how low level their crimes were considered by the police and media. They were no longer newsworthy. What had he expected? Where was the link?

He turned the television off and went into the kitchen, filled the sink with hot water and washed up. His flat was neat and tidy, everything in its right place. Bad thoughts were scrubbed away. The knuckles of his left hand bled. It was a nice evening. He would walk over to the allotments and see who was about, have a chat with Ella if she was there, maybe pop into The White Hart later on for a quick pint.

My body ached from walking and my head from thinking. I was wet and tired, shivering in the cold, saw a church and tried the door. It was unlocked and I went inside. The church was empty. I was the only person there, which was a relief. It meant I could stay for as long as I wanted without worrying that someone would tell me to leave. It was gloomy, but dry and warm, smelled of smoke, candles burning at small altars to the side of the pews where I sat down. The stained-glass window behind the altar dominated the church. It was impossible to not be drawn into the story. The glass was hundreds of years old, but felt so alive and relevant, catching and converting the sunshine. It was one of the most beautiful works of art I had ever seen. I wasn't a religious man, had never been raised in a faith, but I knew the tale. It was the root of my culture and in its way captured the madness of everything that was happening around me. A pregnant woman and her husband had arrived in a strange town and could find nowhere to stay the night. Instead of sleeping on the streets they found sanctuary in a stable. Here, surrounded by the meekest and most abused of God's children, their baby was born. The stable was crowded with chickens, pigs, cows, sheep, goats, donkeys, horses, geese. Ewes sheltered their lambs. Calves stood next to cows. Chicks perched on the shoulders of hens. Piglets rubbed noses on the bellies of sows. Bulls, cockerels, boars and rams looked on with pride. There were no lions, snakes or people outside of this family in the stable, although three rich men did arrive later, following a star and bearing gifts. The meek were going to inherit the earth. It was a new start and everything was possible. Love flowed through the church and I was overcome. But the story didn't end there. It went on and on. The child became a man who told the people to make their own sacrifices instead of sacrificing others. He asked them to take responsibility for their actions, to live in peace, but the rulers needed a pecking order. They tortured and killed him, used their language to distort what he had said. Even now, they call Jesus the Lamb Of God. And this other lamb, the one I am thinking about now, she should have a name. Dolly The Sheep belongs to the vivisectionists. I was shaking again, but this time with anger and fear and my failure. Spring lamb. Nice and tender. Lamb chops. Mint sauce. Sunday dinner after praying in church and drinking in the pub. There is no mercy for the meek. Call her Mary.

The drinker Mike Tanner sat by his kitchen window nursing a hangover. There was a big bag of veg on the table, handed to him by Ella – spinach, beans, beetroot and onions that they had grown together, along with greens from Wendell and one of Sid's pumpkins. He had done well getting this lot home, seeing as he'd stopped off at the pub and ended up having a session with Tony and a couple of the other regulars. He didn't have any work lined up, wasn't really looking at the moment, knew he was slowing down and losing his focus, yet at the same time his mind was speeding up. He hadn't slept well, his dreams coming out into the open, conned by the alcohol. The high of drinking was always followed by a low. Some strong black coffee would sort him out.

He reached for his 'Trotters Independent Trading' mug on the table and raised it to his mouth, blowing on the surface and feeling steam against his face, tasting the hot tar on his tongue. He stretched his legs out and felt a surge of energy. Del Boy grinned. His Reliant Robin was parked in the background, ready to take them on an adventure. There was a cafetière's worth of coffee ready – Italian, strength 4.

Leaning forward, he looked into the gardens from his place in the heavens. Brick walls separated manicured grass from mini-jungles, the four-storey terraces creating a microclimate where plants and trees flourished. He thought about Sid's squash, the enclosures perfect for a bigger operation. Birds, squirrels, hedgehogs and at least one fox lived alongside domestic cats and dogs. Bushes and shrubs boxed in a patch of wild grass immediately below him, and while it was thick with moss and weeds the borders were always clipped. A deflated orange ball had appeared in the middle of the lawn, pulled out of a dustbin or found on the street, brought back by a fox. He hoped it was Lily.

The wall on the left side of the garden had a section missing, the bricks around the gap charred as if it had been blown out by a shell, but this was a peacetime city where the obvious battles were small-time and personal and fought over territory and drugs, organised crime more corporate and hidden. Lily had built a home in the thickest corner of the garden, behind a collapsing shed, knew she was safe with the lady who lived in the flat. Bowls of water and food were left out, but Lily had moved on last year, more recently coming back a couple of times in the hot weather.

He spotted her sunbathing on a bed of ivy spilling from a water tank filled with earth. She sensed him watching, lifted her head, and while he couldn't make out her face clearly he was sure she would be acting coy. He felt guilty, as if he was spying, recognised the expressions he saw on the faces of humans in those of animals – interest, confusion, joy, sorrow, embarrassment, worry, fear.

She was big and healthy and he remembered Kate naming her at this same window, the cubs she'd raised when she was younger. Lily was at least ten, her ginger-red fur dashed with white, and he thought of her as clever and wise, independent and free. He felt there was something special about her, partly due to the years she'd lived so close by, seeing her through the seasons, throwing extra food down in winter. He understood that foxes were hunters and had always separated the hunted in his mind, that they could go into a frenzy when they broke into a chicken coop. Animals usually killed for food. To survive. Here, with dustbins galore, the foxes were strong and lived longer than in the country, and he'd never seen Lily go after a bird or a cat. But he knew he was making exceptions. That's what people did. Made excuses.

Standing in The White Hart last night, with Tony going on about a grand house he was decorating, the size of the bedrooms and attached bathrooms, his eyes had drifted back out to the junction, to the condemned children filling the buses, human and animal faces pressed against the windows, old soldiers dismounting and trooping back into the pub after fighting in a world war. They had done their best and were expected to resume their former lives, but were mentally changed. Many would carry on, their memories buried, while others tried to fit in but failed. Some men came home insane. Each story was different and he doubted a fraction of them had ever been told. Their experiences would have varied, the same as their reactions, these great whirlpools of emotion lasting their lifetimes.

If that bus outside really was heading to the slaughterhouse, full of lambs or piglets, the reaction of the people on the pavements would be one of horror. Despite the leather they were wearing and the meat inside them they would be shocked. And he was sure some of them would try and help the animals inside. A freedom fighter fought for a belief. With the scale of the slaughter surrounding them, the terror that undermined everything positive he saw, why did nobody step forward and take animal liberation to another level? A true soldier killed without anger, remained calm and focused, dedicated to his cause.

A slaughterman was not threatened by those he killed. His victims were defenceless. Harmless. Humans ate the gentlest creatures. A knacker was either oblivious to suffering or didn't care. Either way, he lacked empathy. Some were psychopaths who had found a legal way to torture and murder. The argument that an unskilled man had to take any work he could find had some truth to it, but it was no excuse. Tanner's opposition was moral. Part of a bigger picture. Animal welfare should be at the heart of politics. The green case against meat and dairy was rock solid. These were unhealthy luxuries, a waste of resources. A cause of disease, hunger and poverty.

Could he break the mould and kill another person if it would end the carnage? A soldier had to present two faces to the world. He would have to split his personality. Men had gone away, fought and killed, drunk in The White Hart without anybody knowing what they had done. The ideas filling Tanner's head were exciting and frightening, merged with the information he had collected in the past – the location of slaughterhouses and farms, the names of buyers and sellers, transport firms, suppliers of equipment, those dealing in marketing and propaganda.

Tilting his mug and slowly moving it in circles, he watched the remaining coffee swill and stain the inside, getting it right up to the rim without it spilling on the floor. Lots of people had similar thoughts, he was sure of that – revenge scenarios – daydreams where they dealt out some righteous justice – but it was all fantasy thinking, a release mechanism, and he imagined the suicide bomber who blew up a marketplace and what had tipped her over. Revenge was pointless. There had to be a goal. A genuine freedom fighter would feel that, he was sure. But there had to be anger. He stopped and let the slicks run back down, drank another mouthful, then leaned his arms on the table, holding his head in his hands.

The radio chattered in the background. He didn't remember turning it on. He was on a beach with Kate, eating a picnic, driving from the city into the country, standing outside The Meadows and Elm Cottage. He had dreamed of a pigsty last night, faces appearing over the wall, and when he woke up he thought about the ram. Had it died in the barn? Had they killed the pigs in there? Driven them over from the sty? Slaughtered lambs? Broken the necks of geese so they couldn't fly away to Africa? What did they do with the heads? People thought it was funny to stick an apple in the mouth of a suckling pig – a child that was still being fed by its mother. There always had to be that final insult, the mocking of the dead. Too many people were taking the piss. He stood up and threw his mug across the room, saw it smash on the wall and smear coffee over the plaster.

The radio hummed. He remembered Harry Spalding speaking. Heard him again now. Harry was the brains behind Funhouse Foods. His voice was soothing as he reassured the public. Whatever happened in this mad world, with all the stabbings, bombings and terrible violence, at least the masses could afford to eat well. He was always looking to make savings, determined to supply the most affordable, tastiest meat. Price mattered. The consumer knew best. Business was booming. But questions had been asked about certain practices. He refused to get angry. His critics wanted what was best for his animals and so did he. They were cared for and lived happy lives. What did groups such as PETA *really* want? The country to turn vegan? That was clearly ridiculous. Didn't the presenter look forward to his bacon butty like anyone else? His Sunday roast? A nice lamb chop? The interviewer laughed and said that indeed he did. In a moment he would bring in his other guest, who was waiting on the phone.

Harry spoke about freedom of choice and the right of every individual to choose their own diet. He wanted to stress that he was harming nobody, creating jobs and paying his taxes. He was providing an essential service by growing cheap meat. *Growing* meat? The vegan guest picked up on this after she had been introduced, detailing a range of cruelties and the redundancy of meat in a modern society, arguments which made perfect sense to Mike Tanner. The presenter wondered if she wasn't being naive and even a little selfish. After all, he really did love the taste of bacon, and could never give up cheese. An exchange of views followed.

Harry Spalding was quiet until he was invited to join in. He was relaxed, charming, wanted to put the woman's mind at rest. What would happen to these animals if everyone stopped eating meat tomorrow? Had she thought of that? Animal protein was vital to health. It was all about survival. She should not make the mistake of seeing a lamb in human terms. They were *animals*. She was being sentimental and – if she didn't mind him saying so – rather childish. His voice hardened, but only slightly. It was time to grow up. They lived in a democracy and she was questioning the right of tens of millions of decent, law-abiding citizens to eat the food they wanted. One person was smug, the other increasingly angry. These endless words achieved little. The programme was in the recent past. The radio wasn't even turned on.

A helicopter was hovering outside. A lorry roared through the night. The stench was overpowering. The condemned were inside Tanner's flat. He was standing in the spew of bladders and stomachs, petrol fumes and gas in his lungs. He struggled to breathe. Eyes stared at him through cracks in the wall. He was running across the city, a thermal-image spirit on a police scanner. Macka B boomed. He sat up, his mug next to him unbroken, the plaster clean, Del Boy grinning. Only fools and horses worked.

Tanner went to the sink and rinsed his face with cold water, dried it and returned to the window, looked into a blue sky and saw a helicopter in the distance, moving in the opposite direction, leaving him alone. He refilled his mug, cleaned the cafetière, walked into the living room thinking about the rabbits and the emptiness of the flat, pulled out a box of records and removed albums by Conflict and Crass. He had played *This Is The ALF* in the car after he left Elm Cottage. He would listen to these LPs later on, and while he knew they would stir him up and make him angry, the part of his character he was suppressing insisted. He thought again and searched for *Meat Is Murder* by The Smiths. Added it to the other records. Like Paul McCartney, Morrissey had hit the heights but never backed down. He pulled out some Vice Squad and Flux Of Pink Indians.

The room shook, from the washing machine downstairs or the chopper coppers returning he didn't know, but he left the flat and was on the move, needed to breathe fresh air and feel the sun, wake himself up and live his life. Maybe he would return to The White Hart and lose himself in the crowd, sit in the back bar on his own if nobody he knew was at the front of the pub, but it was too early and the drink would only cause more muddle. He could buy some roses and take them to Ella, but he had seen her yesterday and she'd wonder what was up. Bunny might be about, but he didn't want to talk about seaweed and compost heaps. No, he had to be on his own. He was sick of making excuses for people he knew, all of them meat eaters and leather wearers. It was time to stay away and not let his anger become personal.

How many pigs had built a sty to match the Taj Mahal? Could he name one cow who had walked on the moon? Had a lamb ever won the World Cup? A friend of a friend had come out with these questions in a pub, asking him how he could eat a poor little potato, because didn't he hear it asking for its mummy, and what about those innocent lentils, they felt pain, didn't they, and he remembered the mocking smile of a two-bob cunt who wasn't even original. Bang. He'd split the man's lips wide open. Closed his mouth. That's how he had been then and it cheered him up now, served the wanker right, and he'd walloped him several more times, probably hurt him more than he deserved, seeing as he'd been drinking, and that wasn't so good, not in a perfect world, but fuck him. The bloke thought he could get away with it because Tanner was a vegan, which in his head meant sandals and incense, a lentil-loving pacifist who could be bullied.

When he reached the river Tanner followed the towpath, passed disused warehouses and wharves that were destined to be gutted and revamped and sold to the wealthy of the world, stopped on a brick footbridge barely above the water, looked over at the tower blocks on the other side. At night pleasure boats cruised as far as this spot before turning around, and he had seen their lights sparkle, decks full of figures on special evenings out, heard the music blaring. There was fun and laughter, lively songs he knew, but all he could think about was the stink of their barbecues.

He turned away from the water, walked until he neared a railway station, sat down on a bench across the road in a small public garden. Pigeons cooed. He watched people entering and leaving, moving across the city on miracle trains. These were the chosen ones, the superior species, the strutting two-legged faction that had broken away from the rest of the animal kingdom and taken control. He hated everyone he could see, everyone he knew. He hated their lies. It was true that reality was more complex than any animal lover could ever imagine. Life was not simple. He was naive and sentimental. He loved everyone he saw.

Sentiment was weakness. Empathy had its limits. Bombs, guns and knives were necessary evils. Everything was justified. The mass killing of animals should not be called a slaughter. The factories were *abattoirs*. People paraded their values while a parallel world existed all around them, a twenty-four-hour orgy of organised, industrial violence. Torture, mutilation, rape, murder – every single second of every single day of every single year. It was the terror that never ended. A genocide that was denied yet involved billions of victims. A holocaust that could not be called one, as such words must not be linked to non-human animals. The scale was impossible to comprehend, and because the numbers were so huge, and because the realities so sickening, people turned their heads and closed their eyes and covered their ears and were angry at those who asked them to face up to the truth. They caught their trains and buses and hurried away. They were soft, easily manipulated, and above all wanted to believe the lies. How could they go on living if they did not?

The man Mike Tanner was out of control. The boy Michael had tears in his eyes as he prayed for a happy ending. Mickey Moo was trying to persuade himself that everything would work out for the best. Tanner was in a humid room. It smelled like a sewage works. A giant was standing over him with a stopwatch in his hand. A huge goblin was holding him with one hand and using the other to cut his head clean off. Tanner saw it happen. His naked body ran for a few seconds that seemed like hours. His eyes were blinking. They rolled in their sockets. His head was on a table next to a V-formation of framed photos. There was an apple being stuffed into his mouth. An S&M prop? He wasn't sure. His legs marched on. An endless walking that took him nowhere. The drum inside his chest thumped and echoed in a valley below a golden path on a sandy ridge. His heart strained as that headless body bounced off steel cages, banged into the table and sent the photos of everyone he had ever loved falling to the floor where the glass smashed. Their faces were soaked in blood. More men had arrived. One held up electric tongs, another flashed a knife, a third leered and rubbed his balls. Tanner was a liar and a weakling. He was scared of living. Scared of dying.

Scared as a rabbit... Smelly pig... Dirty cow... Hung like a horse... Black sheep... Judas goat... Just like sheep... Just can't win... Nice bit of gammon... Roast beef... Lamb chop... Traditional... Sirloin steak... Cheddar and Stilton... Fried chicken... Lovely... I don't tell you what to eat... Not hurting anyone... Don't be so miserable... Nothing you can do... Life's too short... Only animals... Can you eat potatoes?... Do carrots scream?... Poor little pea... You think more of them than you do people... Doesn't happen... Making me feel sick... Don't want to hear about it... If we didn't eat them they wouldn't exist... Who cares... Got no memories... Got no emotions... Can't talk... Can a donkey drive a car?... Fly to the moon?... Write a book?... Dogs bite... A cow might trample you... Horses kick... Vicious animals... Stupid animals... Dirty animals... Chop her head off... Cut his bollocks off.... Stick them in the freezer... Bah... Moo... Oink... Cluck, cluck, cluck...

Tanner felt a hand on his shoulder and looked up. For a moment he imagined the lady had come to glue his head back to his body, or maybe she was a vet who was here to slide his balls back into his scrotum and sew the skin together. She asked if he was okay. Did he need a doctor? She must have been in her seventies, but inside her leathery face were two child's eyes that were so blue and bright he felt ashamed. She was clearly scared. He wanted her to know that he was a strong man, not this weakling she saw on the bench.

He pulled himself together, sat up straight and thanked her, said he was allergic to something he'd eaten. It had made his eyes water and his throat sore. A bad mug of coffee. Nuts had contaminated the brew. He had fainted. His vision became blurred. He smiled. This had never happened before. He was fine. Bad dreams. Yes, he felt a lot better. He wiped his eyes. He could see clearly. Thank you for stopping. Crystal-clear vision. Yes, thanks for asking. It's very kind of you, but please don't worry. It won't happen again. Thank you very much. Thank you.

The first time I saw the man driving my dreams was when he was standing inside the tree line of a wood. He was nervous, but didn't move, remained perfectly still. It was after midnight and the moon was nearly full, the scene spread out in front of him radiant, but his head was hidden in the shadows so I couldn't see his face. The wood flanked a road that led to the gates of a factory, the buildings inside protected by high walls lined with wire. There were mesh fences in front of these walls and this created a no-man's land. Light seeped from the factory and sent electricity running along the wire, but by the time it reached the fence it had faded, leaving a faint web. The factory was new and designed for maximum efficiency, isolated but easily accessed, its privacy prized. It was bland. Characterless. The work it did was monotonous. Relentless. The man was noting all this, talking to himself, the words so deep inside his mind I couldn't hear them properly, but I did notice that his hands were clasped in front of his chest, the fingers linked, and I could feel and hear his heart. I was wet from the sweat sticking his palms together, which was odd, as I was standing in front of him and behind him and hovering up above looking down, but nowhere was I touching his body. I wondered if he should go home, but he fought the urge, determined to be brave, and I waited and worried. The time passed. Maybe he had turned to timber. Had I mistaken a tree for a man? A man for a tree? When his head turned I looked in the same direction and saw two white dots. Heard a faint hum. The sound grew louder as fireflies turned to fireballs and meteors and long battery-powered beams. A lorry was booming and blaspheming big-headed towards the factory. The man stepped into the open and hurried to the edge of the road. He was dwarfed by the container when it reached him, and as he looked inside he glimpsed hundreds of lambs, some with their noses pressed through the slats as they struggled to breathe fresh air. He saw their fear and felt their terror and heard them calling out, and for a second his eyes connected with those of a little girl and his heart broke. The lorry flashed past and she was gone, the vehicle shrinking, the sound of its engine fading. The slaughter-house gates opened and it went inside. The man stayed by the side of the road. He felt ashamed. Other lorries followed. He saw pigs, calves and more lambs. His heart was thumping so hard I thought it would crack my ribs. The prayers he had said, his wishful thinking and attempts at persuasion, the peaceful protests and self-control had achieved nothing. He was powerless. A small, insignificant fool. Tilting his head back, he screamed. I saw him clearly in the moonlight. He had no face. No name. I woke up and *was soaked in a pissy sort of sweat. I tried to push what I had seen and felt into the depths of my mind, but it was impossible, and of course it was important to have these dreams as my memories, and my memories as my dreams.*

Smelly Pigs

STEVE COLLINS PICKED up the kettle and realised it was empty, tightened his lips in disgust, couldn't be bothered filling it with water and waiting for the fucking thing to boil, went over to the vending machine and bought a fizzy can instead. He sat down and pulled the ring, drank fast, cold lemonade refreshing a parched throat. His head was heavy from last night's lager and he was pissed off he'd had to come into work, even though it was his choice to do the overtime. He was ten minutes early, opened his newspaper and flicked the pages, stopping at a story alleging gang rape in a luxury hotel.

Five unnamed footballers were in the frame. Cocaine was mentioned. He studied the photo of a naked teenager face down on a pile of cushions, her bum and black stilettos pointing in the air, face turned towards the camera in a saucy pout. At first he thought she was the victim of the attack, then realised she was a model. He carried on through the latest political and religious scandals – MPs accused of fiddling expenses, priests of abusing children. He came to a series of showbiz titbits, turned to the football results, which he already knew. Bored, Steve thought about last night, the laugh he'd had with his friends, glad the wife was fast asleep when the taxi dropped him home.

She'd served him up a nice breakfast and a couple of paracetamol this morning, seeing as he was working, and he'd had time for a good soak in the bath. She'd even come in and scrubbed his back, teasing him when he became erect, soaping his balls and calling him into the bedroom. Once he'd dried himself off and plastered his armpits with deodorant and splashed aftershave over his face, he went and found her waiting, reflected in the full-length mirror at the bottom of their bed. He looked after his body. Work kept him fit and he had two baths and a shower most days. Doing this job, he liked a good scrub. Messy at work, clean at home, smart when he was out and about.

Steve had bills to pay and didn't mind doing weekends, although he preferred his overtime during the week. He lived a busy life and sweated for his money, had debts to service, but it was worth the luxuries – a new TV with all the extras, mobiles for the kids, that holiday last year in Cyprus, a computer he never used but the children loved. That was before he got around to paying the mortgage. He had a lot of outgoings, but his wife worked as well. They got by okay. Life was good.

You made your own luck in this world. Nobody had ever given him a penny. They were a good team, no-nonsense and determined, the memory of her waiting on the bed stirring the blood in his groin. He knew he was the bollocks, loved watching himself in the mirror, alone or with the missus. He'd given her a good seeing-to before he came in, though that girl from last night had been playing across his mind. The wife would never know. It had done no damage to his performance. Probably helped, if he was honest.

One of his workmates strolled in, went to the kettle, and they shared some small-talk as he filled it with water, wondering about the identity of the players involved in the football story. Old Jim was irritated, said a groupie shouldn't be hanging about in a hotel like that if she didn't fancy a good roasting, stuck on a spit and fucked at both ends. She was looking to suck some Premiership cock so couldn't start moaning when she got a dose of double penetration thrown in. His laughter was shrill, chalk scratching a blackboard, but the story didn't interest Steve one way or the other. It was none of his business, though he didn't agree with rape under any circumstances. They should hang anyone who did that sort of thing. Same with paedophiles. Murderers as well. He was tired and wished he could go back to bed.

He saw his wife waiting in the leather boots he'd bought her, and she looked good, fucking loved it, they came right up to the top of her thighs as well. True, she could be a bitch, and was the first to admit it, but he loved her to bits. He shook his head at Old Jim prattling on about spit roasts, left and went in the bogs and had a piss, spat into the urinal, pinched the end of his knob and thought about that woman he'd been talking to last night, her number tucked safely away inside his phone. If the wife found out he was a dead man, but was tempted to call and arrange something on the sly. It would be easy enough.

Back in the tearoom, Steve changed into his work gear, in no great rush as he had a few minutes before he was due to start. He folded his clothes and placed them neatly in his locker, put his mobile on top, made sure the door was locked so none of the lads were tempted. He yawned and walked down the hall, rolling his shoulders and feeling his spine, biceps and calves taut. The noise grew, the rhythm of an operation that was as smooth as it was endless. No second or penny was wasted. He squeezed his fists, thinking about the woman in the pub. A man had to go out and take what he wanted. Had to look after himself. It was important that he was happy.

He listened to Murphy rambling on about some poof who lived near him, beaten up for noncing a kid. Problem was, he hadn't done anything, been near enough killed for upsetting some boys who were vandalising his car by complaining. They'd put it online that he was a paedo, which was fair enough, seeing as he was queer, though if Steve or Murphy had caught them interfering with one of their motors they would have battered the kids no problem. It didn't matter. Steve didn't give a fuck about the man. It wasn't his problem. He had nothing against him for being gay, just didn't care. If everyone took care of their own problems there would be a lot less trouble in the world. He wanted an easy life. Didn't need any hassle.

Steve Collins was a father providing for his family. He strolled through the shopping centre, credit cards ready, treating the wife to those boots and a necklace as well. He was strolling now, following Murphy and Old Jim into the area where they would be working. He made sure everything was in place, imagined the lads further down the line bringing in the first animals of the day. There was a clatter of hooves, and he knew from the schedule that he was dealing with lambs. He checked his tools, held a blade up to the light, the edge razor sharp. Jim was doing likewise, Murphy busy sorting out the hose. They were ready.

Killing animals was hard work – *man's* work – but he had been doing it for six years and it had become a routine. He had the experience, knew how the animals would react, the best way to stick them and achieve clean cuts, which made things easier for everyone. It had taken him a while to get the hang of the job, to make sure every cut counted, but practice made perfect. He only did the sticking these days, preferred it to stunning and shackling, never mind the dressing. Opening up a dead body and pulling the insides out was filthy work. Sticking meant a fair amount of blood, some shit and piss, but if the animals were stunned right he was dealing with easy targets. He felt sorry for the blokes doing the stunning hour after hour, dragging and hoisting the creatures up and sending them down the line. Sticking was the job to have. He enjoyed the killing best.

The boys here were only human, and when one of them was angry or fed up or just hungover he could take his frustrations out on the animals. It wasn't professional, but it happened – kicks and punches, a finger in an eye, an electric shock to the balls or arsehole, short doses of electricity so the pig or whatever was awake when it reached him. Tongs burned out eyes and deformed faces. There were plenty of wounds inflicted before he got stuck in, done here in the slaughterhouse or where the animals were being bred and held. It was the nature of the job. The men had to be strong. It wasn't work for a sissy. There would be chaos otherwise.

Old Jim didn't mind the animals coming through conscious, but Steve got angry if it happened too often. Trying to stab something that was thrashing about made life difficult, wasted his time and energy. Too many arrived this way, but overall the system worked well enough given the numbers they were dealing with over the course of a year.

The hardest part was the repetition. The killing became boring. Endless hours doing the same thing. That's why the men joked, shouting about this and that, reacting to the behaviour of the animals, but he knew there were one or two who really did love their work for strange reasons, sadistic cunts like Old Jim who giggled and talked to himself about fuck knows what. It didn't matter. The killing needed doing. Most people were too squeamish. At least perverts like Jim were in the right place, stuck in here and not out roaming the streets.

For Steve, slaughtering was like mowing the lawn. That's what he told people on the few occasions he was asked, and it was better than stacking shelves, a lot easier than carrying bricks about, and more rewarding than driving a taxi for some horrible fucker who gave all the best jobs to his mates. He thought back to his time minicabbing, the problems he'd had, dealing with people who didn't want to pay their fares, ferrying drunks around, that night he was robbed at knifepoint. It had shaken him up. Just as bad was being bossed around by an owner who liked taking the piss out of him, and this had spread so other drivers joined in. His confidence was dented. His boss was a bully. Coming here had been a blessing.

He had to admit he'd been a bit wild in the past, liked the drink and girls too much, but love had settled him down. Steve was doing well. He had a home and a family, but while there were debts, and he knew he had been caning the cards, it was nothing he couldn't handle. His wages weren't fantastic, but he did all the overtime he could and wasn't going to complain. They'd never been so busy.

Lambs were some of the easiest animals to kill, though he'd done a few goats and deer, and they weren't exactly difficult. If you knew where to stab them it shouldn't matter. These lambs were tiny little things, pretty to look at in a field, but you had to do them young or the meat was tough. If the flesh was left too long it was harder to chew and lost its flavour. Like some women he could mention, and he was thinking of that bird last night again, a good fifteen years younger than the wife. Keen as well. Dirty bitch. He imagined his wife next to her – mutton and lamb. People liked their meat tender. Nothing wrong with that. Miniskirt halfway up her arse. He was sure she'd had a boob job.

The first lamb was hung up and coming through and he could see the cock and balls hanging limp. He'd heard they chopped the bollocks off pigs in Europe but not here, he wasn't sure why, though they did castrate the bulls. Fucking huge knobs those boys had. This first lamb was out cold, not moving at all, brain fried, nicely electrocuted, and he stuck his knife in the neck, cut the artery so the blood gushed out, a small spurt compared to a pig or a steer. He'd done a few donkeys as well. Like the steers, they produced fountains of the stuff. That was the heart doing its job, getting the blood out of the body so the meat wasn't tainted. He heard a hose being turned on, forgot the boy he'd just cut, leaving him to bleed out. His attention moved to the next lamb.

Steve was definitely going to phone that woman up. He worked hard and deserved to play hard. What the wife didn't know wasn't going to hurt her, and anyway, she'd been spending money they didn't have, and on top of that she wasn't ageing well, hadn't shifted the weight from when she was last pregnant. The dirty cow was still worth shagging, but he couldn't be blamed for fancying something younger. That girl wasn't the brightest on the planet, but what a looker. Maybe they could meet up in a hotel.

His second lamb arrived and Steve stepped forward. She was twitching, which was normal, seeing as she was having some sort of epileptic fit, but hadn't been knocked out. At least she was pretty still, trying to move but hardly able, blood seeping from her mouth. Semi-conscious or unconscious didn't matter. He went to stick the lamb but she surprised him by jerking, trying in her pathetic little way to escape, his blade missing the artery so he stabbed the soft flesh of her neck. Blood stained her white coat. She bleated. He stabbed again and she cried out. Job done.

Steve turned and looked down the line. The girl he had stabbed kept struggling, but she was weak and fading fast, bleeding to death. Another lamb approached. His head was clearing. It was an easy start to the day. They had pigs later on. Big noisy fuckers. Harder graft, especially if they weren't stunned right. He imagined that tart from last night wearing the leather boots he'd bought the wife. The hose hissed. Murphy was cleaning up. He was going to fuck her so good she'd be begging for more, screaming her fucking head off. He couldn't wait.

*

Michael was called to the front of the class and asked to read from his news book. His teacher smiled and congratulated him on what he had written about his holiday. She thought it would be nice if the other children heard of his adventures in the country. He was nervous standing in front of the blackboard with everyone's eyes on him, flicking through the pages of his book trying to find the right one, but at the same time he was sort of proud and excited to read his stories out loud. His teacher told the other children to listen carefully. They would be talking about what they were going to hear later.

He found the page he wanted and started, but was nervous and stuttered and the class laughed. The teacher told them to be quiet and encouraged him to try again. There was no need to be scared. Several children sniggered when she said this, and he could feel his face turning red. He thought of Grandad Pop and his storytelling, made himself strong and began again.

It didn't take long before he was into his stride, repeating what he had written down at first but soon adding to it as he gained confidence. He told the other children about his grandfather and how he had gone out to stay in the country to sort out Elm Cottage and that it had been a small farm once or maybe part of a bigger farm – he wasn't sure. There was a barn his grandad never went into and he wasn't allowed to either in case the roof fell on his head but there was a pigsty where he could play if he wanted. It had a trough as well. Some nights the wind howled like a wolf and it was black outside because there were no streetlights so you couldn't see anything except for the stars and the sky was full of twinkling lights. More stars than he had ever seen before. He mentioned the creases on his grandfather's face and how they reminded him of the canals on Mars and that there was a pixie living in the light in the ceiling of the living room. He paused as he felt he should add that this last bit might not be true, but everyone was concentrating hard and his teacher seemed happy so he kept going.

Michael spoke about the rabbits whose family had lived in the field behind Elm Cottage for hundreds of years and how they had burrows under the ground and their babies only came out when the weather was warm and he told them about the day he had walked on his own across the fields but not seen one rabbit even though he knew they were there and probably watching him. He kept going and followed a path that led to a hill and he went up this and when he reached the top he couldn't believe his eyes. He paused again, but this time for effect. He told them how Elm Cottage seemed tiny down below like it was a toy and he was a giant and when he looked around there was a huge white horse in the distance on the side of a bigger hill and this horse was the size of five or six houses though he wasn't sure of that but he did know it was massive.

The class sighed. They had stopped fidgeting when he told them about the pigsty and become a little dreamy when they heard about the rabbits, but this white horse was amazing, and they were even more thrilled when he explained how it was made of chalk and had been carved into the hill by soldiers who were camping there before they went off to war. A hand shot up and a girl asked if the horse was alive. Their teacher told her not to interrupt as they didn't want to break Michael's concentration, but she said it in a nice way and he knew that he was doing okay.

He answered that the horse hadn't moved when he was looking at it but his grandad had told him that the people who lived in the area swore it came to life at night and that its hooves could be heard as it ran along the ridges and down through the fields and sometimes when it was really quiet and the horse was in a hurry it sounded like thunder and the weight of its body shook the land and rocks rolled down from the hills. He had made this bit about the rocks up just now, but looking at the rows of excited faces in front of him he knew it didn't matter as it was part of the magic of his adventure and they didn't care if it was true or not because in a way it was real because it *could* be true.

The class clapped when he finished and as Michael walked back to his desk Sam Norton gave him a big thumbs-up as he passed, the boy's fixed-on smile stronger than ever. Sometimes referred to as Piggy, there were few children in the school who knew their future better than Sam. He was going to be a farmer when he grew up. It was all Sam had ever wanted to do. While other boys played with toy soldiers and guns, pretended to be famous footballers, Sam concentrated on his wooden farm.

He was going to look after different sorts of animals, but it would mainly be pigs. He had a book on the breeds and had brought it into school one day, standing in front of the class and talking about his plans. The children had clapped him as well, as they loved pigs as much as they did white horses and rabbits and that pixie sitting in a lightbulb. Sam even looked like a pig, which hadn't really been noticed until he talked about his farm to the rest of the class, but he was cheerful and chubby and had a slightly turned up nose. If any insult was meant by the nickname Piggy, he didn't see it, and if he'd been asked if it bothered him would have wondered why it should.

Michael didn't know Sam very well, but when he saw the raised thumb and the expression on the boy's face he knew that something was wrong. The smile wasn't right. There were other things Pop had told Michael and he hadn't written these down, having asked his grandfather about the thoughts that were worrying him since they had eaten their pies.

Sitting back down, Michael looked at the back of Sam's head and tried to imagine him as someone who hated animals and wanted to kill them to make money, but couldn't believe that any of the children here wanted to do such a thing. Sam had been so excited and happy when he was talking to the class. It didn't make any sense. But after brooding on this for a while, it suddenly dawned on him that maybe Sam didn't know what the farmers were doing.

There was a break after the lesson and Michael went into the playground with the others and was caught up by Sam, who was still excited by the story of Elm Cottage. He wanted to know more about the place, how big it was and who owned the land nearby, and he tried to imagine the sties, keen to hear about the size and shape and everything there was to know about these pig houses. Michael stopped walking and studied Sam as he spoke, the two of them facing each other among the mass of running, pushing, skipping children. The boy's face was beaming and for a few seconds Michael really did see him as a big, friendly, innocent porker. No, he didn't know what was going on when the normal people weren't looking. Michael asked him what he was going to do on the farm.

Piggy was puzzled. He stepped back and was Sam Norton again, looking at his classmate as if it was a trick question. Either that or Michael was slow in the head. He was going to keep animals of course. He laughed, but in a reassuring way. That's what farmers did. But Michael kept going. What was Sam going to *do*? The boy thought. He understood. First he listed the animals he would keep – pigs mainly, but cows, goats, sheep, ducks, chickens, donkeys and a horse as well – and he was going to have at least a *hundred* pigs. With that many he would have to work extra hard to make sure they had food and water and were warm and had a nice place to shelter when it rained and of course he would look after them when they were sick.

He knew it was a lot to do, but he was strong and would be stronger when he was a man. He would get married and his wife would want to be a farmer and she would help and they would have lots of children. Animals were good for kids, that's what his dad always said. Mum and Dad would live with them. They'd need a big house. More than one sty. A barn or two. Sam liked pigs and he liked people. He couldn't wait.

Mickey knocked on the door of Ronnie's flat. Music boomed inside and after a short wait he tried again, banging this time, but there was still no answer and because he recognised the song and knew it was nearly over he moved back and waited, turned to look out from the landing to the bus station two streets away. From his place in the sky it appeared neat and clean, a plastic model in a grander city plan, the double deckers ten times brighter than they were up close. He put his hands on the wall and tapped his fingers to the rhythm of 'Silver Machine'.

Toy figures stood at the stops. Tin soldiers and lone travellers, couples and small groups, a family that included three children and a pushchair. He had seen the husband and wife treading foot-to-foot a few minutes earlier when he got off his bus and walked through the terminal, wishing they were tucked up at home. A dog barked, but he couldn't see it in the squeezed concrete. The station was dirty, noisy and sullen. Claustrophobic. People were nervous. Some seemed scared. Diesel filled the air as machines choked to death and coughed themselves back to life, the thud of engines adding to the sense of dread. He joined Dave Brock in the chorus, but under his breath.

Busy in the morning and after work, the bus station was quiet by nine and kept thinning out as the night went on. A police notice was asking for information on a stabbing. This came a month after a spate of muggings in the nearby streets, every victim a pensioner robbed and beaten. The gang responsible had been arrested, but now there was a knifeman to worry about. Mickey heard raised voices, saw three youths leaving a bus, one of them kicking the closing doors, thumping the side as it pulled away. They turned and sauntered along, shouting as they went, drawing attention.

Mickey had turned heads as well. One man winced and whistled, a big lump with a cauliflower ear trying to work out the reason for the state of his face, whether he'd been boxing in a ring or fighting in the street. At the hospital, Mickey had claimed his injuries were the result of a hit-and-run driver, the doctor treating him accepting his explanation but angry that anyone could leave the scene of an accident. It had been a job talking the doctor out of calling the police, Mickey blaming the dark and his own carelessness. The specialist who came to examine his head insisted on another scan and that he remain in hospital overnight for observation.

She returned later that evening when he was on the ward, wanted to know what had really happened. It would go no further, but it was important. He told her about the hunt and how he had been trying to disrupt it, that he had lost his friends and been attacked by three men, found himself going into too much detail about the stinging nettles and the ditch, how he had lain there thinking. She listened in silence, checked her watch and left. The next morning he was discharged with a date for a follow-up appointment.

The Hawkwind single ended and Mickey knocked on the door for a third time. He saw movement through the frosted glass and knelt down, lifted the letterbox and greeted Ronnie with one of his animal voices. He hadn't expected Bev to open the door and for a moment was embarrassed, waited as she made sure it was firmly shut before positioning him under the hall light so she could see his head, shocked at the swelling and six stitches. His hair had been shaved around the cut, and because he'd taken the bandage off when the blood kept leaking through, it was out in the open and made uglier by the scab that was starting to form.

His body was bruised black, blue, purple and red. Blood floated under his skin. When he moved he imagined it swishing about, as if the water from the ditch was inside his body. Despite this and some aching ribs he'd been lucky. No bones were broken. His attackers couldn't lose, outnumbering him like that, but their turn was coming.

The more he thought about it, the more he saw his revenge as a mission, an obligation to every fox, badger and rabbit those three sadists had killed over the years. The hounds were treated like shit as well, when they were no longer needed. Those men had had a tiny taste of what he could do, but next time the odds would be even. One against one. They wouldn't like that. He was going to enjoy the look on their faces when he stepped back into their lives.

Bev saw the glint in his eyes and asked if he was all right, and he said no, he was in agony, but apart from that... She agreed. It was a stupid question. Sorry. She hadn't known what to say. It was terrible what those idiots had done. It made her sick. And Mickey regretted his sarcasm, which had been another automatic response, he hadn't meant it to sound harsh, the humour lost between his brain and tongue. He apologised. She hugged him and he kept the pain to himself, Bev leading the way into the living room and motioning for him to sit on the couch, asking if he wanted something to drink. Ronnie would be back in a minute. There was beer and cider in the kitchen. Some of Ron's home brew. He'd try that. Thanks. She left the room.

'Silver Machine' was still spinning on the record player and he took it off, put it back in the sleeve. He was tempted to choose another record, but didn't, seeing as Bev was here and not Ronnie. He sat back down and faced the main wall and its collage of words and images. There were ALF and BUAV posters, smaller A4 sheets on specific campaigns, information sheets and leaflets supporting activists imprisoned for freeing animals from vivisection suppliers and laboratories. A couple of Crass album covers had been opened out and taped up. There were pictures from factory farms that made him depressed and angry. Haunted faces stared at him through bars and from inside crates and out of lorries. Hunched and broken souls that made him want to cry. The people responsible were scum. The lowest of the low.

Coming back into the room with two brown bottles and bowls of Bombay Mix and Caribbean plantain crisps, Bev sat in the chair opposite Mickey as he lifted the beer to his mouth. It hurt his lips and the cut to his gums, but he didn't care. It tasted okay, had a yeasty flavour, like a lot of these homemade beers, and he wished he'd asked for something else but said nothing.

Bev wanted to know exactly what had happened and Mickey went through the details again as she listened quietly, just as the specialist had done, but Bev was visibly upset and he wondered about the unemotional response at the hospital, the difference between the specialist and the doctor. When he was finished she asked if he had done anything to provoke the men, and when he said he had fought back, had a proper go and caused some damage, she pulled a face. What did that mean? He was annoyed. Did she expect him to just stand there and let them kill him? Maybe she read his eyes or an expression, insisted there was no excuse at all for their violence.

Beverley Thomas never responded to provocation. She was always logical and polite and this drove those she was protesting against mad. Endlessly insulted, she had been slapped, punched, arrested, on one occasion cut by a riding crop, on another told she was going to be followed home and raped, but she had never been beaten up like Mickey. Looking past her head to the wall he saw photos of a monkey with a tattoo carved into its stomach; beagles peering through thick wire; cats and rabbits with metal devices embedded in their skulls.

Mickey didn't know how Ronnie could live with these pictures, seeing them all the time, though he did understand that they were there as reminders. Everybody wanted to hide from the truth and Ronnie was no different, but he was refusing to forget, even for a second. There were also images that Mickey loved, photos of masked figures carrying dogs and rabbits to safety after breaking into laboratories, a baby monkey clinging to the neck of a faceless human, thirteen piglets in the back seat of a car. The people involved were heroes.

He realised that Bev was staring at him and had tears in her eyes. She told him that he could have been killed. Murdered. There were plenty of thugs following the hunts, but most were big mouths and hangers-on, only there for the occasion, the sort who weren't prepared to go to prison for their cause. Mickey knew Bev was different, had heard about this shy, legendary figure from their mutual friend Ronnie.

She had served a year for her part in a raid on a firm supplying dogs to vivisection labs, done her time with no regrets and no drama, and Mickey wondered if he could do the same. He would never grass, and neither had she, hadn't given the police any idea where the dogs had been taken either, but he would probably go mad in prison. She was a good ten years older than him and he admired her strength and her pacifism, the long years of activism, knew she was tougher than he could ever be.

There were others like her, brave souls locked away with only the dedicated offering support, their sentences bearing no relation to their actions. He genuinely admired Bev, but even so, he was going to find his attackers. She asked him how he felt about what had happened and he told her honestly.

Bev didn't like this and he wished he'd kept his mouth shut. He knew the score, just do what you had to do without broadcasting it, and he had been carrying out lone, low-level actions for several years, from stickers and graffiti to gluing up the locks of butchers and breaking windows when he could get away with it, one night slashing the tyres of nine lorries used to transport animals to their slaughter. That had been a step up, and he'd done it with Ronnie, who told him seriously to keep it between the two of them, as you never knew who was listening.

Mickey had been nervous in the build-up, but excited when they broke into the yard after cutting through a wire fence, and it hadn't been easy damaging the vehicles, but they had pulled it off. He felt honoured that Ronnie trusted him, as the hardcore activists were tight-knit out of necessity, and he was conscious that he was on the outside. Ronnie was another respected figure, but different to Bev, in control yet very angry.

Bev was telling Mickey about Gandhi and the way he had defeated the British state without resorting to violence, the protests in the American South and the example of Martin Luther King, and if he went out and hurt those men he would be the same as them, and that was no good. The success of the animal-liberation movement depended on non-violence. It was essential. The general public had to be won over, not alienated, and any sort of violence would only be exploited by the other side.

The front door opened and closed and Ronnie came into the living room. He was carrying a big bag of Indian food and the smell reminded Mickey that he hadn't eaten all day. He was suddenly hungry. Ronnie had bought enough for the three of them, and seeing the bottle in Mickey's hand asked what he thought, before he had a chance to reply telling him that he was a brave man drinking that stuff, a lot braver than the brewer who would be enjoying a cold pint of cider with his mushroom biryani, vindaloo sauce and pakoras.

While Frank Norris had done his best to come to terms with the death of his wife, there were still times when he felt her next to him in their bed. The warmth of Anne's body was there in the sheets and pillows, and he could smell her scented soap and talcum powder, once or twice the oranges she loved to eat. This only happened when it was dark, especially in the seconds when he was waking up in the morning, his dreams fading with the rhythm of her breathing, the dying beats of her heart. There was little reason for him to get out of bed, yet he still set his clock, as he had always done, the sound of the alarm a link with the past.

Sometimes, while he was in the bathroom washing before going downstairs, he could hear her moving about in the kitchen, brewing tea and making breakfast. During the week they used to have big bowls of porridge with sugar and melted butter on top, plates of toast and marmalade, while on Saturday it was always a fry-up, a tradition that went back to when the family was all together and they were rewarding their work on the farm and at school. Having rinsed his razor and emptied the basin he would stand on the landing and listen for Anne and be overwhelmed by the silence. She was in a box under the earth in that lonely churchyard he'd be taken to soon enough. The marmalade she made was gone, the empty jars sitting in a cupboard, lined up in rows, waiting for her return.

His mind was playing other tricks. He had become jumpy, fearful even, and that wasn't his way. He was constantly thinking about the past, going back to when he was young and strong and the idea that he could ever be old and weak seemed ridiculous. He had been a dominant husband and strict father, and while this had been for the good of his family, and running a farm demanded a firm hand, he had started to worry that he had been too hard at times. The world was different then and he had to admit he could be moody, short on conversation, and while he believed in discipline he had never hit his wife and only ever smacked his children on the legs and bum, never the head.

He couldn't stop himself brooding. This really was out of character. He had never been the sort of man to question things too deeply. It was better to keep to a routine and follow some simple rules, make a decision and stick to it, not dwell on mistakes. Emotions had to be controlled. Life was a struggle and sentimentality a weakness.

In the first few weeks after Anne's death he had eaten her marmalade at every meal before realising it wasn't going to last long and could never be replaced, so he tried to ration it instead. He heard her voice – *waste not, want not*. That's what she had always said. He supposed it was strange to remember a person for the taste and smell of their marmalade. She was a good woman. A fine wife.

When they were courting they would walk across the fields, holding hands as they climbed a hill. He saw them kissing for the first time, thought about their marriage day and the birth of their children. They'd never had a honeymoon, but they did have a home. There had been some difficult periods when money was short and he was at his wit's end, not knowing what to do. Anne had left him once, gone and stayed with her parents, but she loved him and returned. They had stuck together through thick and thin. What else were they supposed to do?

Apart from the rabbits, there was nothing left of those days. The place was dead without his wife and the children and their animals. He remembered the geese he had kept, how they made a racket when anyone approached and rushed over when they saw him coming. The farm was finished, like the empty land he drove through when he went into town. What was the countryside without animals in the fields? Where were the sheep and cows? He left bread out for the birds and watched as they came to feed, never relaxing, eyes darting in every direction, wary of predators, and they only ventured near the house because they were hungry and knew that they could escape.

He had become very fond of his rabbits. They were something living he could hold and stroke, feel them breathing in and out, their little hearts beating, heads and eyes moving, but much more slowly than those of the birds, curious in a way that cheered him up. They trusted him more than most people ever had, and he had started to worry about their health, as they were getting old, their fur turning grey, but he fed them and had even built a run. Mad as it seemed, they were his last friends.

There were moments when he was annoyed at them for being

his only company, these simple little animals who didn't have the sense to try and break out of their cages. Their ancestors had struggled but never been strong or clever enough to get away from him when he took them into his shed to kill, yet these feelings quickly passed and he regretted having them. He would never hurt his rabbits. The idea of eating them was ridiculous. His back ached and his fingers were bent with arthritis, and he preferred frozen and tinned food, a few boiled vegetables.

One evening, as he sat at his kitchen table, the old farmer sensed he was being watched and turned towards the window. It was dark outside, but the curtains were open and he thought he saw a head, and while he knew it was his imagination it didn't vanish when he willed it away. The creature was hovering in the shadows, a face-less outline, and he felt small and defenceless, unable to defend himself against such a powerful beast. It was as big as a man. He shouted at it to go away, but his words did no good. The monster wasn't scared.

He reached for the bread knife on the table, but still it didn't move. The beast could smash through the glass and climb into the house whenever it wanted. Kick down the door and march inside, reach for his neck and snap it like a twig. Cut his throat, chop off his head, skin his body. Farmer Giles covered his face with his hands. These images swirled through his mind as he tried to hide in the darkness of his palms. When he eventually looked back at the window the figure was gone. He realised he had wet himself and cried like the child he was becoming.

There was no turning back. Mike Tanner was a soldier and would have to control his thoughts in the weeks ahead, crush his emotions, but he had been doing this to a lesser extent for much of his life and was confident. He had moved through doubt, con-viction, fear, regret and guilt in the last few days, but remained strong and determined. The correct decision had been made. His cause was just. He knew what he was doing and right now he was heading home.

He was a faceless man standing at a bus stop with a bag over his shoulder, having left a nearby library where he'd been searching the internet for news. This he had found, but not wanting to leave a trail behind hadn't stayed for long. He had dumped his router so there was no broadband in the flat, and his mobile was in a drawer and not to be used. He had newspapers in his bag as well as provisions, among these a yam, six tins of coconut milk, a jar of jerk. They would keep, but the rest of Pat's tomatoes would not. Plump and juicy, they were waiting in a bowl on the kitchen table.

When he got in he was going to have a cup of tea and a couple of biscuits to tide him over. He was hungry and would get started on the vegan meatballs and linguini. He planned his meal as he waited for the bus, lining the pan with olive oil, gently heating it and adding a chopped onion with three or four cloves of Gupta garlic and a green chilli. While that was turning crisp he'd cut Pat's tomatoes into chunks, add them to the pan with some more oil, give that a minute before squeezing in tomato puree and pouring in a little water, mix this up and lower the heat. Next were chopped mushrooms and dried or fresh basil – Ella had given him some herbs earlier, so he would use her basil probably, or keep it maybe, he wasn't sure, would decide later. The tomato sauce needed to thicken and when it was on its way he would lower the heat again and put the soya meatballs in the oven. These took fifteen minutes and once they were ready he would place them in the sauce one by one, so they were well covered and absorbing the flavours, turn the heat as low as he could so it simmered while he had a bath.

On his return he'd boil the linguini and make a green salad – lettuce, spinach leaves, cucumber, rocket, spring onions – and an oil-and-vinegar dressing sprinkled with garlic salt. The first two ingredients were in his bag thanks to Ella, who he had seen at the allotments. He'd had a chat with Wendell and Maggie, looked for Sid, Bunny and the Guptas but they weren't around. He told Ella that he was going off travelling for a month or two. He didn't know where yet, but somewhere in Europe. It would be a last-minute decision and more exciting that way. It wasn't the big trip he had been planning. That would come later.

Really, he had to be on his own and was saying his goodbyes. He couldn't put Ella, Bunny or anyone else at risk, and would keep away from The White Hart as well. He would return to Bell Street one day he was sure, but had felt sad leaving.

Thinking about those meatballs was making him impatient for the bus to arrive. He was turning into Inspector Montalbano from the detective series *Montalbano*, who was always thinking about food. Montalbano loved to eat, but was no snob, knew the best dishes were made with love and found in local restaurants that were family-run – it was just a shame he ate meat. When Montalbano wasn't eating he was asking those around him if they were hungry. Set in Sicily, the storyline would drift and split, go off on tangents, full of its own quirks and humour. Tanner would sit with a bowl of popcorn and watch the inspector at work, the people and the scenery adding Sicily to his list of places he wanted to visit one day. The land was dry and rocky, but Montalbano lived next to the sea, overlooking a quiet beach, and in the morning he would swim out to clear his head.

The towns were built of white stone rather than red brick, and this crossed into marble on some of the main streets. The buildings reflected the sunlight and were dazzling in the daytime, while the interiors of the houses were dark and gloomy, full of heavy furniture and thick curtains. These rooms would be cool he supposed, an escape from the heat outside, but at the same time felt sparse and secretive. Despite the fading elegance, Sicily seemed earthy and genuine, just like Italian food, which appealed to the masses in Britain. With its warm climate and rich soil, Sicily had a good number of traditional dishes that were either vegetarian or vegan. That was the place to have an allotment. He thought of his Bell Street friends, what they could achieve in such a location.

Tanner liked foreign films and TV series for the landscapes and languages, but also for the different ways of telling a story. The scores were important as well, written by local composers, and while he knew little about Italian music he had been to see Ludovico Einaudi at the South Bank. A classical pianist working with five other musicians, Einaudi performed parts of his *Elements* album in the first half of the show, a selection of other material after the interval. It had been a special night. Sitting in the dark, his eyes had filled with tears as he felt Mum, Dad and Pop sitting with him, and while the music had taken him into the depths of his sadness, he left the auditorium feeling stronger than when he had gone in.

His bus was approaching. It had rained earlier, a heavy down-pour with flashes of lightning, and it was drizzling as the bus stopped and a woman stepped in front of Tanner to board. He said nothing, didn't care, waited patiently as she paused to speak to the driver. They seemed to know each other, as her manner was familiar and the man behind the wheel wasn't hurrying her on, although maybe he was being polite. Terrorists were changing the climate. It was dangerous to be in London. That's what the woman was saying. Tanner assumed she was talking about people's way of thinking, a climate of fear altering the way the world was seen, and she had a point, but then he realised she meant the weather.

Terrorists had stolen a plane the same as when the Twin Towers were destroyed, but this time they were scattering metal filings in the air to create storms. It was going to keep raining for days and wouldn't stop until the river was full and the Thames Barrier broke and the city was flooded and millions drowned. She told the driver she didn't want to die, that she was going to sleep on the roof of a tower block tonight if the rain didn't stop.

Tanner wanted to wrap an arm around her shoulders and explain that everything was going to be fine, but knew that he couldn't. The woman wasn't much over thirty and he wondered what had caused her to feel this way.

When she went inside the driver raised his eyes, but he wasn't making fun of her, more as an apology for keeping Tanner waiting. He wanted to show that he too saw what a mad world they were living in. Tanner liked the driver. He went to work and helped people move around the city, stopped at the right places, didn't have to spread goodwill but did so because that's the sort of person he was. When he was finished for the day he would go home and hug his wife. Maybe they liked to watch *Montalbano*. Two bowls of salted popcorn, coated with soya margarine. The face was big and pale. A union man, respected by his workmates. What you saw was what you got. This was the person taking him home.

Tanner tapped his card and went upstairs, sat towards the back of the bus and opened his bag, took out a newspaper. The front page was dedicated to a big property development by the Thames, the protests of those taking on the builder, council and government. This publication as well, going on the tone of the report. Each body was represented by a spokesperson. Reassurances were released from PR offices as the police were left to deal with the anger directly. The prices of the apartments were obscene. More ghost flats that would stay empty for years, bought as investments while locals slept in run-down accommodation and old soldiers slept on the streets. He wondered if the lady who was worried about flooding would read this story. Maybe she could sneak into the development and spend a few days in the penthouse, somehow evade the security cameras.

Towards the middle of the paper he found a quarter-page piece on a double killing. Two men had been shot to death near their place of work. They were named as Steven Collins and James Ball, and had been on their way home when the attack occurred. Having stopped at a junction less than a mile from their company's gates, they were gunned down in broad daylight. The police believed Collins had been killed first. He was driving the car and his window was lowered. This could have meant he knew the assailant, but there again, it may have been a stranger responsible. The second man died in the passenger seat. The assailant had fired across the slain driver.

Ball was single and lived alone, while Collins had a wife and two children. This information made Tanner jolt, but he continued reading. Their boss described them as decent men who were well-respected by their colleagues. Everyone was shocked. The killings appeared almost paramilitary in style, but as yet there was no suspect and no motive. These were innocent, law-abiding citizens going about their daily business. The investigation was ongoing and the police hadn't ruled out the possibility that this was a random attack, although it did seem unlikely. They were following a particular line of enquiry, but could give no further details.

Tanner was thoughtful. The police were right. The killings could be seen as random. It might be the work of a nutter with nothing better to do with his time. It could also be a crime of passion, part of a family feud, an act of revenge, crime related. The executions meant nothing if the reason wasn't clear. His chest tightened. There was no mention of their occupations. Wouldn't the nature of their work suggest a motive? The public needed to know why Collins and Ball had died.

He realised that he was wet from the drizzle but mostly his own sweat. He was oozing blood, skin searing as it seeped from his veins, and he saw his head exploding as a bullet smashed through the bone. A widow and two children were huddled together and crying. Sobbing. He felt as if he was going to vomit. Breathing deeply, he fought back, regained control, drove that sad family from his mind. He could have no second thoughts. No regrets. Electricity sparked. Knives slashed.

Children were dying in the country's slaughterhouses. Mothers mourned. Lambs were travelling through the night; rabbits sat trapped in hutches; cows were stuck in stalls; pigs groaned in sheds. People loved their ham – the buttocks of a pig salted and pressed flat and packaged and sold and slipped into rolls and between pieces of buttered bread. They craved bacon for their breakfast – the meat taken from the ribcage and salted and smoked and covered in ketchup. Sausages were another favourite – pig flesh ground down and wrapped in the animal's intestines, this stuffed colon stirring the taste-buds. People salivated over crackling, the fat chopped and stewed and chewed. All these body parts could be grilled and fried and roasted and a drinker could stand in a pub and order pork scratchings. Nice bit of bacon, pork, gammon, jellied trotters. There were other treasures. *This little piggy went to market...* Livers. Hearts. Testicles cooked for connoisseurs. *This little piggy stayed at home.*

He put the newspaper back in his bag, turned to watch the world as it passed by outside, leaning against the window as he studied the houses and imagined the lives of the people who lived inside them, all these millions of individuals with their minds split in half.

When the bus stopped at the next red traffic lights he looked down at the gates of a Territorial Army centre, teenagers arriving in camouflaged trousers and jackets and heavy black boots, child soldiers more interested in a weekend camping in the country than a tour of duty in the Middle East. The TA offered them the chance to train and get fit, walk long distances and handle firearms, put up tents and build fires and cook tins of soup and baked beans over a portable stove. Ghost stories were told. There was laughter and comradeship, more marching in the morning. Volunteers crossed moors and passed through woods and followed ridges in weather that ranged from the scorching hot to freezing cold, and all the time they were building up their inner strength and determination, imagining they were heroes. In a few years they would be old enough to enlist full time in one of the services. He watched each boy and girl as they stood at the gates and pressed the buzzer that let them into the barracks and wondered which ones would sign up. Only a small number of people could kill. Not in self-defence or from a distance, but face to face and clinically.

The engine rumbled as the driver continued and he made himself focus on the magic of this bus, the genius of the combustion engine and the inventors responsible, and they were climbing a slope and following a bend, stopping at another set of traffic lights, waiting to turn right, train tracks sheltered by brick walls, and he thought of the engineers who'd built the great steam engines and diesel locomotives, the labourers who laid the tracks and put the machines together, the investors who backed the inventors, the Industrial Revolution taking some of the pressure off the horses that had crisscrossed the city's junctions. To travel on today's public transport was a luxury and an honour.

The bus rolled on, and he made himself trace the designs of terraces and blocks, rows of shops, a school and disused factory, a boarded-up bingo hall, and he considered the heights and widths and shapes of these buildings, the materials used in their construction, the planning that allowed each structure to stand, and he saw the drawings prepared by people who had studied at university and knew about architecture and left nothing to chance, and he noted the state of walls and roofs, the nature of windows that reminded him of eyes and mouths, some tall and narrow, others flat and wide, smiling and frowning, male and female, mammal and reptile, and in certain places the closed curtains were closed eyelids, delicate skin and fur tattooed with flowery patterns, and in one room a skull and crossbones shut out the daylight, but generally he could see into these boxes through glass which was another miracle invention, and he tried to grasp the sort of mind that could dream of a material so clever and so practical, and most of these rooms were private dens where people rested, he was amazed by the range of objects filling them, each one a result of human creativity, all those beds and blankets and sheets and pillows and chairs and desks and cupboards and chests of drawers and shelves that were lined with clocks, creams, hairsprays, deodorants, perfumes, rings, necklaces, earrings, bracelets, and the piles of shirts, pants, trousers, dresses, socks, shoes. Coats on hangers. Posters on walls. Computers on standby.

The gates of the slaughterhouse opened and a car appeared. It moved slowly until it was through the no-man's land outside, increasing its speed as it passed through a further boundary of mowed grass, racing by the time it reached the road leading through the woods. The trees would have been a blur to the two men inside, the air thick with cigarette smoke, a song playing on the radio. The car was going to stop when it reached the junction, held up by white lines, and after a short pause it would turn left or right and take the knackers home. The man waiting for them watched the slaughterhouse through binoculars. The car slowly grew in size. He was impatient. Nervous. Scared. The slaughtermen were approaching the end of the road. They slowed down, ready to turn. The driver didn't indicate as there was nobody else about. It was late in the afternoon but the sun was still strong in the sky, the scene flooded with light, millions of leaves rustling in the breeze. The knackers were talking. They looked tired. One started laughing. I followed my friend as he came out of the trees. He moved fast and I had to hurry to keep up. He tapped on the nearest window. The driver was startled. Turned his head. He lowered the glass. The standing man grunted, but the driver didn't understand. He turned the radio down. 'Sugar Baby Love' by The Rubettes was playing. The driver narrowed his eyes. The man I was with glanced at the passenger, saw a thin mouth tighten. My friend made more noises, sounds he felt they should understand, but they were ignorant and became annoyed. They recognised the gun when it was raised and pointed at the driver's head. I wanted to ask where he had got it, but knew not to, that he would never grass on a friend, and wasn't it true that he had a right to defend himself? To feel safe when he was forced to confront murderers? The slaughter-men were scared, but the good man hesitated. The passenger sneered, stretched towards him, and this made the gunman decisive. He fired into the head of the driver. The passenger was covered in his blood and recoiled, became noisy, reached for his door. He was shot twice. Both of these bad men were still. They weren't so tough now. Two more shots followed. To make sure. These killings were quick and efficient. We kept our nerve and walked away, returned to the wood and followed a path that led to safety, and as I went I felt a rush of satisfaction, broke away from the clear-headed executioner. I couldn't help it, but this was all one big childish dream so it didn't matter, and what followed was done with a sense of humour. I pretended I was a stag who could defeat every hunter. I was a rabbit and a hare running free, a hen who hadn't lost her head, a brave cockerel and no coward, and I was every abused animal in the world. Lamb, pig, cow, bull – I was snorting with joy and sniffing the smells that filled the wood, but when I reached the lane where my car was parked I put away these childish things and became one more thoughtful man driving home in a careful and considerate manner.

*

They were brothers, and if they'd had names they might have been called Peter and Paul, and if it wasn't for the people making money from their bodies they would have been living normal lives, searching for water, food, shelter and warmth. These boys liked to keep active, believed in working together, and being sociable souls they enjoyed messing about with family and friends, pushing and prodding and playing like the children they would always remain. They did their best to stay out of trouble, more than happy to walk away from a fight. Peter and Paul were friendly, loyal, clever and very clean in their habits, and yet the humans who exploited their flesh called them dirty and smelly, as it was important for these people to ridicule their victims.

Peter and Paul could have been labelled Berkshires or Hampshires, Wessex Saddlebacks or Chester Whites, Gloucester Old Spots or Oxford Sandys, Tamworths or British Lops, or maybe a newer breed like a Duroc or Landrace – creatures cunningly engineered by men who liked to play at being God. But these names were based on human boundaries and linked to the business interests that controlled their every move. Peter and Paul were just a couple of everyday pigs.

The brothers were famed for the big smiles that filled their faces and showed off their friendly natures. They were curious about the world around them and, left alone, would happily roam fields and forests for hours, foraging and rooting and rubbing against the trunks of trees, thrilled by the simplest of pleasures. They moved with a roll of the shoulders, a bumping of hips and bums, a wobble and a waddle that humans found amusing, while their ability to balance on two toes – the delicacy of a trapeze artist contrasting with their large frames – only added to the appeal.

Living free lives, they would never have guessed the perversions inflicted on their kind, and yet the very fact that they couldn't imagine the depths to which the human mind could sink was also used against them, as if their basic decency was a sign of stupidity. They couldn't win.

These boys would have loved to spread out in the sun, dozing and dreaming as the rays warmed their bodies, so happy to be alive they didn't need to waste their time fulfilling ambitions which in truth were unimportant, didn't have to create great works of art in order to appreciate nature. They would have been content with their place in the sun. And when they became too hot they'd find some cool mud and have a wallow, knowing they had to protect their sensitive skin. Long snouts added to the strength of their smiles, and they would raise these great noses into the air and breathe deep, ears twitching as they identified the sound of family footsteps, their hearing sharp, sense of smell fine-tuned.

The brothers had been brought to the slaughterhouse by lorry. They were six months old and had spent their lives indoors, restrained by steel bars. They could hardly move in their pens, the pain this caused a constant torture. The sky was a metal roof, the air inside the shed humid and suffocating. They were forced to piss and shit where they slept. Ammonia stung their eyes. The stench of faeces made the pigs sick. Poison filled their lungs. The roof shook when the wind blew, flapping and then banging as a storm exploded. The children trembled. They were being driven mad. These creatures were scared and sad. The abuse they suffered was mental as well as physical.

Leaving the shed had been a shock. Men arrived and released Peter and Paul from their cages and they walked gingerly with the other pigs, muscles groaning as new pressure was put on inflamed and rotting joints, but at the same time it felt good to be moving, to be able to turn and not see bars, and then the walls they knew as the end of their world were punctured and they were driven through a hole called a door, suddenly confused and unsteady as the roof was peeled back and a stunning space spread out above their heads.

They recoiled, and Peter sagged and almost fell, but Paul was next to him and he recovered. The brothers were smelling clean air for the first time in their lives and a cool breeze blew through the yard and past the big machine to their right and swirled around them and felt fantastic on their skin. This new experience lifted their spirits, but not for long, as they were soon being driven into the waiting lorry.

The brothers were still swaying now, inside the slaughterhouse, unsteady after their terrible journey, noses propped against the backs of the other pigs pressed into a holding pen. They were sniffing the air, searching in vain for the freshness of the yard. This new place was very different to the shed in which they had lived. Cold and clinical, manmade chemicals bleached the air, sterilising and burning, and they gave up trying to find the breeze and instead strained their ears, adjusting to the banging of steel sheets, the rattling of chains. One by one, as the pigs tuned into each other's feelings, they began to stiffen.

A strange sound was coming from deeper inside the building, and it was faint at first, hard to separate from other noises, seemed as if it was part of the human world of perfect circles and oblongs, the soulless inventions of scientists and entrepreneurs, and Peter and Paul and their friends, all these creatures who had been imprisoned with each other since the beginning, were struggling to separate it and identify the cause. Gradually it became distinct. They started to shake.

Pigs were screaming. Their voices were high-pitched and distorted and ear-splitting. They were begging for mercy, calling out for someone to help them, and the brothers and those around them started to respond. The fear they had always lived with was turning into something worse.

Monsters towered above the children. They laughed as the pigs squealed and pushed against each other. They rubbed their hands, comically obscene in white coats and hats, one man screeching as he mimicked the pigs' terror, a smirk creasing his wet lips, and Peter and Paul turned their eyes away from the monsters, the familiar smell of family offering a brief reassurance.

Suppressed images of their earlier days were stirring, memories that they had forced into the depths of their minds, remembrances human beings insisted didn't exist. They had dealt with so much trauma over the last six months that when the images returned they did so in an explosion. Their fear and loss had led to a suspension of memory, but the horror had to seep out somehow, and this it had done in their repetitive habits and depression and the open sores on their bodies and the hidden wounds inside their broken organs.

Still they smiled. They couldn't change the way they looked. And the monsters said this was proof that they didn't suffer. But the men in white coats knew the truth and so they made their jokes and these were mirrored in the mainstream – *here's a funny item to end the news – a pig escaped from an abattoir today and held up traffic on the M5 for ten minutes until it was recaptured – we have a picture here of the pig in question – ha ha ha – before it was caught – it could have been knocked down – ha ha ha – but on a more serious note – drivers were delayed for twenty minutes until the animal was brought under control – thankfully it's been returned to its owners and traffic is moving smoothly – a happy ending – except for the pig I suppose – ha ha ha – ha ha ha – ha ha ha.*

The monsters were closing in. One man opened a gate and grunted. Growls of impatience followed from a second. Peter was the more nervous of the two and it was Paul who had kept him going when they had been snatched from their mother, and the horror of that day filled Peter's mind and he could feel his throat burning as the puke rose up. He stumbled now as he had then, the sound of his mother's cries echoing inside his head, the screaming in the distance her screaming, reviving a memory he had done his best to destroy, and he was remembering that big warm generous sow stuck in a crate, covered in her own waste, private parts exposed and abused by human perverts, unable to resist or even move. Vomit filled Peter's mouth.

The children were backing away from the nearest monster, but he was strong and cunning and thought in strange ways, planned ahead to get what he wanted, and the young pigs became confused and panicked as he worked his way along the side of the pen and was suddenly behind them, responded by moving away, through an open gate, a small number separated at this point and pushed towards a door. Peter and Paul were in this group. Boots kicked and drove them on. The screaming was becoming louder, and it was constant, mixed in with human words and laughter. Lights dazzled the brothers as they entered the stunning pen.

The smiles may have been fixed, but the fear of the pigs was clear in their eyes. They tried to huddle closer together, pressing tight and willing themselves to become one, but there were more monsters waiting, a giant marching straight in and pulling and pushing one boy further forward while the others shouted and cowered and trembled. This pig was on his own. A strange device was forced against his head and he fell, legs kicking hard as he had an epileptic fit, trotters clattering as electricity burned and destroyed part of his brain.

Chains rattled and became taut as he was shackled and raised into the air, and he was moving on a conveyor belt, plastic doors pushed open and flapping, the sickly smell of blood rushing in, and Peter and Paul started screaming, their fear turned to terror. And as the pigs saw others being isolated and taken for electrocution more hidden images broke out and Peter imagined himself arriving in the world, a newborn struggling to stand on metal slats, sniffing his mum and loving the family scent and nestling against her belly and feeding on her milk and looking up at this big loving creature and seeing the bars of her farrowing crate and not knowing what they could be, and even though she was smeared with her own shit and forced to piss where she lay, her smell was stronger and he could feel her love.

When his mother tried to turn her head and look at her children there was an expression he wasn't able to identify. It made him uneasy, even though he couldn't grasp the notion of captivity, the invention holding her still, the idea that men would treat a mother and her children like this, that he had been born into a wicked place. But he understood now, knew it was defeat in her face, the hopelessness that could only ever be felt by those at the bottom of society, by the sort of souls who weren't even regarded as part of that society.

Like most sows in her situation, Peter and Paul's mother eventually went insane. The monsters never left her alone, tormenting and abusing her until the depression became so deep her mind shut down. When they were snatched, the brothers stayed together but never saw their sisters and other brothers again. They could have been killed for being too weak, or the boys might have been caged elsewhere, the girls fattened up for slaughter or made pregnant with needles. Their mum was unable to help, had spent her life abused and repeatedly raped, every single child taken from her as a baby. This perversion went on and on and there was no politician or religious leader to save her. No mercy was shown. No escape possible. Instead humans laughed. Made excuses. Said she felt nothing. That she didn't suffer. Her keepers enjoyed their domination. When her reproductive system was exhausted she was murdered. The spoiled and ignorant licked their lips – *Nice bit of bacon... Nice bit of pork*.

Only Peter and Paul were left in the pen. One of the monsters approached and Paul instinctively moved in front of his weaker brother. Cornered and kicked and pulled, tongs were placed either side of Paul's head and an electric charge released. The man doing the stunning was in his usual rush and the current didn't connect, Paul reeling as his left eye burst, the pain sending him tumbling, and the next thing he knew he was sliding and rolling on the floor semi-conscious, his stomach spewing, rolling in the urine of those who had already been electrocuted. Clammy hands tugged at his legs as he tried to stand up, a clamp snapped around his right leg, and he was being hoisted into the air, upside-down and turning in a circle as he struggled to break free, a bone in his leg breaking and pain lancing his body. He was shouting. Maybe he was telling Peter to run and find their mum.

Peter trembled in a corner of the pen as he watched his brother being moved along to another man who stepped forward with a mouth that farted more human grunts, the face angry as he raised a knife and stabbed at Paul's throat, missing the artery, his blade cutting a fleshy part of the neck, and Paul recoiled – *hold still, you cunt* – the knife was pulled back so the man could drive it in again, but it missed a second time – *fucking cunt* – and the monster repeated the motion and this time the blade punctured the artery he wanted – *you fucking deserve this*. Paul's blood splashed across the floor and walls. The slaughterman kept pushing, screwing the steel in, to widen the wound but also because it caused more pain.

Paul was left to bleed to death. Humans didn't want blood in their meat so they used his heart to pump it out of his body. He kept struggling, but each spurt made him weaker, added to the channel below, a specially made gutter thick with the blood of those ahead of him on the line. Paul and the rest of the pigs were being drained alive. As his strength faded, he could no longer raise his head. Eyes fixed on the clotting stream below, he could hear a man whistling as he sprayed the floor down with a hose.

Paul's heart felt as if it was inside his head. It was banging and echoing as it slowly died. This was the thump of the slaughter-house. Broken hearts worked for the men in white coats and the bosses in their expensive suits and those animal-loving consumers who wandered the supermarket aisles searching for bargains.

If he had been free, left alone to get on with his life, Paul could have been strolling in the outdoors right now, in a wood or meadow, up on a ridge maybe, watching the birds soar. He had never known any of these things. His reality was separation and loss, the torture of the pig farm, physical and mental abuse, the stress of trans-portation, electrocution and death. His heartbeat was faint.

He made one last effort and managed to turn his head slightly, looking for his brutalised brother. His flesh and blood. Who would look after Peter now? His heart stuttered – Peter was next – poor little Peter – scared, worried Peter – and Paul's mouth opened and a darker blood gushed out – they had been together forever – and he could feel sludge seeping from his damaged eye – was conscious of the piss running down his chest and along his neck and dripping from his nose – aware of the shit on his back – mindful that his privates were exposed to the world – to the beasts – he was embarrassed – and as he finally died his last feeling was one of humiliation.

Peter was darting backwards and forwards, panicking and squealing, dodging the slaughtermen, and when he was finally cor-nered and dragged forward one of the men pushed an electric prod under his tail, rammed it up his bum and released an electric shock – *that made you jump* – the pain forcing him in the direction they wanted. He was confused and lost, tongs pushed against his head.

Electricity sent him into spasms. He was dazed and felt the thump of his brother's heart as he was raised into the air, and Peter was in and out of consciousness, the separation and imprisonment and stinking air and casual violence and routine sadism and rough injections and the pain of his coughing and sores and infections joining together as a button was punched and machinery rattled, and he was awake and having convulsions, facing the monster who had killed his brother – the eyes were empty – soulless – and the knife flashed and he felt a new pain, heard muttering as the man turned and walked away, Peter left alone to watch his blood pump from his body, and like his brother he was left to bleed to death in a long line of terrified pigs.

There was a photograph I saw of a young man who worked in a slaughterhouse – he had stripped the face from a pig – used a knife to carve off the nose and ears – placed these on his head – he was wearing them as a mask – the ears were rigid and sticking up – the nose long and firm – nostrils looking as if they were made of rubber – a gimmick from a joke shop – to be worn at a fancy-dress party – and when I looked closer I realised that the ears and nose were linked by skin – a forehead and patches of scalp – saw the man was laughing – maybe he really did think he was being funny – but I believe he was trying to impress the other slaughtermen with his callousness – that he wanted to shock – he wouldn't be posing for this picture unless he knew that what he was doing was wrong – for a moment I almost felt sorry for him – but not quite – and I wondered if he had ever been held to account for his behaviour – for the killing – mutilation – the mocking of the dead – his lack of empathy – common decency – and I couldn't help thinking that I should find out what name he used – where he lived – and what he was doing now – go and say hello – but I didn't – this was a long time ago – and there are plenty of others like him – more dangerous people further up the line – the slaughtermen are at the bottom of this particular food chain.

*

The pig farmer looked nothing like the creatures he exploited. He was tall and thin, with wet grey skin and oily black hair tucked behind small round ears. His mouth was long and narrow and tinged purple, a neat powder slash that rarely moved up or down. He was a serious man, the sort who craved routine and believed in the power of repetition, someone who was at his happiest when he was absorbed in the minutiae of his work. Though naturally cautious, he accepted change when he was sure it would be beneficial to business, ready to embrace any new idea or technology that would increase his yield. The farm was running smoothly enough, but it was important to modernise. If asked, he would have described himself as content.

He had no real feelings for the pigs he raised and sent to slaughter, neither liking nor disliking the animals under his control, but he did love turning them into profit. It was the difference between income and expenditure that focused his mind. Expanding this gap had become his mission in life, and while his aim was to achieve the greatest return from the smallest possible outlay, he was clever enough to see that cutting too many corners could be counter-productive. It was a balancing act that required great attention to detail.

His operation was relatively small, which meant there was no way he could compete with the big boys when it came to price, as he lacked their economies of scale, so he outflanked them instead. The corporations could buy low-grade feed at ultra-cheap cost and shrug off losses to growth and disease, the sheer numbers of pigs involved meaning they were able to absorb mistakes, but he enjoyed no such luxury. This made his work more interesting.

The pig farmer was a hands-on boss aware of everything that happened within the boundaries of his empire. Living in sight of the buildings that housed his animals, he had grown up with the smell and noise and was used to the mud and mess, knew the mechanics of breeding and rearing and barely noticed the bones and rotting flesh of the corpse pits. He was master of a kingdom he had taken over from his father, and while there had been arguments when he began intensifying the operation it was essential to move forward. Times changed and they did so for the better. The human population was expanding and more and more animals were being eaten. Meat was no longer a luxury. This was a sign of progress. His fields were filled with sheds, the farm a prosperous pork factory, with all those inefficient, wasteful practices left in the past where they belonged.

He produced big, tasty pigs, which earned him a healthy return per unit. He was by no means at the top end of the market when it came to quality, but was proud of his efforts and the results he had achieved, which were recorded forever in the company accounts. Yet it wasn't the money that interested him so much as the challenge, as he was already a wealthy man and he had no great personal expenses. It was the battle to ensure his will prevailed that excited the farmer.

Those end-of-year numbers – which were calculated and printed by the accountants who handled his affairs, then beautifully bound in leather for which he paid extra – elevated his usual downbeat mood. It levelled the pig farmer out emotionally and left him with a great sense of order. He was eradicating waste and regulating chaos. He was in control.

This man lived a simple life, and while it was one that some people might call boring, it suited him. He was teetotal and didn't smoke, had little sexual desire and maintained a moderate diet, his luxuries limited to membership of a gym and a yearly holiday. His pigs had shown him the importance of regular exercise and over the years he had become very fit.

The creation of protein was an interesting task and reaping a good harvest meant combining the correct feed with a system that prevented his pigs from wasting its value. He spent hard-earned money on their nourishment and the last thing he wanted was the burning of expensive calories. Restricting the movement of his animals meant they put on large amounts of weight, which led to higher returns when they were sold. Watching a large group of pigs being driven into the lorries that would take them away to be slaughtered was fantastically rewarding, the moment when his hard work and selflessness came to fruition. His job was done.

Other pigs would take their place, and once the lorries were gone he would feel a rush of energy and turn back to towards the sheds and lose himself in the well-oiled process that led to success.

He helped to impregnate sows, oversaw the births of their young, stood and watched as tiny piglets appeared from their mother and struggled to stand and suckle at her breasts, and out of habit he would make sure the farrowing crate was secure so she couldn't turn or escape, and then he would start fattening these new arrivals up, docking tails and clipping teeth, injecting the necessary chemicals, making sure they were properly enclosed, picking out the weak and sick and breaking their necks and cutting their throats and dumping their useless little bodies in one of the holes he kept for such rubbish.

The reassuring smell and sound of his pigs surrounded him and were proof of his importance. He heard them coughing with pneumonia, panting from meningitis, and in their painful breathing there were odd occasions when he imagined their stressed hearts beating in the manner of a factory production line, a heaving of bloody cogs, and this seemed natural and wonderful, a merging of nature and industry, a system that despite the mess was neat and efficient.

The pigs' living conditions led to complications. He resented the medical bills, but knew there were cases when he couldn't avoid treatment. Broken bones, infections, cuts, sores... There was always a problem to solve. The hard, metal interiors of the sheds led to injuries, and it was his job to decide which animals to help and which to ignore. Years of experience had taught him where to spend and where to save. He was tough on himself, didn't shirk responsibility, always looking at the bigger picture, considering his options, balancing the pros and cons of every single decision. He made his choices and created history.

A sedentary lifestyle was unhealthy and his pigs were the most extreme examples of this, and so he had learned the lesson and applied it to himself, kept up his fitness with regular training sessions. Pig anatomy was very similar to that of a human being. There was little difference in fact. They were intelligent creatures, their eyes mirrors to their inner feelings. He saw their misery every day of his working life – the resignation and surrender, flashes of fear when he approached, bashfulness when he was dealing with boys and girls and the breeding process, the touching of a sow's vagina, the massaging of a boar's penis, the carriage and transfer of sperm.

The mental collapse of his pigs had shown him how important it was to have a change of scenery. With nothing to do and stuck in the same place month after month, his pigs went mad. He could see the insanity in the behaviour of the older ones, the head-nodding and swaying of breeders who were inseminated and parted from their young and had been through so much fear, mourning and trauma that they had given up. Repetitive behaviour, self-harm, even small outbreaks of violence occurred, though none of this bothered him as it wasn't a threat to growth. His observations, which had already warned him to look after his physical health, extended to a realisation that what happened to the mind of a pig could also happen to the mind of a man. Fitness training lifted his mood, but it wasn't going to be enough in the long term.

A holiday was meant to rest the body, but more importantly refresh the mind. A complete break had profound, lasting benefits. The pig farmer was a man, but he also saw himself as a machine. Looking after his mental health made perfect financial sense. He justified his holidays as investments. The farm depended on his well-being. Without him, it could not function.

He had taken his first cruise more than a decade earlier, at a time when the business was under pressure and he was struggling to cope. That trip had saved the farm. He dreaded to think where he would be now if it had gone under. He had returned home with renewed determination and, through careful cuts to expenditure and the skirting of some restrictive laws, he had turned the operation around. This break had been repeated every year since and he always came back feeling positive. When he smelled the farm in all its piss-soaked, shit-smeared glory, heard the squealing and grunting of his pigs, saw the walls and roofs of his sheds, he fell in love with the place all over again. He couldn't wait to get started, thrilled by the challenges he faced.

Last year he had flown to Singapore and spent three days in a city he admired for its clean streets and strict laws. He had read it was the safest place on the planet and, made bold by this knowledge, he had walked the streets in a fearless manner. From Singapore he had travelled by ship along the Malaysian coast to Thailand, and from there across to India, stopping at Georgetown, Phuket, Kolkata, Chennai, Colombo in Sri Lanka, and finally Mumbai. It had been a peculiar journey through alien cultures. He had taken several tours, but was left unimpressed by the poverty, unmoved by the guides and their endless information. He preferred the comfort of the ship where he could swim and relax with a good book. For the most part, the other guests were undemanding and respectful of the peace he required.

This year he was off to Miami, then cruising across the Caribbean to the Panama Canal and finally up the western coast of Central America, eventually reaching San Francisco via Los Angeles. There were stops scheduled for St Lucia and Grenada and other islands whose names he couldn't remember.

He made sure the cruises he invested in had the best facilities. There was always a gym, cinema and pool, quality dining and entertainment. He couldn't say he was exactly looking forward to this next trip, but knew it was necessary. At least it was certain to be better than the last one. He hadn't taken to the Asian food, especially when they reached India, although the ship itself concentrated on Western cuisine. He made a point of trying the local dishes when he was away, but those he had sampled the previous year only left him feeling sick. These were poor people, held back by superstition. He expected barbecues in the Caribbean, while America was famous for its steaks. He would be fine. He wasn't worried.

The pig farmer took a range of reading material with him when he went on holiday. He had no interest in fiction, preferring autobiographies and history. Communism and fascism were subjects that kept him turning the pages, the sheer scale of their operations never ceasing to amaze him, and he could happily read about the bureaucracy of their regimes for hours. People forgot that these systems were driven by modest men and women who operated behind the scenes, individuals who shunned the spotlight and were happy to deal with day-to-day detail. The Nazis were vilified for their concentration camps, and rightly so, but he was honest enough to admit that they were visionaries when it came to the mechanics of transportation and slaughter. They didn't waste resources on those they eradicated and, taking their logic further, confiscated money and property and even plundered the corpses themselves.

The same rules applied to his pigs, the big difference being that he needed his animals to put on weight rather than lose it, and they of course had nothing to offer him but their bodies. His pigs did have something valuable that the Jews and other subhumans lacked, though – their young. He needed his sows to produce children, and achieving this was another area of his work that he found fascinating.

He had read that the Nazis were inspired by the great beef- and pork-producing companies of the USA, that the Final Solution drew on the slaughterhouses of Chicago, the mass movement and industrial killing of animals in the Land Of The Free. The American stockyards, with their boxcars packed full of living pork and beef on its way to be butchered, mirrored the great cattle-driving Westerns he had watched on television as a boy, and the Nazis saw this large-scale movement of animals and applied it to the transportation of Jews. After the Second World War, the meat industry had in turn drawn on the Nazi example and applied their technology and mindset to another group of subhumans. While he would never want to live under a totalitarian regime, the pig farmer wasn't about to deny the benefits democratic nations had drawn from the work of those able to operate without restraints. He was an internationalist. He believed in the sharing of ideas, the honesty of science, the unrestricted flow of information.

His father had been a great patriot and even now he sold his pigs on the basis of their Britishness, although the idea that British pork was meant to embody the national identity was clearly ridiculous. Pigs were animals and there to be used, and as such existed outside society, in much the same way as slaves had done in colonial times. Meat production was an international affair. This idea of his pork being somehow British was a nice gimmick which he happily went along with, even if he had never grasped the logic. He had no sense of superiority over his customers. They could believe whatever they wanted, vote for whichever party they pleased, worship any god that made them feel good about the future, just as long as they ate his pigs.

He supposed people made connections that didn't exist so they could live with their choices. They said they respected the countryside and the animals they ate, but that wasn't really true. Life was short and selfish. The Nazis targeted the Jews because they were powerful within German society, exploited the killing of Christ and highlighted Jewish control of the banking system and their involvement in the armaments industry. They were scapegoats, outsiders forced to take the brunt of German failure, which in the political climate of the time made sense. But the pig farmer regarded the Nazis as cranks.

He had read that Hitler was a vegetarian and that the SS cracked down on those who were cruel to animals, which was madness. The Nazis were weaklings. How could Hitler, who had fought so bravely in the First World War, and then taken on and beaten the communists on the streets of Germany, be a vegetarian? The Nazis were emotional, wrapped up in myth and fantasy, a bunch of hopeless romantics, whereas the communists showed no such mercy.

The Soviets were also godless, but dedicated to the rule of science. They didn't waste time on spiritual nonsense. They were hardcore materialists and as such tough on their animals as well as those members of the population they considered a threat. If they had been questioned about the lack of equality shown to animals, they would no doubt have justified their behaviour with some ridiculous working-class rhetoric, rambling on about the choices that had to be made and the inherent decency of humans, the sort of rubbish people still lapped up today. It was a nice deflection, but a shame they had to explain themselves. Stalin was a loose cannon, yet he had stayed in power for a lot longer than Hitler, and killed many more millions.

This brought the pig farmer to Mao and China, another brand of communism he was just starting to learn about, and when it came to the unapologetic exploitation of animals he had nothing but admiration for that hard-working, hungry nation. China represented the future, a fast-developing people keen to shed the vegetarianism of their poverty and embrace the carnivorous ways of the wealthy, overweight West. He looked to the East and saw a billion pork lovers waiting to be fed.

With their incredible wealth, the great post-war democracies could easily have moved to a meat-free diet, but instead they had let business interests take them in the opposite direction, adopting a hardline capitalist system of meat production. He greatly respected those who had moved the industry into the modern age, found the propaganda used to hide the realities from the masses nothing short of genius. This had enabled him to fulfil his potential and grow the company.

The pig farmer knew that he fully deserved his break. He was a leader, a producer of food and an employer of men, a good boss who saw his helpers as lacking drive and intelligence. Some were plain stupid, others lazy, and while he accepted they might occasionally release their frustrations at work he had to maintain order. It was a balancing act. He needed people who would accept low wages, and as such he'd had to employ one or two thugs over the years, but as long as it didn't affect productivity he didn't care what his workers did to the pigs. Even so, he ran a tight ship, cracked down hard when the rules were broken.

His father had put him to work early, teaching him every aspect of pig rearing, and as part of his education he had spent a week at a slaughterhouse. He had seen the killing of pigs up close, a nuts-and-bolts process that had left little impression, and yet he would always remember a peculiar incident that had occurred on his final day.

A sow had come through the scalding tank and out of the rotating drum used to remove her hair and was being cut open when several piglets tumbled out of her belly. It was a surreal sight, seeing the umbilical cords stretched and these babies hanging out of their mother with their half-formed faces and mutant bodies bouncing in the air. One or two may still have been alive. He wasn't sure. He had seen plenty of aborted piglets before, but it was the reaction of a middle-aged slaughterman that surprised him. The man went berserk, shouting at the chap in charge, saying how it wasn't right, this was happening too often, the idiot ranting and raving and going on and on, and to this day the pig farmer had never worked out the reason for his anger. It made no sense.

He wondered why he was thinking about this now, as he normally looked forward rather than back. There was no room in his life for nostalgia. He didn't understand why the slaughterman and the sow were so clear in his mind. Then, in an instant, he made the link. He shook his head in amazement.

Two weeks ago he had read an article on a procedure he was hoping to introduce and had followed this up by requesting the relevant literature, but had forgotten to put the documents in the suitcase he was taking on holiday. He left in three days' time and was already packed. The idea was so logical that he wondered why he had never thought of it himself. People wanted the most succulent pork possible, which meant a pig had to be killed when it was young, which was obvious enough, but there were rich individuals who enjoyed novelty food, its rarity meaning they were willing to pay much higher prices. His was a modest operation, but this felt like the big time, a chance to increase his profits like never before.

The process involved the removal of piglets from their mother's womb. The sow was opened up and her young taken from her before they were due to be born. Pork couldn't come much fresher or more tender than that supplied by an unborn piglet. There would be savings as well, as he wouldn't have to feed these animals. His mouth quivered, but remained set, although the purple tinge to his lips did deepen. He brushed his hair back behind his right ear, as it had slipped loose with all this thinking and planning, and as he did so he marvelled at the power of his subconscious, the sheer genius of the human mind.

Mary was four months old and missed her mum. So did the two hundred or so other lambs. It was nearly midnight and she didn't have a clue where she was going, having been bought and sold on and moved several times in the last ten days. Until she was taken from her mother she had spent her short life out in the open and hated this fussy new world. She was used to a field on the side of a hill, grass under her feet and the sky above her head, views of sunrises and sunsets, clean air to breathe. At night she would look up at the twinkling stars and wonder what they were. She wondered about these humans as well. While their movements were slow and they could never have survived in the outdoors as she had done, they had a cunning that made her their prisoner. They stood in small huddles, bodies swollen with fat, smelling of milk as if they were still being suckled. The lambs were being forced towards a lorry and the humans were becoming louder and she could hear a dog barking. Born in winter, she had been lucky to live through the snow and cold when so many others had starved or frozen to death. She had seen the moon and the sun light up the snow and the bodies of the dead, not knowing what it meant. Her mum had loved and protected her, seen her through several storms, as unknown to Mary men had been fiddling with her mother's body. In a normal world Mary would have been born in the spring or summer, when the weather gave her a better chance of survival, but farmers used hormones to bring the breeding cycle of the ewes forward. They needed lambs for the spring. People wanted to eat her at Easter. Christians wanted to celebrate the self-sacrificing Lamb Of God with the sacrifice of an innocent. You couldn't make it up. The men forcing Mary up the ramp and into the back of the lorry were powerful and had their way, the lambs pressed in tight as the container filled up. The doors slammed and they stood in darkness. The lambs called out. The driver started his engine. Metal rattled and the floor moved and they were jolted forward, some of them falling and one boy breaking a leg and crying as the others tried to back off and avoid trampling him to death. The driver changed gears and headed for the open road, choosing one of his trucker CDs and waiting for the guitars to begin, putting his foot down and singing along as the big wheels turned.

DIRTY COW

MICHAEL COULDN'T DECIDE if he should tell Sam Norton what was going on or keep quiet and pretend he didn't know that the grown-ups were killing animals. His friend didn't have a clue that one day he would have to hurt the pigs he loved, and Michael was sure the government didn't pay people to look after them in special cases. Piggy would spend his life doing bad things for money. He was going to be upset when he found out, but if nobody said anything he could go on for years thinking everything was fine, work and save up enough money to buy a farm and lots of pigs and by then he might not have any choice and be forced to kill them by whoever organised it all.

If Sam had a pig farm he would become the sort of person his friends wouldn't want to know and his mum and dad weren't going to like him much either. It must have happened to other children in the past – starting off good and ending up bad. He knew it would be wrong if he didn't tell Piggy the truth, but couldn't think how to do it, would have to choose the right words and pick a time and a place and even then it was going to be horrible. It would be easier to do nothing.

It had taken Michael a while to work out what Pop was getting at when they'd talked about the filling in his pie, and even then he couldn't believe it was true, but the idea that there might be parts of an animal in his food had nagged at him until he asked his grandfather what he'd meant. He seemed unsure how to reply, and this was what Michael was feeling now with Piggy, but then Pop had asked him what was his favourite food?

Michael liked baked beans on toast, chips, toasted-cheese sandwiches, pies and pasties, fish fingers, bacon and eggs. Spaghetti was nice. Roast potatoes. He loved those. Yorkshire pudding. Roast beef. Bangers and mash. Sausages. He hated liver. They had that at school with onions. Pop wanted to know what he liked about sausages. It was the taste, but not the stringy bits or the gristle, and he always had them with ketchup or brown sauce, gravy if there was mashed potato. Grandad opened his mouth to speak and closed it again, Michael following the lines on his face as he waited, imagining canals and Martians. What did he think was inside a sausage?

The boy didn't know, had never thought about it, they were nice in a sandwich as well, his mum cut them down the middle. Michael stopped talking. What was inside a sausage then? Pop leaned forward. A beef sausage was made from a cow. Probably a boy cow. Michael hoped this was a joke and waited for him to say something more, but the face opposite was serious. It couldn't be right. A boy cow was a bull. How did they end up in a sausage? They were killed. But bulls were big and strong. How could a man catch one? They could shoot the bull he supposed, but that didn't seem fair. Pop said farmers sent them to a special place. They called these boys steers. The body of a cow inside the sausages he ate? It made no sense. Pop nodded. Pork sausages were made from pigs. What was in a meat pie?

Pop saw the shock in his face and wondered if he'd done the wrong thing, if it would be better to change the subject or pretend he'd been pulling his leg, but it was important to know the truth. He couldn't lie, wished someone had told him when he was young, that he hadn't walked into that bloody barn. He might be able to back-track and let Michael find out when he was older, but that would be the coward's way. Pop said that he was sorry and continued.

Returning to London on the train at the end of his visit, the countryside had looked very different. The animals in the fields were doomed. Even the lambs. Michael felt sick and found himself looking away from them and towards the horizon. Now that some time had passed he couldn't believe he hadn't worked it out for himself. He must be thick. The words and names used were obvious and the truth was there in the shop windows and on his television. How could anyone miss it? Yet the adverts told strange little stories and it was easy to end up confused and not see any of it as being real. And beef sausages didn't look like bulls. There was no fur for a start. No feet or tail. What happened to the heads? Where were the hearts? He felt the beat inside his chest.

Back in the city he had more questions, but wouldn't ask Mum or Dad as they'd been lying to him, and Pop was still at Elm Cottage. There was nobody he could talk to about the killing. When he went shopping with his mum he wandered off and found the meat section, walked up and down the aisles looking into fridges packed with beef and pork, names he had never thought to link to a cow or a pig, and when he saw lamb clearly marked as 'lamb' he wondered if he had been pretending, somehow lying to himself and blocking out the truth. Body parts were stacked up. The flesh was red and bloody, cut with knives and wrapped in plastic. There were chicken wings, legs and breasts – the shapes obvious. The section was cold and the freezers hummed. He could have been on a spaceship. Except for the smell.

A man stood behind a counter at the end of the aisle, dressed in a white coat and hat. Fish had been arranged in descending layers, their mouths open, the eyes a misty, decaying blur. Ice was packed around their bodies and a poster on the wall showed a cheerful fisherman with a thick white jumper and big grey beard. These fish were the first dead animals Michael had seen and the eyes spooked him, made him hurry back to his mum, and he walked with her for ten minutes before announcing that he was never going to eat meat again. She thought about this, put a hand on his shoulder and said it was good for him and would make him strong, but if he thought about it for a week or so first and still wanted to stop then it would be okay.

He was annoyed at his parents, but supposed she believed what she was saying, even if it was still wrong to kill animals, and as they continued shopping he looked in the trolleys people were pushing to see what they were buying. Chickens, pigs, cows, lambs, fish… When they reached the fruit and vegetables he noticed how fresh the section smelled. There was no plastic or blood, a lot more colour and variety. It felt clean. He hadn't eaten any animals since. Michael was glad he knew the truth. He had to be brave and talk to Piggy. His friend needed to know.

*

Tucked into the backstreets of the city, away from the areas being bought up by Thatcher's yuppies, The Cross Keys was a ten-minute walk from the flat Ronnie had been living in for the last two years and the ideal local for a man of his interests. It had a core of regulars that spanned the generations, well-kept beer, fair prices, good music, and an atmosphere that ranged from the relaxed to lively depending on the day of the week. It soon became a meeting place for Ronnie's friends, and that meant a keen animal-rights group that included the youth known as Mickey Moo.

Landlord Jerry was a thoughtful Irishman who'd been more than happy to broaden the appeal of his jukebox over the years, the record machine's foundations rooted in Chuck Berry and Little Richard, Hank Williams and Dolly Parton, The Dubliners and Clancy Brothers. It had been helped along by the mods and skinheads who'd used the pub in the Sixties, headbangers and punks in the Seventies, and now this jumbled-up late-Eighties mob. It was a rebellious jukebox in the tradition of Mark E Smith and his bingo masters, and like so many pubs and social clubs the music reflected the pub's clientele.

The Rolling Stones, Desmond Dekker, David Bowie, the Sex Pistols and the Pogues had been joined by hard-hitting 45s from Crass, Conflict, the Subhumans and Flux Of Pink Indians, bands that delivered the sort of lyrics Mick Jagger and the rest couldn't touch. 'Bloodsports' by the Style Council and the mighty 'Meat Is Murder' by the Smiths had been easier to get past Jerry than the full-on rage of the anarchists, but Ronnie was persuasive and had talked the landlord around.

Jerry was strict when it came to changes as every record added meant a record removed, and he had to think of his customers, get the balance right, couldn't be upsetting the older Guinness and light-and-bitter men, the ladies with their port-and-lemon and neat whisky. These were hard-working people and they wanted something easier on the ear when they were relaxing, but at the same time he had to consider the younger element, while Ronnie appreciated it might be difficult convincing a sixty-two-year-old who enjoyed singing along to 'McAlpine's Fusiliers' and 'The Foggy

Dew' to accept the militant English vocals of Steve Ignorant, Colin Jerwood, Dick Lucas and Colin Latter.

Ronnie and Jerry had got to know each other pretty well over the first year as the younger man sat at the bar when it was quiet and he was on his own, enjoyed the landlord's stories of a Kerry childhood, the ways of his parents and the Catholic Church, a boxing brother and a sister who became a nun, London when he first arrived and was labouring, and then how he had bought this pub when it was on its knees and got it going again, the nutters he had met across the years.

Jerry was a listener as well as a talker, an asker of questions, and Ronnie explained his concerns – totalitarianism whether left, right or religious; a stifling party-political system; racism and sexism; attitudes towards the disabled and elderly; the murder of non-human animals through hunting, vivisection and meat consumption. Jerry agreed with Ronnie's position on all of these subjects except the last one, but was open-minded and accepted the Peter Singer book *Animal Liberation* when it was passed over the counter one night after closing time, but he did insist that he couldn't see himself ever becoming a vegetarian.

The jukebox was unplugged on Sunday, Monday and Tuesday, and during the day on Wednesday. If anyone asked why, Jerry pointed out that he wasn't running a disco. There were times when people needed to think and talk in peace. He had a pile of cassettes on a shelf behind the bar that he liked to play on occasion – mainly Irish folk and Country & Western, but also a soul collection made as a birthday present by a man called McKenna who'd used The Cross Keys a decade earlier. Jerry had agreed to listen to the songs Ronnie was suggesting if he wanted to bring a tape in.

A recording of *This Is The ALF* didn't go down well at first – not with a man who loved a melody, the fiddle and mandolin – but Ronnie explained Chumbawamba's 'Unilever' and moved into the details of animal testing and fox hunting, both of which Jerry had accepted were wrong. He recognised the berks of Conflict's 'Berkshire Cunt', hadn't thought about the rhyme behind the slang, and Ronnie soon had him considering the lyrics more than the sound of the music.

The compilation included album tracks as well as singles, and 'The Offending Article' by the Poison Girls would have been too much for the jukebox if it had been available as a 45. The lyrics were like nothing Jerry had heard on a record before, the idea of donkeys being sold for sex next to women in the brothels of Port Said really making him think. He'd heard about such a place years before from an old soldier who'd served in Egypt, a man shocked by what he had seen, made to question the use of prostitutes and society's treatment of women. Jokes were made about goat-fucking Arabs and sheep-shagging Welshmen, but nobody believed that sort of thing was true.

Even today, if Jerry met a man who thought raping a donkey in a brothel was funny he would have knocked his teeth out, and if he'd been in Egypt and met the pimps responsible he would have done a lot worse. He had been a bit of a tearaway when he was young, but the years passed and people mellowed, and nobody who came into his pub knew, remembered or cared. For his part, Ronnie reckoned Jerry could handle himself, guessed there were plenty of stories that hadn't been told, which was only right.

Standing at the bar waiting for the landlord to finish serving him, Mickey was feeling the best he'd done since his beating two weeks earlier. Jerry had asked how he was mending and then told him to stay out of trouble, and he had agreed he would. The bruising and pain was almost gone, while the cut on his head was healing with the stitches removed and the shaved hair grown back. He'd had five pints, which dulled the aches that remained, Mickey floating with a couple of songs that had kept him out of a friendly argument at the table where he was sitting with Ronnie and the others.

Steppenwolf's 'Born To Be Wild' and now Creedence Clearwater Revival's 'Lodi' had taken him out of The Cross Keys to an *Easy Rider* highway, the tarmac smooth and empty as it linked the Atlantic and Pacific oceans, and while those neon-lit diners may have been past their pristine best in the Vietnam era, Fifties rockabilly and doo-wop platters still sat next to the heavier Sixties sounds. Mickey had read Jack Kerouac's *On The Road* and the even better *The Dharma Bums* and *Lonesome Traveler*, the author's streams of consciousness linking into the magic of American music and film, the romanticism of the Free World. He knew The Dream was heavy with violence, the theft of land and the extermination of the natives and the horrors of slavery and, like most human societies, the mass slaughter of billions of animals, but the image created by Kerouac was hard to resist. To jump in a car and drive thousands of miles across a wilderness lined with vintage diners and bars was a version of heaven.

Bringing three pints back to the table he handed one to Bev and another to Ronnie, Mickey sitting down and quietly sipping from his glass as he considered the people around him, the different ages and backgrounds. Stereotypes were applied to both sides when it came to the fight over fox hunting. The hunt was promoted as upper-class and upright, toffee-nosed men and women with little clue how to earn a living, eccentrics who loved the countryside and wanted the animals they were duty-bound to control to have a sporting chance. Privileged twits. Nature's guardians. The saboteurs, meanwhile, were an army of bitter class warriors and dropouts who envied the rich their wealth. Violent and out of touch with reality, many were unemployed or unemployable.

Mickey knew it was more mixed up when it came to class, and that the sabs were peaceful and the hunt violent, which was obvious to most people, he guessed, and he could see how the hunt took advantage of that pacifism. It made them braver than they really were, or at least more willing to get stuck in. The media served the establishment and distorted even the clearest truths, and their smears covered every other area of the animal-rights move-ment. Almost as bad was the dismissive approach, the idea that society had much more important things to worry about than animal welfare, pushing the lie that it was an either/or situation.

Ronnie was the one who'd got him involved with the hunt saboteurs, introducing Mickey to a group of people he probably wouldn't have otherwise known. Ronnie had been handing out leaflets in the street and they'd got talking, Mickey wary when he started meeting characters who were different to his usual friends, and yet now it was Ronnie picking up on what Bev had been saying the other day, leaning in close and insisting he was a fool if he thought he could find the men who'd attacked him and have his revenge and not end up in prison.

If Mickey sank to their level he was no better than the hunt and might as well give up. What was he going to do, use an axe or a knife? Buy a gun? Maybe he was planning to kill them? Is that the sort of person he wanted to become? Damaging property was enough. Non-violence was the way to achieve results. Mickey had to think of the bigger picture. If he wasted his time on them then they had won. They were nothing and their time would come. Natural justice. Their crimes would come back to haunt them one day, in this life or the next, it didn't matter. Mickey wouldn't be helping the foxes or badgers or hares if he was running around after terrier-men. Revenge was selfish. What was it? His pride? If he was convicted of assault the judge would love to lock him away for ten years. He had to take the moral high ground. Outwit those wankers. Come on, Mickey knew he was right.

The youth nodded. Ronnie *was* right. Again, he honestly agreed, just as he had with Bev. He felt a little embarrassed, but was also pleased these older people cared about him, and he was listening to what they said, respected their views, and he told Ronnie this, but didn't add that he wouldn't be going out sabbing again. He was a liability. Didn't want to react and let the others down. It just wasn't his way. He couldn't turn the other cheek, would rather be raiding laboratories and burning lorries, and he drank quickly, glad to be in The Cross Keys, heard 'Sick Butchers' and guessed Bev had put it on after 'Lodi'. Crows squawked, a cockerel crowed, a dog barked. There was talk of a nuclear power dump. Yes, that *Neu Smell* EP by Flux Of Pink Indians was a true classic.

Frank Norris had been thinking about his father recently – *really* thinking about him – wondering what his life would have been like if he'd been raised by another man. Like most sons he had looked up to his dad when he was a boy, and when he was older felt he owed it to him to keep the farm going. His father had been hard on the family, but after he was dead Frank still tried to live up to expectations, even if he never knew what these were, had just kept doing the same things year after year, over and over again. It would have seemed like a betrayal to sell up.

The seasons came and went and he saw them through, a cycle of life that farming was meant to reflect in a healthy and honest manner, but they became a straight line when you were working every hour that you could stay awake, a repetition of the same tasks and fears. In truth, his father had been a stranger, as they'd never talked about anything outside of the farm and the jobs that needed doing, and he had no idea what had gone on inside his head. It was only now that Frank was looking back. He had time on his hands and the barriers he'd put up had been broken down by age, and he found himself swinging between sympathy and anger. His father must have had dreams when he was young, but apart from fighting in the war he had never left the local area other than for a week's holiday by the sea every two or three years.

Clearer and less confusing was Frank's love for his wife. He remembered how strongly he'd felt about Anne when they were young and that feeling had never changed, even if it ended up buried under the weight of work. People became used to each other and the romance faded, but he thought that was probably normal. Even so, he was starting to worry he had wasted too much time slogging away on the farm when they could have been living an easier life somewhere else.

He kept thinking back to how Anne had wanted to move away and live in a town when they were first married, but he wouldn't leave the farm, had persuaded her that this was their place in the world. She had pleaded and cried, but he'd won in the end. Maybe he should have listened to her. It might have been better for them both. He knew now that he had lacked courage and ambition, his refusal to consider new possibilities dressed up as strength of mind, determination, loyalty. Frank's thoughts were swirling in circles, tangled in a way they had never been in the past. He couldn't change anything and was stuck out here in this house, slowly going mad.

A few nights before there had been a downpour at two in the morning, and while it was brief the noise woke him, and because it was warm he had got out of bed and gone to the window when he saw a flash of lightning. He had always liked to watch a storm when he was dry indoors, and there was another burst that lit up the land, and for a split second he saw a car on the lane, driving without its lights on, but people rarely came this way and certainly not at night. It was no more than a shape and after a while he wondered if it was a lost horse. As a boy he had been scared of ghosts, especially the horse that was supposed to come out of the chalk and run through the fields, crushing anyone who got in his way. Frank had hurried back to bed, chased by his childhood fears.

Last night he had heard Anne talking in her sleep, the meaning of the words just out of reach, but he was sure she was trying to warn him about something terrible that was going to happen, and when her voice faded away there was a creak on the landing and he had pulled the bedclothes over his head and tried to will whatever it was away. He saw fur and feathers and skin, the muddy paws of the dogs he'd had for friends. He remembered them barking, heard his geese welcoming him home. He prayed out loud for the ghosts of the animals he'd killed to leave him alone. There was a long silence. Tears covered his face. A creature ran across the floorboards and down the stairs and the back door slammed shut, the noise so loud that it woke him up.

Sitting in front of his TV with a tray on his lap, waiting for the six o'clock news to start, Tanner's plate held rice noodles topped with fried bean curd, oyster mushrooms, chopped pak choi and red peppers, the flavours coming from sesame oil, lemongrass, ginger and chillies. There was a bowl of tiny Vietnamese spring rolls to the side, plum sauce for dipping, a bottle of soya sauce on standby. He always started off with chopsticks, but had a fork and spoon ready for when his patience ran out.

He had bought the noodles, pak choi, bean curd and lemongrass from a nearby Thai supermarket, and while the restaurants of Chinatown displayed glazed piglets and crushed ducks in all their brutalised glory, the peasants back home couldn't afford such luxuries. His meal was closer to those being eaten by the majority – carbohydrates, soya protein, fungi, vegetables. This was the people's food and soya beans would be essential when the world turned vegan. It was going to happen, he was sure of that, and the people of the future would look back at their ancestors and feel ashamed.

One of the reasons China had managed to support such a huge population was its diet, with the communist regime confronting the realities of feeding over a billion people. He doubted animal rights came into it, although there was a Buddhist legacy, and the Buddha came from India where the second largest population on the planet ate food that was influenced by more advanced Hindu beliefs. Atheist and religious leaders seemed to have come to the same vegan conclusion, but with China becoming more industrialised and wealthier, meat consumption was increasing, partly driven by the idea that eating pork and beef was a sign of success. He had read about the number of animals being reared in factory farms, this change often driven by snobbery and a desire to mimic the West. Even in India, the emerging middle class saw meat eating as progress. His spirit sagged.

It was hopeless. He was a fool thinking he could change anything, a small man with no power and no influence, daydreaming his life away, creating dead-end nightmares. As his mood dipped down the TV lifted him back up and into a cleaner fantasy. He raised tofu to his mouth as Wagner carried him away with *The Flying Dutchman*, and he kept eating, tasting lemongrass, the music fading as a cool Nordic mist drifted across his screen. A Kraftwerk voice took charge.

His eyes filled with tears and his nose ran, the spices belonging to one world, the car emerging from the mist another. The detached yet earnest narrator was detailing the benefits of owning this particular model. It offered power, prestige, perfection. The three Ps were emphasised. The car glided through the night. Winter turned to summer. North became south. Luxury yachts appeared, moored in a picturesque Mediterranean port. The harbour was a catwalk. Peasants stood in a crowd and watched billionaires eat on deck. Steaks were picked at by stars. A casually dressed man left one of the yachts and walked towards the car, which was parked on a cobbled street. At another location, a beautiful woman was leaving an exclusive discotheque. The car arrived, driven by the billionaire. The woman was impressed. Their eyes met. Teeth sparkled. So did the diamonds on her neck, wrist, fingers. She was up-market and glamorous. The man climbed out of the car and opened the passenger door. The woman leaned in and stroked the leather seats, revealing long legs and silk stockings. She made her decision. The man closed the door and the car sped off. It stopped by the yacht and the peasants applauded.

There was a respectful pause as the advert ended and the news began with a burst of electronica, and this evened out and simmered, ready to turn nasty, building expectations. The fun was over. Important matters loomed.

The screen snapped to an aerial view of the city. The eye of the machine swooped in the style of Batman, Catwoman and Spiderman, semi-human superheroes who descended into the criminal streets of the metropolis, elevating the primitive skills of bats, cats and spiders with the superior moral code of evil-cleansing humanity. The camera settled just above the rooftops and hovered. Its beady eye turned and focused on the bleak suburban wastelands that led towards motorways and factories and into the rural bleakness beyond. It didn't linger, returned to more sophisticated locales, easing forward and picking up speed and skimming towards the core of the city where the grandest mansions, terraces, squares and monuments waited, and these led to the great political, religious and financial institutions at the heart of a mighty civilisation, and Tanner was trying to recognise the streets below – the suburbs, parks, railway lines of London – but the scenery blurred so he could have been above any city in the modernised world, the buildings becoming taller and wider, changing from orange brick to red brick and on into concrete and stone and marble, and he was treated to glass oblongs, squares, triangles and domes, and he was looking at a tinted tower that reflected the clouds and he was going to smash into the windows but somehow slid through and slowed and moved easily across desks and cabinets and filtered through walls and closed doors and along empty corridors and over more desks filled with documents where increasingly important people sat in front of laptops and monitors and he was entering one of these – passing down wires as if he was an elemental – and the wires were smaller and tighter and full of threads that made him think of arteries and veins, and computer chips he imagined as digital hearts.

His tray nearly fell off his lap as he dropped food from his chopsticks and reacted, but he caught it in time, found himself in a room where a presenter waited. The trip was over and she smiled in a serious but welcoming way. Tanner took one of the tiny spring rolls and dipped it into the plum sauce. It was crunchy and tangy, a half-price bargain.

A collage of famous cities and landmarks filled the wall behind the presenter – London, New York and Paris intercut with the skylines of Shanghai, Singapore and Dubai. Glass towers reflected glass towers. Smaller landmarks flashed – Big Ben, the Statue Of Liberty, the Eiffel Tower – along with shots of the workers grafting at ground level, in between skyscrapers that had turned to gold where the sun struck. He saw Chinamen digging foundations, Arabs pouring concrete, Africans building walls. The coolies of the world were clearly glad to be involved. They welcomed globalisation and were keen to join the West. The future was healthy, but there were still battles to be fought.

The lead item concerned the suspension of human rights in a distant land. There were clear pictures shot on a small camera, a good few steps up from the jittery images normally feeding through from mobile phones. The pixel count was high. Realism crisp. Soldiers moved through the dusty streets of a city. The roads were unpaved and the buildings smashed metal and stone. The military had new weapons and uniforms, their heads protected by helmets. They were shooting at youths in sandals, small boys throwing stones against a background of palms. There was a boom of explosives. Tanner noticed a dead dog. A goat stood in an alleyway, nervously looking in every direction. The pictures kept rolling and a reporter spoke to camera. The situation was grave. Civilians were dying. The international community had called for an immediate ceasefire. A meeting was being organised.

More stories followed, shortening in length, and he was only half-listening, had heard most of it on the radio earlier, but towards the end of the programme he focused and increased the volume. A man had been found dead in Norfolk. Unconfirmed reports said that the victim was a pig farmer called Brian McKenzie, and that he had been shot and decapitated. It was being suggested that his death was linked to the recent shooting of two slaughtermen in a car near their place of work. The police had been following another line of enquiry in regard to these earlier deaths, having allegedly found child pornography at the home of James Ball, who was one of the deceased. The police were not commenting at this stage, apart from insisting that the connection was media speculation and unhelpful.

Tanner's nose started to bleed and he soaked the blood up with a paper towel. The first executions could be described as a cull, carried out in a natural setting, while McKenzie had died quietly at home. It was sad when anyone passed away, no matter who they were or what they had done, but he couldn't help thinking about the crimes the pig farmer would have committed over the years, the suffering he had inflicted. When the weather report came on he studied the map, and then the music returned and the visual introduction was replayed, but backwards, at an incredible speed.

In my dream I was a cheerful boy in a porky body, the big smile that filled my face showing off an easy-going nature. I was the kind of character who takes life at face value, always looking on the bright side, content with small pleasures, preferring a joke and a laugh to a heavy conversation. Even so, I knew I was a hybrid and not a proper pig, that I had the brain of a human inside this happy head, which meant I wasn't as nice as I wished I could be. The positive was that I could plan ahead. I had the cunning needed to deal with the farmer who was hurting my brothers and sisters, this backwoods pervert who kept expectant mums locked up so tightly they could barely move. This man raped girls and drove mothers insane, killed their babies, forced children to live in their own shit and piss. He injected them with chemicals and ruined their bodies and sent them off to die in crowded lorries driven by cowboys. I waited for this monster away from the sheds where all those hundreds and maybe thousands of pigs were wheezing and suffering, and I came out of the shadows and greeted him as he walked along the lane towards his clean, neat house. I calmed any fear he might have felt by singing softly in a nursery-rhyme voice about pigs going to market and this one running all the way home. I held my gun steady and guided him so he didn't get lost, and when he sat in his favourite armchair I used shackles to make sure he didn't fall and hurt himself. I searched his home quickly before returning to the living room. It had started to rain and the sound of water hitting the roof was rhythmic and soothing, but only for me, as the pig farmer seemed nervous. Millions of creatures were being abused by men just like this one and something had to be done. We started talking and he asked me why he was here, what had he done wrong? I controlled my frustration and breathed deeply, and when I was calm I tried to explain my motives, but realised he wasn't paying attention. He made a comment about pigs only being pigs. The time for chit chat was over. I was at great pains to act professionally and took no pleasure from what followed. I was quick and efficient. Humane. When I was done I placed an apple in his mouth and went outside. It had stopped raining and I lost myself in the darkness.

Daisy was a mellow, slow-moving soul named after a flower that grew in her favourite field, and lots of people knew her from the stories they had been told as children, the pictures they'd seen in books, but she hadn't gone anywhere, was still ambling along those peaceful country lanes, swishing her tail, moving in time with her big-bellied friends as Jolly Farmer Jones followed in his tractor. It would soon be dark. She was a sensitive creature and the twilight made her nervous, old terrors stirring as the world was redrawn.

The fingers on the tractor's steering wheel were thick and gnarled, but gentle when they massaged her aching breasts, which were swollen with milk and felt as if they were about to burst. Other cows relied on the farmer as well, but he only had one pair of hands and employed helpers, and these kind workers used machines to help with the task, the relief just as welcome. The relationship between Daisy and Farmer Jones was cooperative and organic and based on a deep mutual respect.

Those other daisies filled meadows and ditches and sprinkled the lawns of houses and bungalows in villages and towns and had appeared in manmade parks and the crevices of the cities. Small girls sat on riverbanks and weaved long and short chains. Teachers taught classes to draw delicate stems and small starry heads while a buttery sun shone down on a rolling brown hill that dipped into a valley of green fields where a tumbledown white house stood with bunched red curtains and a blue door and a smiling pink man who held hands with a smiling pink woman as they stood next to a small pink boy and tiny pink girl, and in front of this happy-happy family a crooked yellow path led to a wonky black gate where Daisy Moo Cow stood.

She was glowing, tinged with gold, blooming like the flower peeking over the top of her right ear, and so proud to be sharing her life with these kind people, their round faces and marshmallow bellies topped by carefully crafted messages, the letters and words discussed at meetings where they were approved by the most important executives. Fonts were chosen, sizes decided, colours agreed.

Daisy was burning with the bliss of motherhood. Fortunately, she was producing too much milk. Thankfully, she wanted to share it with her human family. They worked hard to look after her and she insisted on giving them something in return. It felt good to be in a partnership that benefited everyone involved. In fact, she was grateful. The public saw her joy in those big trusting eyes and that wet black nose, while her funny old breasts weren't really breasts but actually udders. Bottles of semi-skimmed and full-fat milk... Pots of cream... Packets of butter... Blocks of cheese... Tubs of yoghurt... Boxes of ice cream... Tasty, natural, nourishing food. Made from love. A hidden love. The sort of love that was forced and best not mentioned.

Daisy was two years old when she was raped for the first time. The men responsible were casual but mechanical, having previously been involved in thousands of such attacks. One spoke of the present he was planning to buy his daughter for her fourth birthday. She knew her daddy worked with cows and had taken a shine to a toy calf, a fluffy little thing with eyes that turned blue and a computer inside its chest which meant it could say some simple phrases. There was a button that set off the voice. It sounded like a cow talking – if cows could talk. Which they couldn't. Even better was the built-in recorder. He could press another button and speak into a microphone and his words were stored inside the calf and his little girl could play them back whenever she wanted. Imagine that.

She was glad he loved animals as much as she did, and with the toy calf she could hear him when he was at work. He was touched by her choice of toy. What would he say? He'd have to think of something funny, shook his head at the cleverness of it all, while his friend wondered how many messages the computer could store. It was amazing what people thought up.

Daisy was scared. The stall she was being pushed towards was very narrow and she didn't want to be in such a tight space. She tried to move sideways, beyond the bars, so she wouldn't be trapped. Daisy didn't like to upset anyone, just wished she could be left alone. Even if she lived to her natural age of twenty she would never understand this human love of walls and roofs, the corridors and gates and pens that made her feel sick. There were no fresh breezes in these places, and she had a keen sense of smell, which in the outdoors could stretch for miles, needed space to move about in as she was related to the gazelle and the antelope, as well as all those millions of sheep and goats already locked into the farming system. She was big and powerful beside these humans, but was by nature timid and hated violence, had never done anyone any harm.

The gate swung and steel clattered, the shock of the sound coupled with her nervousness making Daisy step back so she bumped into one of the men who swore and punched her in the ribs, fear driving her forward into the cage. The gate slammed shut. Her brain was wired up differently to the humans who decided every aspect of her life, and so there was no way she could guess what was about to happen. There was a lull as she fought her claustrophobia, the two men continuing their conversation until a third arrived.

Someone was touching her private parts. She was exposed and embarrassed, tried to turn but could only swivel her head, couldn't see the men behind her properly, and then one of them pushed a fist up her bum causing Daisy to jump and cry out, and he was moving his hand around inside her body, grabbing the cervix, using his other hand to force a gun into her vagina. This double penetration made her shout louder for them to stop, but the beasts took no notice, the fingers in her anus moving in a rhythmic motion, the rapist finally pulling the trigger of his gun and firing semen into her womb.

Daisy's body belonged to these men. She had no rights. People laughed when it was suggested she should. They could do what they wanted, rape her whenever they pleased. It was an experience that never became easier to accept and over the years she was raped again and again. Humans preferred to call it artificial insemination. How on earth could an *animal* be *raped*?

It was important to the business controlling her ovaries that Daisy became pregnant. Time was money. Failure meant no calf, no milk, no revenue. A short while afterwards Daisy was restrained and an arm forced into her vagina, a thick wire held tight in her attacker's hand. She tried to resist, but the beasts had secured her in a specially built contraption, a screen showing them the contents of her womb. These rapes were carried out en masse so the children were born around the same time. An impregnated coil might be inserted or injections of prostaglandin or progesterone given. It made for easier management.

The semen she had been injected with over the years came from bulls she had never met. Indeed, the fathers themselves had never seen a female, as they were bred, selected, isolated. These lads were valued for the quality of their sperm, a network of vets and investors measuring and evaluating the contents of their testicles, the creatures themselves familiar but uneasy with the human hands constantly rubbing their balls and tugging at their cocks. The stud bull was a faceless seed machine for the humans who manipulated his sexuality. In normal circumstances he would have lived with a range of ladies, part of a herd that roamed and breathed clean air, following familiar paths, enjoying natural ways. Kept on a special farm, away from females, deviants used his frustration to their advantage, milking his penis in the same way Daisy and her sisters were drained of their milk.

The first batch of sperm forced into Daisy came from a nameless stud who could well have been called Rambo by the perverts who watched him perform. From his earliest days he had been groomed by sex cases, his body stimulated, mind manipulated, and built up and urged on he was removed from his stable and taken to a younger, more frail bull. The nonces running the show had prepared this boy earlier, using the copper ring in his nose to tie him to a post and stop him running off, then slipping a rubber hood over his head. They thought it was funny to call him Dave, and he was known as a teaser bull, stood blind and defenceless, arse exposed to the rampant Rambo who was led in and encouraged to fuck Dave.

The younger bull was scared and tried to pull away, but the pain was terrible as the ring ripped at one of the most sensitive areas of his body. The beasts were eager for Rambo to mount Dave and encouraged him loudly, Rambo unable to control himself, clambering up with an erection, but just as he was about to bugger Dave the intelligence of the master race was revealed as a human hand reached in and pulled at Rambo's cock and gave it a firm tug, diverting it into a leather vagina. This in itself was a clever invention, and even made from the skin of another bull. Rambo ejaculated. His lust satisfied, he was led away, while Dave remained tethered in the rubber hood, ready for the next stud.

Rambo's semen was expertly looked after and forced into several herds. The eugenics practised by the super-race moulded the non-human/subhuman element to serve the fully human, erasing the physically weak and unproductive and maximising the results of their scientific research. It was a slick operation that left nothing to chance. Dairy farmers abused their cows and were unapologetic. They saw themselves as pragmatic and professional. The propaganda wing of the business had worked wonders, the millions spent on advertising and marketing having convinced the public that the dairy industry was totally different to the meat industry.

Worse even than her rape was the theft of Daisy's children. After carrying her baby for nine months she gave birth and watched with wonder as her little boy or girl struggled to its feet and tried to walk, searching for her milk, knowing what was needed to live. At night her child settled down with her in the straw of their stall and she was content. The rape was a grim memory and she had to move on. To think that this small bundle of life had come from her body was truly wonderful, and she would care for and protect it, and she breathed the air and couldn't wait to get outside and walk with her child to her favourite field. Things were going to get better.

After two days the beasts came and took her baby away. Another gate slammed in her face, leaving her pressed against more cold steel, her calf calling for her as Daisy panicked and shouted, but could do nothing. This happened again and again. Each time she longed for her child's return and looked for them when she was moved, but never saw her sons and daughters again. She mourned and sunk into depression.

Daisy had been taken from her own mother and was haunted by the experience, even if the memory was suppressed. She wasn't the only one of course, as across the world untold hundreds of millions of females were being similarly abused. Daisy was traumatised, exhausted and in constant pain, but would never forget her children. The farmers weren't interested in slackers, needed to make her pregnant again, so within three months of giving birth she was raped again. These sexual assaults would be repeated for the rest of her short life, while other intrusive procedures were carried out on her body, which was defenceless against the desires of her masters.

Her sons were regarded as worthless by-products by the milk industry. Coming from a dairy herd, they weren't going to grow big enough to satisfy the beef producers, so the majority of these boys were killed within days of being born. Some male calves were sold into the veal trade for a period of torture before they were butchered for the richest members of human society. A quarter of the dairy herd was replaced each year, so Daisy's daughters might have ended up suffering the same abuse as their mother. If they were surplus to the farmer's requirements, they too were killed.

Daisy was approaching her fourth birthday and could probably keep going for another year. She was near to collapse, both physically and mentally. She had been made pregnant three times and would soon give birth again. She was being milked three times a day and her breasts were swollen with mastitis. They oozed pus and hurt all the time, her nipples sore from the needles the humans kept inserting to inject antibiotics. They certainly knew how to keep their machines running. Like most of those in her situation, she was also suffering from laminitis, the tissue in her hooves inflamed and lined with ulcers, which wasn't a surprise, seeing as how she spent her winters inside, forced to live in her own excrement. She was in pain when she stood still, more so when she walked.

There were no retirement homes for old cows, no daisy-filled fields or lush meadows where she was going. Once her womb was broken beyond repair, her supply of milk finished, the men and women who lived off her couldn't even be bothered to let her see out her days in peace. It would have cost them little, but they sniffed and strutted and snorted at such a preposterous idea.

Most people probably thought Daisy always produced milk, like a hen laying her eggs, that there were no children involved, no rape or killing. Maybe they assumed that once her working life was over she went to live next to the nice house in the advert, the one that small children liked to draw with crayons. The propaganda machine purred. Once the business people were done with Daisy she would be sent to the slaughterhouse. The industry described the horror she faced there as a culling. Left alone, she would have lived for more than twenty years, but she was part of the nation's dairy herd, repaid for her milk with a captive bolt fired into her head. Sometimes it destroyed the brain, sometimes it missed. Either way she was shackled and hoisted into the air. Daisy's throat was cut and she bled to death.

Mike Tanner joined the morning workers hurrying towards the train station, could smell the still-damp shampooed hair of women and girls as they clip-clopped on high heels, the aftershave of men and youths banging brogues and boots as they trampled along, and when they neared the railway entrance a crowd of figures emerged in trainers, a wave of night-shift workers and cleaners moving slowly with shoulders hunched. He saw this exchange of labour, these cogs in the machine, and when he paused and breathed deeply the heavy stench of leather took him back to the slaughterhouse.

He was on the edge of the pavement as a bus came through the junction and narrowly missed his arm, and when it was past him he looked across to the front bar of the pub where until recently he would stand and listen to the storytellers, their humour and reflections bringing The White Hart to life. It wouldn't open for a few hours yet, but the counter was clean and ready, pumps waiting in a long line, and he would have loved to go in there later but had to keep to himself, couldn't be drinking beer with Tony or tea at the allotments with Ella and Bunny. He turned and left the junction behind, the people thinning out and the smell of dead skin fading.

Twenty minutes later and he was approaching King Harry's Traditional, timing his arrival perfectly as Harry Boy himself had just lifted the shutters from the cafe windows. King Harry's was a godsend for those who craved the Full English but preferred it free from the usual carnage. It was possible to get a vegan fry-up in a lot of places, but these were usually limited to a few basics, while here in the Traditional he could enjoy a proper feast. It was a working-man's cafe that served filling food and charged affordable prices, a no-frills ten-table affair sitting in a row of shops, the difference being that it was solidly vegan. The cafe was a favourite in the area and probably unique in the city.

Tanner crossed the road, the bell above the door jangling as he went inside. A kettle was whistling, Harry's deep voice cutting through the shrill, asking where the fuck had he been for the last six months? He had been worried he'd died. Or worse. Tanner lied and explained how he had been busy with work and life had become complicated, and then he had been away for a while, the older man nodding and saying he looked different. Was he eating his greens? Tanner nodded. Harry changed tack, wondered if he was drinking too much, enjoying late nights with the ladies, and he came around from the other side of the counter and shook his hand, and they talked for a while until the door opened and three builders came in, which was fine by Tanner as he was hungry and didn't want to admit to that period when he had been depressed and stuck inside his flat.

He ordered the St George Special – sausage and bacon (both soya-based), mushrooms, baked beans, grilled tomatoes, bubble and squeak, two rounds of toast and a mug of black tea. Harry Boy wrote it down and called through to the kitchen. The big portions and fair prices were definitely a winning combination, and proved that the native cuisine could be served cruelty-free, the Traditional always busy despite the majority of people who ate there being carnivores.

The Traditional didn't just do breakfasts, which were served all day, as after twelve there were other British meals available – pie and mash, toad in the hole, nut roast, shepherd's pie, sausage and chips, pasty and chips, a soup of the day. The desserts weren't bad either. It was hard getting a seat at dinnertime and some mornings as well, seeing as the cafe was so popular, while it didn't close until nine at night. Harry must have been making a fortune, and could have done even better if he was willing to move to bigger premises, but saw no point – this was where the Traditional had started off and he was happy here.

Pushing sixty, Harry Boy was the son of Harry Senior and the grandson of Harry The First, a private who had been so affected by what he saw during the First World War that he gave up meat and changed the menu of his cafe when he returned home. Watching men being blown to smithereens and left to rot in the mud had changed him forever. The army's treatment of its horses, who were forced into the war and then butchered at its end to save the cost of bringing them home, had only added to his disgust. Seeing them killed and eaten by the same army they had helped defeat, their bodies fed to prisoners of war, had been the ultimate betrayal. The family had followed his lead ever since.

Harry Boy was fit and strong, and his own son, Harry The Youngest, was in the kitchen doing the honours. The property had long ago been bought by the King family, so there was no rent to pay and with the business it did the future seemed safe. Tanner had seen Harry Boy in action, noted the way he handled the punters, knowing everyone's name and making the most of each second, and he was the chirpiest of characters, a man who'd boxed when he was younger and was never going to be pushed about. There was a picture of Harry on the wall, with more and darker hair, holding his fists up for the camera.

The Traditional was pretty straightforward furniture-wise, but the photographs, postcards and horse brasses that filled the walls gave it a rich sense of history. It pissed all over the poncy restaurants that had been springing up with gentrification. The Traditional also destroyed the idea that British food couldn't exist without dead animals. Every sort of meat could be substituted these days, and while it would have been much more difficult in the past – before the easy availability of soya, tofu and bean curd – the Traditional had managed it while adapting to changing conditions. This was vegan food for working people.

Nobody should have been surprised at the success of King Harry's, as in the past meat had been a luxury for most families, and veganism was a logical development for the old revolutionaries. The Levellers and Diggers would have expected today's wealthy society to have erased animal cruelty by now, and probably been stunned to discover that the slaughter had actually increased.

Tanner sat down, the morale-boosting smell of his breakfast soon floating through the hatch, and he cradled his mug of tea when it arrived, sipping at it while he waited, looking again at the photos lining the walls – an assortment of boxers, footballers and soldiers. He focused on a man in a Second World War uniform, a relative of the owner he supposed, a friend maybe. The eyes were steady, but at the same time sad. He was a bull of a man. A human horse. Another traveller through life. No more than bones under the soil now. A plate was placed on the table in front of him, the food piled high. There was no need for unnecessary thinking.

It took him twenty minutes to finish his breakfast and when he was done he sat back satisfied and full. The room was hot and steamy, condensation covering the windows, knives and forks tapping, Frank Sinatra singing in the kitchen. He had never been one for crooners, but had started to think of them in a different way, as a post-war gloss that did its best to cover the cracks in the minds of those involved, a clean-cut sophistication that was meant to mask the madness. He went up to the counter and paid, said goodbye to a busy Harry and left.

Tanner wandered off, full of energy but not sure what to do with the rest of his day, entered an area filled by small factories and storage units, garages where youths worked under cars while middle-aged men drank tea and smoked fags and offered advice, adjusting radios that swung from kitchen crooners to rockers to phone-in callers. He heard a loud voice arguing that the elderly shouldn't be covered by the NHS after the age of eighty, that it would be better if they funded their care privately. Another voice replied that those elderly people had been paying into the system their entire working lives and deserved respect, and what would he want to happen when he was old? The first voice said he would rather be dead than eighty and sick. Tanner had noticed the way the older generations were being talked about in the media, the amount of airtime the subject was given, as if living longer was a problem and these people had no feelings. He could imagine the stress such comments were causing.

He entered a more affluent area where the houses were bigger, their rooms busy with books and paintings, burglar alarms blinking above stained-glass doors, and from here he went into a tiny street where tropical plants grew in terracotta pots, and he didn't know where he was going, just wanted to walk to burn up his breakfast and not think about the things that were happening, the things he had done, followed his feet across a road and through more houses, eventually coming to a parade of shops, turning into a blocked-off side-street where market stalls sold cheap clothes and toys, kitchen utensils and trinkets, secondhand films, and beyond these stalls there were electronics shops and takeaways, the smell of cooking meat stinging the air, and he looked through a smeared window and saw a kebab loaf, beef patties on a grill, flesh pressed by a spatula, oil burning and fat bubbling, turned his eyes back to the street, eateries turning to sex shops, boarded-up windows, drawn-out promises, and there were girls up ahead leaning against walls and patrolling a derelict stretch of road where empty beer bottles stood on the kerbs and several cars crawled, faceless heads behind glass, condom packets on the cobbles under his feet.

The smells were different here, torn bodies rotting in cartons, petrol mixed in with piss, and he saw lorries loaded with children, their scared eyes peering out as they tried to stay upright and breathe the fresh air outside, and he glanced at the girls dressed in leather skirts and shoes, fishnet stockings and boob tubes, wiggling their bums as they approached cars, leaning down and stretching tight fabric tighter. He couldn't believe how busy it was so early in the day, thought of all those females locked up and routinely raped, the exploiters' needles loaded with antibiotics and hormones. Mothers screamed for their kids. They wanted to search for them but were restrained, left to mourn and go insane, drug dealers filling a new wave of streetwalkers with heroin.

The street turned to black and white, and he imagined horses straining, manure on the cobbles, boys used for their brute strength and left to die in the gutter when they were worn out and weak, bullied and castrated. He was dripping wet. The weather influenced everything, the transportation of cattle different in the summer to how it was in winter, and the circles of sex, birth and death kept spinning as he looked at a girl who couldn't have been much over fifteen or sixteen. There was a strong smell of chemicals in the air, every emotion but anger burned away. It was cold and clinical here, a place of vivisection. Blitzkrieg's 'Animals In Lipstick' played at full volume.

Little Michael Tanner was walking past a farm. There were rabbits in cages and he asked his grandad why they weren't in a field. Pop hurried him on, said a bad man lived there. It was only when he was back in London that Michael realised the rabbits would be killed and eaten. He felt guilty he hadn't tried to save them, but then there was that other time, when he was caught in a storm and the same farmer had taken him indoors and his wife had fed him, and he'd wondered if good people could kill animals as well as bad people. What did they do with the heads?

When a girl approached Tanner he asked her age, what she was doing here, said she reminded him of a frightened calf. She stepped back, startled at first, sneered and blew strawberry bubblegum in his face and told him to piss off, what was he, some sort of looney, and he said no, he just loved animals and hated to see them hurt. Her eyes widened and flecks of mascara fell on her cheeks as if they were teardrops, except they were black and dry and melting on her sweating skin, and she told him to fuck off, started shouting. Who are you calling a fucking animal?

She didn't understand. He hadn't made himself clear. But it was important he didn't attract attention as the last thing he needed was the police turning up, and so he said sorry, he didn't mean to upset her, it was the last thing he wanted to do, there was nothing wrong with animals or the comparison, and he walked on, her voice fading into the background, and as he passed other prostitutes he saw mothers and calves with rings in their noses and those big pleading eyes that had made him want to cry in the past, and he heard the clack of hooves, the ticking of body clocks and the gurgle of sperm spurting from needles, the bang of bolts, electric currents, human grunts that made him turn and see the knife of a pimp.

He looked beyond the snarling face to takeaway cows and a couple of farmyard ponces – Ronald McDonald had a farm – this bad man with livestock cash wedged in his pockets next to his balls. Nonces liked their boys broken. Humiliated. Bulls turned to steers. Easier to handle. Homeless kids. Girls and boys. Taken from their mums. Broken cattle full of drugs. Asking for help. News of their children. He studied the castration knife being waved in his face. Tanner believed in staying alive. If he was starving he would kill and eat this pimp. It was important to shut this idiot up before the police came. He dipped inside his jacket and produced his own weapon. The pimp saw this and looked into his eyes for the first time, backed away, turned and hurried off, glancing over his shoulder every few seconds, speeding up.

Reaching a busy high street, Tanner saw a bus slowing down and ran to the stop, was soon on the top deck and leaving the area, and as he listened to the tinny grime on a kid's mobile in the back seats he wondered if he was the only person making these connections. People had to know what was happening to the animals. *Really* know. But the news stories linking the death of the slaughtermen and pig farmer remained vague. He looked at a billboard selling gin. Images were easier to absorb. The top of the board was moving and he realised there were maybe fifty pigeons sitting up there in a row, unseen by the people passing on the pavement down below.

John struggled to stay upright as one of his new pals pulled on his shoulders and pushed at his legs, forcing him to fall sideways onto a steel table. He had been caught off-guard, dreaming his way through the day in the easy-going way that was already his trademark, just hadn't expected this latest bit of rough and tumble. These two-legged animals liked to boss him around, blurting funny noises and knocking him in different directions, and even though they seemed soft and flabby he went with the flow, guessing they had his best interests at heart. Despite the strange things that had already happened he was positive. At two weeks old he could feel his strength building, and while he wasn't thinking of the future in the human sense, he was excited to be alive.

Left alone he would grow into a mighty bull and be admired for his power and presence, an important member of a tight-knit and loyal herd that would roam and reproduce. Not that he had any knowledge of sex. He was a child. Innocent and naive. As the seasons passed he would grow wise and protective, watch the sun rise and fall and feel it warming his body in the spring and summer, see the grass grow and pastures bloom and leaves form and fall. The days would become shorter and the nights longer. He would stand proud in the rain and snow, become a father and know the meaning of life.

While he carried the experiences of previous generations inside him, he was still doing his best to learn about the world, but hadn't expected this toppling-over lark. He was timid, a young boy, no more than a baby, and he tried to stand up, the man playing with him enjoying the game so much he didn't want to stop. John didn't mind some play fighting, enjoyed bumping into the other young bulls, but these humans were clingy, liked to wrap their arms around him, and this didn't feel right. The dread he had been suppressing started to stir.

John really wanted to believe they were his friends, but didn't like their shifting eyes, the grunts that turned to roars, the jerks and twitches that distorted their faces, yet they had to be looking after him and his mum and the others for a good reason.

He waited for the man to relax, slap him on the back and pat his head, and they would get going again, off to wherever they had been heading. John was impatient. He was starting to feel trapped. Claustrophobic. Still his chum insisted on playing this game and so he tried harder to heave himself up, couldn't manage it, wondered if something else was going on. He tried to turn his head, moved his eyes, wanted to see what was happening. His heart was beating fast. He was scared.

John was being restrained on a basic operating table by a man with huge hands, one of them on his neck and the other on his upper leg, the weight of his body pressing down so the boy couldn't move. John could smell rotting meat and sour milk on the human's breath. It was disgusting, but he was becoming used to the stink of the men and women he had met. They used perfume to mask the bad smells, but this only added to the pong.

The youngster's ribs were aching and felt as if they were going to snap. His lungs were being crushed. It was hard to breathe. He was starting to panic, made a big effort to get up, putting all his strength into this new attempt, trying to kick his legs, scrambling to get away from the man who raised his hand from John's neck and formed a fist and punched him hard in the side of the head. The boy was dazed, slumped to the table as the human adjusted his position and spoke to another man who had been standing nearby. John hadn't expected this violence. He was confused.

The second man stepped in close, reached between John's legs and touched his genitals. He couldn't believe it, felt sick, was unable to move his head, eyes at the edge of their sockets. What was going on? This wasn't right. All he could see was the side of the face of the person spread across his body – tight lips, a half-closed eye, heavy breathing. The second man pushed John's legs over and came at him from behind. Fingers grabbed his balls. The boy was shaking. Didn't understand. Wanted his mum.

The man about to mutilate John preferred surgical castration to using an emasculatome or elastration. He had employed the former at one time, used a Burdizzo, a large spanner-like tool that gave a bloodless castration but wasn't always effective. This meant double the work. On the plus side, the procedure could be carried out while the animal was standing, the tail raised over his back and the genitals exposed, the first testicle pushed down into the sac so he could get at the cord. Once this was visible he used the emasculatome to crush it, holding the clamp in place for around a minute, destroying the blood supply and nerves so the testicle wouldn't function. This process was repeated to ensure success. Once he had dealt with the first ball, he did the same with the second. He had made mistakes, used the emasculatome over more of the scrotum than was necessary, when really he needed to target the tubes. He wasn't keen on this method.

Another approach was elastration. He rarely used this technique, but had done in the past, gripping the balls and pulling them down in the scrotum, creating space between the testicles and the spot where the sac attached to the body. A rubber band was then placed around the top of the scrotum, between the groin and balls. Using an elastrator – castration pliers – he stretched the band with his hands and placed it on the instrument before releasing it in the right place. He needed to be exact. Those balls had to be hanging nice and low so the band cut off the blood supply and they dried up and died. He wasn't keen on this method either, as it could be fiddly and there was the threat of tetanus, and it should only be used on calves under a week old. He didn't like these bloodless techniques.

Removing the balls completely was more efficient and left him with a clear result. Job satisfaction was important. The castrator was good at his work and had carried out thousands of operations over the years, knew the standard required to ensure livestock wasn't wasted. He used a Newberry castration knife, which looked more like a pair of forceps. It was a nice bit of kit, well-thought-out and well-designed, a tribute to its inventor. A normal knife was dangerous. These were sensitive areas. The animals struggled and he could easily hurt his hand, or the blade might slip and cut the saphenous vein in the creature's leg. He didn't need complications. Time was money.

Holding John's balls, the man pushed them firmly towards his body, forcing them as far up as they would go, and once he had a solid grip he brought the knife into position with the blade open, placing it halfway up the sac. He squeezed the handles and John jolted and shouted out as the knife cut into his scrotum from both sides. Once through the septum the castrator pulled the Newberry down, dragging it away from the body, slicing the sac open. Blood fell on the table and was soon smeared across its surface. The open wound allowed drainage, something lacking in the other techniques. The man stood back and admired his work. The interesting part was still to come.

He didn't notice John moaning, was used to the effects of castration, but he did see that he was fighting, really struggling, seemed strong for his age, his workmate snorting keep still you little bastard, his feet slipping on the floor. John's attacker was angry, rearranged his footing and dropped his body back down, exhaling so that his weight was exaggerated. The castrator looked at the boy's bulging eyes and warned his friend to be careful, we don't want to kill him – not yet, anyway.

The castrator put the Newberry aside and flexed his right hand. Leaning forward, he slid two fingers into the incision, opening up the wound. The veins and tissue inside the sac were exposed and the testicles clearly visible. He moved a finger deeper inside, curling it around one of them in a pincer movement with his thumb and – making sure his grip was firm – pulled the testicle away from John's body, stretching the cord, making sure the tube was nice and taut and ready for cutting.

He didn't use any old blade for this part of the operation, reached for his emasculator, placed the crimper as near the body as possible before pressing the handles together and closing it on the cord. He counted the seconds, leaving it in place to avoid excessive blood loss. The emasculator was safer than a bog-standard knife, and he knew this from experience, slipping and cutting blood vessels and causing all sorts of damage in the past. These bulls were stupid animals, little more than children, but it was amazing how much they could bleed. A dead calf was useless. The company lost money and he would soon be out of a job. The cord was cut and he worked fast, pulled the testicle, ripped it from the boy's body.

John had never had a sexual urge, but knew his genitals were private and sensitive and shouldn't be touched by a stranger. The monster was squeezing hard, pushing his testicles upwards, pausing as the pain flooded his groin and raced into his belly. John was exposed. Helpless. He closed his eyes, trying to catch his breath, and then there was a cold sensation as a metal object was put on his scrotum and he could feel a new pressure followed by a sharp burst of pain and he realised he had been cut. He was terrified, his mouth frothing, pushed up again, for a moment sure he could break free, but no, he was fixed to the table, the monster pinning him down murmuring shhhhh.

The clamp was removed, but the pain remained. There was more fiddling as the man stripped skin back and slipped fingers into his scrotum, skimming his exposed testicles and the veins and tissue around them, his balls out in the open, the castrator squeezing, pulling, yanking them in the opposite direction. John was in agony and felt as if he was going to faint. There was more coldness, more pressure, and something snapped and the stretching sensation was replaced by the emptiness of amputation. He was bleeding and in shock and wished he could go to sleep, but the monsters hadn't finished with him yet. Not by any means. This was only the start. They were turning him into a bullock and a steer. A change of words. A neat and efficient neutering. Quack scientists swore this mutilation was humane. They told the wider world that the animals concerned hardly noticed.

The castrator dropped the broken testicle into a bucket, said a few words to his friend, who burped, the knife man muttering something else as John was covered in a meaty gas. His abuser continued, reaching for John's privates again and fondling his scrotum, pushing fingers back into the wound. John could smell his own blood, his lungs struggling to cope, and as they heaved he was aware of his heart banging inside his chest, the sound filling his head as the castrator tugged at his remaining testicle, pulling the cord tight so it creaked and was ready to burst and the cold returned and John felt the cutting of a tube and was left without his balls. Castrated, bleeding, broken – the calf lay panting on the operating table.

The castrator was satisfied. It was better to deal with these animals when they were young. There was less chance of complications. The smaller the better, as the operation was traumatic and there was no anaesthetic and a bigger creature would be hard to subdue. Nobody wanted to have their bollocks chopped off.

The company needed quick results. There was no time to waste. Castration was standard procedure, a basic management tool. Farming depended on efficiency, tight financial margins, total control of livestock. The strong had to be crushed. Desires either removed or in the case of studs exploited. The castrator reached for the antiseptic powder. Infection was a possibility. Flies and maggots could be a problem. His work would soon be finished.

The young bull's castration meant he would be easier to control as he grew up, which was important to those who would keep abusing him until his death. It was also meant to make his flesh taste better.

This was the beginning of John's short life. Different men would take him for another procedure soon, using chemicals to burn the buds that would have grown into horns. He would see his days out as a shadow of what he could have become. Eventually he would be separated from his mother and sent to a fattening shed. Not long after his first birthday John would be shipped to the slaughterhouse. A captive bolt was waiting. So was the knacker's knife. They were going to remove his head as well as his balls.

Stephen lifted the cappuccino to his mouth and took a sip off the top. The chocolate-sprinkled froth was smooth and perfect, but when he dipped past the milk to the coffee below he found it was still too hot for his sensitive lips. He placed the mug on the table at which he was sitting and raised his eyes to settle on Claudette, who was nibbling at a low-calorie blueberry muffin. She certainly didn't need to worry about her weight. Claudette was elegance personified – French, artistic, successful and stunning in black leather jacket and trousers, a pair of blue suede shoes with red laces. This was no cheap biker-girl gear, but the height of fashionable chic. The smell of treated skin merged with subtler doses of Chanel No 5, an erotic combination that set the manicured nails of Stephen's right hand tapping on the table-top.

They were enjoying a light breakfast next to windows that overlooked a small Japanese garden. Strategically placed rocks and freshly raked gravel led the eye to a golden Buddha, while snipped shrubs and bushes cascaded in from the sides. The statue was impressive enough during the day, but magnificent at night, when it was drenched in white light. The world's most exotic cultures filled the building's communal spaces, a series of themes easing the minds of the guests, many of whom were attracted by the bohemian nature of the hotel. International, multicultural, progressive – it appealed to the creative end of the corporate market. It was a perfect setting for the conference.

Those attending the event had arrived the previous evening, the majority making sure they were seen at the welcoming party held in the hotel's Green Planet Lounge. A band played gypsy tunes as wine and nibbles were served by staff dressed in traditional Slavic costumes. Stephen, marketing director for a major beef producer, and the man responsible for the award-winning *Beefy Boys* campaign two years earlier, had spotted Claudette the moment she entered the room. He was quick to make her acquaintance, an instant physical attraction escalating as he read and recognised her name tag.

Claudette was employed by a highly respected, quality-cheese manufacturer, and he was surprised to find that such a sexy lady was the brains behind the *Soft Cheese Means Soft Hearts* designs he had only recently held up as examples to members of his staff, a three-strong team he had later been forced to fire. Imagination and empathy were vital in the advertising game.

Stephen had always been a dreamer. He liked to keep his messages crisp and was a dynamic force able to link fragments and form catchy slogans and snappy one-liners, turning logic inside out as he subverted accepted wisdom and created new, more palatable truths. It wasn't all spontaneous genius – he had worked to develop his craft, watching and listening and realising that the masses wanted to be deceived. He pushed his mind to the limit so they would not have to worry. While it was important not to go overboard, it still amazed him when it came to the sort of stories people were willing to believe. He sold food and happiness, and in a brutal business like the meat industry it was essential to introduce light and colour and blend it with humour and warmth, at the same time using the animals themselves to achieve these goals. A big smile never failed.

A young bull was taken from its mother, held down and castrated, fattened up and stunned and had its throat cut so it could bleed to death, and then it was hacked to pieces and sold to the silent majority who looked at his beaming *Beefy Boys* images and actually believed these sad fuckers led happy lives. Stephen was proud of his achievements, the way he was spreading love and peace. He saw himself as a dreamweaver, the brains behind the bulls and the bullshit, a respected pro who greeted Claudette with one of his famous smiles that came straight from an advert, which she mirrored. It was a yin-yang moment. Zen-like. Stephen and Claudette were at the height of their powers.

If, as he believed, Stephen represented the strength and honesty of British beef, then Claudette captured the sophistication of the French and their magnificent cheese industry. Both these whizz kids were ambitious and loved playing to the stereotypes, yet they were also romantics with a shared love of the great surrealist painters and modern thinkers such as Damien Hirst and Tracy Emin. Stephen and Claudette were overflowing with ideas, and there had been an instant chemistry between the pair, a sexual energy they hadn't taken long to explore.

Stephen was a bull of a man, despite his oddly sensitive lips and fine nails, and confident enough to carry off any excesses without appearing brutish. He was proud of his manhood and certainly enjoyed shagging foreign totty, knew he was attractive to the opposite sex, his position within the industry something he exploited to the full. But Claudette was his equal, both as an artist and in the bedroom, her doll-like appearance masking a firm feminism that expressed itself in a liberated libido. They had only just met, but already seemed like the perfect couple.

Miles Davis was blowing in the background, taking his listeners in some free-moving directions Stephen didn't mind but couldn't say he really liked. The music of Miles, Bird and Monk was considered the epitome of cool in the creative circles in which he operated, so when he was in this sort of company he feigned a deeper interest. Claudette was a massive jazz fan, and he decided to increase the tapping of his nails and gently nod his head. She had explained last night, after the band had finished playing and they were enjoying Irish coffees on a cosy couch, how the jazz vibe masked a deeper rebelliousness. She sometimes felt as if she was tripping when listening to Miles, seeing herself as a small part of the fight against prejudice and superstition. She had drunk too much wine, but even so, insisted that hearing this music in such a lovely hotel proved that the black race had arrived at the heart of the white world. Now *that* was progress.

This morning they had woken early and – wrapped in each other's arms and bathed in light – had taken turns talking about their work and the freedom of expression they cherished, the rewards of creativity, the challenges ahead. Stephen had encouraged Claudette to explain the themes behind her *Soft Cheese Means Soft Hearts* work. He knew the imagery well – two cows standing by a rustic gate, glowing with contentment, features manipulated so they appeared faintly cartoonish, enormous smiles filling their faces, love swelling up and lighting their eyes, the masterstroke the addition of headscarves. Polka-dot material topped each head, making them look like milkmaids from the Fifties, and yet the scene was also totally modern and original – fair, democratic, verging on the futuristic.

Claudette spoke for a long time, going into great detail about the fonts and colour schemes she had considered, rejected and finally chosen. The slogan suggested community, a link between species, shared respect, but it also pointed towards healthy eating, a greener sort of existence. She talked about notions of mother-hood and feminism, the bond women would feel with these two liberated worker cows, the tenderness of men for their mothers and sisters, and all the while children could see the innocence of the animals and extend this to the cheese itself. She had tears in her eyes as she spoke of the love she felt for these creatures, and

Stephen was momentarily confused as they ran down her cheeks, wondering if she knew what she was saying, but decided it was the brilliance of the campaign making her cry.

The idea that she could believe her own advertising was bizarre, but she *was* French, possessed the sort of flamboyance and flair he lacked. Her confusion reflected a strand of creative madness. He loved the accent and the seriousness of her words. She was a complicated lady, but above all thoughtful and caring.

Claudette wasn't one of these self-centred people who rambled on about themselves for hours, and she wanted to hear about the *Beefy Boys* campaign, which she adored and knew differed from *Soft Hearts* in its clever use of an edgy sort of humour. Stephen was eager to talk about his own work and began by explaining the nature of bulls, that they were proud and powerful animals, and as such were seen as a representation of masculinity in its most basic form. This was appealing, but people also felt threatened by what were essentially brutal beasts, so he'd had to cut back on this element without making them appear weak. He was able to link his work with that of the men who physically castrated these creatures, and he pursed his sensitive lips and tapped his face with his perfect nails and winced at the thought of having his own testicles removed.

Claudette giggled and lowered a hand and softly squeezed Stephen's balls. He ignored the invitation and continued, running through the thought processes that had led to his triumph, high-lighting last-minute alterations and finally the award he had won and the generous bonus received.

Sitting downstairs together now, with the enlightened face of the Buddha looking out over a gravel ocean, he felt fulfilled. Reaching for his cappuccino he tried again, always surprised by the sensitivity of his lips. They seemed to belong to another sort of man, a pansy or a sissy, but he had come to imagine them as symbolising his gentle nature. On the outside he might appear brash, but really he was kind and forgiving and had never caused anyone any harm.

The coffee slipped easily down his throat and he thought about the statue, recognised the irony in the management's choice. Wasn't the Buddha a passive man who rejected possessions and preached vegetarianism and wandered the land as a beggar? This was a five-star hotel. Dedicated to the rich and powerful. Yet there had been a tramp begging outside when Stephen arrived – dirty and smelly, the man's hair was matted and he spoke in long, roundabout sentences as the *Beefy Boys* creator tried to pay the cab driver. Hotel staff came and moved the vagrant on, but Stephen was still mildly irritated by the intrusion. The tramp needed to have a haircut and a bath and find himself a fucking job.

Claudette was watching the English beef. He had strong features, a firm chin and good cheekbones, and she was sure he would produce strong children. Not that she was looking to become a mother. The opposite was the case. She had her career and looked down on those who produced endless offspring. Women had fought hard for their liberation and she wasn't going to throw it all away. However, she hoped this liaison with Stephen would develop. He was successful and obviously wealthy – as she herself was – and that was a massive turn-on.

She was also impressed at how closely their artistic interests matched. The English were a basic people, a nation of bulls and bulldogs, yet this one appreciated the superiority of the French, Italian and Spanish cultures, knew the art of Picasso, Matisse and Dalí, saw the individuality in Warhol's mass productions and Hirst's work with cows, calves and formaldehyde. She was deter-mined to develop this latter concept in the future, to bring it into one of her projects. It was cold and cruel and brilliant – a strangely soulless work for an Englishman to produce.

Once they had finished their breakfasts they took the lift back to Claudette's room. Living the good life and in the peak of physical condition, they enjoyed their bodies to the full, a man and woman free from political and religious restraints, and as Stephen bonked Claudette he watched in the mirror at the side of the bed, loving her tanned skin and black hair, but more than anything admiring his balls and what he could see of his cock, and he knew Claudette was peering into the glass as well, guessed she was in awe of his crown jewels, but really she was focused on her breasts and the way they aroused Stephen, loving the control she had over her destiny, the choices she was able to make in a modern world where she would never be dominated like all those females who had gone before, all those poor bitches who had been exploited and driven into depression by the evil of men. She wanted the world to share her liberation. The oppressed needed to stand together and unite against every last prejudice.

When they were both satisfied, Stephen arranged the pillows and laid back so Claudette could rest her head on his chest. The first talk was due to start in an hour, but the conference was more about making contacts and consolidating existing networks, even though there were several speakers worth hearing. It was a chance to see familiar faces and discuss changes in the industry, pick up and pass on information. Stephen and Claudette were respected by their peers, and both had noticed the admiring glances at last night's drinks party. They were stars in their fields.

Stephen wondered if he should ask Claudette about her life out-side of work, learn about her family and friends, but he wasn't really interested and for her part she hadn't even considered the idea. Their conversation returned to marketing strategies, slogans and photographs, the software that could improve pictures, human inventiveness, and as they spoke their artistry started to merge and before long they were bouncing ideas off each other and talking about a collaboration, and for some reason they found themselves focusing on Claudette's discarded jacket and trousers, the blue suede shoes that Elvis sang about, and as their brains began moving through the gears instant associations appeared as if from nowhere and suddenly they were outside the limits of meat and dairy and studying the unity of male and female in the form of leather and suede which came from the animals they worked with every day, and they were considering the market and the money that could be made and finally a new anti-fur protest that had been in the news two days before.

The hypocrisy of the protesters was ridiculous and angered these hip young gunslingers. Most people wore leather without a second thought, but for some reason turned their noses up at fur. The campaign had made a splash, which was a surprise given the protest group's limited funds, the masses disgusted by images of skinned animals and blood-splattered models. Stephen couldn't admire those responsible as the pictures were crude and obvious, straightforward reflections of reality. Where was the craft? Where was the challenge? It was much harder to turn the violence of the meat and dairy industries into upbeat, feel-good art. The anti-fur lobby was mean-spirited, lacked imagination and class. Claudette found the campaign extremely childish.

Stephen and Claudette knew they could change these negative perceptions and transform the pro-fur case. The money was sitting in the accounts of the current manufacturers and every firm looking to invest in a new, potentially lucrative market. A fortune was waiting to be claimed and they considered the marketing that had failed to convince people to eat more duck and deer, but if proof was needed that anything was possible they only had to look at the way meat and dairy had been separated. And wasn't there a clear link between meat production and the leather industry? Yet people accepted the lie that it was a mere by-product. These were incredible achievements.

They were energised by this stream of consciousness, exhilarated by the belief that they could see off the *Fur Is No Fun* brigade. They would have to connect the rock 'n' roll rebellion of leather and its inherent masculinity with the femininity of fur, while also admitting the former's attraction to women and the latter's appeal to men. It was a tall order, but if anyone could pull it off...

Stephen began pumping out slogans – *Leather Loves Fur, Tough But Gentle, Soft Fur Forever* – while Claudette stirred up images of grinning foxes and foxy ladies and stockinged models draped in hides, and she was quickly into her stride, adding a Harley-Davidson, Stephen joining the party, humming uplifting snippets of Bill Haley and Clash songs. But they mustn't forget the high end of the market – Chopin playing as a ballroom danced, every woman draped in fur... *Classic Furs, Classical Furs, Slow Fur Waltz* – and then there was the fetish corner – men dressed head to toe in fur, locked inside cages, zookeepers throwing them scraps of rotten meat, slices of mouldy cheese.

They were laughing so hard that Claudette thought she was going to wet the bed. They reined their imaginations in, concentrating on the mass market, the need to make fur as sexy and as popular as leather. That would be their aim.

It wasn't long before Claudette was pulling on her leather jacket. Stephen mounted her from behind, running his hands over the treated skin, telling himself that she really was a dirty cow, reaching for her breasts and telling her she needed milking, and Claudette laughed at this funny man and reached between her legs and grabbed his balls and squeezed, glancing towards the mirror near the bed, tightening her grip and making him yelp, relaxing it as he was slowing down, his hands clasping her breasts so hard she had to tell him to stop hurting her, and he did as she said and apologised.

They watched themselves in the mirror, which was framed by steel and more like a widescreen TV, Stephen and Claudette performing on a stage, strutting along a catwalk, riding high on success and adrenaline and great waves of freedom and the knowledge that they could do whatever they wanted in this fantastic life of theirs. Nobody could stop them – the *Beefy Boys* stud and *Soft Hearts* mademoiselle... This dazzling pair of *Tough But Gentle* untouchables.

The lorry was doing a steady sixty miles an hour, staying inside the speed limit, gliding on the sort of highway every long-distance trucker loved. The road was straight and clear, its surface smooth and jet black, the lorry's lights slicing through the darkness and illuminating the white lines that acted as guides. The driver was singing along to a Country standard. He was a travelling man doing a tough job. A rugged character. Down to earth and honest. He was prepared to work hard for his dough. For his family. Who loved him. There was chicken soup in a flask, part of a picnic his wife had made that included ham sandwiches, salted crisps and chocolate biscuits. He wouldn't be stopping. Had to keep moving. Would rather eat and drink in the cab. There were four cans of Coke in a padded cooler. He had a big plastic bottle for when he needed the toilet. Once he was on the road he liked to get from A to B. Truckers were real men and didn't muck about. Direct and to the point. He had transported lots of animals over the years and enjoyed the late-night runs. There was a magic about the open road when it was dark, but there was also the need to make good time. He was a realist as well as a romantic. The job could wear a guy down at times. It demanded concentration. Sleep was disrupted. But he was on top of his game. In control as he sailed through an empty land, skirting the sleeping towns and cities, the narrow little streets where low-watt bulbs nursed the dreamers, nine-to-five workers stuck in their routines. The peace engulfed him on these jobs, the motorways stretching into the distance as if they were drifting into another dimension. At times he felt as if he could keep driving forever, only had to press his foot down on the accelerator and hit eighty and leave his commitments behind. In his cab he was king. Raised up high. Sitting pretty. A lawless trucker with the security of a wage and home. He was missed. Returned a hero. The cab was comfortable. Nicer than the container. That other dimension. Hidden away and not to be thought about. Unimportant. If he didn't drive this lorry, someone else would. The air was close and humid in the trailer and the lambs swayed as they tried to stay on their feet, the slightest jolt magnified. The driver was singing his head off, saw that he had hit sixty-five and touched the brake, didn't want to end up with a fine. He had the company to think about. Back within the speed limit he relaxed. One song had ended and another was starting. The story of a lost love. The lyrics pulled at the driver's heartstrings and made him think about the meaning of life.

JUST LIKE SHEEP

THE PEOPLE WERE marching. Tens of thousands had come into the centre of the city to show their rejection of government cut-backs and the obscene profits being made by big business and the banks. Many carried placards that read *People First!* The masses were being exploited and deserved better. Their rights had been hard fought for by previous generations, but now they were being stripped back. The general public had become apathetic, bought off by empty promises and easy debt. It was time to wake up. The slogan was also being chanted. Signs jigged up and down and side to side – *People First! People First! People First!*

Tanner stood next to the statue of a general as the protesters passed between government buildings, oblivious to what was going on inside their towering walls. Black windows dotted the white stone, the rooms perfect for surveillance cameras, electronic eyes set back from the glass. Still and moving images were recorded. Spotters trained their lenses on individuals. He lowered his face. Laptops worked their magic. The Apple logo glowed inside a darkened room used as a centre of operations. Pictures had become stronger than words. PR bods sat in soft chairs drinking lattes and reflecting on events. The authorities were progressive in their approach. The images would be studied, edited and presented to the public, used to tell a story and influence opinion.

How many of these protesters knew that a nearby hotel was hosting a two-day conference for the meat industry's propaganda wing? Would more than a handful care? Tanner had sat in the hotel's cafe sipping coffee, flanked by men and women who spent their working lives covering up animal abuse, a Buddha statue nearby, the vegan Siddhārtha Gautama looking on. It said a lot about a society when extra security was considered unnecessary for such a gathering. He'd just strolled in and ordered. The expensively dressed, manicured scum surrounding him were as responsible for the murder of animals as a slaughterman. Maybe more so. Gary Clail's 'Beef' boomed. How low *could* these professionals go?

The *People First!* protesters marched on leather and he couldn't take them seriously. Waving signs and chanting slogans meant nothing when they were wearing another creature's skin. If they wanted genuine change they should get rid of the leather. Give up meat and dairy. He had been on a handful of marches in the past and felt like an outsider, unable to accept the contradictions and lose himself in the group-think. Mind you, he'd been at the poll-tax riot in Trafalgar Square that helped bring down Thatcher, had enjoyed rampaging through the West End as the hamburger and chicken chains were targeted. Animal rights had become part of the bigger picture for a few hours, but then they had been put back in their box. He was determined to wake people up.

Years later he'd attended a pro-hunt rally, nervous there might be a mind-reader present or someone from his Mickey Moo youth. The hunt supporters had been given a dose of their own medicine when the police got stuck in, and this had cheered him up, although not as much as their outrage. He had gone into a pub near Parliament and stood at the bar enjoying their anger. When a man came in dressed as a fox the mood eased. He was wearing a furry romper suit with gloves for paws. The drinkers cheered. Tanner had got talking with a woman in knee-high boots and a riding hat. She carried a crop and talked fast, assuming he shared her views. He was happy to nod along, but when she started flirting he said he was going to the toilet and slipped outside.

Working men had marched here in clogs and flat caps and demanded better wages and working conditions. The suffragettes stood up for those who were denied their rights on account of their sex. Men and women had fought to get the vote, linked by class. The masses showed their opposition to war, nuclear weapons, discrimination, attacks on the welfare state. And vivisectionists had protested for their right to experiment on animals. More than a century earlier medical students and their supporters had rioted in Central London. The *People First!* signs were gathering together.

His liberal democracy demanded tolerance and non-violence,

and so the people carrying these placards were calling for changes in a dignified yet vociferous manner. Most of them channelled their anger. Some banged drums and blew whistles. Others had spent time visiting joke shops and were dressed in amusing costumes. One man walked on stilts while a woman juggled balls. Adults pushed prams and scooters. There were hobgoblin and jester hats. A clown carried a huge teddy bear.

An amplified voice reminded the crowd that they had to fight to protect their *human* rights. Cyclists leaned on mountain bikes worth hundreds of pounds and listened carefully. Some used the latest iPhones and iPads to record the speaker. Couples rocked on the soles of hiking boots. Small rucksacks sat on their backs. There were a few signs that supported communism. Others looked to anarchy, believing that a common decency would flourish once the state was toppled. The crowd was united. They believed in equality and justice. The love flowed.

Police ran to block the path of a group that was breaking away from the main march. They were outnumbered but had helmets, padding, shields, truncheons and pepper spray on their belts. The protesters at the front pushed forward, caught up in the moment, although some were dressed in black and had covered their faces. Cameras were raised to record the clash. Hundreds of hands hung in the air, monitors replaying events a few yards in front of them, and Tanner looked at this bizarre sight and understood that everything was about the spectacle. A Guy Fawkes mask gleamed.

These recordings would be uploaded to YouTube and watched across the world. Angry comments would be added by keyboard revolutionaries. The protesters wanted to show some police brutality, a loss of control by servants of the state, outbreaks of violence that would expose the authorities as fascist. Bottles were thrown. The sound of glass smashing added to the soundtrack. A window was broken. A pixie set fire to a bin. A smoke bomb puffed pink clouds into the air and these drifted and hovered when they reached the walls of the buildings. There was a light in the sky and Tanner heard a helicopter. Chopper coppers watched the ants down below, relayed information and gave directions.

The hacking of the helicopter blades filled his head and drowned out the shouting.

The police had their own cameras. Officers stood behind shields recording over the shoulders of those who were holding them, zooming in on individual faces. He could see others working from the rooftops. CCTV did its job. The black windows looked on. There was no hurry. Early-morning raids would be carried out and convictions secured. Those who didn't break the law but held suspect beliefs were kept in mind. The system was working well.

When the speeches ended the crowd was going to break up and people would feel hungry, excited by the range of food available in the nearby streets. This was a globalised city and the world's cuisine was on offer, from the most exclusive fish and steak restaurants to the cheapest pizza and kebab counters. If Tanner had told them they were hypocrites and should leave the meat alone he would have been met with anger. How could he worry about animals when human beings were being exploited? He watched the crowd. People first? They had always been first.

There was a pub not too far away called The Lamb And Flag, one of his favourites in the West End, and he walked for ten minutes and went inside, a large painting at the far end of the bar showing how public houses and churches crossed over. A lamb stood next to a knight. The English flag flew as William Blake's pre-industrial land filled the background. Tanner ordered a pint and stood alone. The Lamb was surprisingly quiet and he felt deflated, wished he was at home, that he could stop thinking about the self-deception and cruelty of his fellow citizens, silence the words driving him mad.

It was said that the people were just like sheep, did what they were told because they were stupid. If one of them didn't conform they were the black sheep of the family. A child was as innocent as a lamb. An older woman who dressed in a younger style was mutton dressed as lamb. Then there was the Judas goat that sheep mistook for one of their own, humans using them to lead their flocks to their deaths. This goat was named after the man who betrayed Christ. Lambs to the slaughter... These goats were used to control cattle as well. Then there was the Judas steer which, like the goat, was castrated. And weren't hormones sometimes injected into the females so they were constantly in heat? An added attraction invented by nonces. More meat-industry perversion. A young goat was a buckling, renamed a wether when he was castrated. Tanner drank half of his pint.

When humans said language separated them from the animals it was meant to show superiority, but words were manipulated, their meaning distorted. Censorship was constant. External or internal, it didn't matter. Language was turned inside out. The words spoken out loud were often different to those that were not. The ability to deceive was also a means of survival. Where censorship and compromise merged and became a lie he did not know. People accepted the official line as they needed rules to obey. It meant they didn't have to think or worry, were more than happy to accept those PR images of frolicking lambs, playful pigs and contented cows.

How could anyone talk about peace and love and ignore the killing? How could there be a political party that refused to confront the slaughter? Lambs were linked to Christianity, but when it came to the meek Buddhism and Hinduism were way ahead of the Semitic religions. He thought about the Buddha statue and where it had ended up... vegan Siddhārtha... vegan Jesus... vegan laws warped and turned into kosher and halal slaughter... the poll-tax riot... factory farming and the cheap meat it produced... a British animal-liberation tradition that had been battered by a new form of materialism... its anti-viv and vegetarian factions airbrushed from history.

Despite everything he still believed that he lived in a nation of animal lovers. The spirit had been dented but not destroyed, and there was always a fresh wave of youth arriving. Young people were talking about veganism. And in the mainstream, not out on the margins. He was tugged back to his own youth. But nothing had changed when it came to the battle itself. It was there in the music, Propaghandi pointing out that meat was still murder and dairy still rape in 'Nailing Descartes To The Walls'. Fucking René Descartes, the great philosopher who said that you could nail an animal to the wall and it wouldn't feel pain, and even now there were politicians denying that non-human animals were sentient. He patted the brochure inside his jacket, taken from the hotel. Descartes would have fitted in nicely with the speakers listed.

One day meat and dairy would be outlawed, but it wouldn't happen without a fight. There were more and more vegans, yet the streets were full of restaurants that depended on animal flesh, and most people wore leather. The drink was darkening his mood, but he finished it anyway and left The Lamb And Flag, started walking and came to a square where a small crowd had gathered to continue their earlier protest. Mild-mannered souls were doing their best.

He saw a unicycle and watched the teenager riding it, hands outstretched as she circled friends who were setting up tents. The stilt-walker from earlier was wobbling and looked exhausted. There were two young men wearing black top hats and an elderly couple carrying a trowel and small apple tree. One boy set up a speaker and released a strange, sonar-like sound. Tanner went over and discovered that it was a recording of whales talking. He was glad he'd bumped into these eccentrics.

His bus home was near enough empty as it moved along the Embankment and crossed the river, three lone travellers joining him on the top deck at a terminus, and he was already halfway back, rumbling through mansion blocks, street lamps merging with the lights above his head. He pressed his face on the glass and thought about his life and what he was doing and sunk down, couldn't believe what was happening, had to fight and survive, made himself replay his chat with Ella when he'd phoned her yesterday, wished he could join Tony and the other drinkers in The White Hart, and he returned to Norfolk when he was with Kate, tugged back by sketchy reports on the McKenzie death, the lyrics of the Subhumans' 'Pigman' making him strong. It was true – farming was his living and killing was his crime. Where *did* these meat men draw the line? But it was important to concentrate on routine matters and keep his thoughts under control.

As soon as he got indoors he would open a bottle of lager and put on some music. The old reggae men knew the score. A proper

Rastafarian was always vegan. He wasn't an expert on Ital food, but could make a decent meal, or at least one that made his mouth water. First he would put the kettle on. Next heat a saucepan of water and add creamed coconut and Caribbean seasoning, stir this up and add rice and a tin of gungo beans when it started to bubble, turn the heat down and allow his beans and rice to simmer. Putting dry soya chunks in a bowl, he would soak these in boiling water from the kettle. Heating sunflower oil in a frying pan, he'd fry a chopped onion and a tin of sliced pineapple, drop in the fluffy soya chunks when they were ready, mix in two or three spoons of jerk. Near the end mushrooms and green pepper would be added. These had to be crunchy and couldn't be overcooked. He had bottles of hot sauce, but the jerk was spicy enough. Thinking about it, he had some Caribs in the fridge. Maybe even a Jamaican patty. All that was missing was Wendell's callaloo, but there was a tin of that in the cupboard as well.

Four youths came upstairs and sat at the front of the bus, breaking his concentration. They swore and jostled each other, displaying new trainers, jeans and shirts. A mobile played a song he didn't know but liked, seeing how it tracked back to dancehall and the original toasters. He couldn't make out the words, wondered which way it went in terms of the lyrics. One youth was talking too loudly about a fight with a boy and sex with a girl, and maybe he saw himself as oppressed, a poor kid taking what he wanted. If he was treating his own kind like shit he was the same as those at the top. Tanner looked at the clothes and technology and thought about the millions across the planet who had nothing. It was another PR job. More drama. There was always an excuse.

The youths were soon on their feet and thumping their way downstairs, strutting across the road to a parade of shops where three takeaways stood in a wonky row, their windows plastered with adverts for fried chicken, pitta stuffed with lamb, buns spilling slabs of beef and cheese, pizzas piled with salami, pepperoni and a choice of twenty other toppings. There were lots of special offers, pictures to help the people choose. Polystyrene containers and cardboard boxes formed a heap around a bin.

The bus continued and he saw film posters stuck on top of each other, faces peeling and replaced by brighter stars, remembered how excited he'd been going to the cinema as a boy, sitting on a plush velvet seat overwhelmed by the size of the screen and the boom of the soundtrack, and he still marvelled at the genius of a director who let the cinematographer and editor and the rest of the team create a story that would always match good against evil. A series of flickering stills raced into each other and blended visions with reality, these living dreams drawing huge crowds to the movies, the pictures, the flicks.

He passed a town hall that had been turned into an arts centre, one of the many in London that served newly arrived wealth and nobody local. A century before, hundreds of workers had come to hear a Swedish lady tell them the truth about vivisection. Student hecklers were removed. She'd gone undercover in a university and seen the torture of dogs first hand. The council of the day was radical and socialist, erected a statue of a brown dog above a water fountain. After the pro-vivisection riots in Central London, the same mob had tried to smash it up but were given a hiding by the locals. This was a time of poverty. A few years later another sort of council demolished the fountain in the middle of the night.

Tanner's stop was next. He stood up and rang the bell, went to the top of the stairs and saw himself on one of the CCTV monitors. He was fuzzy. Silent. A digital ghost. His face had melted and he felt his legs buckle, grabbed the railing and stayed on his feet. He was sweating. His chest heaved. The image fizzed and vanished, replaced by a shot from the lower deck. He liked to travel on buses and had done nothing wrong. The driver began to slow and he started down the stairs.

I was a little girl taken from her mother and locked in a shed with other frightened children, and when I was old enough to become pregnant evil men led me to a stall and raped me. My first child was a boy. He was snatched after a few days and I was frantic as I tried to save him, but there was nothing I could do. The people who drank the milk I had made for my son didn't seem to understand. My abusers pretended they were kind and caring, swore that I was happy in their special home, but they kept on raping me and taking my children. Grown up and older, I still mourned for my mum, who would be dead; my sons murdered or sent in crates to be tortured and butchered abroad; my daughters killed or living like me; a father I never knew. I was depressed and obsessive, in constant pain, wished I could die, but one magical morning I came out of my nightmare and was free. I found myself inside a human body and was able to walk on two legs, but I could smell my milk on the breath of the people I passed in the street, saw the skin of my children on their backs and feet, and was furious. For the first time in my life I felt powerful. I told myself that the truth was too horrific to suspect, that these people weren't wicked, they just didn't know what went on. I was learning fast, realised that none of this could happen without propaganda. Sickly childish, sadistic lies... I saw myself in shops and magazines and on TV. Everywhere I looked I was smiling. These adverts were mocking me and the professionals responsible were cocky, which meant they were easy to find. I knocked on a door. Swore two of them to silence. Admired the luxury of a five-star room.

Michael waited outside the shops where Piggy stopped to buy sweets on his way to school. He was nervous as he stood on a raised platform, his hands on the railings in front of him as he watched the path that ran through a stretch of grass and trees. The boys had become friends in the weeks after Michael stood in front of the class and told them about his time at Elm Cottage. This was mostly down to Piggy, who was excited to talk to someone who had stayed on a real farm, or at least an old smallholding. He had lots of questions that he kept asking. How many pigs could live in a sty? Would twenty cows fit in the barn? Was there a field where he could keep a horse and a donkey?

People liked Piggy. He was a gentle giant, naive and easy-going, never had a bad word to say about anyone, the direct opposite of

Barry Young, who was in the same class as Sam and Michael. Barry was always ready with an insult or a punch, depending on the other child's willingness to fight back. When Piggy saw him bullying someone in the playground he'd go over and place a hand on Barry's shoulder, tell him that it was nice to be nice. Barry was small and wiry, knew he would be no match for the Norton kid if he ever lost his temper. Piggy was only saying what he believed, but the effect was similar to a threat. Peace was restored.

Like the other children, Piggy had been amazed to hear about the white horse carved into a hill by soldiers, and he went to his local library to try and find a picture, which he did. The shape was as interesting as the size of the horse and that story about it coming alive at night. He drew it on a piece of paper and carried this around with him, showing his family and friends. While he was going to be a pig farmer when he grew up – there was no chance of that ever changing – he would like to have more horses. Maybe he would ride one around his land. He wasn't sure if he would use a saddle, wondered what the horse would prefer and how he could find out.

Michael had decided the shops were the best place to get Sam on his own and say what had to be said. He wasn't looking forward to this, but it would be wrong to keep quiet, to lie and see Piggy make a fool of himself, and he had to admit there were times when he worried that his new friend was a bit slow in the head, because now he knew the truth Michael didn't understand how anyone could not see what was going on. He didn't know how the killing was done, but thought the animals must be shot, and this made him angry.

He was still annoyed at his mum and dad for keeping quiet, and his teachers had done the same. If grown-ups lied about this, then what else were they lying about? They were the ones letting the killing happen, at the same time telling children to tell the truth and be honest. He hadn't spoken to his parents about this yet, but he would, after he had talked to Piggy, which was more important. Sam's dad had built his son a model farm out of wood. It had a house, sties, a barn, water troughs and fences. Toy animals filled it up. Was it possible that Mr Norton didn't know?

Piggy was on the other side of the road, strolling along as the sun shone on his face, turning the skin a brighter shade of pink. Michael could imagine him in the country, sleeping in one of the old sties when the weather was warm, up early and wandering along empty lanes, and if it wasn't for the traffic and concrete and his age he could have been on his way to work in the fields right now. Piggy spotted him and waved, waited for a gap in the traffic, the bag over his right shoulder bouncing as he hurried across. His smile grew as he approached the shops. Life was good, people were kind, and there was no such thing as death.

Michael changed his mind. He would keep quiet. It was wrong to ruin his dreams and things might change in the future. By the time they were sixteen or seventeen, farmers would only be keeping pigs because they loved them. A clamp was removed from his head. Piggy climbed the stairs and joined him on the platform, asked what he was doing here, did he want to come in the shop? Michael shook his head and made a decision. The pressure returned. He got straight to the point.

Farmers didn't look after animals in the way they had thought. Piggy asked what he meant. They kept them so they could be killed and eaten. Piggy didn't seem to hear him properly, took a step sideways and leaned on the railings, looked past Michael, replaying the sentence a couple of times before he replied. Why would they do that? Michael realised he hadn't said it right, had just blurted out the basics, and so he tried again, asked his friend what he thought was in a lamb chop. Piggy shrugged.

Michael said it was obvious – a lamb. It was right there in the name. Piggy thought about this and shook his head. Michael continued. Farmers killed their animals. Lambs, bulls, chickens, cows, rabbits. They killed them all. The pigs as well. Pigs? *Especially* pigs. They killed them and made them into bacon and pork pies and stuffed them inside sausages. Piggy's eyes closed. Farmers killed pigs so people could eat them? Michael nodded. It didn't make sense. How did they do it? How could they get a great big pig inside a sausage? Nobody could keep a secret like that. *Why?*

Michael admitted that he didn't know how they did the killing, thought they used a gun, and then they cut the bodies into pieces, chopped off the heads and arms and legs, and it wasn't even a secret, it was only children who didn't know. The reason the farmers did it was to make money. They were paid to hurt animals. He saw the expression on Piggy's face and talked faster. He didn't want Sam to end up the same way, shooting pigs and cutting their heads off. If he didn't know now he could end up becoming a farmer and it might be too late. What if the government forced him to kill pigs? Michael slowed down. He had only found out when he went to stay with his grandad. He was a good grown-up and didn't eat meat, and it was Pop who had told him the truth. He stopped talking.

Piggy was shaking. His eyes were swollen and tears seeped out. Michael didn't know what to say or do. None of this belonged to their world. Piggy wiped his face and stood in silence with his head bowed, then turned and ran down the steps and charged towards the road. Michael was frozen at first, called after him, began to follow, but Piggy was running fast, hardly slowed down as he went through the cars and into the houses on the other side. Michael was stuck on the kerb as the traffic picked up. Piggy was gone and he could only wait for him to come back. After a few minutes, he started walking to school.

It wasn't long before his teacher was asking where Sam Norton was today. She had seen him on her way in. Nobody answered. She thought for a bit, told the class to keep quiet and went out. Five minutes later she returned looking worried. She told them she had spoken to Mrs Norton and Sam had set off at his usual time. He wasn't the sort of boy who played truant. Mrs Norton was on her way to the school. They were concerned about Sam's safety and she needed to know right now if anyone here had seen him, even if it was before school started. Michael raised a hand.

Sitting in the headmaster's office ten minutes later, he found himself surrounded by three standing adults, two of them leaning over as they talked to him, the other trying to calm things down. Mrs Norton was telling Michael how bad he was to tell her son such terrible things, while his teacher was asking what on earth possessed him to upset Sam like that? Mrs Norton was angry. He knew how much Sammy liked pigs. All he ever talked about was being a bloody farmer. Why did he do it for God's sake? Michael tried to explain that he liked animals as well and didn't want Piggy – sorry, Sam – not to know that he was going to have to kill his pigs when he was older, but this only made Mrs Norton more upset.

The headmaster pointed out that at least Sam hadn't been abducted. He would come into school or return home in an hour or two and, after all, the boy had to find out some time. This seemed to calm Mrs Norton down a little, while Michael started to cry. His mum was called and she came to school and took him home, asking why he had told Sam about the farmers killing pigs and accepting his answer as logical enough. Later that day she spoke to Mrs Norton on the phone, but Sam still hadn't turned up and the call ended in an argument.

In the evening a policeman came to Michael's house and spoke to him with his mum and dad present. Sam Norton hadn't been found yet and they were extremely worried. Mr and Mrs Norton had started to fear the worst. Michael wasn't sure what this meant and asked, the policeman blurting out that anything could have happened – Sam might have jumped into the river, been attacked by older boys, or snatched by a pervert who killed children. Michael's dad swore and shouted that he shouldn't be saying this to a nine-year-old. The policeman apologised.

Michael couldn't believe there was so much badness in the world. The lying never stopped. It wasn't just animals that the grown-ups killed, some of them hurt children as well. It was impossible for him to sleep that night as he thought about what the policeman had said, and he imagined monsters roaming the streets looking for Piggy, and he said his prayers three times with Sam at the start of them, and this continued in the morning at school assembly when the headmaster spoke about Sam Norton and asked God for help. None of the children knew the reason he had gone missing, but Michael felt as if everyone was staring at him. He tried to think where Piggy might have gone, but didn't have a clue.

Three days passed and there was still no news. Searches were carried out, posters put up and appeals made. Divers checked a stretch of river and a nearby pond. He heard his mum talking on the phone, saying that the police had raided the homes of some men who liked little boys. Again, he didn't understand. If they liked boys then surely Piggy would be safe? Dad insisted Sam would turn up and that it wasn't Michael's fault he'd run away, but when he told Pop there was a long silence and he guessed he felt guilty as well. Then on the fourth day a tramp took Piggy into a police station in another part of London. He had been sleeping rough, not too far from the zoo, the man who found him giving him food and shelter and persuading the boy to return in the morning.

It was a week before Piggy returned to school. Mr and Mrs Norton didn't blame Michael now, knew he had wanted to help and not hurt their son. They were just happy to have him home.

Standing in the playground on his first day back, Michael saw Piggy come outside and look around, his eyes narrowing when he spotted him, and he was marching over with his fists clenched, the familiar smile replaced by a glare. Michael was going to get thumped and braced himself, thought that maybe he deserved it in a way, but when they were facing each other Piggy just said thanks for telling me.

It had been a shock, but he shouldn't have run off like that, had ended up sitting on a bench for ages as he couldn't go to school and didn't want to go home either, decided to visit the zoo instead. He wasn't going to be a farmer when he grew up, would do something else, maybe join the army like the old soldier who had helped him out, but whatever he did, one thing was for sure, he would never sleep rough again.

Michael realised that Piggy was gone. He looked and spoke differently. Sam stepped to the side and turned so the two boys were standing next to each other, facing the chaos of the playground. He said what Michael was thinking – look at them running around like idiots shouting their heads off, and that teacher watching is no different, telling us lies and letting pigs die and doing nothing. He hated them for this and Michael agreed, so do I, but what can we do? Sam wasn't going to think about it for a while, not until he was older. That old soldier who slept on the streets and had given him food didn't like people much either. That's why he lived in cardboard boxes, because of what he'd seen them do. He just wanted to be left alone.

Sam started walking across the playground, moving in a straight line, over to the far corner where Barry Young was twisting a girl's arm. She seemed to be crying. When he got there Sam punched Barry in the face and knocked him down.

Michael and Sam stayed friends. Some dinnertimes they would stand at the edge of the playground and watch the other children and barely speak, but usually they joined in a game of football. Sam had stopped smiling and became more of a loner as the time passed. Eventually they drifted apart, changed schools and didn't see each other again, and Mickey Moo and Mike Tanner would think back sometimes and feel sad, wonder what had happened to the boy who loved pigs, the kid known as Piggy.

I was a naive child walking with a man I thought was my friend, but really he was a nonce who held me down on a table while his paedo mate cut into my groin, opened me up and removed my balls. I cried and bled and wished I could run to my mum, but didn't know where she was. These perverts told the world that I was happy, yet insisted I had no emotions, that I didn't mourn or remember much. Within a year of being castrated I would be left brain damaged by a steel bolt, hung upside down and have my throat cut with a knife, but sometimes the good dreams come true and I escaped my nightmare and joined a dairy cow who reminded me of my mother. This made me emotional and I have to admit that I shed some tears. We worked together. Became one. The fact that the rape apologist was a woman made me uneasy, but she should have shown solidarity with her sisters, and when I thought about this properly it made her crimes seem twice as bad. I felt terrible, but had to continue as it would be sexist to make an exception. I didn't torture or rape her, which by rights I should have done to make my point clearly, but I was incapable of such perversion and would rather have killed myself. Even though the silent majority needed to see the horrors in a human context, I was better than her and said so. The castration and murder of young boys was another atrocity that needed to be exposed. The cover-up was blatant and the man in front of me was one of the worst offenders. He had pooed himself, which wasn't pleasant, and kept looking over at the rapist hanging from one of my hooks. He knew how the media worked and was a master of manipulation so I was interested to know what he thought of the camera I was using. I pulled a chair over and sat next to him, and because he was shackled I lifted the viewfinder up so it was level with his right eye. The fiend vomited and I only just avoided the spray. It was a disgusting way to behave in such an expensive room. I went to the window and looked into the night, thought of the Buddha and his code of non-violence and felt my legs wobble, but I stayed in control, had to finish my work before I woke up. This beefy boy should have been castrated for my photos, but the very idea made me feel sick inside. I was a better sort of man.

Mickey Moo sat in the Ford he had rented specially and waited. Tracking down the men he wanted had been a lot easier than expected. The fact he'd found them at all was a result. Knowing the name of the hunt and where it was based, he'd reasoned its core support would be local and had targeted the town and its nearest villages. Trawling their pubs on a Friday night, this was the ninth he'd been to, and as he approached The Stag he spotted one of the terrier-men through the front windows. There he stood with a jug in his hand, holding court as Mickey stopped to watch.

His mate was in the pub as well, part of a six-strong group of men who suddenly started laughing their heads off. Mickey searched for the farmer, but couldn't see him. Two out of three was good enough. It was nearly ten o'clock and he guessed they'd been drinking for a while, going on the way they were swaying and gesturing, and he knew the best time to ambush them would be when they left the pub. Give them a few minutes and bang. There'd be nobody about and their reactions were going to be slower than normal. Sitting ducks – he was the hunter.

These wankers had no clue what was coming next, their minds a long way from that quiet little lane where they'd kicked his head in. It was tempting to go inside and order a pint, stand quietly at the bar in a silent show of flamboyance, as they wouldn't remember his face unless he knocked a glass over or drew attention to himself some other way, were never going to imagine him having the nerve to walk into their local.

Unknown to Mickey they'd celebrated on the night of the attack, had a good session and entertained their friends by explaining how they'd pushed him into the ditch, going into detail as they described him rolling through hundreds of stinging nettles, adding yelps and high-pitched squeals for effect. The attack would be remembered as the day the police went missing and the hunt saboteurs got their comeuppance. Mind you, they were careful who they shared this with, as not everyone approved of fox hunting and they'd broken the law. They had paid a price as well, with one broken nose and two lost teeth to go with the bruises. The lad's reaction had made them think.

Mickey resisted his urge to go inside and returned to the car, moved it up the street and parked so he had a view of the pub doorway. He got out and opened the boot, took out his bag and sat back inside, placed it on the passenger seat. Unzipping the top, he removed a baseball bat and propped it up on the floor. This time he would make sure it was a fair fight. The bat was for back-up, as he was still facing two grown men, and there was no point doing this if he didn't win. It wasn't fair in the true sense of the word, seeing as he was armed and sober and they would be unarmed and pissed, but it was more even than last time. Fuck it, he didn't care. They wouldn't stand a chance.

The sign on the pub showed a white stag with huge antlers being chased by a pack of black dogs. In the distance behind them he could see the outline of a red man on a horse. Whoever painted the sign had put a lot of effort into the work. Even in the dark and faintly lit the stag was majestic. Humans saw the creature's beauty, but hunted and killed him anyway, cut off his head and nailed it to a wall, displayed those antlers as trophies. They would shoot the dogs when they became too slow for the chase, had castrated the horse when he was young and would sell him for dog food when he was old. These people were sordid fuckers. Real scum of the earth.

Living in a picturesque village, with a couple of pubs and a Norman church and a main street lined with beamed cottages, side-roads that it was safe to stroll along at all hours of the night with no muggers to fear, surrounded by beautiful countryside, he couldn't understand the bloodlust of the hunters and farmers. Back in history they had named this pub for a reason, though how many of the regulars outside of the hunt took any notice he didn't know.

Mickey waited. He placed a hand on his ribs, which were still sore, felt the rhythm of his heartbeat behind them strong and steady, eased back against the headrest and thought about Pop and how he used to tell him stories and was more like a friend than his grandad. The sky was so clear out here in the countryside and he had looked at it with Pop when he stayed at the cottage, used to love his science-fiction comics when he was a kid, those strange worlds full of stranger creatures that were somehow familiar, wished he could see a UFO and knew the West Country had its share. Since then he had read about pagans, hippies, Stonehenge, crop circles, spaceships and all the rest of it, but still liked the idea of living on Mars.

He wondered what a Martian would make of the human race – a proper alien and not one from the classic sci-fi films he watched, as these ignored the biggest crime being committed, every story ending with some lines of praise for quirky, imperfect, brilliant mankind. It was bollocks. A more advanced life form wouldn't be following a Hollywood script. They would look at the planet's farms and factories, the slaughterhouses and vivisection labs and bloodsports as much as they would disease, warfare and the inequalities of wealth. An advanced civilisation would know that life was fragile and time was precious. He couldn't imagine they would allow the slaughter to continue.

Something Bev had said was stuck in his mind. These men drinking in The Stag as if they had nothing to answer for could have kicked him to death. The reality had hit him as he was driving out of London. People were brain damaged by a single blow. A blood clot could have formed and worked its way through his body and into his head. He might have had a heart attack from the shock. These things happened, but in the aftermath he hadn't thought about it in the same way as he was now, his focus then on the injuries he could feel.

If he'd died in the lane he would never have had today or any of the days since, none of the years to come, and how would his mum and dad be feeling, and he thought of the future and the things he wanted to do. Painting and decorating was fine, but he had plans and wanted to work with the handicapped or elderly, go off and travel and see the world, meet his soulmate and settle down and have a house with a garden where he could grow vegetables and maybe make cider. The idea that he could be dead made him shudder. He reached into his bag and pulled out the Walkman he'd brought, slipped in a tape and filled his head with a punk sound-track, the words of Beki Bondage and Ian MacKaye.

A bit after eleven people started leaving the pub. He turned off the cassette and waited. The men he was after came outside half an hour later, stood talking for a few minutes before turning and going off in opposite directions. He hadn't expected this, for some reason assuming they would walk together. He had to choose. One was heading down the main street, most likely to the houses at the far end, the other was coming Mickey's way, passing on the other side of the road and walking towards a green. He would deal with him first, then catch up with his mate. It would be easier now that they had split up.

He watched the terrier-man in his rear-view mirror. Mickey felt his head tighten and accepted what Ronnie and Bev had said, that he was here for his pride, and what he was about to do was nothing more than revenge, but they didn't know everything. They were a different sort of person. It was his nature to act this way. The baseball bat felt good in his hand as he opened the car door and got out, and he was careful when he closed it, didn't want to make a noise and spoil the surprise.

If peace could ever exist on Planet Earth then Mike Tanner felt it would be in the botanical gardens he was about to enter. It was packed with plants and trees from across the globe – collected, grown and managed by the best professionals – and he had never been anything but happy here, his mind gradually clearing so he felt content and clean. Experts in horticulture and arboriculture dealt in cultivation and conservation, soil management and maintenance, design and landscaping. Nature, science and art merged. People studied and recorded, ran hothouses and art galleries and put on exhibitions. It had to be one of the best places to work. Showing his membership card at the gate he went inside, didn't think it mattered if you were a specialist or an allotment digger.

He hadn't been to Kew since last year, when he made a picnic and brought Ella. The gardens were thriving, and the fact they couldn't exist without constant love and attention only added to their magnificence. A lot of money was needed and the marketing could only ever be honest. There was nothing to hide. No cartoon packaging required. Positioned next to the Thames and protected on its remaining sides by brick walls and banks of trees, he saw the gardens as a condensing of wonders, a human vision where logic and order was imposed in a positive way, and while there was structure and organisation he knew he was finding sanctuary in a fantasy.

The deaths of two people in an upmarket London hotel had dominated the morning news. A man and woman had been hung upside down from cupboard doors and shot in the head. Their throats had then been cut. Photos of the killings and a letter from the perpetrator had been sent to the police and a national newspaper. These were being studied by the authorities and more information would follow. The pictures were too gruesome to show the public and the police were linking these deaths to the killing of a pig farmer and two slaughtermen. The letter claimed an animal-rights motive. The exact wording had not been released.

Connecting these latest victims to the meat and dairy industries was clearly ridiculous. These were educated young professionals who worked for respected companies, and both had been involved in some high-profile media campaigns. No rational person would see anything wrong in their behaviour, and they had a right to earn a living any way they chose. Creative, confident, dynamic, healthy, good looking and wealthy, they represented the cream of society. The killer's letter said that he had treated them as they had treated others.

The police had no solid leads, but were interviewing known animal-rights activists. One newspaper talked of a sinister underground group made up of fundamentalist vegans, a network of small cells trained in terror tactics, the fanatics involved quite prepared to cause criminal damage in the past. It was believed that only the vigilance of the state had kept them in check. But this lunatic had taken things to another level.

He had been labelled The Butcher by a tabloid journalist, and this had been changed to Bob The Butcher by a celebrity big mouth. The TV channels and radio stations were busy lining up their favourite commentators, and the name was repeated several times. An animal lover was being deliberately confused with an animal abuser, which was as predictable as it was pathetic.

That morning Tanner had sat by the kitchen window listening to his radio, drinking black coffee as the owner of Funhouse Foods defended the meat industry and his firm's reputation. Harry Spalding was a showman, loved the limelight and knew how to promote a hearty image, elements of the Farmer Giles stereotype mixing in with some Billy Big Bollocks, City-boy front. As the head of one of the country's largest meat suppliers he carried a lot of weight in both political and media circles. It turned out that Funhouse had employed one of the victims two years earlier. This made the killing *personal,* although Harry had never actually met the individual concerned.

Spalding's voice boomed as he made his points in a cheery

manner, but he had the ability to insult his opponents while appearing open-minded. He would sympathise with their views before dismissing them with some cutting humour, stirring good people to lose their tempers and appear irrational, and once they had cracked he would backtrack and make himself seem understanding and even vulnerable. The mainstream media loved Harry Spalding. They would have especially liked it when he made a direct appeal to the killer he was calling Bob The Butcher to give himself up.

Harry didn't understand how the death of innocent individuals was meant to achieve a meat-free society exactly, but he wanted to ask the listeners what sort of world it would be without pork pies, sausage rolls, hamburgers and a joint of roast beef? Perhaps the looney tunes responsible had forgotten how fantastic proper food tasted. If he was listening, Harry suggested he try some tasty lamb chops, but to make sure he chose the Funhouse Foods brand. And he laughed. The presenter joined him in this lightening of the mood. The sound filled Tanner's kitchen. Two cowards were sitting in a studio taking the piss, trivialising the suffering and mass slaughter of innocents.

The news reports were missing the point again and Tanner's head ached. Why hadn't the letter been released? Why were the images being suppressed? Well, he knew the reasons. How could people change unless they saw the murder of animals in a human context? Fragrance washed over him and he turned left, had to stop thinking and live in the moment, lose himself in the gardens.

A freshly cut lawn stretched away to his right and the smell of the grass replaced the scent of flowers. Gnarled trees stood to his left. He saw the deep ridges in their bark, pictured them being brought into the grounds a hundred or more years ago. He read the Latin names on the attached plaques and learned a little of their origins. He came to a badger sett, which was right by the path and not exactly hidden. There were no acid men looking to blind the badgers, no baiters to be seen, but those animals wouldn't know this and were reacting to the same peace he felt descending on him as he paused to look at the entrances.

Continuing, he came to another lawn, and this one had exotic grasses growing in the centre, a bulging bed that rose up in tiers. A faint breeze exaggerated the taller clumps, which bent forward and puffed straight and swayed sideways. He listened to the swish and guessed the pampas grass drew the attention of passers-by, but his favourite was a small blue species. Beyond the lawn a narrow glasshouse protected potted alpines, and after passing through it he came to the rock garden. He stood and watched a waterfall before following a path that dipped down between the rocks and boulders, and he thought of the labourers who had built this place and wondered if any of them were alive, and while their names weren't recorded on plaques it was a brilliant, private memorial.

Alpines pushed through gravel and flowed between stones, succulent leaves surreal in the sunlight, a few showing flowers. The gardeners dug grit and sand into the earth to protect their delicate roots from drowning, and he took his time, moving slowly, wondering what it would be like to trek in the Alps or Himalayas, and he thought of his cross-country trip at heights that were nowhere near those to be found in Switzerland and Nepal, but it had been a good time. He was out in the open. On top of his small world with Turner and Nash.

He reached an open space flanked by hedges, shrubs and flowerbeds, came across sculptures made from willow branches stripped of leaves and twigs and woven in and out of each other to form giant seeds and pods. He stood in front of an acorn that dwarfed him and tried to guess what the squirrels thought when they saw this feast. At the main lake he watched ducklings follow their mother as swans sailed past and coots dived. People stood on the bank and smiled. A boy of three or four shouted and stamped his feet, started towards three ducklings that had strayed from the water. Tanner began to move towards the child, stopped as the birds fast-waddled and flopped into the lake.

The boy needed to know that the ducklings were scared, thought they were going to die and were running for their lives, but he kept quiet, couldn't get into an argument. No harm was meant, he was just irritated by the parents who stood there grinning as if the child had done something clever. He had been excited to see the ducklings move and hadn't worked out that they were living creatures, but his mum and dad should have stopped him and explained. It was grown-ups fucking things up. What chance did the children have? Brainwashed from the start.

Tanner crossed the lake on a gently curving bridge, the granite walkway flanked by bronze posts, and he stopped halfway to peer into the undergrowth of an island where the ducks, swans, coots and other birds nested. The banks had been reinforced with rocks to stop them crumbling and falling into the lake. On the one hand humans were burning jungles and driving out the wildlife, while on the other they had created these gardens and an island refuge.

He left the bridge and followed the bank before veering left through pine trees and ferns, passed a pheasant shuffling next to hundreds of slug-eaten hostas, kept going until he was out in the open again, opposite a meadow that had been cut back, a section left for insects. Nobody was about. He sat down on the shorter grass, took his sweatshirt from around his waist and added it to his jacket to make a pillow. Lying on his back he shielded his eyes from the sun. It was hot and this added to his calm. Remembering he had a pair of sunglasses inside his jacket he put these on.

They meant he could watch the clouds – long threads of clever thinking, strands of insight he couldn't read because he didn't know the codes – and he studied the shapes and added faces, felt as if thousands of spirits were drifting along whispering their stories. If one day he could clear his mind for long enough he might be able to hear the colours and see the sounds like Kandinsky and Tchaikovsky, but he was carrying too much grief inside his head, in the depths but not deep enough to forget. Maybe the ducklings saw the boy's shouting as long splashes of paint. Jackson Pollock stamping his feet. Tanner knew it was guesswork. How could he know what another living creature really felt? It was all fiction. Daydreaming. An endless illusion. Empathy – that was real.

He listened to the birds talking in the trees, had read that once upon a time humans communicated by singing. The idea of men and women chirping and whistling was a nice one. Everybody loved music. The lyrics and storytelling. And closing his eyes he drifted, saw himself out in the open and running towards a wood, beyond the city walls that had been keeping him hidden and safe. He was exposed and in danger, changed his shape and raced down an abandoned path with ditches on either side, but these were spreading into a latticework of canals where chainmail frogmen lurked, and he was being chased by human-headed dogs, purple rat-girls spitting poison, bronze spiders and copper ants, and as he ran he saw the shadow of a steel-clawed hawk on the land, heard the chop-chop of chopper-copper blades. It was true what the radio said. These mutants had been built by Funhouse mechanics and released to hunt traitors like the vegan nutter who had turned on his own kind. The trees behind the ditches were flickering silver and white. It must have snowed. Zooming in he found millions of sheets of oven foil tacked to their trunks. There were runaways in the wood at the end of the path and he was being urged to hurry by pixie-looking children hiding in the ferns. One day these boys and girls would be teenagers and adults, grow old and return to the beginning, think in more innocent ways.

The people in the wood had been forced to sleep rough on greenwood streets, and he was breathing hard and stumbling and nearly falling, knew he had to stay on his feet and not tumble off the hill and the path and into the ditch. If he didn't stay upright he would be kicked to death – in the country or the city, it made no difference. He had to avoid the feeding frenzy, the stamping feet and electric shocks. Clammy hands reached out, trying to drag him into those nettle-rotten gutters thick with farmyard bones. The nonces were sniggering and snickering and sneering. They were going to poison, castrate, rape, murder, disembowel, decapitate, skin and dismember him like they did all the others they caught, and he realised he had to assume the nimbler form of a four-legged sprinter if he was ever going to reach the trees and the ordered gardens he loved. He had seen himself as a piglet, a calf and a lamb, but they had been brutalised and broken, so hobbled by fear they could barely move. He turned himself into a stag and sped away from the chopper coppers, but when he reached the trees he was too tall, his antlers were going to become tangled in the branches, and so he shape-shifted again and was a hare entering the wood, coming to an overgrown brick wall and squeezing through a tiny crack.

Tanner sat up and took his sunglasses off. He wiped the sweat from his face, stood and wandered into a hollow that was damp and empty of people, the way flanked by moss-covered stones. A smaller path led into a bamboo garden, the edges tight so he couldn't see what was around the corners. The bamboo grew in clumps or ran free, yellow canes drooping over his head, moving gently and in silence. There was a wooden building and he went inside, felt cold and trapped and left, sat outside and enjoyed another unique zone, breathing in the rich smell of loam, reaching down and taking a handful in his right hand and letting it slip through his open fingers.

There was a Mediterranean garden he liked and he retraced some of his steps to find it, reached a small row of cork trees standing in sand and gravel, continuing through to herbs such as rosemary, thyme and lavender – big bushes that filled the air with their scent. He sat on a bench and thought about Maggie and her allotment, knew she would be impressed and wished he could bring her here as he had done Ella. He lost himself in the setting, half an hour later walking to the Japanese gate with its three linked gardens dedicated to peace, activity and harmony. The planting was formal and he assumed Zen, and he sat on a stone seat and dismissed a comparison, looked at the raked gravel that represented water, using the scene to try and empty his mind.

The hours passed, and after a cup of coffee he visited the Marianne North Gallery, which was another of his favourite places in the gardens, the building packed with the paintings of a Victorian woman who had travelled and recorded the world. She had privilege and money, it was true, but he admired her greatly, wished he could have done something even a fraction as brilliant. After forty minutes he continued and went into the biggest of the glasshouses, climbed the stairs to the balcony, water spraying and dripping from pipes, the cooler air a relief when he went back outside.

There was an area near the rock garden that a lot of visitors missed, and his wonky circle took him back to an avenue lined with house-brick columns, railway sleepers balanced across the top. He was tired and sat on a bench, lifted his head and followed the longer beams running lengthways, fixed with cracked concrete and iron bolts. It was a rough construction, made from available materials, in the aftermath of one of the world wars he guessed, or at least during harder times. Whatever the truth it was different to the grand buildings, glasshouses and follies elsewhere, felt more like the Bell Street allotments.

Vines climbed the bricks, thick roots bulging at the base of each column, arms clinging to the lower levels as fingers reached towards the sun, tendrils spreading along the beams and forming a roof of partial shade. The leaves were green, red and purple, and would change again with the seasons. A gardener would sweep the leaves up when they died, build a huge pile where they could turn to compost and be used as a mulch, a scale of production that would send Bunny into orbit. He wished he could bring him here as well. Wendell too. Mr and Mrs Gupta. Pat and Sid. Tanner missed the allotments.

He sat here for a long time, as content as he could be, and when he heard human voices they were timid and seemed to be singing, and he wondered if he was dreaming again. His brain took a few seconds to adjust. Two figures stood by an arch. A boy and a girl were peering down the avenue. They were in their early teens, and when a smaller child appeared they moved apart so he could stand between them. A few seconds later they stepped forward to give a man and woman space. This family was tall and thin and thrilled by the climbers. Five frail humans gaped at the fine details of a canopy alive with butterflies and bees.

They didn't say a word. Didn't need to. Tanner was sure they were sharing their thoughts. They reminded him of ducklings as every few seconds a limb jerked as a new idea seemed to pass between them, and then they were glancing left and right, moving over to inspect some nearby roses.

When the father looked at Tanner and shyly nodded he didn't

respond. He was stunned for some reason. Couldn't move. No offence was taken. It didn't matter. Tanner watched as the family admired the petals and thorns, heads moving in time, the girl glancing over, and then the older boy, followed by the mother and finally the child. He managed a smile this time and everyone grinned, and then they all shifted as one and examined the avenue from the outside, raising their eyes to the beams. The father was speaking, his voice low, riding another frequency. Heads bobbed. They looked at Tanner again, but quickly, as if they sensed a sadness and didn't want to intrude.

He was confused, trying to work out why he was shocked. They weren't unusual in their shabby clothes and clumsy bodies, but even so, they were like nothing he had seen before. It was the aura they gave off. They were indecisive and awkward, as if they hadn't grown into their limbs, and yet they were wise. Frail and peaceful, but with brains that buzzed. They reminded him of lambs, not ducks. The family was humble. Gentle. They worked together as one unit. But he had seen humble and gentle humans before. Individuals who were mild-mannered. No, these people were *meek*. And they were on the move, off through the roses, shrinking in size, leaving Tanner to catch his breath.

The buck with the tombstone teeth and twitching nose was pressing his forehead against the kitchen window as he peered inside. He was careful to keep quiet and still, as he didn't want to disturb the sad soul inside, an old man who was turning into a boy. Farmer Giles drank tea from a mug, steam rising into his crinkled face, drifting around the sides as if he was bathing his skin in a cloud. The figure outside was here on a mission and didn't want a fuss. The moon was nearly full and lit up the land. It was a time for some childhood dreams to come true.

The farmer had kindness in him, and even when he was in his prime and raising animals to send to the slaughterhouse he'd been ready to care for strays. But how many rabbits had died at his hands? Were these creatures in the hutches their descendants? How many other animals had been killed here? The creature at the window had thought about this a great deal and had decided that in this case he was going to hate the sin and love the sinner. He wouldn't be seeing Farmer Giles again. He moved away from the glass and did what needed to be done, walked into the fields with a load in each hand.

When he reached the hill and was in a good position he stopped to ease his aching arms, but also to look back at the house down below, and he pictured the farmer inside when he was a boy, sleeping in the same bedroom and eating in the same kitchen, back at the start of his life, open-minded and eager to please, doing as his father said. The child would have loved and admired his dad, which was natural. Perhaps he had feared him as well. How could an outsider know the things that were said and done? This was his education and he had to obey. When he was older he could have changed, made different choices, but maybe he'd been too scared.

Frank had been aware of the face at the window, hoped that if he pretended it wasn't there it would go away. This it had done, but he knew the beast could return whenever it wanted. He went and checked that the doors and windows were locked. Frail and fed up, every muscle in his body ached as he sat back down and hunched over the table, and when he finally stirred himself he emptied the dregs of his tea in the sink and couldn't be bothered to rinse the mug out, stuck it on the draining board and went upstairs. He left the lamp next to his bed on as he had become scared of the dark. He knew it would be another miserable night, but it wasn't.

The old farmer slept soundly and woke up feeling better than he had done in years. There were no remembered dreams or odd sounds, and he was surprised to realise that he was happy. He couldn't recall the last time he had felt this good. Not for months, years, decades. He hurried out of bed, washed and noticed his back wasn't hurting as it normally did first thing. Once he was down-stairs he made himself a bowl of porridge and some tea, eating and drinking fast, amazed by his hunger. When he was finished he put carrots in a big bowl, cut and added cabbage leaves, took it outside for the rabbits.

He stopped by the wall and looked out over the fields, and while he felt the same loneliness he had always carried inside him, even when he was married and raising his children, and when he was a child, he was optimistic. Why, he couldn't say, but he had a new energy as he walked towards the hutches, saw that the rabbits were still asleep. Normally they had their noses pressing against the mesh as they waited for their breakfast, and this made him feel good. He tapped on the first roof, but there was no movement, so he reached down and opened the door to the room where the rabbits slept. He squinted and pushed his head forward, reached in and moved the straw about. The hutch was empty.

He hurried to the next one, but again there were no rabbits inside. He started to panic, scared they had been taken by a fox, but the hutches had been properly shut and no animal he knew of could open a latch and close it again. He checked the last hutch. All of them were gone. He couldn't work out what had happened, remembered the face at the window, guessed it was a real prowler, a man or a monster, but still a thief who would break their frail little necks and skin them and cut off their heads. The tears spilled out and he sat down hard on one of the rickety chairs he kept next to a wooden table, the place where he rested in the sun and thought and drank tea, his rabbits watching him and listening to what he had to say. He was totally alone now, but worse was knowing how scared they must be, how they would suffer.

He stared at the empty hutches for a long time, felt as bad as he had felt good when he woke up. This was the end. The farm was falling apart and he might as well be dead. He didn't know what to do with himself, sunk against the table and saw an envelope on the ground. Trying not to fall as he bent down to pick it up, he opened the envelope and read the letter inside. He clapped his hands and shook his head. He saw his father and thought how angry he would have been if he'd seen these words, removing his belt and taking his rage out on his son. Frank felt fantastic.

The rabbits were on their way to an animal sanctuary where

they would live in a field, and while they would be free they would also be protected and have a shelter to sleep in at night. He shouldn't worry. These hutches were small and claustrophobic and it was the kindest thing to do. Frank didn't know where this place could be, but he trusted the stranger. He pictured it in his head. Kind people lived there. The old man was a small boy, but in the best possible sense, imagining the creatures he loved running around and stretching their legs and digging holes. He was filled with wonder. Farmer Giles was happy.

Harry Spalding normally stayed until nine o'clock when he was at head office, but it was past ten now and he was knackered, yet it was a healthy tiredness and he wasn't going to complain. He had achieved a lot today. Easing back in his specially made chair, soft leather caressed his shoulders and hips as he lifted his feet so they were propped on the desk, taking a few minutes to wind down and reflect on his achievements. This was the best form of relaxation.

Funhouse Foods had made him a millionaire many times over and the company kept growing. It had a life of its own and he couldn't have stopped it expanding if he'd wanted to, which of course he didn't. He was elated. Size was everything. He laughed – big cock, big balls. His firm was hung like a fucking horse.

He lit a cigar and drew the smoke into his lungs, felt manly flavours boosting his mood, sucked on the tobacco for a while before standing and walking over to the drinks cabinet and pouring himself a generous cognac. He took a sip, rolled the spirit around his mouth and swallowed, returning to his chair and lifting his feet and settling back down. Life was sweet.

He'd never imagined he would reach such heights when he started out. Harry had been ambitious from the off, and he grafted, starting at the bottom and learning his trade. From castrating young bulls to having his own bollocks licked by a posh tart dressed in their skin, well, it didn't get much better. He had done enough shitty jobs in his younger days to make him appreciate every penny of his wealth. Unlike a lot of people, he had earned his fortune. A man had to be strong to kill animals. It wasn't easy work, but he had never been scared to sweat, and he had seen the big picture early on.

Essentially, humans were scum. Once he understood this, the rest was easy. There were no limits to the depths to which they would sink, but most of them needed to make excuses and justify their behaviour, and not just in public either, but in private as well. Knowledge was power. He was the man in the know.

People needed food. They could do without most things, but they had to eat. Most were also tight-fisted, which reflected their pinched and mean natures. Supply the cheapest meat on a large enough scale and a good businessman would end up rich. He knew the meat industry inside out, had learned about every aspect of the trade, seen all the corners that could be cut. The breeding and raising and killing and butchering of animals was a mechanical process, the saving of money and flouting of laws a piece of piss, but it was his grasp of human nature that had made the difference. He had built his empire by using his brain, putting a knowledge of basic psychology to excellent effect.

These days he could ask for anything and his wealth meant it was delivered gift-wrapped. He had travelled the world and stayed at the finest hotels, sampled the best food, drink, drugs and sex the planet had to offer, and yet he hadn't really changed. He was still the same old Harry Spalding, a man who enjoyed the simple pleasures. He replayed his visits to South East Asia, because while money could buy him the same services at home, he trod much more carefully here.

His animals hated shitting in their living quarters, and while he didn't give them a choice, he was the same. He didn't want to ruin his life with one careless act. He was off the radar in Thailand and the Philippines, had come to realise just how slippery the pole of human degradation could become. Clever men had been caught out in the past, targeted by tabloid hacks with chips on their shoulders, wannabes jealous of the high rollers. These journalists resented the success of strong men. The greatest achievers were generally the best deceivers.

Everyday whores were easily had most places in the world,

ordered by phone or text, picked up in a hotel lobby, but in the East he had taken them off the streets, fucked them hard and made the dirty little bitches squeal. They looked more like monkeys than dogs, while their high-pitched voices reminded him of squealing piglets, brittle-boned hens scratching at his wallet with their red-painted nails, but even though the best ones were truly stunning the endless supply of cunt became boring and he had soon left the worn-out fannies of those fifteen- and sixteen-year-old peasants behind, craving tender young flesh that wasn't infected with Aids or chicken flu or swine fever or any other of those diseases haunting the tropics. He could do without any of that, thank you very much.

One good thing about the Orientals was how they were turned on by youth. Western culture took it some of the way, but was too inhibited by the remains of a near-dead faith, hampered by out-of-date laws. He could see this desire bubbling under the surface, the people craving tender flesh the same as those men they branded paedophiles. He saw it in their gluttony, the babies he bred and killed to satisfy their lust, the same lambs they regarded as the epitome of innocence and religious purity. He found this self-deceit funny. Their longing was clear in the skimpy clothes they bought their kids, the music they listened to and films they watched. They milked their young like the cows supplying all that butter and cheese they ate. The stupid cunts were only lying to themselves if they denied the sexual nature of the meat industry.

The Orientals would eat and sell anything that had a pulse. Educated pimps in expensive suits had brought the slums to his hotel room, enticing innocents from their farmyards and delivering them to his bed, and he had enjoyed plenty of girls who hadn't reached puberty, and even though he knew it was dangerous, that if he was caught he would end up in jail, he couldn't resist the temptation to experiment. His cock became hard as he remembered the sex. Dumb brats crying like the lambs he was having slaughtered in their thousands back home. They didn't know that he killed babies for a living, had done the dirty work himself enough times in the past.

Harry had accepted he was on thin ice and backed off before he was betrayed, although maybe it would have gone no further than a bribe. Of course, he couldn't keep taking the risk. Prison would have killed him, and so he drew on his famous discipline and moved out of that world, furious at the law-makers restricting freedom of expression, the meddling of Western democracies, taking his rage out on the ladyboys he picked up in safer areas, a series of trans-sexual freaks castrated and mutilated like the young bulls he turned into steers, and he remembered how these people groaned as he fucked them, and he thought right back to when he was a young man forty years before and how he had fucked some of the animals where he worked, shagging sheep in their pens for a laugh, when nobody was round, mutton dressed as lambs, the fucking ladyboy cunts.

The Taffs were sheep-shaggers and the rag-heads were goat-fuckers and any silly cunt who pulled a boiler was a pig-fucker. He stubbed his cigar out in the ashtray. It was a long time ago, but he'd done pigs, lambs, calves, even a goat. Cunts, arses, the lot. They struggled and tried to speak, made their odd noises, but there was no escape and no real punishment if he was caught. Nobody cared as long as they didn't see him in action. Comedians made endless jokes about it and the public laughed long and hard, said it didn't matter, but most of the thrill was that he knew it did. Animals had the same fears as humans. They were children. He understood this and enjoyed their terror. Why lie? He was being honest. But only with himself.

He swilled cognac around his mouth. People were rich with credit and growing fat, clogging their arteries and ruining their bodies in an orgy of consumption. God, he really had fucked a good few beasts in his younger days. Their terror was an aphrodisiac. They were debauched times. Good days. He had it all now, but was still an ordinary chap with exotic desires, had merely progressed and become more daring. Why abuse animals when his money meant he could do the same to humans? He was Harry Spalding – a multi-millionaire with a heart of gold. The media loved him. The system was run by careerists and it was easy to manipulate them when you were rich. He put on the charm and reassured the ignorant masses with a cheerful routine.

There had been tough periods when he started out, back when he was borrowing and in debt, and that had been exciting in its own way, but nothing like the risks he took later. Abusing animals was fine, encouraged by law, but when he got carried away and nearly killed that subhuman ladyboy in Thailand, well, that could have been the end. He had left the country the next morning and never been back. It was a narrow escape. He was wiser now and his sexual appetites were starting to ease, today's pleasure was in the money he accumulated and the power it brought, and through this power he had respect, which really was little more than a mix of self-interest and fear – which he preferred. He had done no real harm. Excess was part of a successful life, his mistakes the lessons a clever man learned.

He wasn't resting on his laurels either. He played hard, that was true enough, but still wasn't shy to put in the hours. He had ideas seeping out of his arse. New markets were crying out for exploitation, but he would never forget the essentials, because that's where his fortune had been made and it was what kept making him richer. It was the bread and butter of life – beef for the Sunday roast, turkeys at Christmas, lambs to celebrate spring. Pork and chicken every day of the fucking week.

Most people were thick as shit, little better than the animals he killed. They had few real morals. If the price was right they would do anything he asked. The law-makers were no better, and he had met a lot of them over the years, plenty of arse-licking politicians who were going through the motions, talking bollocks in public as they continued with their bullshit and bullying in private.

He flicked cigar ash on the carpet. He was paying for the cleaning so might as well get value for money. No reason to make things easy for the lowlifes. Immigrants most of them, dozy cunts from backward nations, refugees who couldn't even speak the language, but they worked for peanuts compared to the natives and that was a good enough reason to use their labour. Still, they were lazy fuckers and needed something to do, so he liked to spread the ash about.

He remembered that trouble with the unions, but it had passed.

Socialists talked big, but the leaders all lived in expensive houses. He didn't mind the men he'd dealt with, knew they were on the fiddle, blokes who had seen an opportunity, and there was nothing wrong in that. It was a dog-eat-dog world and their ethics only went so far. They had the same needs and desires as anyone else. Liked their Sunday roast and didn't give a fuck about the suffering on their plates.

Nobody had helped Harry, apart from his father who'd given him ten grand to start up. Another ten when his business looked like failing. But he was the one who had made a success of his life. It wasn't rocket science, and there were times when he'd had to be tough on those working for him, but he didn't give a fuck what they thought. He paid their wages and most people were whores who would bend down and let him fuck them up the arse as long as they got their money. There were one or two over the course of his life who couldn't be bought, but he had airbrushed them from the picture. They could piss right off.

He returned to his mantra – *people had to eat* – and they would scoff any old rubbish as long as it was presented in the right way. Education and background made little difference. The rich wanted to be told what to eat as much as the poor. The correct packaging was essential. Make it look good on the outside of the container and nobody gave a toss what was inside. Cut off the head and rip out the ugly bits, remove the fur, skin or feathers, inject the chemicals needed to stop the meat rotting and give it a glow, add a sauce to disguise the bland taste, and the silly fuckers were falling over themselves to hand him their cash.

The name Funhouse Foods was a stroke of genius and he took full credit. The slaughterhouse was his funhouse. For most people it was a house of horrors, but that wasn't going to make them buy his meat. He had toyed with the name Fun Farm Foods, as the public loved the idea of Farmer Giles and his happy band of animals, but it reminded him too much of those funny-farm asylums full of looneys, the sort of demented scum the government spent millions on keeping alive when they were nothing but a drain on society. Not that he paid too much in the way of taxes, his accountants masters at maximising the loopholes and dodges every government put in place for entrepreneurs such as himself, but what he did hand to the taxman he wanted to be wisely spent. It was the same with the national-health system. Close the fucking thing down. It was full of scroungers.

He puffed on his cigar and considered the problems facing society. He had made quite a few media appearances over the last couple of years and had enjoyed the attention, was clever enough to know what to say and what to keep to himself. It always came back to the packaging.

When he thought about it, what the government should do was donate the mental cases to science. They were worse than his pigs. He didn't have a problem using such people for experiments, or to test cosmetics on. Fucking anti-vivisectionists wouldn't know what to do about that one, and he liked the thought of those woolly headed animal-loving do-gooders running around squawking and flapping their arms like spastics. Most of them were eccentrics. Gormless pacifists. Clueless fucking cunts.

He considered the targeting of that research centre by the animal-rights mob a while back. A couple of the staff would call known activists and make their rabbits and mice scream down the phone to wind them up, and when the antis responded with some mild protests that went further than their usual ineffective peaceful efforts, well, the police had started raiding houses and using the terror laws to rush them to court where they were sentenced to some harsh prison terms. He loved the unfairness of it all, and it *was* unfair, but it served the wankers right. He adjusted his feet and refilled his mouth with cognac.

Harry Spalding thought about the man he had christened Bob The Butcher. He was a fool for putting himself at risk, but could well change the approach of the animal-rights movement with his decision to kill for the cause. This might feed into the mainstream, at least in terms of the sympathy vote. There were signs of this happening on social media. A lot of people were excusing his actions. The authorities hadn't realised it yet, but this one man was threatening the status quo. It was odd, as their sentencing was over the top when it came to animal rights, and he decided they were in denial. It was the only explanation.

Bob was a serious danger to the meat and dairy industries, but the wider establishment could also be in for a shock. The police were talking about him as if he was a mindless terrorist, which was a mistake. One of Harry's contacts had told him that in the first letter sent to the authorities the killer had claimed he was a soldier. Harry agreed.

Bob had been operating at a low level at first, killing slaughter-men and a pig farmer, but those last two deaths showed he was evolving. That brought risks. Outside of their families and a few friends, who was going to mourn men who cut the throats of lambs and tormented pigs? The slaughtermen were easy targets, the sort of morons who did his dirty work for him, while the farmer was a small-timer knee deep in pig shit. Those advertising whores were more interesting. It was a step up. Bob was climbing the ladder of animal abuse. And there was the move from a straightforward shooting to a shooting with decapitation and an apple in the mouth – a nice touch – and now a shooting with the cutting of throats and two naked bodies left hanging from slaughterhouse hooks. And this last attack had been photographed and accompanied by a second letter. Bob's mission was clear.

Still, the man was weak. If he'd really wanted to show the world what went on he should have raped the woman and cas-trated the man, not written about it in his stupid note. He should have fucked Claudette and filmed himself in action. Flashed his knife and tortured Stephen, cut his balls off for the camera. Done it nice and slow. Made him suffer. But no, Bob had bottled it. Bob The Butcher? More like Bob The Bottler.

It wouldn't be long before he was arrested and locked away in an asylum. Maybe they'd change the law in time and the vivi-sectionists could get to work on the soppy cunt. Imagine throwing your life away for a bunch of animals. The man was a fool, yet Harry admired him, respected what he had done. He was clearly a loner. One honest man surrounded by millions of liars. But what a waste. It was only ever going to end in tears. Fuck Bob. He returned to his own life and the success he had made of it, and especially the triumphs to come.

The more he had the more he wanted. He would never tire of success. It was an ongoing process, which suited him, seeing as he had always been restless. He had never bothered to marry, preferring to stay single and play the field. Not that a wife would hold him back, he just didn't have time for that sort of hassle. Women were slags. He had his fun. Invested wisely and enjoyed himself. There was a villa in the south of France, a yacht in the Mediterranean, an apartment in Manhattan, his properties in England.

He was at the level where he could delegate and have time away, and he did this to an extent, spending periods in the USA and Europe and Dubai, and while he was always in contact and made the important decisions, after a while he missed the hustle and bustle of being at the Funhouse office, always came back to London refreshed and eager.

He took his feet off the desk and leaned over the proofs he had been studying earlier. While he had taken chances in his life, risked everything for young cunt and arse, he was a meticulous planner, forward-thinking and inventive. People followed their leaders, did as they were told, and even those silly fuckers who shouted about free will were easily persuaded. He was planning a big promotion on lamb and targeting the younger generations. He was doing it in a range of sauces and coatings, and the packaging was clean, colourful and *cool*.

A lamb beamed from the proofs – begging to be eaten. There was no pain but plenty of gain. This was Funhouse Foods after all. His cartoon pigs were everywhere.

They had that silly cunt off the TV lined up for the promotion. Personally, he thought Andy Six was a wanker, with his arrogance and the rubbish he spoke about healthy food, which Harry could have appreciated if it was a marketing gimmick, but he had met the man and he seemed to believe what he was saying. It was pathetic. Talk about conning yourself. The public loved him and Six revelled in the attention, preening himself for the cameras, lost so deep inside the media machine he had forgotten it even existed. He wasn't cheap, but hadn't asked any awkward questions and was a worthwhile investment. He would attract a new wave of celebrity-lovers to the Funhouse brand.

Removing his cigar from his mouth, Harry blew smoke into the air, watched it shoot out in a column before spreading across his office, and he ran his eyes over the wood panelling that oozed old money and class, the sculptures that always impressed visitors, pride of place given to photos that showed him with leading public figures, men and women in high office, politicians and bankers, influential characters whose determination and ambition he shared. They were pragmatic, hardened realists, yet on the surface courteous and open to different views. He had never met a vegetarian or a vegan in these circles, which was a pity, but there again, maybe not. He had to charm his business contacts, not rip the piss out of them.

He heard the sound of a trolley in the corridor outside, the shuffling of feet, and while the cleaners changed regularly and he didn't remember their faces, there was one that stood out. He hoped she would be working tonight. She was as black as they came, from some African hellhole by the looks of her, a refugee of war or famine, probably gang-raped by another tribe, riddled with disease, but despite this she had a pride he found attractive. It reminded him of an odd strength he had seen in his animals, and he appreciated that it was a strength he could never match. They were crushed, with every possible crime committed against their bodies, traumatised and driven mad, and yet they retained their dignity while the scum he employed had only their apathy and violence. This used to make him angry, when he was still on the front line, but he was way beyond that now. Even though she was poor, this cleaner was a noble woman. It was a huge turn-on.

He would watch her limp and kneel to pick up the waste bins because she couldn't bend properly, and she hid the pain, and for a few seconds he might see the crack of her arse and her limbs through the cheap trousers she wore, and his cock filled with blood. He knew she was beyond buying. He could do nothing to her that hadn't already been done, except maybe end her life. She was out of reach and it made her attractive in a way he just couldn't explain. Last time she cleaned his office he had masturbated as soon as she left, filling a handkerchief as he sat at his desk.

He stood up and walked over to the window, flicking ash as he went, but making sure he didn't tread it into the carpet. There was a knock on his office door. He told the cleaner to wait, finished his drink and refilled the glass, returned to his desk and positioned himself comfortably in his chair, called for her to enter. The door opened and he saw that it was a different cleaner, which was a shame, but he reasoned that the woman he liked was on another rota, and would be along later in the week. The cleaner lumbered in with a trolley and bent down to empty the bin by the door. Harry took no notice, started to pack away the proofs in their folder. He would leave when his office was done, lock up and get going. It had been a good day. Nodding thoughtfully, he inspected the last piece of artwork again.

The smiling face of a lamb looked out from the edge of the design, the centre of the packaging dominated by six golden nuggets. The lamb was inside a circle, which had a perforated line around the outside, to indicate it was a stamp of approval. Maybe from the lamb itself. He didn't know and doubted the idiots who bought this shit would either. The suggestion was enough. The words *Fun-Sized Nuggets* rested above and below the animal, each letter inside smoother versions of the nuggets, so it resembled a child's building blocks. The team involved in producing the artwork insisted there was a graphic link to the teenage market, although Harry was more keen on the connection to the building blocks of life. Nourishment, playtime, endless fun. He had chosen the lettering personally. He was going to make a lot of money out of this happy little lamb.

The vacuum started and he remembered the ash, raised his head to tell the cleaner not to miss it, but the man was working behind him and before he could turn he felt an arm loop around his neck and clamp his head, a hand covering his nose with a piece of perfumed cloth. Harry Spalding reached for the emergency buzzer on his desk but was unconscious before he could call for help.

Mary was at the edge of the container and doing her best to stay next to the wall. She had been moved short distances in the past few days, but this trip was different. They had been travelling for a long time and the lambs were struggling, the air hot and humid, body waste and petrol fumes adding to the stench, making a lot of them physically sick. It was getting harder to breathe and their hearts were beating fast, but it was the roar of the engine they heard. The journey was a long-distance balancing act, the only relief coming when the lorry was cruising and didn't jolt. Mary could see some of the outside world, the darkness solid at first but then as her sight adjusted she began to make out the shapes of hedges and trees and she thought of her mum waiting for her in that small overgrazed corner of the universe where she'd lived, and when the outlines vanished she raised her eyes and focused on the stars and remembered the smell of her mother, the sunsets and sunrises, the different moons, wondering if this was the same sky they had looked at together. A boy banged into her as the driver braked. She knew him from home, saw that he was bleeding above his right eye. The wound was deep and she sensed he had given up. The curve of the road changed and the motion took him away from her in a wave of falling lambs, back into the middle of the container. She couldn't see him in the blackness, turned towards the night outside, and she was half-dreaming in her exhaustion, trying to believe she was with her mum, and if she wished hard enough maybe it would be true. One star seemed brighter than the rest. She wondered what these pricks of light meant and if they were alive in the same way that she was alive. She was young and the changes were coming fast, and even though she stayed on her feet she dozed on and off until the stars crashed down to earth and woke her up. The lorry was slowing. The light outside was bright. A brutal glare that had nothing to do with the heavens. Gates slammed. Metal vibrated. The breeze was gone and a new smell filled the container. The rumbling stopped as the driver turned off his engine. There was a brief silence and then the doors swung open and men appeared and started shouting. The lambs moved back and cowered. They had reached the slaughterhouse.

No Mercy For The Meek

IT WAS NINE days after the execution of Funhouse Foods boss Harry Spalding that Tanner cracked. Spalding's death dominated the news. The police had received a recording of the killing which confirmed it as the work of Bob The Butcher, and the contents of the film were truly horrific. Spalding had been castrated, to the sound of a human imitating a bull. Raped with an iron bar, while the killer mimicked a cow. Stunned with electric tongs, stripped and hung upside down, and once he had regained consciousness his throat was cut to the sound of a lamb bleating. The footage showed Spalding's corpse impaled on a hook, the point protruding from his chest, while a pig oinked off camera. Spalding had then been decapitated and his head placed on a table next to the skull of what looked like a devil. A cockerel crowed. The body had not been recovered.

The castration and rape allegations were soon retracted. There had been some confusion over what Bob said happened to cows and bulls and what had been done to Harry Spalding. It was an honest mistake, pointed out by a journalist acting on a tip-off. Even so, the victim's genitals and buttocks *had* been exposed on camera. As with the photos taken at the scene of the hotel killings, the footage was too graphic to show the public, but details had been released in the hope they would shock people into refocusing their efforts on identifying the person responsible. The authorities were also keen to put a stop to the small but worrying cult building up around the perpetrator.

It was again important to stress that these killings had nothing to do with animal welfare. Livestock was well treated and humanely processed in professionally run abattoirs, and these were closely monitored by government officials. The health of animals was important to everyone involved in meat and dairy production. Nobody loved chickens, pigs, cows and sheep more than those who worked with them on a daily basis. Donkeys, horses, rabbits, ducks and deer were among the other species slaughtered, but not in the same numbers. Every single creature was shown respect. Harry Spalding had emphasised this on numerous occasions. Animal welfare was the industry's greatest concern. This latest atrocity merely showed that Bob was a cold-blooded killer who needed to be caught, convicted and locked up for a very long time. Life must mean life.

If he was opposed to meat eating, well, there were plenty of peaceful ways in which he could express his beliefs. Such violence had no place in a liberal democracy that had been founded on notions of tolerance and freedom. This sort of cruelty belonged to less-prosperous, unenlightened times. It was medieval. The rights of the individual were under threat. Rich or poor, every man, woman and child was entitled to eat and drink whatever they wanted. It could be argued that democracy itself was at stake.

Tanner followed the story closely. He watched his television and listened to the radio, sat in his local library and read newspapers and searched the internet, was especially interested when psychologists and other experts analysed the nature of the killer. While it was agreed that Bob had gone further than before with this latest attack, opinions differed when it came to his motivations.

There were those who believed he killed for pleasure, but that the thrill lessened each time, forcing him towards more extreme acts in order to satisfy his bloodlust. Others felt his behaviour reflected a need for power, which could be related to a poor upbringing, or possibly a wealthy one, where expectations had not been fulfilled in adulthood. He might be a former soldier, so dehumanised to suffering he was unable to stop a repetitive process. A repressed hatred of animals was possible, expressed in a false love of the same. He could even be an ex-slaughterman repenting for his work, or someone with a grudge, a man sacked from a company involved in the wider industry. A real-life butcher perhaps.

There were numerous possibilities and these offered a series of permutations which led to a feeding frenzy for an ever-hungry media. This led to more speculation, which in turn created new theories and some exciting debates. The fact that the establishment still wouldn't talk about the meat and dairy industries truthfully, and so were blatantly ignoring the reasons for the executions and the way they imitated the abuse of animals, was pushing Tanner to the edge. Someone in the government had to stand up and be honest and demand change.

Representatives from the main animal charities and animal-rights groups were interviewed and condemned the killings, clearly fearing the publicity would put their work back years. The public expected a peaceful approach. Tanner respected their positions. They followed a different set of rules. How could they say anything else? Maybe they were right, but he didn't think so, and he wondered how many of these individuals secretly sympathised with Bob's work.

Beyond the mainstream, there were plenty of people who under-stood the executions, while others celebrated what they saw as revenge attacks. Social media showed varying levels of support for the actual killings, but the direct connections to animal abuse were clearly made. A Facebook page was started that enthusiastically backed Bob The Butcher – or Bobby Four Legs as his supporters had started calling him – and it had more than ten thousand followers when it was shut down one week later. Another was then opened. While Bobby's motives were ridiculed by the establishment, his support continued to grow.

Since the killings had been linked and the reasons made clear, four slaughtermen had been beaten up and treated in hospital. A pig breeder was covered in manure, chained to a wire fence and stabbed in the leg. The offices of an advertising company running a campaign that excused the abuse of cows had been burned down in broad daylight. Butchers' windows were being regularly smashed. Lorries used to transport animals to slaughter had also been targeted. This wave of activism was said to have been inspired by Bobby Four Legs.

Tanner was pleased, but unless the masses rejected meat and dairy the campaign would be a failure. Censorship was the prob-lem, and this was internal as well as external. The police were painting a freedom fighter as a psychopath. There were loud, official voices insisting he was insane, but again, if a soldier was professional and derived no satisfaction from his job then how could this be true? Men were rewarded for far greater acts of violence. Even so, the death of Harry Spalding had shaken Tanner. The work of a slaughterman was merciless. Depraved.

He waited for the mainstream coverage to deepen, but it didn't. The machine denied the crimes inflicted on animals and turned the story around. It was being rewritten as a serial-killer tale to attract viewers and advertising. Horror meets reality TV. Evil men were talked about as if they were somehow relevant. One expert compared Bob to the degenerate child killer and farmyard nonce Fred West, the mass rapist and sadist Ted Bundy, even the demented characters in *The Texas Chainsaw Massacre* who, perversely, were slaughtermen. He remembered talk of head cheese, the murderer Leatherface, the meaning he had taken from the film.

West and Bundy were the sort of scum Tanner saw as examples of the perverted nature of meat and dairy. This so-called expert was taunting him with deliberate distortion, and yet what if the wider analysis was right, if Bob had lost the plot. Yet the killings were executions, part of a mission that involved the self-sacrifice of Bobby Four Legs, a man who was trying to do good. Instead, he was being blamed for the crimes of others. This wasn't new, but there was only so much he could take.

They said Spalding was tortured, but this was a lie – *humane slaughter is quick and clean* – that he had been treated unfairly – *Mr Fair wears a funny little hat* – nobody deserved to die that way – *which was the point* – Mike Tanner was confused – a *stupid dog chasing his tail* – and he was scared – *scared as a rabbit* – perhaps they were right and he was wrong – *stupid animal – bull in a china shop – headless chicken – running in circles – a pig in a barrel – vicious circles – savage circles.*

He could hardly breathe. The air was thick with the memories of people executed for crimes they couldn't believe they'd committed, and his lungs were being crushed, the ceiling pressing on the roof of his skull. He was a lamb in a lorry. A drowning rabbit.

A pig bleeding to death. A tethered girl raped. A boy castrated. A man shackled and about to be dipped in electrified water and scalded. Voices screeched. Visions fizzed. It was impossible for anyone to kill and not be corrupted.

He didn't sleep for two days and when he finally dozed he was in an ancient prison, locked away with the lost souls of the world, a heaving mass of clucking, squawking, oinking, mooing, bleating, neighing, whispering four-legged and two-legged folk. His block housed ducks, geese, rabbits, pigs, cattle, sheep, deer, goats, donkeys, horses – both male and female. There were human beings – broken spiritually, mentally, physically. Every creature was praying and begging God to leave his ivory tower and save them, but there was no response and they were starting to believe the rumours – that there was forgiveness for sinners but no mercy for the meek – that God didn't exist. The prisoners had been branded subhuman, but changes were coming as a recent arrival explained, the news worse than anyone had expected. Non-human animals had been categorised plant life by the immortal Controller Harry. Religious and political leaders were backing him from their own ivory-trade towers, lenses zooming in on the scum in the yard down below. Examples would be made. Executions performed. Tanner didn't want to die here, but the guards couldn't understand what he was trying to say, imitated and mocked his speech, called him names, swore he deserved whatever he got. Two of them knocked him over and took turns kicking his head. They sneered and spat sound, a hissing that scorched his ears as he tried to protect his skull with his hands, panic gripping the yard as his thoughts flowed from a tannoy and merged with the prayers of the block. The tallest column – Babel Tower – was stuttering. His body belonged to Harry Spalding. *I fuck you good, fuck you hard, fuck you so good you cry for your mother... my friend.* The guards left him curled up and bleeding. Wanted him conscious. And hauling himself up he joined the crowd packed tight against a wall. There were no toilets and the smell was rancid. Mothers searched for their children, some of them stopping to ask him for help. He was sorry. He could do nothing. Controller Harry roared. This was his own special barn. Welcome to the Funhouse. Tanner fought to breathe as the guards returned and dragged him from the yard. He was dumped in a cell. The drum keeping him alive skipped beats, speeding up and slowing down, lost its rhythm. He was alone. His heart was in his head. A chopping sound filled the room.

Moving to a window he looked outside, couldn't see the helicopter, but it was above the house and getting closer. The police had come to arrest him, and while he had done nothing wrong they would lock him up forever. Closing the window, he went into his bedroom and filled a bag, grabbed his jacket and wallet, double-locked the front door and was quickly outside and on the move.

The air was thick and clinging, heavy with fear, and I was exhausted, saw the bright lights and was dazzled for a few seconds, before the ghosts turned to men. They shouted and raised sticks and I was pushed into a holding area. Some of the children in our group were taken by a doctor and I heard whispers that he was a vivisectionist with a preference for the very young, but I was still clean-minded and found it hard to believe. The rest of us passed through open gates, a sign telling us that this was a place of joy. Our masters called us non-human, said we were dirty, full of fleas and lice, riddled with disease, and they blamed us as if it was our fault. We all looked the same to them and the guards were angry when we tried to speak. The man in charge of the camp lived outside its walls, but I could see him at a window in his control tower. He was holding a glass in one hand and a cigar in the other. He was older than the guards and these days he gave orders and kept his hands clean. Controller Harry was a showman. A multi-millionaire. Untouchable. He could do most of what he wanted inside his polite society, but there were no limits when it came to us lot. The system needed Spalding for the messy jobs. He had its full support. This increased his confidence. Made him a big mouth. Brought him out of the shadows and into the limelight. The lessons of the chicken killers and knackers, the pig farmer and propagandists of the beef and dairy industries hadn't achieved enough. It was important to move further up the pecking order. Spalding had power and protection it is true, but he was vulnerable to the subhuman element. This meant it was easy to come in under his radar. He was sitting in his office and didn't take much notice of the cleaner with the hunched shoulders and bowed head. He thought I was a weakling, someone who crawled on his hands and knees with his snout in the dirt, and that was his mistake. I was Henna The Hen and the brothers Peter and Paul Pig, Daisy Moo Cow and her friend Johnny Moo and Little Mary Meek, but I was also the nutter who was going to tan this bad man's hide. I shared some sweet dreams and carried him off in the back of my silver machine, took him out beyond the cameras and into the wilds. And there he sat, comfortable and warm, tied to a chair but not gagged, free to speak his mind. We talked and talked. If he'd been able, I know he would have hurt me, but I felt a strange bond with him as he didn't try to deny the truth. He revelled in his cruelty, and when he began boasting I held my tongue, let him continue, even though his stories made me sick. I wondered if he saw this as his confession, a way of repenting, but after a while it became clear that he was incapable of remorse. Seeing that I was upset and sensing weakness he became aggressive and told me not to be a fool. We were the same, knew that human beings were scum, but I honestly did not, and I told him so. He sneered. Said I was soft and would never cross the lines I needed to in order to make my points. Work for him and I would be rich. Perhaps he could help me with my mission? It would be fun. I was too conservative. Lacked imagination. Eventually I had enough. My anger erupted and he was suddenly scared. I could even have lost control and enjoyed what came next. I don't remember. He begged for mercy. I showed him none.

The hotel was cheap and not very cheerful, but the owner had little interest in his guests, which suited Tanner. He was tired and needed a place to hide, somewhere he could rest and work out what to do next, and so he was happy to hand over a week's rent in cash and watch the notes being held up to the light and counted twice. A framed photograph dominated the wall behind the reception desk. Pilgrims circled a shrine, each one dressed in white, their numbers and clothing emphasising the importance and purity of the occasion. Mugshots of religious leaders were arranged around this central picture, their stern faces glaring at Tanner, who only saw the reality.

Each year hundreds of thousands of sheep were packed into ships across the world and transported to Saudi Arabia. The pilgrims needed sacrificial lambs and there were plenty of business interests eager to oblige. Many of these creatures died on the journey, while those who survived arrived in a traumatised state. Back on dry land, they were separated and taken away by individuals, families and slaughtermen to have their throats cut. More than a million sheep, goats, cattle and camels would be killed. Tanner wanted to grab the arrogant cunt opposite and shake some decency into him, but he had to stay out of trouble and get off the streets.

The room was small and musty, but clean enough, the window four storeys above an alley, facing a brick wall. More importantly, there was a door that locked. He had his privacy. If he kept his head down he would be left alone. Living like a monk, he would stay sober, quiet and humble. This was his cell, more monastery than prison house. There were two bathrooms at the end of the corridor and plenty of shops nearby. He had shelter, warmth, food and drink. And money. Nothing was free in this world. Eventually he'd need company, but for now he was glad to be alone. He laid down on the bed and slept, didn't remember his dreams, woke up drenched in sweat, his head throbbing.

For the first few weeks he was outside and walking by eight in the morning. One minute he was a failure, the next a monster, his reasoning ruined by flashbacks and waves of guilt. Horror films played in his head. He was two people. A split personality. He marched harder to drive the images away, blisters forming and breaking on his heels, soles and toes, but he hobbled on, only stopping when the pain was unbearable. Back in the hotel he cleaned his wounds and covered them with plasters. After taking a shower, he stayed on his bed for the rest of the night, watching the news on a small-screen TV, skipping channels, searching for information, but after a while there was nothing.

He ate in his room as he didn't want to be outside after six o'clock. Apart from buying and ordering food in shops and cafes, he rarely spoke. A bakery supplied him with bread, a Greek-run deli with hummus, tahini, vine leaves and olives, a local supermarket everything from samosas to peanut butter and fruit. During the day he stopped in the emptier canteens and restaurants, but resisted pubs. Setting his alarm, he pretended he was a nine-to-five worker with somewhere to go, and after so much exercise he climbed into bed exhausted, which blocked out his dreams. This was the aim, even though he felt rough when he woke up. His feet mended and were hard, but now he feared he was going to burst, his lungs splitting and his body caving in on itself, leftover skin slipping into the sewers. He kept going and by the end of the first month his thinking had flattened out.

In the past he would have loved the area around the hotel. There was a fruit-and-veg market and stalls selling clothes and music, rows of junk shops full of furniture and books and ornaments, the generations overlapping and filling the maze fanning out from a railway station, but he wasn't determined enough to see the positives. He knew he was conning himself and killing time, would soon need some proper human contact.

The highlight of this period was the Ganesh Bhelpuri. A small restaurant lifted from a sleepy Dravidian village and dropped into a quiet London side-street, it was Hindu and strictly vegan, specialising in food from the south of India. Dosas dominated, but they also offered thalis and many other dishes, while the bhelpuri starter was one of the best things he had ever tasted. He ate here two or three afternoons a week, the owner Heramb waiting on tables and showing him to his favourite next to a six-foot statue of the elephant god Ganesh.

Their two long conversations were a joy for Tanner. The first took place two weeks after he turned a corner and discovered the place, and when the restaurant was empty. He'd mentioned the statue and Heramb sat down with two cups of masala tea, and just listening to another person talk was a relief, Tanner's own input unimportant. He felt awkward at first and was over-cautious, guessed this was how a person ended up when they were ostracised by society. The owner was a gentle character who understood the opposites, how something could both be and not be.

He had done the Ganesh up nicely, his clientele a mix of Indians and English, the Hindus drawn by familiar dishes, a fair number of the others attracted by the cruelty-free nature of the food at first, and then by its flavours. It was a lighter cuisine than that served by the standard curry house, and the framed pictures on the walls were a lot nicer that those in his hotel reception. Photos, paintings and batiks stretched the imagination with their vibrant colours and content, Hinduism linking human and non-human animals. It felt open-minded, like Buddhism. And a lot different to the one-god religions of Christianity, Islam and Judaism, where nature existed to serve the master species, an arrogance that bled into their attitudes towards non-believers.

Tanner especially liked the picture of a temple in Madurai, a full-colour photo that showed a range of Hindu gods carved from stone, a supernatural pantheon that mixed human and non-human animals and hybrids of the two, Ganesh himself being the best example. The elephant god was half-man and half-beast, and he reckoned that was a pretty good way to be. Heramb meant 'Lord Ganesh' or 'a respected and calm person', which summed him up, and Tanner thought about his own name and the grim trade of one or more of his ancestors, wondered if he had been shaped by unconscious memories that had formed an ingrained guilt. It would make sense.

Heramb told him about the Jain monks who covered their mouths with cloth to avoid swallowing insects, and the Zoroastrian towers where the dead were left for the vultures to return their bodies to nature. They discussed reincarnation and how it related to Hindu and Buddhist thought, and how there was a time when Christians shared this belief, and hadn't it been altered to ensure the masses obeyed their leaders' rules and worked hard for a place in an eternal heaven? It was interesting to learn that the Hindus regarded Jesus as an incarnation of Shiva, and the two men agreed that Christ would never have eaten meat.

Christians, Muslims and Jews were meant to protect the weak and vulnerable, and shouldn't eat anything with blood in its veins – not cut an animal's throat and drain it from its body. Christians in the West stunned their victims before they bled them to death in factories, and Heramb wondered if this was a throwback to a pagan root, which was maybe closer to Hinduism. Stunning could be seen as a sign of guilt. It certainly admitted that animals experienced fear and pain. Kosher and halal slaughter was meant to recognise the taking of a life, even it was a brutal throwback and he doubted many people were moved by the deeper significance.

Tanner didn't know if he was guiding the conversation or if Heramb was reading his mind. He began to worry and went to the Ganesh less often after their second conversation, imagining that people could hear his thoughts, or that he was talking out loud and didn't realise. But he loved the food, focused on it when he was eating, taking his time and savouring every mouthful, tasting the ginger in the bhelpuri and thinking of the Guptas. He enjoyed his king-size dosas, the mango juice and masala tea afterwards. He stared at Ganesh, one of the most popular of the Hindu gods, and knew that until recently a lot of Christians would have feared him, seen a mutant that reflected the evil of human beings.

Tanner had been stopping in two different libraries to read the newspapers and check the internet for news of Bobby Four Legs. Wary of electronic trails, he mixed things up and tried not to stay too long, one day searching for Sam Norton and finding out where he worked and what he had done with his life. There were lots of online discussions about the killer and his cause, one link leading to another and drawing him into the web. By the end of that first month the story had died down. He still travelled to different areas to take money from cash machines, leaving as quickly as he could. The police could well be hiding what they knew. Apart from his hotel and the libraries, he realised that the Ganesh was the only place he regularly went each week and decided to stay away for a while.

Autumn arrived and the air cooled, and while his lungs were strong and no longer felt as if they were about to explode, he was hit by the chill. Frost covered the morning pavements, forcing him to take more care, and he started to spend longer in the library nearest to his hotel, sitting in the reference section among the rows of heads bent over books. He'd always had a respect for learning, but it meant little to him now. Society was rooted in lies. The great buildings served conformists. Exhibitions and lectures dealt in distractions. The architects and artists were driven by reward. All the films, songs, concerts and books being promoted meant nothing if the foundations were rotten. The slaughter of innocents was denied. Culture had been celebrated as slaves were transported from Africa and the Jews were sent to the gas chambers. He walked less and less, stayed in the library for hours, sat in cafes and coffee shops watching the world passing him by.

Eventually he'd had enough and found a pub. The Crown was a ramshackle old gin palace, a proper boozer, and while it still had its original fittings these were dusty and largely unnoticed by the regulars. There was a core of drinkers, among them a handful who started at opening time. There was a hush during the day, a spiritual, chapel-like atmosphere that reminded him of the back bar of The White Hart. The beer was cheap and the pipes clean, while the only food on sale were crisps and peanuts, which meant it was free from the gastropub stench that had ruined so many pubs in recent years.

He had two pints each day in the late afternoon, took his time drinking them, quickly on nodding terms with a few people, but even so, he kept his distance. There was no Tony holding court here, none of the bustle of the junction, which was fair enough. He was a loner, had no wisdom to pass on and was keeping his opinions to himself, just wanted to relax around similar characters, and he wondered if he had moved beyond words, everything that needed to be said better left unsaid inside his head. He was sick of the endless mental arguments.

The weeks passed and he arrived earlier and left later, became more friendly with the other drinkers. It was raining a lot, the city cold and the days shorter. He was content to hear familiar stories – tales told in mumbling, nervous voices – rambling opinions that twisted and turned and came full circle and summed up the confusion they all felt. There were no agendas in The Crown. No plotting or planning and little forward-thinking, and he was left to drink at his own pace. He made himself think about each pint, never got drunk enough to lose control. There could be no rows. Careless words would cost him his life. He knew alcohol was a depressant as well as a stimulant, that his highs would be followed by lows, but he needed to create fresh visions, enjoy the rare bursts of clarity, determined to lose himself in a new routine. It was important he ate when he returned to his room as he needed to soak up the alcohol and weigh himself down for the night ahead, and so he kept his food supply stocked up and enjoyed some proper feasts.

It wasn't all sweetness in The Crown. There were moments when differences were exaggerated by the hops and barley, and insults, threats, punches followed, but the blows landed were wonky and did little damage. These tiffs were broken up by peace-makers, while one of the bar staff would lean on the counter and warn those involved that they would be barred if they didn't behave. Glances might be exchanged afterwards, but the reasons for the disturbances were soon forgotten. Tanner kept out of the way, watched these clouds of anger burst and rise into the air where they broke apart and merged with all the other emotions pushing at the ceiling, and he reasoned that there must be well over a century's worth of thinking drifting through the pub.

When he mused over a pint like this his mood was warm and idealistic, and he had to admit that he could be naive and foolish. In the creased faces of the drinkers he saw his own deeper sadness and disappointment, but understanding as well. There was always humour and hope in The Crown, an acceptance he respected but couldn't share. In this gathering he no longer saw lambs and pigs entering the slaughterhouse.

He became friendly with one man in particular, a giant who dressed in black and greased his hair back, a rougher version of

Johnny Cash, but there was a perfume-like fragrance about him which didn't fit the craggy face and brooding presence. Teenage doses of aftershave hid an odour Tanner knew yet couldn't place. Johnny wore a heavy ring on the middle finger of his right hand, and there were times when he tapped the protruding crucifix on the bar or a table and Tanner placed a palm on his own chest to feel his heartbeat, which seemed faint and far away, as if it belonged to another person.

The two of them would stand at the bar and swap a few words, after a couple of pints sometimes move to a quiet table or corner. Johnny always looked tired, but when the drink livened him up they talked freely, although only in private. The other man dominated, even if his delivery was slow and meandering, but this suited Tanner, who enjoyed the sound and had little to say.

One afternoon, with the temperature plummeting outside, Johnny commented on the cold night before, how he'd thought he was going to freeze to death and would have to find another blanket, and if he was living indoors it would be an electric one. Did they make them with batteries, so it didn't need a plug? After a few seconds Tanner realised that his friend was sleeping rough. The clothes were scruffy and frayed, even if Johnny was more dapper than anyone else in the pub, but he would never have guessed. He said this out loud, Johnny telling him about his cave and how it was protected by enough concrete to save him from a nuclear explosion. Buried under a flyover, cars and lorries passed non-stop over his head, the drivers oblivious to his existence. He spoke in a whisper. There were several of these bunkers hidden behind a forgotten yard, the only way in through a hole in the fence.

There were others who shared his secret hideaway, and he named them as Sailor Steve, Mr Morrison and Arklight. Sometimes Steve brought Dorothy back, same as in the *Wizard Of Oz*, and he laughed – they were living deep under the yellow brick road. It was the first time Tanner had seen Johnny smile. His cave was dry and safe, plus he was shielded from the propaganda that filled the airwaves and had driven him crazy. Tanner frowned. The tiredness and slow delivery made sense, and the smell masked by aftershave was the same transient odour he lived with in his hotel, which he was starting to hate.

For the first time he realised that Johnny was fragile, wondered if he was seen in a similar way, and the fact he'd been oblivious to something that now seemed so obvious was a worry. He knew that his appearance had changed, and he looked around the pub to see if he was being watched and pitied, but this was the wrong place. He wasn't going to stand out in The Crown. Johnny was sure he would find Arklight interesting, given his animal politics and vegan beliefs, and this shocked Tanner as he was certain he hadn't mentioned the subject.

Johnny tapped his cross on the table and continued. Arklight had started off in the military, moving through the ranks and leading commando raids before leaving to become an agent and finally an interrogator for hire. He had been shaped by politics and later money, done some terrible things before finding God. Johnny laughed again, but sarcastically this time, went on to explain how he himself had moved in the other direction, realising that organised religion was a form of politics, which he hated. They were the two main pillars of control. Politics and religion – the twin towers. The terror was within, but again, he wasn't saying anything that they didn't already know.

Tanner was worried, watched as Johnny drank faster and talked about the seasons, how he had the funds for food and drink, and if he was desperate could find a bed in a shelter, but preferred to stay outside. Bad things happened to boys when they were locked up and couldn't escape. God wasn't listening and didn't give a fuck. He raised his eyes quickly, scared that he had been heard, while Tanner hoped he hadn't been thinking out loud at the same time, speaking when he thought he was thinking, and maybe all this time he had been trying to say nothing he'd been babbling away like a nut job.

The ring stopped tapping and Johnny looked terrified, Tanner overwhelmed by the man's sorrow, but then he mentioned a fresh start and cheered up, followed a different line. He only used a shelter when the temperature dropped below freezing. Life wasn't all bright sunshine and birdsong. If he could survive the next few months there was spring to look forward to and then it would be summer. There again, the lighter evenings and longer days could be dangerous. He never let his guard down. Homeless people he knew had been beaten, raped, stabbed, set on fire, splashed with acid and one bloke had been murdered.

After silently considering what he was about to say for a few minutes, Johnny explained how he had woken up one morning and accepted that the majority of people were beyond redemption. He left the church that same day, rejecting the priesthood and his congregation. Tanner almost choked. He'd never had Johnny down as a priest, but with the black clothes all he needed was a dog collar. Reading his mind or responding to his words, Johnny produced the collar and put it on. It was dirty and torn, but still came in handy.

More time passed and Tanner was eating breakfast in a different cafe every morning, diluting the previous day's alcohol with three or four mugs of coffee. He didn't return to the Ganesh. After a short stroll he would sit in the reference library and scan the newspapers, when he was finished move next door to the lending library to use the internet. There was no news of Bobby Four Legs or Bob The Butcher. The police were surprised the killings had stopped and reasons were suggested. It was possible he'd been driven insane by the ferocity of his last attack and committed suicide. Or died of natural causes. He might be in prison for an unrelated offence, in hospital for an operation, in another country planning his next move.

The investigation would not be scaled down and police officers were working around the clock. It was all about survival now, staying free and alive, because the retribution would be harsh when it came, and Tanner kept to the rules he'd set himself, although these did change as he became less active. He tried to drink slowly, reflectively, absorbing the nourishment. He listened to the prayers of the other men in The Crown, fashioned stories from fragments, forcing himself deeper into a dimension where there was no such thing as horror.

It was inevitable that he would stray and one day he was in the pub for ten hours straight, drinking and talking fast, and while it felt great he stayed after Johnny left, the beer knocking down the barriers he had put up in his mind. When he finally stumbled outside at closing time he could hardly stand. It was freezing cold and he slipped on some ice and fell, heard the roar of a bus, smelled the grime and dirt of the street, and he thought of what he had done and heard and smelled and saw the slaughterhouse. Using a railing to pull himself up, he made it back to his hotel and collapsed on his bed and didn't get up until after eleven the next morning.

He had breakfast and an extra cup of coffee and decided to give the pub a miss. It would be better to never return. He was angry with himself, went to the library with a hangover, out of habit but also because it was warm and he loved the smell of the books. He couldn't stand his soulless room, its stale air and the loneliness he felt and the sight of the owner. Breathing in the reassuring flavours of paper and ink he felt himself reviving, went to the newspaper rack, reached forward and reeled back, stunned by what he saw on every front page.

He chose a broadsheet and a tabloid and took them over to the far corner of the library, sat down at an empty desk and began to read. It was hard to believe. He felt as if he was hallucinating, lost in one of his nightmares and unable to wake up, regaining consciousness in another realm. It was no dream. The headlines and standfirsts told him that Bob The Butcher was dead. He had been shot by police marksmen after attacking a livestock market. There was his face staring back, real name Steve Nash – *a hardcore animal-rights fanatic.*

Tanner closed his eyes and tried to slow his breathing down as his heart hammered. The whole library was going to hear the thump thump thump and zoom in and see his thoughts. It took a minute, but he regained control, opened his eyes and continued.

Steve Nash had killed nine people and wounded fifteen more with a rifle before being wounded by a farmer who happened to have a loaded shotgun in his car. Forced to retreat, Nash was pursued by the police who followed him back to his house where he took refuge. Once inside, he had gone upstairs and covered the street from a bedroom window. Armed officers surrounded the property. He had refused to negotiate and swore he would never surrender, shouting that he had attacked the market to draw attention to the plight of the animals being held there – sentient creatures who were terrified and would soon be murdered. He wanted people to know what was going on. Those responsible were criminals and deserved to die. Meat was murder. He wished he'd killed more of them and talked this way for another ten minutes before firing a single round. He was then gunned down. Witnesses reported a large number of shots.

Once the police had secured the scene they'd searched the house and found the walls of a box room covered in newspaper articles relating to what Nash had called the Four Legs War. There were also maps detailing the locations of abattoirs and connected businesses. The HQs of the big food chains were marked and certain products highlighted. Chillingly, a list of names and addresses was pinned to a board. These people had not been identified by the police, but there was speculation that they could have been targeted next. Nash had clearly wanted to escalate his reign of terror following the slaying of Harry Spalding. There was still no indication as to the whereabouts of the Funhouse boss, but once the police had examined the premises in greater detail surely his remains would be found and given a proper burial.

Tanner read the coverage in both newspapers before taking them back to the rack and returning with others. The reports were similar. At last life could return to normal for all those innocent people who supplied the public with their meat and dairy. They didn't have to be scared any longer. One editorial took great pleasure in telling its readers how Funhouse Foods had survived the loss of its charismatic leader. Profits had dipped a little it was true, but things were picking up, with its latest PR push a huge success. The company had refused to bend to the warped will of Harry Spalding's killer. Its shareholders deserved better. *That* was bravery. A fine tribute to a decent man.

Poor Steve Nash. Tanner saw his head ripped apart as he replayed that grim footage of the Kennedy assassination, more shells thudding into Steve's chest and breaking his heart. Those who believed in a conspiracy liked to describe the Kennedy murder as a turkey shoot. One broadsheet had reported a sustained attack on Steve's house by elite snipers. He hadn't stood a chance, but the propaganda machine was already purring as it described his raid on the livestock market as a mad rampage. Tanner knew that Steve had been driven by the purest of motives. He was a hero.

Taken alive, he would have had a chance to stand up in court and explain his reasoning. It would have offered the sort of public platform long denied the animal-rights movement. The reporting may have been distorted by a complicit media, facts omitted and lies told, but such a trial couldn't be ignored and would attract huge attention. All those making money from the slaughter would be happy Steve was gone. The police had done their job.

Two of the market dead had been named, short biographies painting them as the non-violent victims of a psychopath, but Tanner saw their occupations and identified a rapist and a murderer. Hastily drawn profiles of Steve were included in several publications. There was a photo of him as a youth and Tanner checked his age – thirty-three. Someone close must have supplied the information, but why would they? Three convictions were listed – two for criminal damage, another for theft. All of them were animal-related. Good old Steve.

Tanner saw him as a young boy who was sure that if he wished hard enough the grown-ups would stop killing animals; a teenager who hoped words could change minds and end the slaughter; and a frustrated adult knowing that he was powerless and that nothing he thought or said made any difference. Finally he had taken the logical step and adopted the system's methods. And Steve was still young. He'd had a long life ahead of him.

There was no questioning of the meat industry in any of the papers. No mention of atrocities. No attempt to understand the killings. When he had finished reading, he tried to imagine how Steve had felt as he was chased and cornered by the state, realising he could either go to prison for the rest of his life or die in his own home. Steve had confronted the establishment head on, breaking cover to operate in the open and make his stand. He would have been scared like anyone else, but more than that defiant, knowing he was right. Maybe his death was his statement.

Mike Tanner stood in the street and pulled the zip of his jacket up, tucked his chin into the collar. The wind screamed and spat rain in his face. To his left was the pub and his hotel. He looked ahead and saw Christmas decorations. The faithful were preparing for their animal sacrifices. He blew into the air and watched a cloud form and dissolve. He had everything that could identify or incriminate him inside his jacket. Turning right he walked away, gradually fading into the winter gloom.

Tanner didn't return to the hotel or drink in The Crown again. After learning of Steve Nash's death he wandered the streets for several hours, wishing he could sit and talk to someone who agreed with the executions and shared his respect for the bravery it had taken to carry out such a raid. What would Ronnie be thinking? He remembered Sam Norton after the boy had been sleeping rough. Peaceful Piggy thumping a bully. What did he feel? The Meadows was a sanctuary that took in homeless animals – Jeff and Sandy would be sad. All life was precious.

When it was dark he went into a park and found a place under the trees, sat with his back against a trunk and tried to sleep, but his mind was racing and the cold made it impossible. Images were spliced and sounds chopped. He saw his parents on their deathbeds, the job he'd had for so many years, marriage and divorce, the road he had taken, choices made, a life that had passed. Steve Nash was dead. Around five in the morning he finally dozed off, leaving the park at ten. He washed in the Gents in a supermarket. There was a canteen that was empty and the staff hardly saw him. He was an invisible man eating a breakfast of vegan sausages, mushrooms, baked beans, tomatoes, toast.

In the early afternoon he took a bus home, but couldn't go back to the flat and avoided his street, stayed onboard as it passed through the junction, and looking into The White Hart he was sure he saw Tony standing at the bar with a pint in his hand. Thirty seconds later he wondered if it was a trick of the light. While he would have loved to go inside and listen to Tony's stories as if nothing had happened, or visit Ella and hear her plans for next year's planting, he couldn't show his face. The police were watching. His friends could well be under surveillance.

He thought about the allotments and a few stops later got off the bus, walked to Bell Street and stood by the fence. Nobody seemed to be around and he thought about going into one of the sheds and staying there for the night, but then he spotted a figure in the distance and reckoned it was Wendell working on his brassicas. He really did like it up here in winter. Tanner wished he was somewhere warm, but didn't want to be indoors. Even the bus had felt claustrophobic.

He wanted to go over and say hello to Wendell, sit down and chat over a mug of tea, return to the summer and dig the soil and do the rounds, but he was toxic and had to be alone. Wendell didn't deserve the trouble he could bring. Looking across the allotments he thought about pumpkins and lavender and compost heaps, startled by the scarecrow in the distance. It had always made him jump, standing there in the sun and rain, never moving but thinking its thoughts. Tanner left and couldn't avoid taking a bus across town, sweating by the end of the journey and relieved to stand on a corner in an area he had never been to before. He didn't know what to do next.

It started to drizzle and he walked away from the shops and into an abandoned industrial estate. A billboard advertised more luxury apartments. The drizzle quickly turned into a heavy downpour, and he hurried to the ground floor of a disused multi-storey car park. From here he watched sheets of water shatter on the ground, billions of shards scattering to fill the potholes and form oil-slick puddles. Thunder detonated. Gunfire echoed. The clouds swirled in thick bundles and if they fell to earth the oxygen would be pushed into the heavens and kill him like a landed fish, crushed and alone, suffocating and suffering in silence, unable to speak or show his pain.

Would Steve Nash see the beauty in a black-and-white scene like this one, or did he prefer colour and light? Frans Masereel and Lynd Ward had their approaches, Turner and the Nash brothers theirs. Nothing seemed fair. Steve was dead in a morgue, naked and exposed. Pathologists stood around his corpse swapping opinions. A stranger was giving Tanner his freedom, but what if it was a trick? Either way, it was too late. There was no going back. Steve had died quickly and in the public eye, while his death would drag on and it might be months before his body was found.

He was finding it hard to breathe, went to the stairs and climbed five flights, lungs heaving as he struggled to move his aching legs, and when he reached the top he was panting and took several minutes to recover, finally raising his head and looking over a roofless, empty floor. When the rain died down he sucked air into his chest and tried to rid himself of the crushing sensation, but the guilt was clogging and he was another headless chicken running in circles, flapping broken wings... A porky boy spinning inside a machine that had been invented to strip his body of hair ready for dismemberment... A cow with a fist up her arse... A calf crying as nonces ripped off his balls... A lamb dangling from a chain... A donkey on her way to slaughter carrying an unborn child in her belly... A scared rabbit soaked in greasy oil-drum water...

Tanner walked over to the perimeter wall, placed his hands on the top and rubbed the crumbling surface, looked out at a city that was faint and fading, a fudge of misty lies where the people faked concern and took the easiest options. Words were meaningless. The Meadows and Elm Cottage were a long way from Steve Nash's small-town home in the North. Police officers would be scouring the countryside near his house, searching in vain for Harry Spalding's body.

Leaning forward and looking down to the ground, the drop was sheer and fatal, with none of the summer romance of his long-distance walk. He was thirsty and hungry, cold and exposed, but didn't have it in him to find a room for the night. And he was alone. Totally alone. He saw his flat and its radiators, the fridge and cooker, bed and chairs, music and books, the easy life he could have had if he had only been able to conform. Drink, food, shelter, warmth. Companionship. For the second time in his life he thought about killing himself. He could jump and be dead in seconds. But the thought receded. There had to be some sort of life after death, and if there was then suicide would achieve nothing. Anyway, he was too much of a coward. In truth, he wanted to live.

A chalk horse appeared on the horizon, pushing through the mist, its concrete back smooth and sleek, the head at an odd angle, and it seemed to be moving with the fading light. Designed by engineers and built by navvies, the flyover's origins were in local council and national government, the needs of infrastructure and commerce, the movement of citizens and transportation of goods. Living down below was the legendary Johnny Cash and a few of his trusted friends, among them Arklight – a man of politics. Inter-rogator and torturer. Using the same voltage as a slaughterman, Arklight could have become a dictator, creating thunder and con-juring up the dirty rain that led to chemical attacks. He had attached wires and inserted tools. Johnny had explained how Arklight loved electricity. And yet the man had changed and found religion. He had repented. He fed the rats that lived in a derelict yard.

The flyover offered Tanner protection from the elements and the monsters, Johnny's friendly face and the chance to talk, but he recoiled from the idea. He was better off up here on his own, living in the clouds, and pulling away from the edge he returned to the stairwell. The rain started up again. It was heavier than before and lightning split the sky. He sat down and leaned against a wall, enjoyed the show for a while, and when the darkness closed in he slept.

Tanner stayed at the top of the stairs for two days, walking to the wall and scanning the London skyline, staring at the concrete horse, replaying the last year of his life until his hunger finally forced him down to the ground. This bird's-eye view of the city suited him and he planned to stock up on food and return, but in the street a gang of youths threw stones and threatened to stab him if he didn't fuck off. He headed for the busier areas where there was protection in numbers, and over the following five days slept in doorways, a park and the previous night a subway.

It had been a mistake going underground, even though one of the men down there had given him a cardboard box to add to the blanket he'd taken from outside a charity shop. He'd felt like a Christmas present, packed up and ready for shipping, and while he slept he turned into one of the ten million turkeys who were being murdered to mark the birth of Baby Jesus. He woke in the early hours, plastic wrapped around his dismembered body, tore it off in a panic, took his blanket and got out of the subway.

It was over a week since he'd left the hotel and sleeping rough had changed him more than he could have imagined. His mind had slowed right down and he shuffled when he walked. Concentration came in small bursts, his inner talk switching from sparks of lucidity to a trance-like mumble. He had never felt this way before and was constantly thinking of food. His current account was empty and he had no more cash, approached strangers and held out a hand as he had seen others do, and most people passed by, some embarrassed and others annoyed, but a few handed him coins and each time this happened he felt warm inside.

Homeless men and women struck up conversations, asked a few questions and offered lots of good advice. They were happy to share information and their friendship if he wanted it, but he regarded himself as diseased and didn't want to infect anyone. He recalled the philosophers he had met in the pubs he'd used over the years, found another sort of knowledge in those who were living on the streets, and in brief exchanges he glimpsed lives changed by tragedy, illness, exploitation. He was part of a sub-class now, feeling the cold like never before, and for some he was the lowest of the low, belonged to the dregs of society.

He had made his choices and wasn't sorry for himself, but felt the suffering of the people he was meeting who were worse off than he could ever be. There were a couple of times when he saw hatred in the eyes of those he asked for money. Not disgust, but pure loathing. Despite everything, he was shocked. These people would seriously hurt him if they were allowed, and yet they looked normal from a distance, their fury hidden behind bland facial expressions. He saw them pinching children, strangling pets, burning tramps. They obeyed the rules and thought they were strong, but they were bullies and weaklings.

Scientists blinded mice and rats, grew cancers and tumours, yet outside of their laboratories these animals were stronger than humans and could adapt and survive on the streets of a major city, nesting and breeding and scavenging for food. Tanner saw them in the darkness as he searched the bins behind restaurants and in front of takeaways, stuffing carbohydrates into his mouth, cold pasta and rice, chewing on stale bread and biscuits. He found meat and chicken, but stayed vegan.

The cold cracked his lips and rainwater soaked his clothes, seeped into his pores so he heard it swishing around inside his body, filling cavities and settling in stagnant pools. He walked with his head down and no longer had a sense of time. Studying himself in the mirror of a public toilet he saw how far he had sunk. He was unshaven and ragged. Filling a basin with water he washed his face the best he could, but the dirt was ingrained. He groaned. Men glanced over. Something reeked and he realised it was him and felt humiliated, knew what people must think when they saw him coming. He was conscious that he was confused and vulnerable, stumbled out of that grim subterranean world of cubicles and urinals searching for space and light.

His body was covered in tattoos, carved letters forming scabby words and slogans and sentences that curled around his arms and legs, ran along his back and chest, the ink loaded with accusations. Scratching like mad his arms were raw and weeping, tattoos tightening as the condemnation cut deeper, and it was only the cold that stopped him from bleeding to death. There was ice in his kidneys and soon they would be cut out, sliced and packaged and placed in a freezer. His head was suction-wrapped in polythene, ready for a shopper to take home. Entrails, brains, eyeballs – people would eat anything if it was cheap. Or expensive.

There was no more beauty in snowflakes and he hoped it wouldn't snow. There was nothing good about this world. Not when you were hungry and dirty and at the mercy of the weather. There were places he could go for shelter, decent people offering to help the likes of him, but he resisted, and didn't know why, just sure that he didn't want to be trapped. Nobody could be trusted. Every smile was a lie. Every sentence a trick.

It seemed like he had been walking forever as he approached a grand street lined with department stores, and he decided to brave the crowds and follow it, as it would be busy with buses and taxis and their exhausts would warm him up. He drew fumes into his lungs and they tasted good, heating his heart and boiling his blood. He was a machine that needed gasoline. A tin-can robot man.

The street was brightly lit with signs that sold entertainment – cultured plays and films, comedies and dramas, seasonal and feel-good shows – but this extravaganza was best enjoyed when a man was wearing clean clothes – solid soles on his shoes, thick socks, long johns under heavy trousers, a shirt and jumper, a heavy coat, maybe a hat to keep the heat inside his skull, gloves to protect his fingers from freezing solid and snapping off. The next best option was to stay near the traffic which had come to a standstill, so he walked on the kerb, arms out, keeping his balance, but even though he was absorbed in the smell and sound of the engines he couldn't ignore the panel of light in a shop window. He slowed and stopped. Stood and stared. Moved over to the glass.

He stood outside the department store and gazed at the display. His face was one huge smile and tears trickled down his cheeks. His mind was calm. Baby Jesus was safe in his manger. His mum and dad stood on either side of him, and around Mary and Joseph the meekest creatures had gathered. Up front were lambs and a couple of ewes, behind them pigs, cows, donkeys, horses, chickens. Cotton wool mimicked snow yet Tanner knew that they were warm. Beyond the stable giving them shelter came three wise men bearing gifts. It would soon be Christmas. He looked up and down the street, loving the tinsel and fairy lights, returned to the display, pushed his face up against the window.

He felt an arm wrap itself around his shoulders and he was small and his father was big and protecting him from evil. The embrace didn't scare him, although when Dad's fingers squeezed tight before disappearing he wondered if it was a warning. Mum held his hand. Grandad Pop's face appeared in the glass, but only for a second. His mother released her grip. Rubbing his palms together he looked to the Christmas tree behind the nativity scene, admired the glass balls and wooden ornaments and delicate strips of glitter, the angel at the top, a winged girl with a wand in her right hand, showing off the miracle of flight. Glancing sideways he saw the hampers.

Bottles of champagne and chutney nestled against headless birds who had been stunned, scalded, slaughtered, decapitated, plucked and gutted for some festive-season fun. They were wrapped in plastic, advertised as organic, stickers showing them in their natural state. There were sliced meats on display, jars of pâté, tins of *foie gras*. It was Christmas and people were looking forward to some time off and wanted to celebrate with a spending spree. The seasonal massacre was well under way, the murder rate rising as he looked back towards a plastic Jesus.

There was a revolving door next to the window and he watched shoppers leaving the store with body parts in presentation cases, wrapped in paper and tied with ribbons, more treats for the spoiled brats of the world. The stickers made him sick – happy turkeys, pigs, lambs, cows, deer, fish. A middle-aged man came outside and stopped, searching for a taxi, noticed the tramp and sneered. His disgust was obvious. He wore gleaming leather shoes and Tanner saw skin being ripped from a bull's back, knew he himself was subhuman, one of the beasts, someone who was meant to stand in his own piss and shit, and so he took a few steps, undoing his flies as he went, started spraying.

It took the snob a few seconds to realise what was going on. He shouted and moved forward and then back, finally turned and retreated into the mass of bodies moving in columns. Tanner went back to the shop. The crowd parted. He splashed the door with dehydrated, dark-yellow urine. He was a dog leaving his scent. A poor man making his mark.

People shook their heads. Some pointed and stared while others looked away. Men and women turned children's faces from the disgusting sight. Someone called him a pig. A guard dressed as a doorman rushed out of the store and told him to stop, that he was behaving like an animal. It wasn't right, acting as if he was mental, but Tanner had finished and he shook the last drops off and zipped up, returned to the kerb and was on his way, keeping his balance the best he could.

He left the main street for the smaller side-roads, felt stupid making a show of himself like that, but he had hardly known what he was doing, just didn't understand how these individuals couldn't see what was happening in their name, how they could live with the insanity. There was a church up ahead and he tried to enter, barred by another security guard who asked if he had a ticket for the service. Tanner shook his head and tried to explain that he wanted to speak to the spiritual leader of this church, that it was important. The guard apologised. This wasn't possible. The tramp asked again. He needed to know why so many children were being killed, why Christmas was celebrated with the massacre of innocents, why the lambs of God were being butchered. A holy man could change everything with a single sermon. The guard shrugged and said that he should leave as he would upset the worshippers. Otherwise he would have to call the police. It was a private event. Sorry.

Tanner shuffled along and came to the centre of government, the heart of the greatest democracy on the planet. If the church was unable to help him then surely a politician would. They responded to reason and dealt in fairness, and he approached the policemen at the main gate, armed and ready for the next terrorist attack, asked one of them if he could see the MP responsible for animal welfare. He needed to know why the slaughter hadn't been stopped yet. Especially at this time of year. It didn't make sense. All the MPs had to do was pass a law. But the man didn't understand and told him to leave, that he should go before he was arrested.

Tanner saw himself locked in a cell with no window or room to move. The officer became more friendly, suggested a homeless shelter. They could give him a bed and a hot meal. He shouldn't be sleeping rough on a freezing night like this one. The policeman pointed to the nearby bridge that crossed the river.

The concrete path stretched out on either side of the homeless man. There were no more Charlie Chaplins, no gentlemen of the road, just runaway kids and traumatised soldiers, broken males and females, sad souls who thought too much and didn't know what to do with themselves. The tramp was sitting on a bench, looking at the floodlit buildings on the other side of the river, the homes of democracy and religion. In the first of these MPs searched for ways to make society richer and fairer, and while they differed in their approaches they put party politics aside in the run-up to Christmas and celebrated with stuffed turkey and all the trimmings. In the second, spiritual thinkers honoured Christ's message of peace and love with the same meal.

The stone surrounding Tanner was turning white as frost formed, and he hunched further into his jacket, couldn't believe he had pissed in the street like that, out in the open as if he was mad. It proved he was finished. Those last traces of self-respect were gone and he was overwhelmed by the things he had done, knew it was his time to die. He would wait for the cold to end his life. He could freeze to death right here, and if it snowed he'd turn into a snowman and then when it was warmer he would melt and vanish. That was going to take a while, though, and really he should go over to the wall and jump into the river and let the current carry him away, but he didn't want to drown.

There was movement to his left and he waited for two shapes to appear, watched as they grew in size and became more distinct. Neither of them seemed to be worrying about the weather – the man wearing a black suit and the woman a leather jacket and short skirt. She was balancing on high heels and had a paper hat on her head. The man blew a tiny horn that unfurled a strip of plastic.

They'd been to a works party and were drunk and eating from a polystyrene carton, sharing the food inside, slowing down and stopping, leaning against the riverside wall.

They stayed there talking for a few minutes, peering into the water, looking across the river to the floodlit buildings, and the carton was placed on the wall and they kissed, the man running his hands down the woman's back and pulling her close. After a while they separated and moved away from the wall, the man picking up and dropping the carton. The contents spilled over the ground and he swore, bent down and scooped it back into the container, stood and held this out to the woman who shook her head and seemed angry. An argument started.

Tanner hoped he wouldn't be noticed, but the woman pointed over and said something he couldn't hear, the man following her finger with his eyes and holding his nose, and while she stopped and watched he strode over, blowing the horn. Tanner looked up at the drunk and tried to ignore the expression on his face as the carton was held out, the man telling him to treat himself, it had been on the ground and he didn't want it, but it was a treat for a smelly old tramp. Tanner shook his head.

The man was offended. He should take what he was offered, not turn his nose up. Tanner was making the place look dirty – dressed like a scarecrow, begging and poncing – didn't he know he was scaring off the tourists. The man blew the horn and tried again, but the tramp explained that he was a vegan and didn't eat animals. Didn't eat animals? It was a fucking kebab, what was wrong with that? It was made from a dead lamb and why would anyone want to eat a child? The man's face clouded over. A smelly animal should eat a smelly animal. He dropped the carton into Tanner's lap. Eat it, you ungrateful cunt.

The woman joined them and wanted to know what was going on, and when she heard that the kebab had been offered and this scumbag wouldn't touch it because he was a vegan she cocked her head and said they should charge the dirty bastard. The man puffed up, eager to impress his sexy colleague. He worked hard and paid his taxes and didn't have time to waste on those who didn't pull their weight. Useless cunt. No good to anyone. The woman was becoming excited and the man rolled his shoulders and told Tanner to go on – eat the fucking kebab. What difference did it make? The lamb was dead. It would have died in vain otherwise. What was wrong with him? Sitting in the freezing cold like a fucking animal – *fucking animal*. He was smelly and needed a bath. The woman shouted smelly pig – *smelly fucking pig*.

Tanner didn't respond. A nursery rhyme played in his head. The story of Old MacDonald.

Ronald McDonald kicked him in the leg. The tramp didn't want any trouble. Taking this as a sign of weakness the man made a series of threats, but Tanner shrugged and looked along the concrete path, which apart from the three of them was deserted. The woman told him to pay attention and he did as she asked and added a grin which seemed to upset her and she started talking in a silly voice, asking him about that poor lettuce in the kebab. What about the tomato and onions? She bet he killed defenceless potatoes. Didn't he hear them screaming? Calling for their mummies. How about the carrots he cut with a knife? The chickpeas? Lambs were made to be eaten. What was the point of living if you couldn't enjoy some KFC or a Big Mac now and then?

Rachel McDonald slapped Tanner in the face, and while it didn't really hurt he was surprised, saw the spite in her eyes and wondered if he'd met her before when he was trying to beg, and she was becoming hysterical, as if looking at her was an insult, and she hit him again and again before Ronald eased her aside and had a proper go, thumping Tanner in the mouth. This time it did hurt.

Maybe he deserved to be treated this way. They were young and drunk, but it was no excuse. He saw cowards. The alcohol made them think they could get away with anything. Their violence was suppressed and starting to bubble over. They were the ultimate conformists, the same follow-the-leader bullies who would happily export food as a local population starved; sacrifice others for a single god or leader; manage the slave trade and practise genocide. They were international and could be found right across the globe.

He thought about the unrecorded animals and this lamb in pitta bread, considered dogs that bit their tormenters and were killed for their impudence, and the horses that reared up and the bulls that charged and all those other creatures who were too timid and terrified to fight back. They turned their heads and looked away and hoped they would be left alone. He did the same. Turned the other cheek. Rachel scratched it and Ronald told him to eat the fucking kebab.

Perhaps this loving couple would enjoy an 'Old MacDonald' singsong? The tramp lifted the kebab to his mouth and saw that they were suddenly unsure. He was damned if he did and damned if he didn't, one of the doomed – the doomed and the damned – like all those lambs on their way to their deaths at this very second. He bit into the kebab. Chilli sauce, onions, lettuce, a wax pepper, the flesh itself. He felt it sitting in his mouth, could taste the herbs mixed into the meat.

Tanner knew he could kill these two idiots if he wanted, that he was stronger and more deadly than they could ever be, but he didn't care, this was his society and he was out on its margins, had broken laws and deserved to be punished. More punches landed. He had done what they wanted and this made them powerful. Ronald pulled him from the bench and he fell to the ground, and he didn't resist, just let it happen.

He was being kicked in the body and head and closed his eyes so he couldn't see his attackers. The blows were painful but ridiculous. In his mind he was a bleating lamb, a squealing pig, a lowing cow – and these two might like it if he cried out 'Old MacDonald' style. They were united in their hatred, aroused and almost frenzied, and later on they would mate and feel invincible. So he bleated, squealed, lowed. Decided to crank the volume up. Heard himself baaing and oinking and mooing. And even though these sounds were muffled by the meat and some of it fell out of his mouth, they caused a reaction.

The McDonalds were confused and for a moment scared, stopped what they were doing, and he rolled over on his back like a dog waiting to have his tummy tickled. How dare he make these noises? He was meant to suffer in silence. Why wasn't he terrified? The woman's face contorted as she stepped back and bent down to take off her shoes.

Tanner watched as she steadied herself and put one of them on the bench, turned the other over and then crouched down and started hitting at his head with the heel. It was sharp and cut his hand when he raised it to protect his eyes. She was going to blind him if he wasn't careful, and while he hadn't cared if he froze or was kicked to death a minute ago, worn down by his short time on the streets and the cold that had worked itself inside his body, he was bored. These people were vicious and gutless and had no imagination.

He stood up and pushed Ronald away. Young McDonald wasn't sure what to do. The tramp had changed, seemed like another person. Rachel was still and he reached over and pulled the shoe from her hand and threw it towards the river. She was furious, but didn't speak. He head-butted Ronald, who fell to the ground with a broken nose. Pulling Rachel towards him, Tanner spat the unchewed meat into his hand and forced it into her mouth, squeezed her jaw shut and told her to eat it all up. He returned to Ronald and kicked him in the head as he tried to stand, knocking him clean out. Rachel was sitting on the bench and spitting the lamb out, Tanner telling her that he was vegan and didn't eat non-human animals, that he had tried to make this clear earlier but nobody was listening.

The city was full of cameras and he couldn't hang about, left the riverbank and was on his way, and when he reached an empty side-street he trotted and heard a horse's hooves echoing on cobbles and through the hills, but he was soon tired and walked instead, fifteen minutes later slowing right down, feeling confused and dizzy and starting to fall.

Mickey Moo was floating in a ditch. The water was warm and supported his back. A frog croaked. He knew he'd been beaten up, but his battered body didn't hurt. Bullies had found him when he was vulnerable and couldn't control themselves. He tried to recall the details, if he'd fought back and had his revenge, remembered leaving London and heading into the darkness, visiting a series of village pubs before he found two of his attackers. There they were – fox-hunting, badger-baiting, rabbit-ripping scum – drinking and joking as if nothing had happened.

He waited in his rented car with violence on his mind. If there was no mercy for the meek there could be no rest for the wicked. Once they left the pub he was going to dish out his own brand of justice. His older self was praying that his younger, peace-loving side had triumphed. Mickey could have maimed or killed both of the terrier-men and got away with it back in the days before CCTV took over, but he'd changed his mind at the last moment and returned to London. It was one thing to plan such an attack, but another carrying it through, plus it felt wrong picking them off when they were drunk and unable to defend themselves. In the end, he had listened to Ronnie and Bev, and was reaping his reward. Mike Tanner was on his way to heaven, drifting through space with the meteors and the stars.

The light was becoming brighter and forcing its way through the lids of eyes he had to keep shut. He shifted to avoid the glare and winced as he felt the bruises on his body and the cuts to his head. It was a relief knowing he hadn't hurt anyone. He was a man of peace. There was someone else, though, a figure in the shadows, a man who was prepared to kill. The beams of a lorry exposed the face of Bobby Four Legs. Tanner started. He remembered everything. Steve Nash had died proud and unrepentant, while he'd fallen apart. He didn't know where he was, and hoping for the best he opened his eyes.

Tanner was on a bed in a white room, covered by a red blanket, wearing a blue shirt he had never seen before. The walls and ceiling had been painted in a brilliant gloss that magnified the sunlight coming through the window. His pillows were clean and smelled of lavender. He sat up and tried to work out what sort of place this was and how he had got here. The only sound he could hear was the ticking of a radiator, and focusing on this he counted to sixty and marked the minute. Nothing changed in that time. He was warm and comfortable.

Flopping back and closing his eyes again, he enjoyed the sheer luxury of a bed. Maybe he was in a home for runaway boys, a secure unit that demanded discipline in return for protection from the perverts circling outside. Celebrity chefs would try to use their fame to infiltrate the institution, but the staff were vigilant. Yet he was no boy. Perhaps he was in a young offender institution. A short sentence warning a wayward youth that unless he mended his ways he would end up a lifer. But he was no youth. No, it made more sense that he was in prison, the due process of law passing him by, and he could have no complaints. But this was no prison.

There was a knock on the door. It opened a crack and a head appeared. The hair was short, the face cheerful, clean-shaven, familiar. The man was of a similar age and had a steady gaze, a decency that was obvious. He came in and sat down, asked Tanner if he felt okay, told him there were showers at the end of the hall and there'd be a meal served in a while. Tanner had been discovered outside the shelter, unconscious on the pavement. He'd clearly been attacked. The temperature had dipped well below freezing last night and he was lucky. He could have died. Tanner wanted to explain, but wasn't sure what to say. The manager said to tell him later, but only if he wanted.

Taking the towel, soap and clothes he found next to his bed, Tanner went down the empty corridor to the bathrooms, entered the first one and locked the door. He was soon naked in front of a mirror and looking at the mess he'd become. His face was thick with stubble, skin covered in grime, hair matted. Worse were the sores that seemed to be leaking blood and pus, dirty little oil slicks that ran along bony ribs. His arms were covered in scratches and there were bruises everywhere, puncture wounds to his right arm and shoulder where he'd been hit with a high-heeled shoe.

Next came the smell. While it rose up from his armpits and groin, he imagined it oozing through his pores, and the thought of parasites living under his skin made him hurry and turn on the shower. He could mend this much faster than it had taken to happen. There was a constant supply of hot water and he stood under it for a long time, scrubbing himself as clean as he could. It was the best wash he'd ever had. He needed a shave and haircut, but that could wait until tomorrow.

Dressing in the clothes he'd been given, they felt strange and alien, as if they might transform him into a previous owner, but he was grateful to the generous souls who donated to charity and would make them his. Walking back down the corridor he could smell food and followed his nose to a canteen where twenty or more people were eating a thick vegetable soup with doorstep slices of bread cut from a bloomer. He was served by a friendly lady who told him to come back for more if he was still hungry after he'd eaten this lot, and he went over to a long table and sat on his own, dipped the bread into the soup and watched the goodness soak in. It tasted fantastic.

Checking the room he saw a mixture of ages, both sexes, a few loners, people sitting in twos and threes, everyone quiet as they ate, and in a much better state than some of the poor sods he'd been around recently. He looked for the manager, but he wasn't around, watched a young woman in a baseball cap go up for seconds, and when he was finished he did the same.

Tanner slept through the afternoon and when he woke up he asked for a razor and shaved his face, then had another long shower before eating again in the evening. This time it was a chick-pea curry with rice and salad, and the boss had cooked this one himself, with the help of the woman in the baseball cap, the two of them serving it up. When the meal was over there was a commotion at the main doors as a couple of drunks tried to come into the shelter, but the manager was quick and firm and turned them away. The people inside had to be protected and Tanner admired his strength. The doors were locked and the shelter was quiet again, the manager sitting at the front desk.

Later that evening Tanner went and joined him. They drank tea and ate biscuits and talked about easy subjects – the music they liked and bands they'd seen, the area around the shelter, foreign travel, their lives and families, the jobs they had done since leaving school. Tanner learned that as soon as his friend took charge here he'd changed the menu and put everyone on a vegan diet. The people at the top didn't share his morals or grasp the deeper logic, but accepted it was cheaper to cover every option with one meal. There was a decent number who came to the shelter that just wouldn't touch meat, while the rest would eat anything that was tasty and filling. Tanner said he was glad, being vegan himself.

They talked about the treatment of animals and humans and how the two crossed over and couldn't be separated, and eventually Tanner was asked what he thought about the attack on a slaughter-house in California. He knew nothing about this and listened to the story of two animal-rights activists who had shot and killed thirteen slaughtermen in an operation they'd dedicated to the memory of Bobby Four Legs – the liberationist Steve Nash. For his part, the manager found it hard to feel sorry for the dead men, even though he knew he should. They'd been happy to murder on an industrial scale – it was like a fascist whining about their human rights when they'd committed genocide, or a communist claiming to have killed millions in the interests of equality.

He paused and apologised and seemed embarrassed. They were just words. He wouldn't hurt a fly. Even so, he hoped the people involved weren't caught. The American legal system was brutal and all about revenge. Sam changed the subject, wondered if his old friend had ever been back to that house in the country, the one he'd talked about in front of the class. What was it called? Elm Cottage. That's right, Elm Cottage. Did Michael remember when he'd wanted to be a farmer? Tanner nodded. And Sam Norton smiled in his cheerful, piggy way.

After three nights in the shelter, Tanner headed home. A train took him to a bus which he caught to some familiar shops and from there he walked the rest of the way with a bag of food in either hand, bought with money lent to him by Sam. Drizzle coated his freshly cut hair and a freezing wind blew into his face, but he didn't care. He was upbeat and positive. Nobody was hunting him and he had done nothing wrong. Good people had helped him out of the gutter and saved his life when he was on his hands and knees. It had been a test. He had survived.

If he'd been meant to die he would have frozen to death leaning against a tree or curled up in a doorway, been set on fire in a subway or stabbed in the street by creeps, jumped off a car-park roof or into the river. Or ended up blinded and brain-damaged by a stiletto heel. True, he had been confused and lost his way, vested interests swaying him with their propaganda, his conscience manipulated, and while it would take time to fully recover he would be a better man in the future.

When he entered his street he was excited but nervous, his face raised towards the rooftops as he focused on the windows of his flat, relieved when he saw the same curtains hanging. The pavements were empty and he stood outside the house for a full two minutes, waiting for the police to come running. It was now or never. Nothing happened. And why should it?

He reached into his jacket and realised that he'd always guarded his keys. Some would say he had lived like an animal, and it was true he'd experienced hunger and a different kind of fear, but he'd always had hope and the chance to escape, an ability to unlock doors and pass through walls. In the hotel he had a private place in which to hide, while out on the streets he'd been threatened by a gang of youths and attacked by drunks, seen flashes of spite and hatred in the straightest of citizens, yet he was a human being and had a level of protection. The same rules didn't apply to animals.

He went into the house and climbed the stairs, opened his front door and walked inside, closed it quietly, put the bags on the kitchen table. It started to rain. He'd made it just in time. Picking up the kettle and taking it to the sink, he listened to the pipes splutter as they pumped out water, filled it and left it to boil as he turned the heating on and checked the flat. Apart from a lot of dust everything was the same. He put a bath on and went back into the kitchen, made himself a mug of coffee, sipped it as he put the food away. Cutting a slice of the five-grain loaf he added hummus and pepper, ate this by the window as he looked into the gardens and found Lily watching him from the bushes.

He had a bath and stayed in the water for ages, topping it up when it cooled, steam filling the room and moisture dripping from the walls and ceiling, and despite his showers at the shelter he still had dirt to scrub away. Afterwards he stretched out on his bed for a couple of hours and dozed before dressing in clean clothes and going into the kitchen where he made himself a meal of roast potatoes and parsnips, soya sausages and stuffing, steamed broccoli and sweetcorn from a tin, a jug of mushroom gravy. He ate this with a bottle of Carib he found in the fridge, and lots of cranberry jelly and ketchup.

Asleep by ten, he woke up at nine. Drinking coffee as he wandered through the flat, he decided to give it a clean, opening all the windows to let fresh air in, then dusting and hoovering and mopping, and when he was done he closed the windows again and turned up the heat, sat down to relax. He chose a radio station that specialised in easy listening, and when the weather forecast came on it predicted a white Christmas, and he couldn't help picturing Bing Crosby and Danny Kaye singing on a Technicolor film set. Drink, food, shelter, warmth, friendship, love. It was a wonderful world.

Tanner stayed indoors for four days, and when he finally went out it felt fantastic to walk through streets he wouldn't have to sleep on, knowing he could return to his flat whenever he liked. He phoned Ella to say he was back, went round that afternoon with a bunch of flowers and she gave him a big hug. They sat drinking tea and eating biscuits, talking about the seeds she'd bought and the plans she was making for next year. He was keen to start digging and looking forward to seeing the allotments. She said that it was nice to have him home.

When he tried to start his car the battery was flat, so he took it out and charged it up, and once the engine was warm it ran smoothly enough, offering him the mobility a walking man lacked. He felt free when he was behind the steering wheel, as if the world was opening up again, and he moved from side-roads to high streets and on towards two- and three-lane highways, swapping houses for factories and churches and fields, just kept on driving. He even played some of his favourite songs.

Eight days after his return he strolled into The White Hart and ordered a pint, saw the men gathered at the other end of the bar and went over. Several nodded and Tony stopped talking. Tanner raised his glass in a toast and said it was good to be back in England. A drinker mumbled something about sunshine and the bloody cold. Tony tapped his pint against Tanner's and drank, and then he got on with his story as the buses stopped at the junction outside and the window rattled and a crowd formed at the crossing as they waited for the lights to change.

Snow fell and settled and turned the city into a winter wonderland. Adults became the children they had once been, leaving the warmth of their homes to build human figures in back gardens and on commons and inside parks, remembering what it was like to believe their wishes could come true. Fresh flurries arrived, adding depth and softness, and looking into the sky as they descended Tanner marvelled at the number of individual snowflakes, moved by the knowledge that no two were the same. Old beliefs flickered, the idea that words could make a difference returning. It was the best sort of fantasy. He threw bread down to Lily, who was around a lot more, and lined it up on his windowsill for the birds, and was thankful he wasn't sleeping outside.

Sam had been on the phone. Tanner would spend Christmas Day at the shelter, for the company but also to help serve dinner. While the bad memories remained, he had managed to blur the details. He remembered Elm Cottage as if it existed in another dimension to the tinsel-covered city, saw the place before the snow fell and added its sugar-plum coating, the house cut off and drowning in loneliness. He thought about the farmers left behind, the emptiness of the countryside and the terrible things that happened there, needed to lose himself in London and its people and was grateful to Sam.

It was Friday night and he took his time walking to The White Hart, extra careful on icy pavements, stood at the bar with a glass in his hand listening to his storytelling pal. While he hadn't converted Tony to the vegan path yet, it was only a matter of time. The man had a heart of gold, the energy and humour of a boisterous child. This particular tale was full of clever turns, but even so, it was the unity that made people smile. The drinkers here were different to those in The Crown, controlled their fear with the repetition of work and the security it offered. His attention drifted to the buses outside, their drivers cautious on treacherous roads, the decks crowded with spirits.

Inside the pub the faces were clear and animated, everyone full of the Christmas spirit. It was the season of excess, an orgy of spending and feasting. He could have labelled everyone here cowards, hypocrites and selfish cunts, insisted the human race was lost in its self-centred arrogance and greed, but these were his brothers and sisters and he needed to believe that his species was weak rather than evil. They were big babies, overgrown kids building snowmen and adding carrot noses. He needed to belong. He didn't want to be alone.

Change was on its way. An MP had gone missing. The morning news said he had been having an affair with a researcher and that his wife had only found out the week before. Neither woman knew his whereabouts. The police were concerned. Terrorist involvement hadn't been ruled out. Tanner wasn't surprised by the MP's infidelity. He was a sleazy individual who had been excessively critical of the freedom-fighter Steve Nash, and had made some mocking remarks about those being murdered by the meat industry. He should have been working towards a vegan future, but had instead been guilty of voting for the eroding of already weak animal-welfare laws.

Interestingly, a prominent clergyman had vanished on the same day. This man should have been promoting peace on earth, yet did nothing to challenge the obscenities being excused by his religion. He had publicly condemned the animal-rights movement on a number of occasions and was corrupting what should have been a spiritual tradition. He was as complicit as the politician. Tanner imagined them tied to chairs somewhere quiet, with time to reflect on their behaviour.

The two incidents hadn't been linked, but he felt that one day they might. There could be no more emotion. The war on terror was moving to a new stage. Prayers went unheard and words were ignored. The same lies and excuses were repeated on an endless, brain-dead loop... *We need meat to survive... It's natural... Traditional... You think more of animals than you do of people... I like the taste... A chicken's the same as a cabbage... Pigs don't have emotions... Cows have no memory... Lambs don't feel pain... They're just dumb animals... God says it's okay... It's legal... The law... Survival of the fittest... You don't mind killing a potato... What about a poor little carrot? ... Ha ha ha... Animals are treated well... Humanely slaughtered... Two by two... Off they go... Just like sheep... Ha ha ha... Ha ha ha....*

Laughter boomed and shook the big window at the front of the pub. Tanner realised that Tony had finished his story. He'd missed the punchline, but it didn't matter. The barmaid was pouring and he could smell her perfume over the softer scent of the beer. He sniffed leather shoes, coats, jackets, belts and handbags, the bodies of innocents stripped and tanned and treated and wrapped around the ruling class, the men and women who stood here with their intestines stuffed with blood and rotting meat. He saw jaws grinding on flesh and lips sucking on bones, limbs jerking and wings flapping, throats being cut – right now as the Christmas slaughter took place.

Tanner reminded himself that it was important to stay strong, to hate the sin and not the sinner. He thought about Steve Nash and those two Americans staying free, the suffering children of the world and the scared kids drinking in The White Hart. It wasn't their fault. They needed to see what was happening. To be brave and accept the truth. His mind cleared. He was focused and looking to the future.

*

Christmas was over in a single day. The snow turned to slush and once the people had feasted they boiled turkey and chicken bones in pans and made soup, snacked on beef and pork leftovers, and the new year came and was celebrated with a mixture of sorrow for the time passed and hope for the good days ahead. In January the hard-working millions sighed and went back to their jobs, lowering their heads and concentrating on the important tasks that needed performing, and while this selfless desire to work was accompanied by some justified complaining, they accepted it was worth it to pay for the luxuries of life. The system wasn't perfect, but there was a fairness about it, a belief that each and every individual was essential and that society couldn't continue without their contribution.

On the twelfth day Baby Jesus and the Virgin Mary and their friends from the stable were packed up with Joseph and the three wise men and put away until next year. Lambs were wrapped in soft clouds of cotton wool and joined by cows and calves, pigs and piglets, chickens and chicks, horses and donkeys and goats, and as time passed and the ritual was repeated the paint chipped off their plastic bodies and the smiling faces blurred, but the masses were sentimental and kept them until they became too worn out to use and then they were thrown away or given to a jumble collection for the poor. Replacements were bought.

The new year saw resolutions broken as people became absorbed in their work and the important things in life, like keeping a roof over their heads and food on their tables and heat in their houses and hot water in their pipes and electricity in their wires and light in their bulbs and petrol in their cars and shoes on their feet and clothes on their backs and music in their ears and films on their screens and credit on their phones and smoke in their lungs and drink in their bellies and rings on their fingers and bells on their toes. They had more vital issues to deal with than the brutalities of farming and the horror of the slaughterhouse.

Diets were abandoned. Abstinence was fine in theory, but this was the real world. People missed the Christmas excess and the arrogant among them became angry at those who questioned their consumption and wealth. This was a free country. Democracy meant that every desire had to be satisfied. It was unfortunate others had to struggle, but what were they supposed to do? Below these workers was an underclass deemed misfits and freaks, and below them the non-human animals, the real subhumans, and within this kingdom there were the hunters and the hunted, and it was the most peaceful creatures that the dominant species butchered.

Thick rain fell and a bitter wind blew. There were floods. Homes were destroyed. Carpets ruined. Stock markets fell. Currencies crashed. Media-driven scandals distracted attention. Great football competitions would soon be decided. Divas released love songs. Rebels talked about revolution from penthouse suites. The days became longer and the intensity of the light increased as the planet shifted. Cold snaps came and went, and during this supposedly quiet time between Christmas and spring the monsters were busy perverting nature, fiddling with ewes so that their lambs would be ready for another seasonal slaughter. Easter was coming. The killing machine was fine-tuned and relentless. Profits soared. And on their packaging and posters and stickers and in every new bit of slick advertising the animals kept smiling.

A knacker kicked Mary in the belly and sent her running in the direction he demanded. The building was busy and noisy and men were coming into the pen and picking out individual lambs. The children were screaming. A boy was electrocuted and Mary could smell his fur burning as his head snapped back. Metal clasps were put in place and his body rose into the air, dangling from a chain as a conveyor belt took him away through heavy plastic flaps. A monster grabbed Mary and she was on her own. Tongs were pressed against her head, electrodes positioned on either side of her brain. The person who was about to stun her was chewing gum that smelled of mint and as Mary squirmed and tried to escape she wet herself, the man grabbing her jaw and squeezing and turning her face around, taking a few seconds to stare into her eyes, and the human smiled and released the electricity meant to start an epileptic seizure. The tongs were only kept in place long enough to put her in a daze, Mary shackled and hoisted up and moved down the assembly line. She felt the flaps hit her body and was semi-conscious when she reached her killer. The slaughterman stepped forward and stabbed her in the throat, the blade opening up Mary's carotid artery. The pain shocked her awake and she felt her heart thumping in time with the blood spurting into the gutter below. There was no escape and her terror was complete. And as the blood drained from her body it took the fading memories of her mother and the fields where she'd lived with it, small pops of starlight bursting in a night sky as her brain slowly died. When her heart stopped beating she was passed to the people who would dress her – which in human double-speak meant the opposite. They stripped the little girl bare, cut her head off and dumped it in a steel container with the others. Her torso was sliced open and her insides ripped out. The skin was tugged from her body and the flesh inside removed. Cleavers hacked at her bones. Mary was dismembered, frozen, wrapped in cellophane, transported in a lorry and a van, placed in a supermarket fridge. Stickers were attached that showed her beaming with joy. There was no need for any of this, but people liked the taste of her flesh. It was traditional. Habit. Business. The company responsible had worked hard to separate Mary from her body. Millions of sheep would die in Britain this year so what did one lamb matter? She didn't even have a name. Not really. Nor did she have a memory, emotions, feelings. It was wrong to compare her to a human being. Those making money from her death swore there was no suffering involved. They wanted the public to rest assured that the animals were happy. And so the killing continues, behind closed doors, out of sight and out of mind, deep inside the slaughterhouse.